Stefanie London is the *USA TODAY* bestselling author of contemporary romances and romantic comedies. After sneaking several English Lit subjects into her 'very practical' business degree, Stefanie worked in the corporate world. But it wasn't long before she became bored with writing emails for executives and turned her attention to romance fiction. Stefanie's books have been called 'genuinely entertaining and memorable' by *Booklist*, and her writing praised as 'elegant, descriptive and delectable' by *RT Book Reviews*. Originally from Australia, she now lives in Toronto with her very own hero, and is currently in the process of doing her best to travel the world. She frequently indulges in her passions for good coffee, lipstick, romance novels and anything zombie-related. For more information on Stefanie and her books check out her website at stefanie-london.com.

J. Margot Critch currently lives in St John's, Newfoundland, with her husband Brian and their two little buddies Simon and Chibs. She spends equal amounts of time writing, listening to Jimmy Buffett's music and looking out at the ocean—all the while trying to decide if she wants coffee or a margarita.

If you liked *Faking It* and *Forbidden Sins*
why not try

The Debt by Jackie Ashenden
Cross My Hart by Clare Connelly

Discover more at millsandboon.co.uk

FAKING IT

STEFANIE LONDON

FORBIDDEN SINS

J. MARGOT CRITCH

MILLS & BOON

First Published in Great Britain 2019
by Mills & Boon, an imprint of HarperCollins*Publishers*
1 London Bridge Street, London, SE1 9GF

Faking It © 2019 Stefanie Little

Forbidden Sins © 2019 J. Margot Critch

ISBN: 978-0-263-27388-5

MIX
Paper from
responsible sources
FSC™ C007454

This book is produced from independently certified FSC™ paper
to ensure responsible forest management.
For more information visit www.harpercollins.co.uk/green.

Printed and bound in Spain
by CPI, Barcelona

FAKING IT

STEFANIE LONDON

MILLS & BOON

To all the readers who emailed me asking why Owen never got his happy-ever-after…

This book is for you. xx

CHAPTER ONE

Owen

I KNOW IT'S going to make me seem like a cruel bastard, but there isn't much in this world that pleases me more than getting the drop on someone. The element of surprise is my catnip. I love the moment my target realises they've been duped. Maybe it's because nobody ever expected a thing from me.

Who actually thinks the class clown will amount to something? No one.

So yeah, I like it when the tables are turned. Especially when my target comes in a five-foot-two-inch package filled to the brim with bristling indignation.

"No." Miss Indignation shakes her head, a frizzy brown ponytail slapping her ears like she's a puppy shaking off the water from an unwanted bath. "Can't we pretend to be brother and sister?"

"I'm not sure which part of this meeting you misinterpreted as a negotiation, Anderson." My old boss, Gary Smythe, raises a bushy silver eyebrow. "This is your first assignment as a detective. I thought you'd be champing at the bit."

Hannah Anderson, now known as Detective Senior Constable Anderson, straightens her shoulders. "Yes, sir, and I'm very grateful for the opportunity—"

"Then I suggest you quit shaking your head like you're trying to dislodge something."

I snort and stifle the noise with a cough. Neither one of them buys it. We're sitting in a meeting room at the Victoria Police headquarters. It feels strange to be back. I'd never planned on returning to Australia, let alone to my old job. But that's life, right? The second you think you've got your shit together, fate punches you in the nuts.

"Yes, sir." Hannah looks like she's about to erupt. She clutches her coffee cup in a way that tells me she's trying to mentally crush my skull.

Nice try, Anderson.

"Not exactly the warm welcome I was hoping for," I chime in, returning her fiery glare with a cocky grin. If there's one thing that makes Anderson blow her stack, it's people who take life less seriously than she does.

Spoiler alert: that's literally everyone.

"Shut up, Fletcher." Gary takes a sip of his cappuccino. He's drinking out of a mug that says "I like big busts and I cannot lie" with a picture of a pair of handcuffs beneath it. A white line of milk foam caps his Ned Flanders–style moustache. "If you want someone to fawn over you, then pay your grandmother a visit."

"Will do, sir."

Anderson rolls her eyes. If it's not completely obvious at this point, she kind of hates me. Well, *hate* might be a strong word although she *has* said it before. It's a weird kind of hate. The kind that feels prickly and cold but is really a front for a gooey centre of white-hot attraction. Yeah, she has the hots for me and she hates herself for it.

So I'm scoring another point in the bastard category, but that pleases me very much.

"We're going undercover," I say, leaning forward against the table and not even trying to hide my glee. "As man and wife."

I swear she somehow manages to tell me to go fuck myself with her eyes. "Right."

"We thought we'd put this to bed before you left." Gary frowns.

He told me the pertinent details before I submitted my leave at Cobalt & Dane, the security company I work for in New York City. A folder with everything required for this undercover gig—ID for my new identity, keys and an access card for the apartment I'm going to call home for the next month, and surveillance info that's been collected to date—is already in my backpack.

This is an evidence-gathering mission, in the hopes of convincing the higher-ups to put together a task force. And I'm going to enjoy the heck out of being cooped up with Anderson.

"So did I, Boss." The name comes out of habit. Gary Smythe will always be "Boss" to me.

We'd cracked the old case before I left for New York. But organised crime is a tricky beast. You think you've cut off the snake's head and suddenly it grows back. If there's one thing I've learned over the years, it's that greed is unrelenting.

"It looks like one of the relatives took over the family business," Gary continues. "We suspect they're running the operation out of an apartment complex in South Melbourne. We've secured an apartment for you. You'll move in on Monday morning and make friends with the neighbours."

Easy as pie. I love making friends.

But I suspect Anderson might have trouble with that. Friendliness isn't her strong suit.

"I want you two to get reacquainted. Finish your coffees and figure your shit out." Gary pushes up from his seat, his belly straining against his navy uniform shirt. Today he's in office dress—proper trousers instead of the tactical ones, and a black tie at his neck. Probably had a meeting with the big boss. "See if you can keep from killing each other."

"Our reputation precedes us," I say as Gary exits the meeting room, leaving me alone with my soon-to-be fake-wife.

"*Your* reputation precedes *you*," Anderson corrects me. "Mine is nice and quiet. The way I prefer it."

"Always so argumentative." I lean back in my chair and fold my arms over my chest. Unlike her, I'm not dressed in uniform since I'm here as a consultant.

They might be able to drag me back for a case, but I'm not signing any long-term contracts. I'll do this job as a favour for my old boss. I like the guy. I *don't* like the life I left behind. Too many demons. The second this job is over I'm getting my ass back to New York.

"Look, this is my first assignment as a detective," she says, nailing me with her wide brown eyes, "And I know you have a penchant for wreaking havoc, but I will not let you screw this up. You might have left this life behind, but this job is important to me."

Anderson is all spit and polish, just as I remember. Perfectly pressed shirt and slacks, neat ponytail. She's clearly catching up on paperwork before her big move into a detective's role. I bet she stayed up late last night shining her shoes.

"Message received, Anderson. No tomfoolery."

"You should start calling me Hannah. Get into the habit so my surname doesn't slip out in front of anyone while we're on the job." She sticks her thumb into her mouth to chew on a nail, but then thinks better of it and folds her hands in front of her. Outside the meeting room, people wander back and forth—some in uniform and others in civilian dress. "I wanted to keep our first names the same. Make it easier to remember. Although I still don't see why we can't be brother and sister. It seems ludicrous that *anyone* would think I'd marry you."

"Oh yeah, speaking of which..." I dig my hand into my pocket and pull out a worn velvet box. Anderson's eyes widen as I flip it open, showing her the old, ornate ring nestled inside.

The ring is legit. It belonged to my mother and since I'm never, *ever* getting married I'm pleased to use it for something. It wasn't her engagement ring— that one lives with my grandmother. But my mother loved jewellery enough to have a personal jeweller on retainer when she was alive, so I wasn't short on options for this fake proposal.

Fun fact: I don't need to work. My parents were rich. Like, travel around the world on a private jet rich. Like fly in a bunch of diamonds straight from Antwerp rich.

Not that I want anything to do with the money. It's been sitting in a bank account for the last fifteen years while my financial adviser plays with crypto-currency like he's got a great big pile of Monopoly money in front of him. I told him to pick the riski-est ones and not even think twice if he lost the lot. He didn't, not by a long shot.

And for this job, I'm going to have to embrace the upper-crust lifestyle.

"You've got to start wearing this," I say.

Anderson blinks. "This is *not* how the fairy tales led me to believe a proposal would happen."

The gold band cradles an interesting stone in a smoky shade that's somewhere between brown and grey, which is nicer than it sounds. It's surrounded by tiny white diamonds that glimmer under the ar-tificial lighting.

The ring is unusual and pretty, like Anderson.

"I guess I'm not doing it right." Clearing my throat, I slide off my chair and drop down to one knee. "Detective Senior Constable Hannah Anderson, will you—"

"Fletcher!" she squeaks, and several people outside the meeting room snap their heads in our direction. She gives me a shove and I fall to one side, laughing and landing on my palm. She snatches the ring box out of my other hand and shoves it into her pocket. "Are you trying to give me a heart attack?"

"What? I thought I was being nice."

She shakes her head as though I'm the biggest idiot this side of the Yarra. Which, to be fair, might be true. "Couldn't you find one of those gumball machines and get me some crappy little trinket? I'm going to freak out wearing this." She pats her hand over the pocket containing my mother's ring. "This is…real."

"Yeah, it is. Topaz or some shit. And we're going to be tracking a band of jewellery thieves. Ever think of that? Might be good to have a sparkly conversation starter."

Her expression tells me it was a good call but there's no way in hell she'll say it aloud. Anderson—sorry, *Hannah*—doesn't like to admit when other people are right.

"We should meet early on Monday morning. I've arranged for Ridgeway to drive a van with some boxes to the apartment building."

"What's in the boxes?"

"Nothing much. Files and stuff. But we have to look like we're moving in."

I grin. "It's a new adventure for us. Newlyweds getting their first place together. You'll have to practice looking excited."

"I don't know if I have it in me," she drawls. Then she stands. Even with me sitting and her standing, she doesn't have much height on me. What did I call her back then? Pocket Rocket. "Monday morning. Seven a.m."

"Seven?" I groan. "Who moves into a house that early?"

"People who are excited to be living together." She picks up her coffee cup. I'm already imagining how strange it's going to be to see my mother's ring on her finger. For some reason, it doesn't repulse me as much as it should. "Don't be late."

"Seven a.m. it is, my darling wife."

She rolls her eyes again and I contemplate warning her that the wind might change. But this time I hold my tongue. I'll have many hours ahead of me to drive her nuts. Gotta take the perks of the job wherever they come. I pull the file out of my backpack and scan the summary page containing the key details of our assignment. Seven a.m. at 21 Love Street, South Melbourne.

Love Street? Sounds like the perfect place for a fake marriage.

CHAPTER TWO

Hannah

OWEN'S LATE. I'm shocked…not.

I bounce on the balls of my feet, trying to ignore the strange feeling of the ring on my left hand. The big stone chafes me, reminding me constantly that it's there. It's irritating. Like the man who gave it to me.

It's also insanely beautiful and makes me feel like a princess, but I'm not telling a soul *that* little piece of information.

"Have you got a coping strategy in place?" Max Ridgeway leans against the small van parked in the loading dock of the place that will be my home until this assignment is over.

21 Love Street is the kind of place I would never actually live. It's one of those "boutique" apartment complexes—only six stories in height, with a grand foyer and all the trimmings. It's not meant for people like me, people who grew up with a family crammed into a house without enough bathrooms to go around.

Sure, this place isn't the most expensive building in the city…but it's *well* beyond my means. And we're going to be living in one of the penthouse suites.

So yeah, you could say I was feeling a little out of my element. And that was *before* my "husband" arrived.

"A coping strategy?" I ask.

"To avoid homicide."

I laugh in spite of the strange churning in my stomach. "No. I need one, though. Any tips?"

Max adjusts the dark cap covering his thick brown hair. He's dressed in plain clothes, like me. Civilian-wear. Old jeans and a hoodie. Blundstones. He skipped his morning shave, too. Now he looks like a furniture removalist instead of a cop.

"Don't take things too seriously." He winks. "That'll only give him fuel."

Max gets along with both of us. He's good at his job and I respect him a lot. His wife, Rose, gave birth to their daughter, Ruby, about six months ago. Now he spends most of his free time at home with his adorable family, so I don't see him as much as I used to.

He was in Manhattan for a while, when he met Rose, working with Owen in the private security field. They're pretty tight. Have been since we were all in the academy together in our early twenties. But I don't hold that against Max. *He* didn't have anything to do with "the diary incident."

I check my watch. "Owen is going to be late to his own funeral one day."

"You've got the wife act down pat." Max's eyes sparkle. "Although I hope you're not planning to accelerate his funeral."

"Ha," I say drily. "That's entirely up to him."

A cool wind whips past me, ruffling my hair. Today I left it down and it feels like the first time in forever that I've ditched my standard scraped-back style. But it's all part of the act. Anything to help me get into character. For the foreseeable future, I am not Hannah Anderson. I am not the only girl in a family of rough-and-tumble boys. I am not awkward and shy and trying so hard not to let other people see it.

Last night, I sat down with all my files and a cup of tea to work on my story, so that when I arrived at 21 Love Street, I would be Hannah Essex. Lady of leisure, newlywed, a woman obsessed with shiny, material things. A pretty magpie.

My polar opposite.

I wonder if my boss is screwing with me, pushing me into the deep end to see if I sink or swim. I could think of a dozen other female officers who would be *way* more convincing than me. Who are prettier and look like they *could* belong in this world.

Meanwhile I burned my thumb while straightening my hair this morning so I'd look like Owen's wife, instead of his poodle.

"Party people." Owen announces himself with a *whoop*, sans apology for his tardiness—as expected—and slaps a hand down on Max's back. When he leans in as if to kiss me, I place a hand on his chest to stop him getting too close. "That's a chilly greeting."

I chide myself. He's right, of course. We have to be in character now, even if I want to strangle him with my scarf. "The concierge manager is due to meet us in ten minutes."

"Ten minutes?" Owen looks at his watch. "I thought you said seven a.m."

"I did. And I booked the move-in for eight, knowing your lazy ass wouldn't be here on time." I shoot him a smug grin. "So you're early."

"She got you there." Max chuckles and heads to the back of the van. "I'll start getting these boxes out now and we can load them straight onto the flatbed."

"I'll help."

I resist the urge to join in and speed up the process. Hannah Anderson is a hands-on person who can lift a box with the best of them. However, Hannah Essex is worried about her manicure. I glare at the pearly pink polish I applied last night. I'd toyed with the idea of fake nails to compensate for my terrible nail-biting habit, but I have to draw the line somewhere. The last thing I need is a nail flying off while I'm chasing a perp.

"Mrs. Essex?"

For a second the name doesn't register, but then my brain kicks into gear and I smile at the man and woman approaching me. "Yes, that's me."

"Welcome to 21 Love Street." The woman is older—late sixties, maybe seventies—with a genuine smile and a neatly pressed uniform of white shirt and grey slacks. "I'm Irma and this is my colleague Dante. Looks like you're all ready to move in. I understand you've already picked up your keys and access cards."

"Yes." I stick my hand out to shake Irma's and then turn my smile to Dante, who's about my age. "Nice to meet you both."

"Dante will set the elevator to freight mode and make sure you get up to your level okay," Irma says. "Let us know if you have any questions at all."

I give my thanks and wait while Owen and Max finish unloading our boxes onto the flatbed trolley. Owen is wearing a pair of fitted jeans and a simple V-neck grey jumper that sits close to his body. A heavy silver watch decorates one wrist. The neat, casual outfit is at odds with Owen's overlong dirty-blond hair, which seems to be permanently two weeks overdue for a haircut. The thick strands kink and curl at the back of his neck. At one point in my much younger, much *stupider* years I'd fantasised about running my hands through it, about kissing his full-lipped, smart-ass mouth.

"She can hardly keep her eyes off me." Owen looks smug as hell and I realise I've been caught staring.

"Newlyweds?" Dante asks with a knowing smile. I want to punch them both.

"We're so very in love." Owen walks toward me with that careless rolling-hip gait that makes women adore him. I can't walk away. Can't break character. "Isn't that right?"

"It sure is." I tip my face up to his, aiming for a loving look while hoping he can hear the obscenities I'm screaming at him in my mind. As he lowers his lips, I turn my face so the kiss catches my cheek. Nice try, Fletcher. "And I'm also madly in love with this apartment. Are we ready to go up?"

Owen chuckles. "My wife, the drill sergeant."

"Tell me about it," Dante says as he leads us through the loading bay into the building via a room where recycled waste is kept. I make note of my surroundings, mentally jotting down details about building access points. "I've been married for two years now. My wife is about to have our first baby."

"That's sweet." I try to sound like I mean it. But my mind is on the job…well, it should be. And it should definitely *not* be occupied with the enticing way Owen's butt looks in those fitted jeans.

Dante leads us to a bay of elevators, one of which is open and protected with heavy-duty fabric. "You're good to go. Shouldn't take more than three or four trips, by the looks of it. I have to stay in the loading bay to make sure we don't end up with any traffic jams, so I'll see you when you come back down for the next load."

Max, Owen and I squeeze into the elevator with the trolley and boxes. The door slides shut.

"The whole team is taking bets on who strangles who first," Max says as we rise up to the top floor. "Money's on Anderson, ten to one."

"Ten to one?" Owen's lip curls in disgust. "Traitors."

"It's better odds than you deserve," I mutter, my

thumb rubbing over the ring on my left hand. I can't stop touching the damn thing. It's driving me nuts.

The other thing driving me nuts is the smell of soap on Owen's skin—creamy and warm, like sandalwood with a hint of vanilla. I don't remember him smelling that good in our academy days. Though, to be fair, I don't know if many guys in their early twenties shower as often as they should.

I should *not* be thinking about what Owen looks like in the shower.

The glowing green numbers count up to level six. I really need to get a hold on my imagination—because this assignment is going to be difficult enough without giving him *any* indication that I still harbour an attraction to him. And I don't. He's awful and childish and irreverent and not the kind of guy I would ever marry because I like serious men who do…serious things.

Ugh. I'm no good at lying, even in my head. I train my eyes on the glowing numbers. Maybe if I don't look at Owen, I won't get affected by whatever hot guy voodoo he's using to mess with my head.

When we reach our destination, the elevator opens with a cheerful *ping*.

"Apartment 601." I exit with more speed than is necessary. As I march toward the front door, I dig the key out of my bag. "Home sweet home."

The apartment is bigger than anywhere I've ever lived, including my family home that housed five of us. Even though we're only six floors up, we have a lovely view of South Melbourne made even prettier

by the buttery morning light. The apartment itself
has been staged by someone who knows the fine
line between style and comfort, and there's a mix
of textures—light, warm woods and soft grey fabric
and faded gold metals—that make me feel instantly
at ease. The neutral tones are brought to life with a
few pops of colour, including a vibrant sunflower
yellow chair and a canvas splashed with shades of
teal and lavender.

"This'll do," Owen says as he walks in. Max follows with the trolley. "Not really my style, but it
looks like we have money."

No kidding. I spot a Herman Miller Eames chair
in the corner of the room, and it looks like the real
deal. Those things cost more than what I paid for
my first car. I dated a guy once—*very* briefly—who
owned one of those chairs. Talked about it like the
damn thing was his child.

"I'll get the next load of boxes," Max says. "And
I'll make conversation with the concierge guy, see
if I pick up anything interesting."

Owen nods. "Good idea."

The second the door swings shut behind Max, my
body is alight with awareness. The tingling sensation of being watched is an itch beneath my skin. At
one point, I'd craved this with all my being—a moment alone with Owen.

"We'll have to make sure we don't damage any of
this furniture," I say in a desperate attempt to keep
my mind where it belongs—on work. "Budget won't
accommodate eight grand for a chair."

"And how do you think we're going to damage the furniture, huh?" Owen walks up beside me, and I feel his presence right down to my toes.

"Not like *that*." I don't need to spell out that sex isn't part of playing man and wife for this job. Owen might be a larrikin, but he's not an asshole. In fact, the one time he had the chance to take advantage of our situation—the time I *asked* him to—he declined due to "personal ethics" and I never quite got over the humiliation. Even thinking about it now makes my stomach churn. "But I do remember one young recruit who managed to break both a dining chair *and* a bed frame in one evening."

"Harmless fun." He slings an arm around my shoulders and I force myself not to lean into him. "It's been a long time, Anderson. I missed you while I was in New York."

I snort. "I didn't think about you once."

"Liar." He laughs and his delicious scent fills my nostrils again. Damn it. How does he smell so freaking good? "You ready to take the bad guys down?"

"Absolutely." This time my response is genuine. I love my job and I'm damn good at it. "They won't even know what hit them."

CHAPTER THREE

Owen

IT TAKES LESS than a day for us to argue about every little thing—our approach for gaining the trust of the people in the building, where to set up discreet surveillance…what flavour pizza we should get for dinner. She wanted Hawaiian. Gross. Pineapple does *not* belong on pizza.

We compromise and get Thai food instead.

"We should be talking to people already," Hannah argues. Her dark hair started the day floating around her face, brushing the tops of her shoulders, but now it's pulled back into a messy little knot. "You think they want to pay us for sitting around? That might be how things work in your cushy world, but we're wasting taxpayers' dollars right now."

"Sorry, I was under the impression you were a detective senior constable, not the chief commissioner." I spear a piece of duck and make sure I get some coconut rice on my fork, as well. Damn, it's good. "And cushy, my ass. My job keeps me fit as a fiddle, and don't think I didn't notice you staring earlier."

When some women blush, it's like a delicate pink flush over their cheeks. Hannah's blush goes *everywhere*—over her cheeks and nose, down her neck and under the edge of her simple black T-shirt. But my favourite bit is how it colours the tips of her ears.

"I have to stare. It's not often I see a class-A idiot in the flesh," she snaps.

The defensive comeback bounces right off me—I've been called worse. No-hoper. Slacker. Troublemaker. I saw my eleventh-grade science teacher in my first month of being a constable and her eyes almost popped out of her head. To say most people didn't expect me to do much with my life is an understatement.

Have you done much with your life? Really?

I promptly ignore that inconvenient thought and file it away where it belongs: in the corner of my mind marked "shit not to think about."

"You've got such a way with words, Anderson."

"It's Hannah, remember? You can't mess that up." Her cheeks return to their usual colour as she tucks into her Pad Thai. "Now, back to work. We've got to get out and talk to people."

"Have you ever met a newlywed couple who wanted to become BFFs with their new neighbours the second they got married? No, they want to fuck like animals and not leave their apartment."

She rolls her eyes. "You *would* think that. How many times have you been married?"

"Zero. But if I *did* get married, I wouldn't make hanging out with the neighbours my first priority." I reach for my Coke. "However, I do agree we can't sit in here all night."

"Then what?"

"We go for a romantic evening walk in the garden."

She looks at me like I've sprouted a second head. "A romantic walk?"

"It will give us a chance to scope out the property, look for anything out of the ordinary and find some surveillance points."

"And then we can talk to anyone we come across?"

I sigh. "We don't need to talk to them yet. It's not a good idea to come across too eager."

"Is this some weird guy logic?" She narrows her eyes. "Like needing to wait three weeks before you call a girl after a date?"

I raise a brow. "If he's waiting three weeks, he's not interested."

She stabs at her dinner like she's trying to make sure it's dead. Either that, or she's imagining it's me. "I'm talking hypothetically."

I would usually take the opportunity to stir her up some more, but for some reason I don't want to talk about Anderson's dating life. It makes me feel a little stabby myself, so I move the conversation on. "If we come on too strong, we might tip them off. We need to seem interesting, so they come to us."

"And by 'seem interesting' what you really mean is 'seem rich,' right? We need to make ourselves a target."

"Exactly. And it needs to be subtle. We can't *look* like we're trying to get anyone's attention."

She makes a sound of frustration that's music to my ears. Winding her up is way too easy. "So we have to attract attention without looking like we want it, and we have to avoid talking to people so they want to talk to us? Doesn't that seem a little counterintuitive?"

"No, it seems like the right way to do things. Trust me, I know how these guys work. Last time—"

"Yes, last time you brought down a crime ring almost single-handedly. I remember the bragging." She shakes her head and scoops up a pile of noodles with her fork. "Why *did* you move to New York, anyway? It seemed like you were on the rise, and then suddenly I hear you've taken off."

Speaking of things to file under "shit not to think about…"

"I'm a free spirit, baby." I use the smile that comes naturally to me—the one that's been convincing people for years that I don't give a crap about anything. "I go wherever the whim takes me."

She shakes her head and concentrates on her meal. In the silence, I watch her. I liked Anderson the second we crossed paths in our first week at the academy. She's smart—if a little traditional in her approach to things—and she's calm in a crisis. I've seen her outrun some of the fittest men I know to take down a bad guy. I've seen her talk herself out of dangerous situations and I've seen her stick up for some of the most vulnerable people in the communities we serve. Despite my teasing, I respect her a hell of a lot. She deserves to be a detective.

And I can't take my eyes off her.

"Who's staring now?" She smirks at me with a self-satisfied expression that's a flashing cape to a bull.

"You have a little something..." I lean forward to point at an imaginary spot on her cheek and when she moves I flick her nose with my finger.

"You're such a child," she says, rolling her eyes. But that doesn't stop her dabbing at the imaginary spot with a napkin. "Fine, let's try it your way tonight. Romantic walk in the garden...but we might want to bring a bucket in case I need to puke from the pressure of pretending to be attracted to you."

"Who's the child now?" I mutter, stacking the empty containers and stifling the grin that wants to burst forth. If I'm going to be back in Australia, then at least I have some fun to distract me from the growing list of things I don't want to think about.

CHAPTER FOUR

Hannah

THERE'S A SURPRISING amount of garden space out the back of 21 Love Street, considering we're in South Melbourne. From what I've read on the building, this used to be a big warehouse lot that was rezoned to accommodate residential construction. The original building was torn down, but instead of filling the space with a huge apartment tower, they went for quality over quantity. It makes for a nice change from the other massive towers popping up all over the city, which are slowly blotting out the light in increasingly cluttered streets.

There's a shared barbeque area with tables and chairs adorned with striped cushions. A curved path leads to a communal vegetable garden already budding with zucchini and thick bushes of thyme and mint. I take a moment to crouch down and breathe in the enticing scent. A lemon tree fills one corner, bursting with yellow fruit. Several lemons lie on the ground, half-consumed by some creature who must have stumbled across the bounty.

That's when I notice a small single-door gate next to the tree. Between the darkness of the evening sky and the fullness of the lemon tree, it's somewhat concealed.

"See that?" I turn to Owen. "It would be pretty easy to slip in and out here at night without being seen."

The sky isn't too dark yet—but soon it will be. There aren't many lights in the garden, beyond the barbeque area and the entrance to the building that houses the indoor swimming pool. This part of the yard is shadowy and private.

"I'm assuming it's locked," Owen says, taking a closer inspection. "There's a latch and a padlock, so it's not accessible with the key cards."

"That means it's not for resident use. What's behind it?"

Owen jumps up and wraps his hands over the edge of the fence, hoisting himself up. I suck in a breath at the sight of his muscles bulging beneath the sleeves of his jumper. He's always been fit, but the last few years have filled his body out in a way that sets off a warm burn in my stomach. He's broader in the shoulders, fuller in the arms, rounder in the butt. But his waist is still sharply defined in that delightful V shape that tells me he hits the gym regularly.

"An alleyway," he confirms and I nod, hoping he hasn't caught me looking again. "We'll take a look down there tomorrow, see if there's any evidence of people hanging around."

"So there's four ways into the property that I've seen—front entrance, car park, loading bay and this door." I tick the options off my fingers. "I doubt they're hauling bags of jewels and cash in and out via the front door. If we're talking about the kind of money that Ridgeway mentioned…they're not sneaking that through in a gym bag."

"And the car park has as much surveillance as the front entrance. There's cameras all over," Owen adds. "In the loading dock, too. This might be a hand-off point."

We know jewels are coming into this building thanks to a diamond cuff that had been fitted with a tracker. Unfortunately, the person who'd stolen the cuff from the small exhibit where it was being shown as "bait" had done a good job skirting the surveillance cameras. After that, the trail went cold.

The current estimation is that the thieves lift the items and bring them to 21 Love Street where a jeweller strips the gems out. Then the gems are sold either individually or in lots and residual metal from the settings and chains is sold to a gold buyer who melts it down.

By that method, there are no pieces of evidence floating around which might provide a trail back to the operation. It's smart. And while it might not provide the same kind of cash as other criminal activities—such as drug production or trafficking—it's a good place for would-be criminals to cut their teeth. The larger worry was that the Romano crime family had a new figurehead. This case wasn't simply about stopping theft. It was about gathering information so we could go after the bigger problem. But there wouldn't be budget for a task force unless we could prove that the Romano crime family was back in action.

"Someone's watching us," Owen says quietly.

The words cause goose bumps to ripple over my skin as my brain switches to high-alert. It's like the air has dropped a few degrees, and suddenly I'm conscious of every little detail around me—the whisper-quiet sound of footsteps on grass, the scent of cigarette smoke coiling into the air, the shifting shadows of the lemon tree as a breeze causes the leaves to shudder in the wind.

"Kiss me," he says.

"What?" I resist the urge to turn and look at whatever he can see behind me.

Owen's fingers encircle my wrist and he pulls me closer, further into the dark shadow of the lemon tree. "We're a newlywed couple out for a romantic stroll…so let's look romantic."

Shit. I have no idea what he can see and I hate being the one in a vulnerable position. But protecting the cover *always* comes first—before my comfort zone, before my own desires. Only now, the cover and my desires converge, and I wind my arms around Owen's neck. He takes a step back and hits the fence, allowing me to pin him there.

We don't have to kiss, not really. Holding my head

close to his would have been enough to maintain our position as horny newlyweds, but my lips part before I can logic my way out of doing what I've dreamed of since I was a fresh-faced academy trainee. I press my mouth to his and his fingers tighten at my waist, pulling me closer. His lips are firm and his grip is confident and his tongue slides along mine in a way that makes my knees buckle. God, he tastes even better than he smells—like earth and man and a hint of spice. Delicious.

My fingers drive through his hair, fisting the lengths so I can hold myself upright. I don't protest as his hands slide down my back and cup my ass, because there's not a single cell in my body that *doesn't* want this. I've kissed a few guys before—some of them weren't bad. One or two were good kissers.

But Owen is a master. He kneads me in a rhythmic way that makes my sex throb, like he's simulating the tempo of fucking. But it's the moment he yanks me up an inch and jams me firmly against him that takes my breath away. He's hard as a rock and his jeans do nothing to conceal the thick, curved length of his cock as it digs into my belly. *That* isn't part of our undercover script.

Because kisses can be faked and affections can be feigned, but a hard-on tells me that maybe I'm not the only one who's super into this right now. And that's a terrifying thought, because it's easy for me to hate Owen for rejecting me all those years ago. For teasing me about my crush on him. It's easy for me to write him off as someone who's totally wrong for me.

But unfortunately, I've never stopped lusting over Owen Fletcher. Now the floodgates have been opened and I have to live with him as man and wife. Screwing your co-worker isn't exactly a great career move.

But something tells me that I'll be going to bed with this kiss on my mind every damn night until we either crack this case, or until I give in to the feelings that have been haunting me for the past decade. Right now, as I writhe against him, I'm not sure which option I prefer.

CHAPTER FIVE

Owen

HANNAH FEELS LIKE heaven in my hands, but she kisses like the devil. Dark and sinful and so tempting my mere mortal brain has no hope of withstanding her. When I pulled her toward me, I hadn't expected her to respond with such enthusiasm. The kiss was a legitimate action to maintain cover and within the boundaries of our work.

The wood in my jeans was *not*.

I'd been prepared to keep my hands at ten and two—high school dance style—until the second she'd rubbed against me, purring like a kitten and taking a lit match to my decency. The sound coming from her mouth scrambles my brain, making me think of long sweaty nights and the feeling of thighs clamping down on my head. My fantasy woman always has dark hair and dark eyes, and it didn't occur to me until right now that Anderson could be that woman. She *has* been that woman…more times than I will ever admit.

But Anderson is a family woman. A heart-and-soul kind of woman. A forever woman. And that means we'll never be anything more than friends.

Her lips work against mine, her tongue sliding into my mouth as she presses herself against me. Grinding. I'm pinned to the fence, my body temperature skyrocketing. I want nothing more than to spin her around so I can use the fence to brace her back while I drag her legs up and encourage her to lock her heels behind my back.

But this is work. And this kiss is veering into the space where one of us is taking advantage of the situation—only I don't know *who.*

"He's gone." I whisper against her lips. It's dark outside and I can't see the details of her expression, but I feel the effects of the kiss in the puffiness of her lips. In the quickness of her breath.

"Well," she says shakily. "*That's* a relief."

"Yeah, I got the impression you thoroughly hated that." The teasing comes easily, naturally. It's like breathing for me. Like walking.

But what I really want is to tell her that she's got me hot and bothered. That I'll have to scrub this memory from my mind if I have any hope of keeping my focus on the case. But my focus is no better than a crystal glass thrown against a brick wall. It's thousands of irreparable glittering shards. I want to punish that sweet mouth of hers and haul her over my shoulder so I can take her straight to my bed.

"What now?" she asks.

I want to stay in this bubble forever—me and her.

That kiss. The feel of her subtle curves against me. "We take the show back to the apartment."

"What?" she squeaks, stepping back suddenly. No longer covered in the shadows of the tree, the moonlight bounces off her face—off her wide eyes and lush mouth. I bet the tips of her ears are bright red.

"We're newlyweds who've gotten distracted by a kiss and now we're heading back home to finish what we started." I grin and step forward, causing her to back up. "Do you have a problem with that, darling wife?"

She rolls her eyes and turns, heading back across the garden. In a few strides, I catch up to her and sling an arm around her shoulders. I'm surprised to find a smirk on her lips. "I think if anyone thoroughly enjoyed that kiss, it was *you*, by the way," she says.

Our footsteps fall in time. "What powers of deduction did you use to figure that out?"

"You're going to make me say it?" She shakes her head. There's more light overhead now as we approach the barbeque area and her ears are definitely pink. "It was pretty bloody obvious."

"I have no idea what you're talking about."

She opens her mouth to respond, but we're interrupted by a group spilling out of the building and into the shared barbeque area. There are three men dressed in casual attire, laughing and carrying food. Two of the men look to be brothers and all appear to be in their early thirties.

"You're new." One of the brothers points a pair of

tongs in our direction. The others wave and set themselves up around the barbeque. "Level six, right?"

"Word travels fast." I stick my hand out. "Owen.
This is my wife, Hannah."

The W-word rolls off my tongue *far* too easily and
it stirs something uncomfortable in my gut.

"Dom." The guy is built like a bear and has a grip
to match. "That's my brother, Rowan, and our mate
Matt."

"We moved in today," Hannah says, her smile a
little too wide. I reach for her hand and squeeze—
hoping it looks more loving and less like the warning it is. Rule number one of being undercover, never
offer more information than you need to. "This
morning, actually. We've been unpacking all day."

She's nervous. Hannah is like a fountain when
she's nervous, which normally I am *all* about. But
now is not the time for verbal diarrhea. I squeeze
her hand again.

"It's a great building." Dom nods. "Ro and I
moved in about two years ago."

If it's true, it doesn't really seem to fit the time-
line, since the activity only started up within the
last six months…but that's a *big* if. Could be part
of their cover story. I'll get my hands on the building management documents and corroborate that
information.

My eyes drift to the two men firing up the barbeque. They're laughing and joking. Matt is dressed
in all black and he could very well have been the
shadowy figure who interrupted us in the garden.

"How did you all meet?" I ask.

"Matt went to high school with us. He's a chef."

Rowan looks up from the barbeque and grins. He has a cavalier air about him, like he's a bit of a joker. "You wouldn't know it with the way he butchered this meat. Looks like it was done with a hacksaw."

"I can't work magic with shitty tools," Matt grumbles. Unlike Rowan and Dom, he's fair-haired and has sharp grey eyes.

"What do you do?" Hannah asks, looking up at Dom.

"Ro and I run the family business, an art gallery."

I have to actively conceal my surprise. Dom looks more like a bricklayer than the owner of a gallery—though admittedly, I know as much about art as I do about bricklaying. Zip.

"I run all the events," Rowan says, wandering over and handing his brother a beer. "Deal with the temperamental artists and mingle with the buyers."

In other words, he's a professional party boy. Could be a good cover, getting to mix and mingle with all the big players in Melbourne and making connections. Maybe he scopes out the targets.

"And I make sure my brother doesn't blow all our profit on champagne and canapés." Dom grins. "You should come and visit us sometime. I'm sure we have something perfect for your new apartment."

"That would be lovely." Hannah brings her hand to her chest, so the stones on her engagement ring wink in the light. The gesture is subtle—authentic—which is why it's perfect. I watch Rowan and Dom carefully, noting the way their eyes drift down to Hannah's hand. "We were saying today that we'd like something special for the bedroom. Our old pieces don't feel quite right anymore."

That's my girl. She's finding her feet in the role now, which I know to be far from her real "true blue Aussie" life. I've met her family—her dad was a sergeant before he retired. Nice bloke. For some reason, watching Hannah in action brings back the surge of attraction I've been trying so hard to keep under wraps. What can I say? Capability gets me hot.

"Isn't that right, Owen?" She looks up at me with those luminous brown eyes and I wonder how in the fuck I am going to get to sleep tonight.

"Yes, dear." I say it with just enough of a patronising tone that I get a chuckle from Rowan. It makes me feel like a class-A dick, but it's part of the act. Still, I can practically hear my grandmother scolding me. "Whatever you'd like."

"We've got an opening for a new artist later this week. Why don't you join us?" Rowan looks back to where Matt is throwing the steaks onto the grill. The sound of searing meat hisses into the night air. "I'll put an invite into your mailbox."

"We're number six-oh-one," Hannah clarifies, looping her arm through mine. "It's nice to meet you. Enjoy your barbeque."

The men turn their attention to their dinner and Hannah leads me inside the building.

"What do you think?" she asks as we're in the elevator.

"Not much to go on, but the gallery thing is un-expected. They don't seem the type."

"Agreed." She bobs her head. "And I know what I'm doing, okay? You don't have to freak out every time I open my mouth."

"You seemed a little nervous."

"I wasn't."

I would call bullshit, but I cut her some slack. Hannah's nerves only ever come from wanting to do a good job. This position means everything to her. She told me week one of our academy training that she was going to make detective by thirty-five and she's a couple years ahead of schedule.

It's a tough job and competitive to even get the opportunity. She's probably thinking about all the things that could go wrong.

"If I seemed nervous it was more likely revul-sion," she adds. But her clipped tone is all bark and no bite. "From kissing you, I mean."

"Whatever helps you sleep at night, Anderson," I reply. "So long as you look the part when we have an audience, that's all that matters."

The way she kissed me is playing on my mind, however. It wasn't the kind of kiss I expected, and she could easily have kept it low-key. Faked it.

But that *wasn't* faking it, for either one of us.

I'll have to do my best to ignore the burning chemistry and hope she'll do the same. Because I have a feeling if Hannah asked me to fuck her sense-less tonight, I'd have a *really* hard time remember-ing why it's a bad idea.

CHAPTER SIX

Hannah

DAY TWO OF my fake marriage and I'm already questioning why I didn't put up more of a fight when Max suggested bringing Owen back for this operation. I should have nipped it in the bud. But oh no, I had to go and think the golden boy's shine might have worn off with absence. Mistake number one.

Mistake number two was not pushing the brother-and-sister undercover plan harder. But like any good public servant, I fell into line.

Mistake number three was kissing him. Well, kissing is kind of a soft description. I basically dry humped him against the fence.

Cringing, I shake my head. Last night I acted out of line—unprofessional. Owen made it clear *years* ago that he wasn't interested and yet I threw myself at him the first chance I got. Pathetic. He's probably having a good laugh about it.

But what about the fact that he was hard enough to drill holes?

Natural physical response. Endorphins. Adrenaline. Pick a reason.

It's like the universe has designed the perfect situation to test me. This morning I burned my toast while getting lost in my imagination. Getting lost in a fantasy starring him. How am I supposed to do my job when I can't even make a bloody piece of toast without screwing it up?

Ugh, don't think about screwing. Don't think about screwing. Don't think about screwing...

"Whatcha thinking about?" Owen walks into the kitchen, a pair of tracksuit pants riding low on his hips and a white T-shirt clinging to every muscle in his chest. His blond hair is damp, which makes his blue eyes even brighter.

It's borderline disgusting how attractive he is.

"I'm thinking about the case." I busy myself by putting the dishes away from our dinner last night. "Obviously."

"Obviously." Amusement dances in his voice. "By the way, this arrived. I noticed it when I came back from my run this morning."

He's holding a crisp white envelope in the kind of paper that usually signifies something fancy—weddings, galas, charity balls.

He grabs a knife and slips it under the seal at the back, slicing the envelope open. Inside is a single piece of paper. It's grey and industrial-looking, with rough edges and an asymmetrical shape but the fancy gold-and-white font screams money.

"A personal invitation from Galleria D'Arte to

join Dominic and Rowan Lively in presentation of artist Celina Yang." Owen looks up. "It's a cocktail party tomorrow night."

A cocktail party. Great. Unfortunately, the work budget doesn't extend to fancy wardrobe purchases, and I'm pretty sure Owen doesn't own a tux. Or is a tux more black tie than cocktail? I have no earthly idea.

"What should I wear?" I bring my thumb up to my lips, ready to bite down until I remember that I need to look the part. No more biting my nails.

"Cocktail dress?" Owen supplies less-than-helpfully.

"I don't own any." I have one dress that *might* pass at a nice restaurant since it's black and simple. The last time I wore it was to a funeral. And if it passed muster at a funeral, does that mean it's no good for a cocktail party?

Damn it. When it comes to outrunning the bad guys and clipping on handcuffs or diffusing a tense situation, I'm at the top of my game. But I don't do parties and dresses and high heels. How am I going to convince *anyone* that I'm a trophy wife?

"You go. I'll pretend to be sick," I mutter.

"Do we need to go shopping?" Owen places the invitation on the kitchen counter and leans his forearms against the sleek marble. "We can get you something to wear."

"That's not an appropriate use of the budget and you know it." Maybe I can slap on some fake leaves and pretend to be a potted plant, Scooby-Doo style.

"Don't worry about the budget."

I sigh. "Of *course* I worry about the budget. There are more important things to spend that money on and I can't be seen taking advantage of the situation to fill out my wardrobe."

"I'll cover you." When I raise a brow, Owen shrugs in that careless way of his. "I'm a consultant and I have expenses. No big deal."

"I'll pay you back," I say. The thought of him footing the bill for a dress feels totally and utterly wrong, but if I'm being honest my five-year-old Target dress isn't going to cut it for an upper-crust gallery event.

"Stop worrying about the money." He turns and heads toward the spare room, which he's graciously taken so I can have the master suite with the more private bathroom. "Go grab your things."

We catch the tram to Collins Street, where the designer shops sit like glittering beacons of unattainable style. The only time I come to the "Paris End"—aka the section with all the fancy stores—is to have the odd drink with friends. But Owen whisks me into the Gucci store like he's done it a thousand times before.

We bypass the shoes and bags and head into the quieter part with the clothing. "This is excessive," I say under my breath. "Can't we go to Myer?"

Department stores are a little more my speed. And I'm already wondering what kind of payment plan I'll need to buy a dress here. I love my job, but it isn't for the thickly padded pay cheque.

"You need to grab everybody's attention. We're drawing them to us, remember?"

We walk into a room with huge screens playing footage from a runway show. The models are wearing strange, avant-garde creations and they all look terribly unhappy. Biting down on my lip, I glance around the store.

I walk over to a simple dress in emerald green with a ruffle draping from one shoulder all the way to the hem. It's not my style, but it looks like something my undercover alter ego might wear. But when I glance at the price tag, I almost faint.

"We need to leave," I say under my breath as a well-heeled sales assistant approaches us. "Please."

"Hannah, it's fine." Owen touches my arm like we really *are* a married couple and that only makes my stomach swish harder. I'm going to send myself into life-long debt for a cocktail dress.

"Can I help you?" The woman has a cool confidence that I immediately envy. But maybe I could learn a few things from her to help bolster my persona.

"My wife is looking for a cocktail dress," Owen says when I remain stubbornly quiet. "We've got an important event to attend."

The woman's gaze sweeps over me, assessing my size and shape. Her fingers drift over a rack of clothing, and she pushes the hangers to one side to reveal a hot pink monstrosity that looks like some cruel fashion joke. When she notes my expression, she immediately moves to another rack.

"What kind of an event?"

"A gallery exhibition." I can barely find my voice. I *hate* feeling so out of my depth, and over such a stupid thing, too. I've had a gun pointed directly at my face and yet I'm scared of a few metres of silk?

"Ah, so you might want something artistic." She taps a well-manicured finger to her chin. "How daring are you?"

Not very. Not even a little bit. "Uh, I'm probably more classic than daring."

"She's very daring," Owen says, his gaze scorching me from the inside out. "My wife doesn't see it in herself, but I do. She's got a spark like nobody else."

Does he really see that in me? Or is it part of the doting husband act?

My head and heart have been a jumbled mess ever since Owen set foot back in Australia. I thought I'd gotten over it all—over the desperate desire and humiliation. Over the way he'd looked at me, with clear eyes while mine were glassy with champagne, as he'd told me that he wouldn't sleep with me because he valued our friendship. The humiliation had burned me to ash, and it made his act now all the more painful to swallow.

Because despite the time that had passed, I still wanted it to be real.

The woman's face lights up as she pulls another garment from the rack. It appears to be a blazer made of reflective black material. "Is there a pair of pants to go with that?" I ask.

She ushers me to a changing room. "It's a dress

made to look like a blazer. It's classic *and* daring, to suit both what you see and what your husband sees."

When she closes the door behind me, I stare at myself in the mirror. Even with the flattering gold tones of the change room and the specially engineered lighting, I don't love what I see. I'd never call myself ugly, but I wouldn't say I'm anything special to look at, either. Brown hair, brown eyes, eyebrows that could do with some TLC. I've always viewed my body for what it can do—for speed and strength and agility—rather than looks. And I've told myself over and over when relationships fizzled, that it was because men are intimidated by strong women.

But now I wonder if I'm a bit…boring. Unsophisticated.

"How's it going in there?" Owen's honey-smooth voice jolts me out of my negative thought spiral and I shuck my jeans.

"This is my worst nightmare," I admit. Somehow, without having to face him, it's a little easier to be honest. "I can't afford anything in here and I feel like a little girl playing dress-up."

The silence stretches on for a beat more than is comfortable.

"Firstly, the dress is my treat. And secondly…" The lock rattles lightly and I can tell he's leaned against the door. "You need to stop being so hard on yourself."

I raise a brow at my reflection. It's the most un-Owen-like thing he could have said. I'm down to my bra and undies now, and pulling the blazer/dress thing off the hanger. It's surprisingly heavy, and I notice it's covered entirely in glimmering beads.

"You deserve to be where you are because you work harder than anyone else. Because you're smarter than anyone else. Maybe more people should be like you, rather than you trying to be like someone else."

The statement warms my heart, kindling an old fire. I can't help the goofy grin that stretches my lips as I slip into the dress. The sales assistant was right—it *is* the perfect mix of classic and daring. The long sleeves and padded shoulders give a structured, powerful vibe and the short hemline and plunging neck are sexy as all get-out. But the fact is I *am* a girl playing dress-up. Because I would never wear this dress, and I would never be with a guy like Owen who flits from one thing to the next, always chasing a new whim.

I like him. I always have. But I need to remember what I told myself all those years ago—it's a good thing he rejected me. Because a guy like him would chew me up and spit me out. I need to find a relationship where I'm an equal partner, where the other person is invested as much as I am. And unfortunately, I'm *always* more invested than the other person.

When I open the change room door, Owen's eyes widen. "Wow."

He's looking at me like it's the first time he's seen me. But I don't want to have my *She's All That* moment right now. Because this transformation is a lie—like the ring on my finger and the apartment we're sharing. I'm never going to be the "after" picture in some "ugly duckling to swan" advertisement.

I'm not sure I want to be, either.

"Thanks." I swallow my awkwardness. "Don't get used to it. I'll be back in leggings tonight."

I refuse to let his reaction affect me. If there's any attraction here, it's not because of who I *really* am. I can't afford the delusion that there will ever be anything between us…no matter how much I can't stop thinking about that kiss.

CHAPTER SEVEN

Owen

BY THE THIRD day of living at 21 Love Street, we've met a number of our neighbours in passing. Hannah ignored my suggestion to let them come to us, and I have to admit she's playing the role of social butterfly well.

We've met a communications manager and her investment banker fiancé from level one. A quiet schoolteacher named Ava and her friend Emery, who live in the apartments next to Rowan and Dominic on level five. I'm thinking they could be a good source of information on the brothers' activities. And Matt the chef lives on level three. We haven't seen anyone on level six—I suspect the other penthouse might be owned by someone who travels a lot. There are also two young families on the first floor, and an older woman on level three who seems to keep to herself but gave a friendly wave in the mailroom as I pretended to inspect our mailbox.

Nothing suspicious yet. Based on what we have,

I feel Dom, Rowan and Matt are worth looking into further. Which is why Hannah and I are waiting outside L'Arte Galleria in a line to have our tickets checked by a beefy guy in a black suit.

"This place is fancy," Hannah whispers. She's hanging on to my arm and has a black trench coat covering her new dress. That dress has been on my mind *all* day. "I bet they have Swarovski-encrusted toilets."

I snort and make a poor attempt of covering it with a cough. We step forward in the line and she's careful to keep her balance on a pair of pencil-thin stilettos that I bought to go with her dress. They have a mirror-like silver finish and they're doing amazing things for her legs. Hannah had argued that they were impractical and that she wouldn't be able to chase after anyone in them—but tonight we're gathering information. No running required.

"Tickets?" The beefy guy has a nose that looks like it's been on the losing side of a few fistfights and he's built like a brick wall. Is that OTT for a gallery? I'm not sure.

Hannah hands our invite over and the beefcake scans a small barcode on the back of it. "Mr. and Mrs. Essex, welcome."

Interesting. I don't remember giving our surname to Dom when we spoke in front of the barbeque, but he obviously got it somehow. I press my hand to the small of Hannah's back and we're ushered into the cloakroom area. It's chilly out tonight—rainy and damp in that typical Melbourne early spring way—

and so we offload our outerwear. I try not to stare as
Hannah shrugs out of her coat, revealing her long,
lean legs and a scandalous triangle of chest. The
bare skin contrasting with long sleeves looks edgy
and sexy. She's put on a little makeup and fluffed
out her hair, so that it falls in shiny brown waves
to her shoulders. I don't quite understand why she
made that comment about being a little girl playing
dress-up yesterday, because she looks every bit the
perfect Mrs. Hannah Essex to me.

"Shall we?" I hold my hand out to her, and she
takes it. There's that blush again, tinting her cheeks
and neck and the tips of her ears.

"Stop looking at me like that." The words are spoken low, for my ears only.

"Like what?"

"Like you're a wolf who's gone weeks without a
fresh kill." Her hand slips into mine. "And I'm a big,
dumb deer who's stumbled into your path."

I pull her close to me as we weave through a large,
modern archway which opens into the gallery's main
room. The exhibition is…not quite what I expected.
Sculptures dot the room, abstract shapes that somehow manage to look erotic—like bodies entwined—
without actually resembling anything at all.

The lighting is low, except for a few strategically
placed red spotlights which give the room an almost
club-like atmosphere. Electronic music plays over
the speakers, but not so loud that it inhibits conversation. There are waiters circling the room, wearing

blood-red tuxedo jackets and carrying trays of pink-tinted sparkling wine.

Hannah cocks her head. "This is different to what I thought it would be. Although, to be fair, my experience with galleries is limited to that one time I went to NGV on a high school excursion."

"Same."

Even living in New York hadn't tempted me into the local pastime of spending hours staring at things my brain isn't creative enough to process. I'm more of a hands-on guy. This is a bit...cerebral.

"They're kind of sexy." Hannah steps closer to the sculpture nearest us. She leans forward slightly, her eyes narrowed and a cute little wrinkle in her nose. "Is that weird?"

"It's not weird at all." A woman appears beside us, her dark hair shaved on one side and reaching down to her shoulders on the other. "This collection is about capturing the feeling of oneness that two people experience in love and lust."

"This is your work?" Hannah straightens and puts on a smile.

"Yes, I'm Celina Yang." She extends her hand and Hannah accepts it.

"Hannah Essex, nice to meet you. The pieces are very...thought-provoking."

"Thank you." Celina smiles. She's a striking woman, barely more than five feet two and wearing flat shoes. She's dressed in red to match the theme of the event—a dress that looks as avant-garde as her work. Two large diamonds glitter in her ears. "I take a lot of inspiration from my own relationships."

"Looks like you have some good relationships," Hannah comments. Then she looks up, as if the comment had slipped accidentally. "I mean…the sculptures are beautiful."

That's my Hannah. Smooth as sandpaper.

Celina laughs. "Being comfortable with one's sexuality is a very pure thing, despite what society might lead you to believe. Sex is when we are at our truest and most vulnerable."

I watch Hannah inspecting the sculpture. This one is two pieces of twisted material—a shiny black that's so glossy it looks like there's a fine layer of ice over it, and a matte, velvety black.

"You can touch it," Celina says. "This is meant to be an interactive exhibit."

For some reason Hannah's eyes flick to mine as her hand comes slowly—hesitantly—down to the sculpture. At first she brushes her fingertips over the sweeping curve of the matte black material, but then—as if enjoying the feeling—she presses her palm flat over it and moves it along in one smooth but firm stroke.

This shouldn't turn me on. It's a sculpture that looks like nothing. An adult version of Play-Doh. But watching her hand move, growing bolder with Celina's encouragement, has all the blood in my body rushing south. What the hell is wrong with me?

"Try it." Hannah holds her hand out to me, tempting like the devil herself.

I step forward and allow Hannah to take my hand. The sculpture is strangely soft beneath my fingertips. As I glide my hands back and forth, it changes from smooth to rough.

"It feels so strange," Hannah says.

"It shows the dual-edge of a toxic relationship," Celina says. "The very thing that can feel good and comforting, can become painful when turned on us."

I watch as her eyes drift across the room. There's a man standing by himself, his long figure encased in a black suit. He's fair-haired and when he turns, I recognise Matt instantly.

"Some people are no good for you, even if you want them to be." Her hand toys with one of her earrings, the large clear stone looking almost pinkish from the red spotlight above. "But it looks as though you two don't have that problem at all."

"We have our ups and downs," Hannah says, winking at me. "Right now, I'd say we're up."

Who *is* this woman? The Hannah I know is prickly and has a tongue that could slice bone. But now she's soft and flirty. It's part of her act, of course—Hannah Essex rather than Hannah Anderson.

"Well, you should think about getting one of the sculptures for your bedroom. Never helps to inject the room with more sensuality." Celina smiles and her hand drops away from her earring. "If you're interested, I can help you pick one that will be a good fit."

"Thank you. We'll definitely consider it," I say.

Celina moves on to the next cluster of people.

The room is moderately full, but there's still plenty of space to move around. I notice more people interacting with the sculptures now—touching and getting close. Hannah sticks by my side as we drift on to the next piece—it's a harder and more aggressive shape made of gold and silver. The two pieces of metal bow away from each other before coming back to twist into a small spire at the top.

This time Hannah doesn't hesitate to reach out and touch it. "Do you think it's true what she said?"

"About what?"

"That sex is when we are at our truest and most vulnerable?" Her eyes don't meet mine and I wonder what game she's playing—is this about our cover... or something more?

My memory drifts back to the night she propositioned me. We'd graduated from the academy and there was a huge house party—one last hurrah before we were all scattered across the state. Many new constables work in rural areas for a period of time, finding their feet and helping communities that don't have much police coverage. Hannah had never been a big drinker, so the champagne had hit her hard. She'd been falling all over me, giggling with her cheeks and ears pink and hair mussed and eyes wild.

I'd never seen a more beautiful woman in all my life.

Don't you want to kiss me? she'd asked. *I've seen you look at me and I never knew if it meant anything but I hoped it did. I'm not supposed to like you because you're dangerous for a girl like me...but I do.*

Dangerous. The funniest thing about it was that if anyone was dangerous in that scenario, it was her. Because she was smart and beautiful and courageous and so kickass it made me want to burst. But I'd been with a girl like that before—where I'd loved as hard as my teenage heart knew how. The day I'd lost it all I'd broken into so many pieces no one knew how to put me back together.

"Owen?" Hannah cocked her head. "You didn't answer my question."

"I guess it's true." I shrug. "I'm not sure I would say it's a vulnerable thing, though."

It never was for me...not after the first time. These days, sex is blowing off steam and scratching an itch. It's fun and enjoyable, but it's never about vulnerability. In fact, being vulnerable is the thing I avoid most in life. Because getting close to someone has never worked out well for me in the past—I've lost a mother and father and a brother and a grandfather and the girl I loved.

That's a whole lot of loss for one heart to handle.

"Yeah, me either." She looks as though she's seriously considering Celina's words. "Sometimes it's just about fun, right?"

CHAPTER EIGHT

Hannah

GOD, WHAT AM I saying? This whole event has my head mixed up. I'm wearing a revealing dress, touching erotic sculptures and talking about sex with my colleague. This is *not* who I am.

I should have my eye on the prize. I should be hunting out Dom and Rowan and trying to figure out if they're part of the jewellery theft ring we're supposed to be tracking down. But it's like I've inhaled some kind of drug and my brain is in a lusty pink fog.

The way he looks at me, with those intense blue eyes, makes the rest of the room evaporate. I've wanted a lot of things in my life—to climb the ladder at work, to have the respect of my father and brothers, to one day have a family of my own. But I've never wanted another man as much as I want Owen right now. The years have grown my desire for him, making it stronger and more unwieldy.

He encircles my wrist with his fingers and tugs

me closer, as any husband in love with his wife might do. I tilt my face up, trying to read him. But Owen's poker face is world class. He's a master joker, a friend to all...and known by none.

"What are you doing?" he asks.

The heat from his body melts me and I pull my hand away from his grip and press it to his chest. His mother's ring glimmers. "Making conversation."

I'm not, though. I'm dancing around something I know I shouldn't be doing. A suggestion which has occupied me with increasing strength from the very second we were left alone in our apartment at 21 Love Street.

"It's not a smart conversation," he says.

"Because you're going to reject me again?" I don't know why I'm setting myself up for this.

"I should."

Should. It wasn't a yes, but it wasn't a no, either. "Because we work together?"

Owen's lips lift into a smile. "That should be the reason *you* keep your hands to yourself. I've got no interest in rejoining the force."

"Then why?"

"Because you don't want casual sex."

His assumption that he knows me so well— regardless of how accurate the statement is—annoys me. Okay, fine, so maybe I already know sex with him wouldn't be casual even if it was a one-time only deal. So what? I'm a grown woman and I know how to deal with the consequences of my actions.

"That's my decision to make," I reply. "And I

haven't voiced what I want, so I'm not sure why you think it's your place to tell me."

We're close now. So close that if we swayed it would look like we were slow-dancing. The people around us might assume the intimate chatter between us is verbal foreplay—and I guess it is. I can't seem to do the sensible thing and back away, because the moment I heard about his move to New York, I thought I'd lost him forever.

Who falls for the most unattainable guy in the world and expects to survive without any bruises on her heart? I'm a fool.

But maybe a few bruises would do me good. It's been so long since I did anything that wasn't work. And yes, I want to solve this case and prove my boss made the right decision to promote me...but this could be my last chance to have the man who's always occupied my head. What happens behind the closed doors of our apartment isn't anyone's business.

This was *precisely* why I wanted us to play brother and sister...because I knew that one kiss for the sake of playing a role would be enough to unlatch the feelings I've locked up tight for far too long.

"Then tell me, Hannah. What do you want?"

Out of the corner of my eye, I spy something that gets my intuition tingling. And, as much as I desperately want to keep playing this game with Owen, the case *does* come first. "Matt and Celina are arguing."

"Huh?" Owen blinks and I entwine my fingers with his, pulling him toward the next sculpture in the exhibition. "Where?"

"Your nine o'clock." I lean over so it looks like I'm reading the little gold plaque. "They're standing by the hallway."

"Got it. She looks pissed."

I let my gaze drift casually in the direction of the argument. A few people have noticed and are moving away, so Celina and Matt head down the dark corridor together, disappearing into another part of the gallery.

"Think it's something?" I ask. I stand and lean my head against Owen's shoulder, so we can speak without anyone hearing.

"Not sure. Did you notice her earrings before?"

I nod. "Big stones. Could be fake, though."

"We should try to get a photo to compare to the list of stuff that went missing in the Collins Auction House robbery." His voice is low, gravelly. He could be reciting a shopping list and still make it sound like the sexiest thing ever. "I had a funny feeling about them."

"Me, too."

I walk forward, unhurried. Partly because I don't want to draw any attention, and partly because it's the only speed I can maintain in these damn heels. Owen is beside me, his hand still in mine. I feel as though my body is burning up. We receive curious glances from other people in the room—but nothing that gets my police officer senses tingling. My dress demands attention and Owen…well, he's always got appreciative eyes on him. The open-collar shirt and grey suit pants make him look every bit the hot Aussie millionaire he's supposed to be.

We slip past the gold sign that tells us this hallway is "for staff use only" and follow the voices.

"Then why did you invite me here?" Matt sounds irritated and in the quiet pause, I can hear sniffling. "I thought we agreed to part ways after…"

I shuffle closer to a bend in the hallway, and I can tell they're just around the corner. Celina is definitely crying.

"Can you walk away so easily?" she asks. "After everything we shared?"

"*You* were the one who said you couldn't do this anymore. I was ready to go all in."

"No, you weren't. Because you would have listened to me if you'd cared at all about my feelings."

It's a lover's spat. Nothing more. I'm about to motion for Owen to head back the way we came, when she mutters something under her breath.

"Here, take these bloody things. I'm not going to wear something you *stole*." There's a long pause and the sound of something dropping against the floor.

"Don't be ridiculous, Cel. They were a gift." Matt sighs. "Does it matter where they came from?"

My brows shoot up and Owen nods. This could be something—because I am *damn* sure she's talking about the earrings.

"Yes, it matters. It should have mattered before but I was willing to look past your…unethical activities." She huffs and the sound of shoes knocking against the floor makes my heart kick up a notch. *Shit*. They're coming this way. "You promised me you'd get out of that stuff. It's dangerous."

Owen backs up as silently as possible. The hallway isn't long but I'm moving slow and a little unsteadily in these heels…we're not going to get back out before they come around the corner. And there's nowhere else to go.

As I sense a flash of movement, Owen pushes me against the wall and his lips are hard on mine once more. It's even better this time than it was the first—because anticipation has been fuelling my every movement. My every waking moment. I open to him like a flower, my body warm and pliable in his hands. The soft groan that comes from the back of his throat is everything.

The scent of his cologne winds through me, and like a creeping vine it wraps around my heart and lungs. I'm intoxicated by him. Enraptured by the way his hands smooth over the fabric of my dress, tracing my boyish shape and making me feel every inch a desirable woman. They tell me a perfect lie and I'm in too deep not to believe it.

I slide my tongue along his, tangling my fingers in his hair and taking my fill. By the time we're done—pink-cheeked and breathing a little heavier—Celina and Matt are gone. I turn my head in time to see Matt walking out of the gallery on the other side of the room. Celina is mingling with the guests as though nothing happened.

"Did you see anything?" I pull back and right my dress, which has ridden up my thighs.

Owen shakes his head. "No. I was a little distracted."

It's a problem. These kinds of distractions lead to cases going unsolved…or worse. We've lost good men and women in the past when someone makes a mistake. When someone has their eye on the wrong thing.

Guilt surges through my veins. I've got this amazing opportunity in front of me and I'm letting my libido lead me astray. I *know* this thing with Owen won't go anywhere, but I can't let it go. Maybe sex cravings are like food cravings? If you want something sweet, the best way to dissipate that feeling is to nibble on some chocolate.

"What did you make of the whole 'unethical activities' thing?" I ask as we slip back into the main room.

"It's vague, but it cements Matt as someone to keep an eye on."

The gallery is much fuller now and it's harder to get close to the sculptures. So we tuck ourselves away in a corner, pretending to inspect one of Celina's few charcoal sketches. This one depicts a woman with her face screwed up with pleasure. The blurry figure of a man is behind her, with his hand at her throat. It's intense. Sexy and a little dangerous and it socks me in the chest.

"She's talented," I murmur, watching Celina weave through the crowd.

There's no sign of her tears now. Her face is radiant as she works the room—touching arms and leaning in close to create a sense of intimacy geared toward making people open their wallets.

"She's not wearing earrings anymore." Owen slips

a hand around my waist as we spot Rowan across the room. His face lights up in recognition and he heads over. "I think we need to make sure you get a business card for Ms. Yang. A private consultation might be a good chance to get some information."

I nod. "Maybe putting something like that in our bedroom might spice up our sex life." I say it partially for Rowan's benefit, loud enough that he'll hear us acting like a regular married couple.

But heat flares in Owen's eyes—turning the icy blue to pure flame—and his fingers flex at my hip in a way that's instinctive. It's *not* for show. I'm convinced I'm not the only one being drawn in by this carnal tide. He feels it, too. Underneath the teasing and the butting heads, there's something simmering.

But he won't pull the trigger. Why? For a long time I thought it was because he wasn't attracted to me. But the way he looks at me now, darkly engrossed and with an intensity that threatens to burn me alive, I reconsider.

The fact is, I can't keep going around and around like this. My brain is like a spinning top, and I need to focus. Tonight, I'm going to do something stupid, something that proves I'm a glutton for punishment.

I'm going to proposition Owen again.

CHAPTER NINE

Owen

I LEAVE THE gallery with Hannah close to 11:00 p.m. We stay longer than most, chatting to Rowan and Dom. Rowan told us in hushed tones that Matt and Celina had a tumultuous relationship—on again and off again. Their strange work hours and the pressures of their perfectionist tendencies had put them under a lot of strain. Before we left, Hannah got a card from Celina and promised to call for a private appointment.

Now, Hannah and I stroll along the Southbank Boulevard. I'd suggested a cab, but she wanted to walk. Processing time, she called it. I'd rather be back at 21 Love Street and straight into a cold shower, because her dress is turning my resolve to mush and her gently smudged lipstick has me thinking about what I could do to further ruin her makeup.

Sparkling lights bounce off the Yarra River as we walk, and the night air is filled with the sound of music and laughter. This part of the city is full of bars and restaurants and, despite the chill in the air, people are out in force.

"Do you think much about the academy days?" she asks me, out of nowhere.

"Sure. They're fond memories." I'd made a lot of friends back then—though many dissolved after I left. It's something I've learned over the years—when you hang out with ghosts for too long you can easily become one.

She steps up to the railing overlooking the river. "Was it hard to walk away?"

"No." Self-preservation is the easy route.

"Not even a little bit?"

"Are you mistaking me for someone with a heart?" I aim for a joking tone and miss by a long-shot. "I left my grandmother two months after my granddad passed. I was her only other family…and I left. Like a coward."

Shit. Why did I say that?

The sincerity shines out of Hannah's eyes like she's turned into a fucking Care Bear. I don't want her to look at me like that. I'm not a person to be saved. Hell, I'm not a person to be loved. I operate best in the middle ground between friend and acquaintance.

"Why did you go? I'm not buying the whole 'I'm chasing a whim' thing."

"You don't need to buy it because I'm not selling it."

Nobody from my police force days is aware of my past, except for the people who run the psych evaluations and the superiors who looked over my file before I entered the academy. I haven't told a single person unless it was absolutely, one-hundred-percent necessary. Not even Max knows, and he's the closest friend I've ever had.

"You were missed," she says quietly, almost as if reflecting to herself. "By a lot of people."

"By you? I thought you hated my guts."

"I did…for a bit." She leans against the railing and tilts her head up at me—all lashes and big brown eyes and a sweet expression that's softer than anything I've seen from her before. "It's hard not to hate the guy who made you a laughing stock."

"You were hardly a laughing stock."

"Really?" She pushes back up to a standing position and folds her arms. "Let me see if I remember this correctly. You snuck into my room, found my diary and decided to do a dramatic reading to a bunch of my peers."

"Firstly, I didn't sneak into your room. I was visiting Vanessa and she opened the door. Secondly, it wasn't like I had to scavenge for the damn thing. It was right there on your nightstand…in a box. Under a picture frame."

Okay, fine. It had been hidden and I'd hunted it out.

Hannah rolls her eyes. "And how do you explain busting open the lock, huh? Did it fall off when you picked it up because your hands are so strong no metal can withstand your grip?"

I laugh and the feeling drives all the way through

me, loosening my muscles. Thawing the ice cage around my heart. She always had that effect on me. It's hard not to like a girl who can make you laugh from down deep.

"I may have encouraged it to open," I reply. "With a paperclip."

"You picked the lock on my diary like a ten-year-old boy!" She's blushing again and I know we're thinking about the same thing.

Hannah Anderson, who'd always seemed like this straitlaced, buttoned-up good girl, had been harbouring some dark and dirty thoughts…about me. At the time, I did *not* expect to see my name on those pages. She'd always acted like I was a bug to be swatted. Or some gum stuck to the bottom of her shoe.

When I decided—in my young, stupid brain—that it would be a good idea to read her diary, I had not planned to make it a show. But my roommate had caught me, demanded to know who it belonged to and rounded up a bunch of guys to listen in. I *never* divulged Hannah's name. Ever.

But someone obviously figured it out.

"Do you remember what it said?" she asks. She's luminous under the moonlight and street lamps, her dress glimmering through the gap between her coat lapels. That peek of bare skin is everything and nothing—the best kind of tease.

I want him. Even though I don't truly know what wanting is because I've never slept with anyone before. But I want to send everyone away for one night—just one—so I can lose everything I have to him. I want to know what it's like to be fucked. Will it hurt? Will he lie with me afterward? I have no idea if I'm even on his radar. Owen could have any girl here, but I want him to have me. Hard.

The words were forever imprinted on my brain. They'd circled like vultures, preying on my sanity and concentration. The night she'd come to me after we graduated, with sooty eyes like blackened pits, my fucked-up brain hadn't been able to shut out the darkness. The second I started to feel anything about Hannah, all I could think about was the dead girl I'd loved more than anything else.

"You do remember," she says. "You just weren't interested."

"Believe me, it wasn't like that. I only took the damn diary because I wanted to know more about you and being a dumb kid, I didn't think I could ask." He shook his head. "I never meant for anyone else to see the pages."

"Water under the bridge now," she said with a shrug. "It's not like it stopped me doing anything I wanted to do...well, not most things anyway."

I don't respond to the innuendo hanging in the air. We shouldn't be talking like this—not when we've got shit to do and a case to close and not when I'm leaving the second it's all over. "Nothing will ever stop you, Anderson. You're a force."

"Why do you say sweet things like that when I'd rather you say something dirty?"

My head snaps toward her. "Don't tempt me."

"Why?"

"Because I can't go there. Not with you."

Her face falls and I want to explain. I want to tell her that it's nothing to do with her and everything to do with me. I want to tell her that it's because I'm not capable of treating her the way she deserves to be treated. That I can take her to bed, but that will be it, and I don't know if I can handle the look on her face when I leave after it's all done.

"It's…" Fuck. I'm *so* not good at this. I can walk away from my troubles like a boss, but staying and talking…I suck at it. "You're hot, okay? It's nothing to do with that."

She tilts her head in a way that reminds me of an adorable puppy. "So it's not because there's a lack of physical chemistry."

I laugh. "Hell no. That's not it at all."

We're still standing at the river, and a group of drunk girls totter past giggling and singing. On the water, there's a cruise boat stuffed full of partygoers. Music floats toward us and so does the sound of laughter and cheering. They're all so obliviously happy.

"I'm not asking for a ring, Owen." She nudges me with her elbow. "I already got that."

"What *are* you asking for?" I go against my better judgement with that question, but the air is burning up around us and we're standing close enough that I could capture her lips with mine.

"One night." Her chest rises and falls with a big breath. "Get it out of our systems. I'd like very much to be able to concentrate on the job and I just…can't. Not with the tension distracting me."

One night, no strings, with the girl I've crushed on ever since she walked into the first-day induction session at the Victoria Police Academy. It would be so easy to say yes.

"No." The word comes out a lot weaker than I'd hoped.

"Why?"

"Because the whole one-night thing doesn't work when you know the person. It's all fine to say we'll act like it never happened, but we both know that's bullshit."

"What if I wasn't me?" There's a darkness to her expression, a simmering heat that pulls me in. "What if I was someone else?"

"What?"

"I'm already playing a role. Hannah Essex." She wriggles her fingers and my mother's ring glints in the light. "I can simply change roles and be someone else."

She wants it that badly? My fingers twitch and my cock is aching for release—I've been in a semi-state of excitement for days and this is only making it worse. How long before I break? How long before my willpower is a billion glittering shards?

"Surely you're not intimidated by a bit of role play?" Her tongue darts out to moisten her lips and I'm about ready to fall to my knees in front of her.

"I'm not afraid of role play." I grit the words out.

"Then I'm going to be in that bar, ordering a

drink." She turns and points to a little hole-in-the-wall place with the ambient glow of low-hanging lights. "If you come find me, we'll pretend to be other people for the night."

Bloody hell. "And if I don't come find you?"

"Then I have my answer."

She turns and walks across the tree-lined boulevard, pausing at the edge of the bar to shrug out of her coat. Her dress glimmers, like stars winking at me, beckoning me closer. I catch the flash of her toned, bare legs and those shiny silver shoes before she disappears inside.

CHAPTER TEN

Hannah

MY HEART IS pounding a million miles a minute as I enter the dimly lit bar. The place is full, but not bursting. A beautiful curved bar in gold and pearl-white wraps around the back two corners of the room. Ornate pendant lights emit a warm glow, and velvet chairs dot the space, where people sit drinking and talking. Most wear suits or pretty dresses—they've probably come from seeing a show at the Arts Centre.

When a couple vacate the bar, I claim one of the empty seats.

Will Owen follow me in here? Is he outside stewing over his decision or has he already started walking home? I can't get his words out of my head.

Nothing will ever stop you, Anderson. You're a force.

When it comes to work and my career, I've worn that label with pride. I'm ambitious and I have the respect of my colleagues and superiors. But the second I shrug out of my blue uniform, I somehow shrug out of my confidence, too.

"What can I get you?" The bartender smiles.

"A French 75, please." I'm craving something fizzy.

My eyes stray to the door, where a couple walks in. They're arm in arm and so into one another that the room shoots up a hundred degrees. Is it pathetic that all I want is for someone to look at me like that? I'm an independent, intelligent woman but…

Just once I want to be *that* girl. The girl who gets the guy, the girl who stops traffic. Is it so bad to want to feel desirable? To feel sexy and coveted and beloved?

The bartender places my drink on a coaster and I pay. Bubbles race to the top of the champagne flute, where a delicate curl of lemon peel sits, curving over the edge of the glass. I stare at it for a moment, hanging in a delicious limbo between fear of rejection and the possibility that I may have something exciting in front of me.

The cocktail is tasty, dry champagne with a hint of sour lemon. As I watch the door, I twist Owen's mother's ring. I still haven't gotten used to wearing it. But for tonight it's on the wrong finger. I slip it off and transfer it to my other hand.

I turn back to my drink and run my finger over the rim, trying to make it sing like I used to when I was a little kid. I count my breaths in and out, clinging to hope.

Please come to me.

I remember how mortified I was when I found out my diary had been read aloud. I knew Owen had done his best to conceal my identity. But people talked and theorised—we all wanted to be investigators, after all.

Rumours spread. I'd denied it, of course. And then the diary had turned up back in my room seemingly of its own accord. I knew he'd put it there. And part of me had been excited that he knew how I felt. Unfortunately, nothing had come of it.

"Is anyone sitting here?"

I turn toward the deep voice and swallow back the excitement surging through my veins. Owen has a dangerous edge to him. His usually playful smile is nowhere to be found, and his vibrant blue eyes hold me captive. Will he play my game?

"No, please." I gesture toward the empty seat next to me. "It's all yours."

He eases himself onto the bar stool and signals to the bartender. 18-year-old Talisker, neat. I've never seen him drink anything but beer. He looks at me while the bartender pours, his expression smouldering and unreadable. The corner of my lips lifts into a smile, inviting him closer. He knows what I want, so now the ball is in his court.

I hold my breath…waiting.

"I'm James," he says.

My thundering heart almost trips over itself with joy. It's happening. "Annabel."

"Are you from around here, Annabel?" An American accent has crept into his voice that's doing funny things to my insides. Is he drawing on his time in New York?

My mind spins. I don't have a backstory planned—I don't know who I'm supposed to be. Hell, I have no idea how this role-play thing is supposed to work. Perhaps part of me never thought he'd say yes…

"I'm in town on business." I sip my drink. "For one night."

"Just one?" There's that cheeky twinkle.

"Yes. I'm…" Think, dammit. "A researcher."

"And what do you research, Annabel?" The way he says my fake name sounds like sex itself.

His drink arrives and he brings the heavy glass up to his mouth, tipping his head back. As he swallows, I watch the muscles working in his throat and I find my own totally devoid of moisture.

"I research the five senses and their effect on the human body." My creative mind kicks into gear and it's like slipping a costume over my head. "Such as how the other senses increase in strength to compensate when one is no longer accessible."

"That's an interesting field of research."

"It's very hands on."

Our bodies are turned toward one another, my legs crossed so that my knees sit between his open legs. Owen leans one arm on the bar and watches me closely. It's different to every other time he's looked at me.

"How do you test those things?" he asks.

"It's pretty simple. I can show you right now, if you like?"

He nods. "Sure."

"Close your eyes."

There's something deeply appealing about having this strong man under my spell. Owen is physically fitter than most men...even most cops. He's easily over six feet, broad-shouldered and has the kind of sculpted, muscular arms you'd expect of an action hero. But having him here in front of me, eyes closed, while he awaits my instruction makes me feel all kinds of powerful. I usually only get that surge of confidence at work.

But this is purely personal.

I take the lemon rind from my cocktail and slowly bring it under his nose. I see the recognition in his facial features, even though he doesn't open his eyes. "What do you smell?"

"Lemon."

"But a second ago you had no idea it was there."

I leave the peel there for a second before placing it on a napkin on the bar. Then I lean closer to him, being sure not to touch him. When my lips are right by his ear, I blow cool air onto his skin and he shudders.

"With your eyes closed, everything else feels more intense. Your sense of smell and touch compensate for your lack of sight." I place my hand on his thigh, feeling hard muscle beneath the fine fabric of his trousers. "It's something that helped our ancestors when they had nothing but the moonlight to guide them."

Where the hell is this coming from? I've fully embraced the role—Annabel, the sexpot researcher. It's helping me be less like my typical awkward self, and more like the woman I *wish* I was.

"In fact," I say, pausing to clear my throat. "I'm here recruiting test subjects."

Owen's eyes open and he looks at my hand resting on his thigh. "What are the requirements?"

"Single men between the ages of thirty and thirty-five. Must be in good health." I let my gaze roam over his body in a way I've never done before.

I dwell in the details of him—in the blond hairs dusting his arms where his sleeves are rolled back. In the way his Adam's apple protrudes at his neck. In the sharp cut of his jaw and the hard slash of his cheekbones. In his bluer-than-blue eyes and full, curved lips. He's so attractive it borders on obnoxious. *All* the female recruits had a crush on him— charming Owen, who could befriend anyone. Who was always quick with a smile and a joke.

He was a boy, then. And now he's filled out into this complex, mysterious man.

"Anything else?" he asks.

"Must be free for one night of testing," I reply. "One *whole* night because...I like to be thorough."

"Sounds like I fit the bill." He knocks back the rest of his Scotch and I'm so nervous and excited

I'm worried my heart is going to bust its way out of my rib cage. "I don't suppose you have a spot open tonight?"

"Actually, I do."

CHAPTER ELEVEN

Owen

MOST PEOPLE DON'T know this about me, but I make decisions with care and consideration. No one expects the joker to have much going on upstairs…but I do. I let my head take the lead, instead of other less reliable parts like my heart, or my dick.

Tonight, however, is a rare exception.

My head is literally screaming at me to back away from this bad decision. But all the blood in my body is currently supporting another appendage. Hannah—posing as a sexy researcher named Annabel—slides from her bar stool, her eyes never leaving mine, and I'm done for. No amount of worrying about the case—about tomorrow—is going to stop me from taking the delicacy she's dangling in front of me.

I follow her from the bar and help her into her coat the second the night air hits us. It's colder now, spitting with rain, and I tuck her close against my body. "Where does your research take place, Ms. Annabel?"

She looks up at me and I see the cogs turning. She's considering whether we should go back to the apartment. That's not a good idea. A hotel will make it easier to keep sex and the job separate.

"I've got a room we could use," I say, leaning into my role of anonymous travelling businessman. "If you don't mind working out of a hotel."

"That sounds great," she says breathlessly.

We walk along the river's edge, our heads bowed to the fine, misting rain and our hands entwined until we reach the Crown Entertainment Complex. The hotel here is swanky to the max and has a price tag to match. The only room available is a suite and the nightly rate makes Hannah's eyes bulge but I hand over my credit card and within seconds we're whisked up to heaven. The room boasts an incredible panoramic view of Melbourne, with glistening lights and a luxurious white sectional facing the window.

I can already see how incredible she'll look laid out on it—naked, with the moonlight dancing on her skin—while I feast on her. My body is tightly coiled, like a spring. There's a pressure building inside me that's been growing for years.

"Please remove your coat," Hannah says in a formal voice. She's already hung hers on a stand by the front door. "If you could also remove your shoes and socks, that would be most helpful."

The clipped, efficient tone makes me smile. I bend

and untie my dress shoes, toeing them off and removing my socks, as instructed. She hangs my coat
next to hers and when she walks back to me, she's
holding a tie in her hands. It looks to be made of the
same fluffy white material as a bathrobe.

"I'm going to blindfold you now, so we can begin."
She waits a moment and I give her a quick nod, letting her know it's okay to proceed.

I've always known Hannah to be a take-charge
kind of woman, and it thrills me to know it trans-
fers to the bedroom. I love being in charge, too, but
there's something insanely hot about a woman who
wants to take pleasure into her own hands. Tonight,
I am willing to be her test subject—to play this role
and revel in whatever that mysterious brain of hers
has planned.

She wraps the blindfold over my eyes, tying it in
a secure knot behind my head. And then nothing. I
can't detect her movement, because the plush carpet
absorbs the sound of her stilettos.

She makes me wait.

The seconds tick by and my desire grows like a
storm, swirling and building, rising until it fills me
completely. When her soft touch brushes the front
of my pants, I'm hard as stone and aching for her.

"Ready?" she asks, her lips brushing my ear.

"I've never been readier."

We've both waited a long time for this.

CHAPTER TWELVE

Owen

IT DOESN'T TAKE long for the blindfold to work its magic. In seconds, I feel my other senses ramping up to accommodate for my lost sight. The gentle kiss of cool air is amplified where my collar sits open, and it's so quiet I can hear the *pitter patter* of rain against the windows. I smell the rain, too—in her hair as she moves around me, mingling with whatever fruity shampoo she uses. I'm driven immediately to the edge of sensation, to the edge of wanting.

There's a tug at my shirt. She's undoing my buttons...slowly. I sense her teasing through the way she pops each one open with an agonising pace.

"You must be doing well to afford such a fancy hotel room," she says, tracing the V of skin at my chest with her fingertip. But the sensual touch does little to hide the curiosity in her voice. The question, no matter how it's posed as part of this role play, is genuine.

"I'm doing well, but money doesn't make the man."

"It certainly doesn't," she murmurs. She works her way to the last of the buttons and then pulls the hem free. "Money doesn't buy decency."

I know the opposite is more likely—money is the reason I have no family. Money is what caused them to be taken from me. "Greed brings out the worst in us."

I would have burned all my parents left me if I'd been allowed. A teenager—blinded by rage and grief—has no use for zeros in a bank account. Because whatever future they might have secured—education and houses and finery—means nothing to an orphan who only wants his parents back.

"I'm feeling a little greedy now." Her hands toy with the buckle at my waist. "Is that so bad?"

"This is totally different." And *this* greed, I can handle.

The buckle makes a metallic *chink* as she yanks the leather through the loops on my suit pants. The sound of my zipper being undone slashes through the quiet air—through my thoughts. I'm about to embark on a hot night with a woman I've wanted for a long time. I need to get my head out of the past.

As if sensing my need to retreat from this conversation, Hannah says, "I'm going to strip you completely. Then we're going to see how you respond to different stimuli."

"Like what?" The anticipation is a fist around my cock. I'm desperate for more, desperate to see what she has planned.

"I can't tell you that. I need to measure the…

strength of your response." Her voice is low and husky.

She shoves my pants down my legs, dragging my boxer briefs with them, and helps me free. I'm totally naked now, and knowing that she's fully dressed makes this even hotter. My cock bobs up against my stomach, hard as concrete and oh-so-ready for her. But after a few seconds of nothing, I realise that Hannah has disappeared.

The silence is broken by the click of her heels over tile—has she gone into the kitchenette or the bathroom? I don't know the layout well enough to tell. There's a brief rushing of water, a dull, metallic sound and then that damn clicking again. I let myself dwell in the vision of her legs in those heels. Hannah is muscular—always devoted to stamina and speed. And her daily runs haven't been interrupted by this case. She gets up at the crack of dawn every morning without fail.

I know the purpose of her runs aren't for physical appearance, but there's no denying the activity has given her shapely legs and a firm ass. Both of which have been on my mind since our kiss in the garden.

I wonder where she is now. The clicking has stopped, and the robe tie is a surprisingly effective blindfold. I need to relieve a little of the tension, and I hesitate only a moment before reaching down to wrap a fist around my cock. I don't think I've been this hard in years. Never mind the fact I lost my taste for casual sex some time ago. But this…is not that.

Not casual. Not meaningless.

I stifle a moan and I run my fist up and down, giving a little twist at my swollen head. I imagine it's her hand doing the work, pleasuring me. Exploring me. Pulling the tip of me to her willing, open lips. My balls are tight. Achy. Never mind that I rubbed one out in the shower this morning, trying to make sure I kept my desires in check.

So much for that.

"Owen, uh… James…" She loses the role play for a moment, her voice ragged-edged with need. "I need you to stop that so we can properly start testing."

I release myself, reluctantly. But it's clear she was watching me for a while before she told me to stop. I can hear it in her voice. Dirty girl.

"Anything else I should refrain from doing?" I ask, letting my words come out slow and lazy.

"Just follow my orders," she replies. "If I don't tell you to do something, then don't do it."

CHAPTER THIRTEEN

Hannah

I'M SO OUT of my depth. I can only hope my voice sounds more commanding than I feel. Because right now, I want to melt into a puddle at Owen's feet.

His body is a masterpiece. Hard sculpted muscle shapes his arms, shoulders, legs and abs. A dusting of blond hair creates a delectable trail from his belly-button all the way down to...

God. I can't tear my eyes away. Of course he's perfect everywhere. Watching him touch himself, watching those slightly rough, strong tugs and the way the swollen head of his erection poked out the top of his fist... Let's be real, I'm already a puddle.

"We're going to start with scent," I say. I've found a bowl of fruit in the kitchenette and I've selected an orange. I press my fingernail into the flesh, piercing it. The ripe scent of the fruit's flesh comes through. "What can you smell?"

I bring the orange under his nose, trying hard

not to think about how I want to rush through this and sink straight to my knees so I can take him in my mouth.

"Hmm, fruity." His voice is roughed up, desire-laden. God, it makes my toes curl in these ridiculously high heels. If a man can have that effect with his voice, what will happen when he finally touches me? "Citrus. Orange or mandarin."

"Very good." I've collected a few items for us to use in this role play: a glass of chilled water, a fork and an individually wrapped chocolate. A condom that I'd stashed in my purse…just in case. "How about taste?"

I peel back the rind from the orange and extract a small piece of flesh. Coaxing his mouth open with my thumb, I wriggle the fruit between his lips. He readily accepts it.

"Definitely orange."

The chocolate is next. I unwrap the foil and see something flicker over his face—like he's trying to figure out what the sound is. But I don't give him any clues. Instead, I pop the chocolate into my mouth and take my time enjoying the small, decadent moment. Then I press into him, bringing my lips to his, and he responds hungrily. The taste of chocolate mixes with the orange he's just consumed.

"Tastes like a Jaffa," he says, bringing his strong arms around me. "So sweet."

"Not yet," I rasp, pulling out of his grip. I want to draw this out—because I have the power now. I'm in charge.

And the second he gets his hands on me I'm going to fold like a house of cards.

"Am I not a good test subject?"

"You're not very good at following instructions." I pick up the fork and press the spiked end into his thigh—not enough to hurt, but certainly enough to elicit a response. His erection twitches and his hands ball by his sides. "How is your sense of touch?"

"Heightened." His voice is wire-tight.

I trail the fork over his chest, letting the metal scrape lightly against his skin. I imagine the contrast feels good—a little pain, followed by something softer. I press my lips to his neck, breathing in the faded scent of cologne on his skin. Sucking so the blood rises to the surface.

The soft imprint of lipstick fills me with a sense of warm possessiveness—like I've claimed him. Marked him.

"If you want this to last more than five fucking seconds, you're going about it all wrong, Hannah." He speaks softly, the growling sound like a fine blade along my nerve endings, making my body sing. "I'm breaking character to tell you that."

"We're almost there," I purr, emboldened by the effect I'm having on him.

I'm not quite done toying with him. I step back and watch him for a moment, let my eyes have their fill. Then I bring my hands to the zipper that runs down the side of my body, keeping my dress in place. I drag it down slowly, letting the sound slice through the air. Then I shed the garment, making a show of dropping it to the ground.

"What can you hear?" I ask him.

"Are you…?" His hand twitches, as if he's going to touch himself again but I make an *uh-uh* sound. "Are you undressed?"

"Almost."

I'm in lacy underwear, heels and no bra. But I hook my fingers under my waistband and drag the black silk and lace down over my hips. I step out of the underwear and dangle it from one finger. Then I move closer to him, draping the silk over his swollen cock. I drag it up his length, wrap it around him and rub the silk over his skin.

"Hannah," he growls.

"Annabel," I correct him as I pull the underwear back and whip it across his stomach. His body jerks and his nostrils flare, but not from pain. Oh no, it's all pleasure now.

"Annabel. Is that…?"

"Yes."

He stifles a groan. "I want to touch you."

"Not yet."

I toss my underwear onto the floor and slowly sink to my knees. The water glass beckons and I take a big mouthful, relishing the slide of the cold liquid down my throat. But the water isn't intended solely for hydration.

I take another big gulp and set the glass down. I saw the tip once in Cosmo, to drink cold water or suck on ice cubes before giving head. The sensation is supposed to be amazing for the guy. It was one of those cheesy articles: *Ten Ways to Pleasure Your Man* that I used to laugh at with my girlfriends back when I thought blow jobs were all about the guy.

But right now, I want nothing more than to take Owen into my mouth and suck him until he forgets why he ever said no to me. Until he understands the giddy, lust-fuelled attraction that turns my brain to jelly.

I don't want to be the only one feeling this way.

"What are you doing?" he asks, his hands reaching forward to see if I'm there.

I brace one palm flat against his stomach and lower my mouth to the tip of his cock. It's beaded with pearly liquid, and I wrap my lips around him.

"Fucking hell." His fingers drive through my hair, flexing against my scalp in a way that mixes the sharp snap of pain with a whole lot of pleasure.

He's hot and pulsing on my tongue—tastes and smells earthy in a way that's one-hundred-percent masculine. Yeah, this isn't just for him.

"That…" He grunts. I release him for a second and look up, catching the way his head lolls back as I continue to work him with my hand. "Christ, that feels good."

I lower my head down again and relish in the power cursing through my veins. I've never felt like this during sex. Never felt like I could bring a man to his knees. But the sounds coming from his mouth tell me all I need to know—for now, for this moment, I'm in charge.

CHAPTER FOURTEEN

Owen

THE CONTRAST IS enough to undo me. Hannah's mouth is somehow hot and cold all at the same time. Her fingers form a tight ring at the base of my cock and her mouth works over me in a way that feels so good it makes my head spin.

I keep a tight grip on her hair, pumping my hips back and forth. But I want to see her now, because I'm the kind of guy who likes to feast with my eyes. I yank the blindfold off and toss it to the floor.

Holy. Freaking. Shit.

Hannah's naked, except for her glossy mirror-finish heels, which poke out behind the round curve of her ass as she balances on her knees. Her lips are swollen, wet. Her cheeks are flushed the prettiest shade of pink…the tips of her ears, too. With each bob of her head, her dark hair brushes over my stomach and thighs.

"Look at me," I command.

Hannah tilts her face ever so slightly, enough to

angle those big brown eyes up. But her mouth continues working me—her tongue circling my head, her
cheeks hollowing as she applies the perfect amount
of pressure. It's even hotter with the eye contact.

Sparks shoot through me, and I feel so damn alive.
I haven't felt like this in…years. The whole time I've
been in New York, I've been a shell. A hardworking,
hard-partying shell.

"Testing time is over," I growl.

"Can't hang on?" she teases, rocking back on her
feet and standing.

If I thought the heels made her legs look good before, then she's damn near goddess-level now. Her
body is incredible. She's got these strong, broad
shoulders which I never really thought would be a
sexy feature, but they're perfection on her.

"You're so beautiful." I'm not sure this kind of
talk is meant to be part of our one-night, this-isn't-
really-us deal. But I can't help it, the words are gone
before I can contemplate the consequences.

Her gaze drops to the floor for a second, her dark,
sooty lashes shielding her expression. She doesn't
know what to think and neither do I. All I know is
that I want her. Desperately.

"I feel like we're not doing very well at this role-
play thing," she says.

"Are you kidding me? That water trick was…
Fuck." I step toward her, my hands zeroing in on
her hips. Her skin is soft and silky, and she feels
like heaven. "I think you blew every one of my five
senses."

"Four," she corrects me. "No sight, remember."

"If you don't think I'm getting my fill of that right now, then you're dead wrong."

We're in the middle of the hotel room and Hannah's body is backlit by the cityscape outside the window. Lights sparkle and wink, and off in the distance some fireworks bloom over the Docklands. They're not close enough to hear, but I spin Hannah around so she can watch.

"Look." I point, as I guide her to the window. "What a view, right?"

"It's beautiful," she breathes. I'm behind her and she presses her palms to the glass. "Fireworks always make me happy."

The explosions of green and purple and red create silent music in the distance. I lean forward, lining her back with my front. "Keep your hands there."

I run my fingertip down the length of her spine. Then I curve my hand over her hip, pressing my palm to her stomach before driving it slowly down, and gently delving between her legs. Hannah shifts, widening her stance. Inviting me in. She's wet. So fucking wet.

I slide my fingers through her pussy, dragging the moisture toward her clit. The sensitive little bud is so swollen, she jerks against my hand with even the softest touch.

"Oh no." Her head drops back against my shoulder.

I still. "Do you want me to stop?"

"God, no. It's…" She turns her face and looks up

at me shyly. "I have a feeling it's going to be over way too quickly."

"Luckily there's no limit on what we can do tonight. I'm yours until we check out." I circle her clit with my forefinger, enjoying the way she rubs against me. My cock is nestled against the top of her ass. "All damn night."

"Good," she sighs, "Keep going."

Tremors are already running through her and my fingers are soaked. In the reflection from the glass, I see the faint outline of us. Her legs are wide, and her face is screwed up with pleasure. I, on the other hand, look like a man possessed—eyes wild and hair mussed and jaw tight.

I'm worried the second I sink my cock into that tight pussy I'm going to blow my load quicker than a teenage boy on his first fuck. But like I said, we've got all night. I want nothing more than to watch the sun come up while we're bleary-eyed and satiated and aching all over.

She gasps and rocks against my hand. "I'm going to come."

"Don't hold back, baby. Take what you need." I work her, rubbing my finger against her clit. Faster, a little more pressure, helping her to ride the wave until she's shuddering, whimpering. Until she's calling my name like I'm a goddamn deity.

Hannah slumps back against me, aftershocks causing her to tremble. I scoop her up and she loops her arms around my neck, like I'm her last tether to earth. I know, as a guy, making her come should have me feeling high on sexual power. But it's this—that trusting, easy, sweet way she leans her head against my shoulder—that has the power to break me.

I get to the bedroom, stopping only to retrieve the condom she's thoughtfully supplied, and slowly lower her onto the plush covers. Then I slip her feet out of her heels, dropping them to the floor one by one. We've left a breadcrumb trail across the hotel room—discarded clothes, abandoned items from our "sensory testing" experiment. Now it's just us with nothing in our way. We're in a perfect bubble, where yesterday and tomorrow don't exist.

A thought niggles at me, telling me that it's naive to think this won't impact tomorrow. But I'm so far into the fantasy nothing can drag me away. The only thing that could stop me is Hannah herself, but her big brown eyes stare up at me—her lush mouth parted—and she's a picture of wanton lust.

"I never thought this would happen," she says, her voice close to a whisper. "I thought you would always be an unfulfilled wish."

I slide my hands up her thighs, parting her. My thumbs trace circles against her fair skin and she shivers, propping herself up so she can watch. "You should be spending your wishes on someone better."

I know the second the words are out of my mouth that I've said too much.

Hannah cocks her head. "You never struck me as the kind of guy to have an inferiority complex."

"I don't."

I simply know what I'm capable of and what I'm

not…and where I foresee it causing problems. But the easiest way to deal with questions I don't want to answer—the way I *always* deal with it—is to distract the person asking.

I kiss the inside of Hannah's knee. It's the softest of kisses, a bare graze of lips and her skin ripples with goose bumps. Oh, Hannah. She's still sensitive from the orgasm I gave her a few moments ago. Still reeling from the pleasure.

I want to draw this out—stretch the anticipation until neither one of us can take it—but I can't. For too long, I've denied myself what I wanted. What we both wanted.

I slide my hands under her ass and pull her to the edge of the bed, setting my mouth on her pussy like a man starved. She bucks against me, fingers driving through my hair and nails digging into my scalp. Her words aren't fully formed and she squirms—wanting more and less and in equal measure. She tells me to keep going when I pull back for the briefest second, blowing cool air across her swollen skin in a way that makes her back arch against the bed.

Then I'm on her again. Feasting on the honeyed taste of her, licking and sucking until she rolls her hips, grinding herself against my face. Yes, baby. Take it. Take all of it.

"Owen," she moans, the keening sound like a shot of pure adrenaline. "Yes!"

I'm wired, like a spring pulled tight. The need to drive into her is pounding in my head like a religious chant.

Take her, take her, take her.

When she comes, her fist flexes against my scalp and she clamps her thighs around my head. It feels like her orgasm goes on forever; she rocks until she's wrung every last bit of pleasure from it. Watching her flop back against the bed—one arm flung over her eyes—is a picture I'll never forget. Moonlight dances over her skin.

"You're so beautiful." I climb onto the bed, grabbing the condom, and encourage her to come with me.

Propping my back against an obscene number of pillows, I tug her closer. She straddles me, her knees digging into the soft cotton on either side of my legs. For a moment she hovers there, her eyes locked on mine. Like she's looking for something—but what, I have no idea.

Hannah leans forward, her hair brushing my cheek. I feel her lips at my ear, her warm breath sending anticipation slicing through me. "Don't be gentle."

"You want it rough, huh? You want to make sure you're not walking straight tomorrow?"

She pulls back, her pupils blacker than ink. There's a glazed look to her now, like arousal has dulled her edges. Like she's sinking into sensation. "Yes."

She plucks the condom from my hand and tears the packet open. Squeezing the tip, she places it over the head of my cock and begins to roll it down. Condoms aren't usually sexy. Necessary? Hell yeah. But part of the foreplay? Not really…until now.

"Keep talking," she says, her eyes meeting mine like smoke and fire.

She likes the dirty talk? Can. Fucking. Do.

"Spread your legs, baby. I want to make sure you're soaking wet before I stick my cock in you." I grab myself with one hand and angle toward her, dragging the tip through the slick moisture, rubbing back and forth in a way that makes her mewl. "You're so wet. So ready for me."

"I am," she breathes, her chest rising and falling with choppy breath.

I reach behind her and sink my fingers into her ass, guiding her toward me. She feels like heaven, like sin and temptation and all that's right with the world. Planting her hands on my chest, she shifts so that I'm pressing against her entrance.

"Sink down slowly," I command. "I want to feel every little bit until I'm in as far as you can take me."

"Yes." The word is a hiss.

She bears down and takes me inside her. She's so tight I have to press my head back against the pillows for a second so I don't lose it. But damn, it's like she was made for me. We fit together perfectly.

"So full," she gasps, her forehead touching mine. She presses down more, taking me inside her, stretching to accommodate me.

"That's it. Slowly." I press a kiss to her lips, my hands rubbing circles over her ass to relax her. "Don't tense up."

I feel the movement as she gives in and slides down the last little bit. It's everything—and I sit there for a moment, still and quiet. Giving her time to adjust. Hell, giving myself time to adjust.

I'm fucking Hannah Anderson.

My mind spins. The amount of times I've jerked off in the shower to this very fantasy… God. I don't even know how many times. All I know is that I never thought I'd be here. That I shouldn't be here.

But that I want it more than anything.

"I'm good," she whispers.

If only she knew that I needed that moment of stillness as much as she did. But I'll never let on.

"You trying to tell me to hurry up and fuck you?" My voice is low, gravelly. "Greedy, greedy girl."

This Hannah is different to the woman with the blindfold. She enjoys being in charge, but I think she equally enjoys letting someone else sit in the driver's seat. It's exciting, how open and curious she is. How playful.

"You want a quick and dirty one-night stand, huh? You want to be thoroughly fucked? Tomorrow you're not going to be able to take a step without remembering how good it felt to have my cock in you. I'm going to leave you satisfied and sore, so when you sit that pretty ass down you'll have to squeeze your thighs together."

"Bloody hell." She's practically panting as she wriggles against me, frustrated. Not wanting to wait.

I fill my hands with her ass, lifting her up so I can

tease her for one more minute. So I can see the plea in her face before I give her what she wants.

"Owen."

My name is like a prayer and a sentence all at once. I'm lost to her, lost to how good we feel together. Lost to the reality that I've well and truly screwed myself for the rest of this job. Because I won't be able to forget what she looks like—wild-eyed and open-mouthed. I won't be able to forget the way she looked up at me as she sucked my dick. The way she teased me, taunted me. The way she sees everything.

I'm a goner.

"You feel so good." I thrust up into her, driving hard and deep. She's so wet there's no resistance at all. "I'm going to bounce you up and down until I feel those beautiful thighs shake."

"I..." She's incoherent now. Babbling pleasure sounds that started off as words but ended up as sighs and moans and gasps.

Wrapping my arms around her, I move us to the edge of the bed so I can plant my feet against the ground for leverage. When I stand, she locks her ankles behind my back and clings to my neck. She's all muscle, but she's still light enough for me to carry. Light enough that I don't need to lean her against a wall.

"Don't drop me," she gasps.

"I've got you."

Her mouth is on mine, ravenous. Can she taste herself on my lips? Her body is soft in my hands, letting me control the pace. I slip my hands under her thighs and move her body how I want it. How it feels good.

I slide her up and down my cock, flexing with each stroke as I go deep. I start off slower, taking my time but soon I'm losing control. My balls are achy and full, and they slap up against her with each stroke, drawing me close to the edge. She smells like faded perfume and perspiration, a potent combination. And her lips are firm and smooth, her tongue driving into my mouth as I screw her senseless.

"Oh God…yes, that spot." She bows in my arms and her internal muscles start to pulse.

I've got no hope of hanging on now, as she draws me deeper. I hold her tight and thrust up, pounding into her over and over as we chase release. I'm so close, our pleasure is a pinpoint and I chase it. I shut my eyes, going back to what she did to me before, letting my other senses take over.

"Owen," she whispers into my ear, her voice hoarse. "I want to feel you come."

I'm a dead man. A slave to pleasure.

There's nothing but the smell of her, the subtle saltiness on her lips. The sound of skin slapping against skin. And the feel of her—hot, wet, tight.

"Hannah," I groan, bouncing her up and down, my movements stiff and jerky.

Then I go deep one last time and I shatter, my cock pulsing inside her as I come. Hard. It's that moment that she tips over, too, her body squeezing mine so tight I think I might faint from the intensity of it all. After a moment, I stumble back to the bed and drop down, folding us onto our sides while I'm still inside her.

The shock waves of orgasm ripple through us and she curls her hand into mine. I want to hold her forever.

CHAPTER FIFTEEN

Hannah

I WAKE COCOONED in plush, expensive sheets, like I've been sleeping on a thousand-thread-count Egyptian cotton cloud. The pillow cradles my head and sunlight streams in between a gap in the blinds, bathing the hotel room with a buttery glow. I wonder if I've been smiling all night. Every part of me aches—I'm overworked and overloaded. I'm satisfaction personified.

But when I roll over, my hand automatically reaching for him, reality jolts me. His side of the bed is cold and the sheets are pulled up neatly, which is a surprise. Normally I sleep twisted in my sheets, the endless spinning of my mind causing me to toss and turn. So either Owen screwed me so good that I slept like a log…or he tucked me in and rearranged the sheets when he got up.

Thinking about that gives me a funny feeling in my chest.

I push up and swing my legs over the edge of the

bed, my mind churning. The idea of putting on that sexy black dress this early in the morning makes me cringe, so I settle on wrapping myself in a fluffy bathrobe.

What is it going to be like between us this morning? Will he be remote and act like it never happened? Will he tell me he had a good time? I'm not sure which is worse. Because as much as I had the time of my life last night—and got *exactly* what I wanted—I'm far from getting it out of my system. In fact, I want nothing more than to search him out and drag him into the shower.

"For all you know he already left," I mutter, scrubbing a hand over my face.

A rustle on the other side of the room startles me, and Owen walks into the bedroom from the little corridor that leads to the rest of the suite. "No dice, Anderson. You can't get rid of me that easily."

"Don't high-flying businessmen usually take off at first light?"

"Well, this *is* my hotel room. So I guess you should have been the one to take off." He's wearing jeans and a fitted black hoodie, and looking every bit as delectable as he did last night in his suit pants and shirt.

Wait a minute… "How did you get changed?"

I hadn't even given a thought to what might happen this morning, and whether or not I'd need to do the "walk of shame" back to 21 Love Street. Although that term strikes me as dated—there's nothing shameful about having sex. They should really call it "the walk of blisters" because lord knows putting on those wretched heels again will be hell on my feet.

"I went back to the apartment."

That's when I notice Owen is carrying a calico bag over one shoulder. "I didn't even hear you leave."

"You were dead to the world." The corner of his lips quirks up and it's the sexiest expression I've ever seen. Not quite a smile, not as hard as a smirk. Just something crooked and imperfectly in the middle. "And I figured you probably wouldn't want to head home in that dress from last night. It's chilly out."

My heart melts. "You went all the way back there to get me a change of clothes?"

"It's not far." He shrugs, as if suddenly trying to downplay the kind gesture. "And there's coffee on the table out there."

Okay, now I *really* melt. The way to my heart is not with chocolate or flowers or any of that gooey crap—it's with a so-strong-it-punches-you-in-the-face coffee. Almost as if the fumes of caffeine are carrying me, I drift past him into the main room of the hotel suite. Two white takeaway cups sit side by side—identical except for the black Sharpie scribble. A flat white, his. And a triple-shot latte, mine.

"Come to mama." I take the cup in my hands and bring the liquid gold to my lips.

"I ran into Rowan this morning." Owen picks up his coffee and sips. I catch a glimpse of us in the mirror and we look like a couple who's been together forever—him with his hair mussed and stubble on his jaw, and me—looking equally mussed—wearing a robe. "He mentioned there's a barbeque on for building residents today. Apparently, they do it once a month."

"Seems like a very social building." The place where I live currently is nothing like that. "Might be a good way to meet some of the other residents…if you think it's time to start talking to people."

I can tell my teasing hits the right spot when Owen shoots me a look. "Very funny. But yes, I agree we should go."

"What do you know, we finally agree on something."

Owen puts his cup down and stalks forward—I see a hint of the fire from last night. A fire which has burned me so bad I'll never lose the scars. Last night was…everything. Everything I knew it would be, everything I hoped it would be. Everything I was terrified of because there's no way in hell one night will ever be enough.

"I think we agree on something else." He reaches out and traces the edge of the bathrobe, starting near my collar bone and going all the way down to where the belt is knotted at my waist.

"What's that?" My voice trembles.

"That you're crazy hot."

I'm not sure I agree on that, but I like the way I look reflected in his eyes. I'm the best version of myself—the most confident, the most desirable. I'm not ready to leave the hotel. Like a junkie, I need one more hit. Just one more…

We're entering a dangerous place, going back on the agreement we made for this to be a one-night thing—if we're breaking our own rules already, then what hope do we have of controlling the beast we've unleashed?

What hope do *I* have of protecting my heart?

Because I know Owen is worried I'll want more than he's willing to give. Truth be told, I'm worried about that, too.

He tugs on the knot, loosening the fluffy fabric and letting the robe fall open. "Fucking hell, Anderson. You've got me hooked."

"I thought you were supposed to call me Annabel," I say. I wish I could get out of my own head and go with the flow. I wish I could indulge in my desires and stop always worrying about the consequences.

If he keeps touching me, I know I'll give in. I'm powerless when it comes to him—but that doesn't mean I'm not worried about getting hurt.

"Yeah, I totally forgot about that when I woke up this morning." He rakes a hand through his hair. "You'll always be Anderson to me."

His statement makes me feel simultaneously better and worse. The role-play game was fun, but it was never going to give us a free pass to forget what happened.

Here and now it's us.

"What happens in the hotel stays in the hotel?" he says with a cheeky smirk.

Boundaries. I'm not sure they'll work but it's

enough that my rule-loving brain puts a checkmark in that box.

"What happens in the hotel stays in the hotel," I echo.

"You weren't ready to leave this morning, were you?" he asks.

I shake my head, biting down on my lip. "Not even a little bit."

His head dips to mine with a force that makes me gasp. The roughness of his jeans is heaven and hell against my bare thighs, the friction driving me wild.

The kiss is raw, possessive. His tongue claims mine and he tastes of coffee. He backs me up against the sturdy wooden table and his hips pin me in place.

"So good." The words come out muffled against my throat where his teeth scrape against my skin.

"I want to touch you." My words trail off into a groan as his lips find the hollow at the base of my throat.

"You'll touch me when I say you can touch me." His grin almost melts me on the spot. "I'm going to pay you back for making me wait last night."

Oh God. Is there anything sexier than a guy in control? Last night I had fun, but I love knowing that Owen can flip the tables on me. He keeps me guessing.

He's so hard, and the length of him digs into my belly. I'm panting and desperate, my thighs clenching to quiet the sensation that's gone from an insistent throb to a roaring. "But last night—"

"I'm not pretending to be an anonymous business-

man now." He lowers himself, grasping my wrists
and holding my hands in place before setting his lips
on my skin. He's kissing my breasts, gently tugging
on my nipples with his teeth. Each little nip makes
my knees shake. "I'm me and you're you."

I nod, my voice lost. I'm me and he's him. We're
us. Ourselves…no pretending. It's risky as hell. But
while we're here, we're not working the case. It's a
line of separation.

What happens in the hotel stays in the hotel. Or
am I clutching at straws?

"Ditch the gown." Owen releases my hands and
steps back.

I shrug one shoulder out of the fluffy robe, and
then the other. It slips heavily to the ground. He's still
as a statue, legs grounded in a stance of pure mascu-
linity. One hand rakes through his hair.

Owen whips the hoodie over his head and takes
his T-shirt with it. I automatically reach out to him
but he catches my hand and spins me around. Bracing my hands against the table, I arch back to press
against him.

"What did you say to me last night? Don't do anything until I explicitly tell you to." He nips at my ear
lobe, his face buried against my hair. "Keep your
hands on the table."

I force myself to breathe slowly. I've never had a
guy make me feel like this before. He's controlling
the pace, but not in a way that makes me feel infe-
rior. I'm almost relieved. He's taking the lead, taking the pressure off my shoulders.

Suddenly, my back is cold and the sound of a zipper cuts through the air, followed by the soft thud of fabric hitting the floor. Then warm flesh presses against me from behind. Hot palms skim my thighs, the curve of my butt and my hips.

"Please," I whimper. "Oh my God, please."

"Slowly, Anderson. Don't rush it." He kisses the back of my neck while he slides his hands all over me, mapping me. Learning me. "Just enjoy."

How could I not? His hand slides up my front, cupping my breast and thumbing my nipple until I'm sagging against him. My hands curl over the edge of the table, but I'm in serious danger of dissolving onto the ground like a melted ice cube.

"Can I touch you yet?" I need to be active in our lovemaking. If this is the last time I can have him, then I don't want to be a bystander.

He doesn't respond but he guides my hands behind my back and down to his cock. The guttural moan tells me he wants it as much as I do. The soft glide of my palm over his steel-hard erection makes me throb.

"I want to look at you."

"Bossy." His amused tone makes me smile. "I thought I was in charge."

"I let you *think* you're in charge."

"You're a handful." He spins me around and I drink him in, the flushed cheeks, wild blue eyes and a body fit for a museum sculpture.

"*You're* a handful." I stroke the length of him, swallowing at the satisfying weight in my palm.

The cool air makes my nipples peak further. As if he senses my need, he drops his head to one stiff peak and draws it into his mouth. The hot wetness of his lips and gentle flicking of his tongue has me squirming against him, squeezing him and stroking him firmly in response.

"What did I say about going slowly?" he growls.

"Going slow is for wimps." I grin wickedly.

"Temptress." His eyes flash and he hoists me over his shoulder, a palm landing down on my butt with a loud crack.

"Oh!" Warmth spreads through me and I'm tingling all over.

He carries me to the bed as if I weigh nothing, and he sets me down with a gentle reverence. For a heartbeat he only looks, his eyes like blue fire and his face set into a mask of wonder as if I'm the most beautiful woman in the world. In that moment, I feel as though I am. But the spell vanishes when his face morphs into one of pure heat.

"Get on all fours," he says.

Biting back a moan at the sexy command, I comply and climb onto the bed, facing away from him and sticking my ass in the air. It's like he has the controller to my body. The rustling of a foil packet gets my attention. I'd only stashed the one in my wallet last night.

"Where did you get that?" I turn to look over my shoulder.

He breaks his confident-Owen façade for a minute and a shy smile slips over his face. "I stopped on the way back to the apartment. Just in case you wanted…"

He was thinking about it. Thinking about me. I whip my head back around so he can't see how I'm slayed. How does he do this to me? But before I can spiral, he's behind me.

"All good?" His voice is softer now, thick with desire.

I nod.

"Say it, Anderson." His lips trail down my spine. "Nice and loud."

"Yes." I swallow. "I want this."

Then he's filling me, burying himself deep. Each stroke brings me closer to the edge. He slips a hand around my waist and dips between my legs, finding my sweet spot.

"I don't even want to know how you're so good." I press back into him, receiving each long, deep thrust with pleasure.

"Build-up. Years and years of you tempting the shit out of me."

I press my face down into the bed covers and lose myself. The sounds of us fucking—skin slapping and hard breathing and hearts thundering—fill my head. It's so good I can't speak anymore. I'm melting into sensation.

So good, so good, so good…

"Fuck, Hannah."

My name is a strangled plea on his lips, and it's enough to send me over one more time. I shudder, my body spasming with pleasure. It sets off a chain reaction, and he's thrusting deep. His body covers mine, and he whispers dirty things into my ear. Telling me all the ways he's thought about having me, all the ways he wants to have me.

I know it's the sex talking, but I let myself believe for a second that it's real.

Then he pushes deep inside and follows me into oblivion. As the fireworks fade, he lowers himself onto the bed and pulls me against him.

"Good?" His hand traces designs over my thigh. Each touch is feather-light, worlds apart from where we were moments ago.

I nod, unable to form words. My brain stutters like he's short-circuited me.

"I didn't hurt you, did I?" There's a sweet note of concern in his voice, perhaps a tinge of regret.

"No, you didn't hurt me." Not physically anyway. Emotionally...I don't know yet. God, this is awkward. Why can't we stay in post-sex bliss forever? "So...uh, what now?"

For a moment he doesn't say anything. But then he gets up and heads into the bathroom to dispose of the condom. Looks like he's not sure the best way to handle things, either. Maybe it was too soon to ask...

But there's a part of me that always needs to know my next step. It's how I operate in my job and in my life. Ambiguity is the enemy.

"We get back to work." He grabs the bag with my clothes from the table. I can see he's picked up a few things, perhaps unsure what I might want to wear.

The gesture is sweet, but the magic is all gone. It's my own fault. I knew I would feel like this.

"Back to work." I nod. "Right."

It's not what my heart wants to hear, but I shake off the disappointment. If I feel bad, that's on me. Unrealistic desires and all that.

I hurry into the bathroom to change. Which seems a little useless considering he's seen me naked a lot in the last twelve hours. My body is one thing, however. My emotions are totally another.

"Are we…okay?" he asks through the door.

"Sure." I doubt it convinces either one of us.

"I told you there was a reason I kept away, Hannah."

I swallow. Damn him, when he says my name like that it always reaches inside me. Makes my heart squeeze. When I'm Anderson, he's all playful and fun. Owen the Joker. When he calls me by my rank, he's trying to get under my skin. And when he says Hannah, usually it's with a coating of sarcasm because I've told him off.

But this is different.

It's softer. More. Everything.

I can't handle that right now. I need a less vulnerable emotion to cling on to, something that doesn't make me seem like the weaker party. I choose frustration.

"What is that reason, exactly?" I ask as I tug my outfit on. "If you really want me to understand then why don't you tell me something real?"

"Messed-up childhood. What else do you need to know?"

Everything. I don't need to know it, but I want to. For some reason—and against every bit of sensibility in my usually *very* practical brain—I want to be closer to him. And it hurts to be held at an arm's length.

"Life is short," he adds. "I want my life to be as easy as possible."

"Wow. Stick that on a motivational poster and I'll hang it on my wall." I roll my eyes. The sentiment disappoints me, because it doesn't fit with the man I believe Owen to be. He does care…even if he doesn't show it. "Don't you think everyone would be happy with an easy life? But spoiler alert, life *isn't* easy."

I come out of the bathroom and spear him with a look. I'm not buying this BS.

"Is this the point where you tell me things happen for a reason?" he grunts. "I've heard that recycled bullshit a thousand times over."

"So you're going to do this case and then return to being a party boy in New York?"

I'd heard stories from Max—that Owen had a sweet bachelor pad and liked to hit the clubs on a regular basis. It seems like a complete waste to me. Owen is one of the best officers I've ever worked with—despite his inability to show up on time. He's a joker, sure. But he's got a sharp mind and a desire to do good.

"How do you know I was a party boy in New York?" He folds his arms across his chest.

"People talk."

"Fucking Max," he mutters. "What did he tell you?"

"Nothing much, just that you've been acting like you're twenty-two instead of thirty-two. Clubbing, drinking..." Probably sleeping around, although Max never actually said it and I *certainly* don't want to think about it. Especially not now. "Avoiding commitment of any kind."

"I'm committed to my job."

"The new one?" I shake my head. "You wanted to climb the ranks. You wanted to protect the people in this city, make Melbourne a safer place."

He stares at me, eyes smouldering and jaw pulled taut. But then he shakes his head like he's telling himself not to bite. "I'm going to walk back to the apartment. Clear my head."

The door swings shut behind him and I sink down onto one of the dining chairs surrounding a small glass-and-chrome table. This is the Owen I know—the one who walks away when things get real. The one who dodges tough questions and close connections.

This is your own fault. You pushed for more when he was very clear about what this meant to him.

I bring the coffee to my lips and tip my head back. Yep, it's stone cold. Ugh.

I look around the fancy hotel room, remembering how last night made me feel. How this morning made me feel. The power that surged through my veins. And the pleasure...oh, the pleasure.

That kind of connection only comes when there's more than sexual attraction between two people, but I have to accept that Owen has made his stance clear. He's not looking for anything real.

And for the sake of this job, I have to be okay with that.

Later that afternoon things are a little tense with Owen and me. We've been circling around one another all day. But the barbeque is a great way to meet some more of the residents and perhaps find out more about our prime suspect: Matt. So we have to suck it up.

The weather is chilly—but the sky is clear and bright. Lights have been strung up and outdoor heaters emanate a warm glow. The covered area has great views of the lush green garden and vegetable patch. For a moment, I forget I'm in the middle of the city and I imagine that's *exactly* what the property developers were going for. It's a slice of outdoor heaven in the middle of the big smoke.

A group of men cluster around one of the barbeques, and I immediately spot Rowan, who seems to have everyone enraptured with one of his stories. Three women sit at one of the tables, chatting and drinking wine. Several more people mill about, shaking hands and smiling.

"It's Hannah, right?" A woman with huge brown eyes and a kind smile stands and motions for me to take a seat.

I recognise Ava right away. She's the schoolteacher from level five, and she lives next to Rowan and Dom. I liked her instantly the first time we met—she's warm and welcoming. A little shy, but I imagine if she wrangles four- and five-year-old kids all day then she can probably dole out the whoop-ass when it's required.

"Good memory." I pull out a seat and get settled. Owen waves before heading toward the group of guys.

"I'm so glad you came," Ava says and I get the impression she means it. "It's a really social building to live in. Let me introduce you around. I think you met Emery already?"

I turn to the woman next to me—she's got a slight build and sharp eyes. Both times I've seen her now she's been wearing a *Game of Thrones* T-shirt. This one says You Know Nothing. "Nice to see you again."

"Likewise." Emery nods. "Always good to get some fresh blood into the building."

"And this," says Ava, "is Drew."

Drew is stunning. Long blond hair in a perfect Gwen Stefani platinum, smudgy dark eye makeup and a sleek all-black outfit. She's got the sexy goth thing down pat. "Hannah, was it? Nice to meet you. Don't get attached—I won't be around long."

"Yeah, yeah." Emery rolls her eyes and reaches for an empty wineglass. She pours me some white wine and hands it over. "Little Miss Jetset can't stay in one place."

"You travel a lot?" I ask.

Drew nods. "I'm a flight attendant and usually I'm based in London. I was in Dubai before that."

"Such a glamorous life," Ava says with a sigh.

I sip my wine. "What brought you home?"

"Wedding." She says the word like it makes her physically ill. "Hate the damn things. But my sister is signing her life away, so I gotta be there."

I blink. "Oh, that's…lovely."

Emery laughs and slaps her hand down on Drew's back. "I knew I was gonna like you."

"An old friend lives in this building," Drew says. "But she travels a lot, too, so that worked out perfectly. Staying with my parents on top of the wedding would have been too much to handle." Drew's gaze sweeps over me, taking in details. Her eyes are a pale silvery blue, almost ethereally lacking in colour. With the dark eye makeup, it's a striking combination. "That's a big hunk of stone there. You're married?"

"Yeah." I nod and give her the practised smile that should accompany my answer—serene, happy. Not showing an ounce of the confusion and frustration that's been swirling in my head ever since this morning. I point over to where Owen stands, chatting with Matt. "That's my husband."

"Cute." Drew winks. "How did you two meet?"

"University. We had some of the same classes." We're keeping our stories close to the truth, thereby reducing the chance we might slip up given it was my first time undercover. Swap police academy for university and we could use pretty much any of our old stories and make them feel authentic. "We were friends for a long time first. He didn't want to date me, actually. But I won him over."

"Look at how in love she is!" Ava sighs dramatically. "You can see it all over her face."

Heat floods my cheeks and I gulp down some of my wine. I'm not *that* good an actress, and it terrifies me that Ava can see something I don't want to show.

It's good for the cover story. And you are *a good actress, that's all this is.*

But I know that look comes from somewhere deep inside me, a part I've been hushing for years. I like Owen...a lot. Last night was more than sex to me even if it wasn't to him.

"You must be one of the lucky ones." Drew leans back in her chair and her eyes drift over to the men. There's something in her expression that's difficult to read. "To find a guy who won't promise you the moon and then vanish the second he gets what he wants."

Ava and I exchange a glance, while Emery nods empathetically. I get the impression there are two opposing views on love in this little group. I can't help letting my gaze drift to Owen. He's talking and laughing.

God, he's gorgeous. When he looks back at me, catching my gaze with his, I'm ruined. But I need to get my head in the game. I'm not going to hang my hopes on a fantasy.

"So give me the lowdown," I say. "Who's who in this building?"

That's what I'm here for. Information. A clue as to who might warrant our attention. Because, for the first time in my life, I'm struggling to keep my focus on work and I can't drop the ball now. Not when I've finally gotten to where I want to be.

"Well," Ava says with a cheeky grin. I suspect the sweet schoolteacher might enjoy a little gossip, which is good news. "Looks like your husband has already met the Lively brothers."

"Rowan is a grade-A playboy," Emery chimes in, the edge of her lip curling. "Thinks he's God's gift to women."

"He's not *that* bad." Ava rolls her eyes. "Sure, he's a little cocky but he's a nice guy."

"She's only saying that because she's had a crush on Rowan's brother, Dom, since the day she moved into her apartment." Emery shoots me a smug grin as she reaches for the wine to top herself up. "Dom is a great guy, actually. They run a gallery together, family business."

"Yes, I went to one of theirs shows," I say. "What about their friend, the chef?"

"Matt?" The two women exchange glances and eventually Ava offers a strange little shrug. "He's… intense."

"What do you mean?"

"I get the impression he's got some issues. He was dating this woman for a while and it's this on again, off again thing. We could hear them fighting sometimes when we were visiting a friend on his floor."

"Yeah, they *loved* a bit of drama." Emery taps

her chin. "But he went off the rails a bit after the last split. Quit his job and holed up in his apartment. Dom hinted that he'd fallen in with a bad crowd."

Interesting. Ava and Emery continue on with their assessment of everyone who lives in the building—from the cute young couple with the newborn twins, to the glamorous older lady who apparently was the muse of some big Australian designer back in the day—I struggle to pay attention. Matt is definitely still at the top of my suspect list.

When my gaze swings back around to the rest of the barbecue action, I find Owen looking right back at me. The intensity of his stare sends a shiver down my spine and my traitorous body reacts, priming me for what I want—more. More of last night. More of his lips on mine. More of his hands romancing my body.

But I have to keep my eye on the prize and, unfortunately for me, the prize is *not* another night of fantastic sex with Owen.

CHAPTER SIXTEEN

Owen

"WAIT, SHE WANTED *how* much?" I shake my head.

"Twenty thousand dollars," Hannah replies. "And that was for the little sculpture."

Hannah had her meeting with Celina Yang this afternoon, following up from our visit to Dom and Rowan's gallery a few days ago. Now we're having a drink and bite to eat at the pub across from 21 Love Street. The great thing about this pub is that if you sit at the bench that runs across the front window—and put up with the rock-hard stools—then you have a perfect view of the entrance to our apartment building.

It's been two nights since the barbeque. Three since Hannah and I crossed a line and did things I can't get out of my head. Just long enough since we fumbled the "morning after" that Hannah is finally opening up to me again. Frankly, it's happening sooner than I suspected.

Not that it makes me feel any less guilty about the

way I handled it. I shouldn't have ended the conversation by walking out like that. But I *always* retreat when it comes to that stuff.

"I almost choked on my coffee," she continues. "I mean, I know she's an amazing artist but geez! Who has that kind of money for something so... frivolous?"

"Lots of people would say art isn't frivolous." I'm goading her and her narrowed expression says she knows it, too.

"Twenty thousand dollars on anything that doesn't serve a functional purpose is frivolous." She's nursing her beer, bringing it to her lips every so often but not taking more than the barest of sips. Eventually the waitress will try to move us on, so they can seat customers who'll drink more. But for now, we have time to wait. And watch.

Thankfully this spot is out of the way of the other tables. It affords us some privacy to talk, while keeping an eye on the building. Apparently Matt is going out today, and we'll tail him to see if we can dig up any more information.

"So, what did you say?"

"I told her that you'd promised me something special for my birthday and I was interested, but that I would *not* be purchasing my own present." She rolled her eyes. "I sounded like such a tool."

"You stayed in character then, that's a good thing." I grab one of the corn chips sitting on a platter between us and dunk it into the guacamole. "Shitty thing about this job number four hundred and two:

most of the time we have to pretend to be awful people."

She nods. "Every morning I have to remind myself 'who' I am, you know. Like this—" she gestures to her hair, tight black jeans and low-cut silk blouse "—isn't me. The woman who expects her husband to buy her whatever she wants, no matter the price tag."

"You got something against rich people, Hannah?" It's come up a few times now, her discomfort with money.

"It's not that. I just…" She shrugs. "My dad worked his ass off for very little, always taking overtime and doing the unsociable roster to bump up his pay. My brothers and I were grateful to have him home so we could eat a meal together, never mind buying a game console or designer jeans. I guess it seems sometimes when people have a lot of money they think 'stuff' is the end goal. Status symbols, keeping up with the Joneses. To me, that's not the stuff that matters in life, you know? I want quality relationships. Not money."

For a second I'm rankled by how easily she references her desire for relationships. The way she talks about her family is a thorn under my skin. It's easy to say relationships are important when you've never had the people you love ripped from your arms.

But this conversation isn't one I want to have with her, and work is the perfect excuse to avoid it. "What about Matt? Did Celina mention that she saw us in the hallway when they were arguing?"

Hannah grabs a corn chip and scoops up some

guacamole. "I actually brought it up, pretending I was embarrassed we'd heard them arguing but reassuring her that all couples go through it."

"Good move."

She crunches down on the chip. "Apparently they had a 'passionate and turbulent' affair. She said two personalities that big are bound to clash."

"Did she say why they broke up?"

"Not exactly. Only that he got in with a bad crowd. Which is exactly what I heard at the barbeque. But that could mean anything. Drugs, maybe. Gambling. Regular deadbeats of the non-criminal variety."

"But Rowan and Dom are not 'the bad crowd' then?"

Hannah shakes her head. "I didn't get that impression. My gut tells me they're not involved, unless he's using the gallery in some way."

"I agree." Nothing about Rowan or Dom raises any red flags. They appear to be open books, decent blokes. I've met a lot of criminals in my time and I don't get that vibe from them. "I haven't turned anything up."

That was the frustrating thing; *none* of them had a criminal record. After feeding information back to Max and the team at headquarters, Rowan, Dom *and* Matt were cleaner than a freshly scrubbed shower. They didn't even have any shitty misdemeanours on them. Nothing.

"Something is staring us right in the face, but we can't see it yet." Hannah wrings a napkin in her hands.

As if on cue, a figure exits 21 Love Street. It's

Matt, wearing a dark bomber jacket, jeans and boots. His head is bowed and he's tapping away at his phone.

"See that?" Hannah asks subtly, as she leans over to grab another chip.

I love watching her slip into work mode. There's a sharpening of her attention, a laser-like focus that comes to her big brown eyes.

"Got it."

From where he's standing, Matt can see straight into the pub windows. It's a plus for our visibility, and also a minus. If we watch him too closely and he looks up at the right moment, he'll catch us. If he does, we'll wave and make out like we're calling him to join us.

"Suspect is crossing the road," she says softly. "Approaching the pub. He's entering now."

A few seconds later, the front door of the pub pushes open and Matt strides in, heading straight for the bar. There are two bartenders—a man and a woman. Matt approaches the man, who's covered in tatts—a sleeve on each arm, and one that stretches up the right side of his neck. He's got a gauge piercing in one ear and a chunky set of rings on one hand. The kind of rings that would bust up a face in a fistfight.

Hannah has lost visibility now, as her back is partially to the bar. I turn, pretending to lean into her all while giving myself a better view of the suspect. "He's talking to the bartender, but he's not sitting. Now he's taking something out of his jacket."

She raises a brow. "What is it?"

"Envelope. Possibly cash."

Matt looks behind him, but his gaze doesn't swing in our direction. There's a lot of telltale signs that someone is nervous—sweaty brow, fidgeting, difficulty maintaining eye contact. He doesn't display any of those things, but there's a frenetic energy to him. Something that seems a little...off.

It's those details—the small inconsistencies—that often unravel a criminal's plans. They're also what make some cases hard to crack, because we can't arrest someone based on a "feeling." Well, I can't arrest anyone full stop. I'm only here to gather information, to try to make a link between this case and the one I worked five years ago.

"He's going out back," I whisper. "Bartender is going with him."

Hannah turns to see where they're going. The two men disappear into a door marked *staff only*.

"We should follow them," Hannah says.

"We'll get stopped in a heartbeat. Or it will *look* like we were following them." I rake a hand through my hair and then I'm struck with an idea. "I wonder if this place backs onto an alley. We could go around."

"I've got a better idea." She slides off her stool and musses her hair so it looks a little wild. "Stay here."

"Don't even think about it." I reach out to grab her wrist, but she dodges me, giggling as if I've said something incredibly funny. Then she turns, weaving through the tables in a way that's ever-so-slightly unsteady, like she's a bit drunk.

Dammit, Hannah.

I sit on my stool, stewing for a bit. I know what she's doing and I know it wouldn't be the first time an undercover cop got intel by pretending to be drunk. Hell, it wouldn't be the *thousandth* time. But we don't know what's back there. We don't know where the exits are if she gets trapped. We don't even know what the plan is because we don't fucking have one. We were supposed to be keeping an eye on Matt by waiting until he left the building and then slipping out of the pub to follow him discreetly.

Only we'd had no idea he'd walk straight into our stakeout spot.

I do *not* like the idea of Hannah going back there alone. The female bartender doesn't even give her a second look—after all, there's nothing unusual about a tipsy girl in a pub. Hannah makes out like she's headed for the ladies' room and when she clumsily sidesteps two women coming the other way, she ducks into the same door Matt went through a few minutes ago.

Then she's gone.

Immediately my body reacts with visceral displeasure—my heartbeat kicks up a notch and my pulse pounds in my head. I don't like this at all.

She'll be fine. Hannah is a perfectly capable police officer and she knows what she's doing.

But I've already broken out into a sweat, my palms itching as I rub them down my thighs, trying to quash the sensation. No, something is wrong. I can feel it in my bones. I get off my stool and try to follow her. But my plan is foiled when I attempt to enter the staff door and a big, burly guy comes out the other way carrying two plates.

I attempt a casual laugh. "I'm sorry, my wife had a bit to drink and I think she went through here."

"I didn't see anybody."

"Is that the kitchen?"

The guy looks at me suspiciously. "Yeah. Kitchen and our loading dock. But I didn't see anyone."

The loading dock.

I head out the front of the pub and immediately curl around to the right. If there's a loading dock, then there's a way for vehicles to get in.

I race around the corner, my heart thudding like a fist pounding against my rib cage. In my mind, the worst-case scenario is already playing out. Hannah surrounded, vulnerable. But my mind is playing tricks on me and suddenly I'm seeing something old.

Photos. Blood splatter. Bullet holes. Mum. Dad. My brother. The girl I thought I'd be with forever.

"Hannah!" I call as I turn the corner.

I'm panicking. The feeling washes over me like sickly sludge, addling my brain and my ability to think. I see her. She's talking to a group of men and one of them grabs her arm. There's a smile on her face, but it's brittle like old plaster.

Fuck.

I storm up the alley, dodging the stinking garbage bins that smell like rotten food. There are three guys, one of them is Matt. If I go in too hard, we might lose any chance of being able to talk to him later. I could

royally screw this up. But no amount of logic will
stop me now, not when I see the guy who has Hannah's arm in his meaty grip tugging her away from
the group and further down into the alley.

CHAPTER SEVENTEEN

Hannah

I'M IN CONTROL HERE. I have to tell myself that because fear charges through my veins like a shock of electricity, filling me with jittering energy. I'm in control.

Sure, beefcake number one is holding my arm so tight I'm sure he's going to leave a bruise. And okay, of *course* I would feel safer if I had a weapon handy. But I know how to handle a big guy. I know exactly where my elbows and knees need to go. And I know, beyond a shadow of a doubt, that he thinks I'm a dumb drunk girl and based on that he will underestimate me in a fight. Which I will *absolutely* use to my advantage.

"C'mon, pretty girl." He leers at me with his colourless eyes, and his puffy lips curve into a smile. "Let's go this way."

Dark hair, dark eyes. Heavy brow and bulbous nose. Tattoos on his right arm that peek out from his cuff. They're coloured tatts. Faded, though. Details rattle through my brain at lightning speed, all getting logged away so I can compare them to mugshots Max provided us at the beginning of the assignment.

"No," I say in a kind of singsong voice my room-mate uses when she's had a few too many Chardon-nays. "I don't want to go that way."

I glance at Matt, who doesn't even try to inter-vene. And he knows who I am, because I saw it on his face the second we made eye contact. Not that he mentioned it, however. He acted like he'd never seen me before. I'm pissed he's willing to let a neighbour get into trouble like this, but his inac-tion tells me something important. He's scared of these guys.

"I want to talk." I bat my eyelashes at beefcake number one and then a waft of rotting garbage hits me. I don't need to pretend to be grossed out by that, so I let my natural reaction play out. "Why are you hanging out in such a stinky street? Haven't you got anywhere nicer to go?"

"We're conducting business, sweetheart," beef-cake number one drawls.

"Are you garbagemen?" I giggle and sway on my heels. "Is that why your business is out here?"

"Do we look like garbagemen?" Beefcake num-ber two glares at me. He's also dark-haired and dark-eyed, but seems cleaner cut. No tatts that I can see.

"She's a stupid drunk bitch," Matt says, almost snarling at me. But the action feels a little forced, like he's trying to draw attention away from me.

Speaking of drawing attention...

I catch sight of Owen rushing up the alley toward

me, his face filled with worry. Shit. He's going to blow everything. I'd hoped to poke around a bit more, see what else came out. I can handle these guys, especially since there are a ton of security cameras focused on the loading bay. They wouldn't do anything in plain sight, so all I have to do is make sure I don't stray too far.

"What the fuck?" Beefcake number two swings his head around and jams his hands into his pockets as Owen approaches. "Can I help you, mate?"

His tone has the acid-dripping edge of someone who is definitely *not* greeting a friend. Owen catches the cue and slows, arranging his face into an expression that's more world-weary than fearful. "Just looking for my wife. She has a tendency to wander off when she's drunk."

Beefcake number one raises a brow and looks at me. "This guy's your husband?"

My mind spins. If I lie now, I might get more information out of these guys, but at what cost? Who knows what they'll do to Owen. Not to mention that Matt would be curious as hell. I can't risk it.

"Oh, hey." I make my voice syrupy sweet as I wriggle out of beefcake number one's grip. "There you are!"

"Here I am," he mutters, rolling his eyes. He looks at the three men and shakes his head. "A word of advice—don't get married."

I pout and allow him to lead me back down the alley, past the graffiti-covered brick walls and a seemingly endless collection of stinking garbage bins. Eventually, we curve around a corner and find ourselves on Love Street.

"I had that handled," I say, tugging out of his grip. My drunk act is totally gone now. "I told you to wait inside."

"While that giant monster tried to drag you into some abandoned corner? There were three of them, Hannah. You're not invincible." It's only now that I notice how absolutely and totally pissed he is. I don't think I've ever seen Owen this mad before.

But he's not the only one. "You didn't even give me a chance. How long was I out there? Barely five minutes. Not even. Three minutes."

I storm over the street, letting my resentment flow freely. It doesn't matter if people see us fighting, because we can chalk it up to me being an "angry drunk." Neither one of us says a word until we make it into our apartment. But if Owen thinks I'm going to let him off the hook, then he's about to have a rude shock.

"You impeded this investigation," I say as I dump my bag onto the couch and kick off my heels. I'm keeping my voice low, but I can tell he understands how pissed I am. Good. "I could have secured important information."

"You could have gotten yourself in a whole lot of fucking trouble." He's vibrating now. The emotion pours off him like a wave, washing over me and mixing my feelings up. Usually, when someone cuts my grass like that, it's because there's doubt over my capability. The force doesn't have as much misogyny as it used to, but it's still there.

This, however, is different. Owen seems genuinely worried about my safety. But ultimately, that doesn't matter. The job comes first.

"*I'm* the detective on this investigation." My voice is low, hard-edged. Soft enough that nobody walking past our apartment would be able to hear, but loud enough that Owen gets the message. "Not you. So that puts me in charge. *I* call the shots."

"I'm not going to sit on my hands while you act like some dumb rookie, Anderson." He rakes a hand through his hair. "Do you have any idea what could have happened? Do you have any goddamn idea what the world is like out there?"

"Do I have any idea?" I shake my head. "What do you think I do all day? Write reports and apply my lipstick?"

"Fuck." He's pacing now, moving back and forth like an agitated cat. "I know you can handle yourself. This isn't… I didn't say it because you're a woman, all right? It's got nothing to do with that."

"Then what is it, huh? Would you have busted in on Max?"

"Probably." He lets out a sharp laugh. "Once a worry gets in my head…"

"I work on the street every day dealing with the community. Dealing with bad people. I know what I'm doing." My tone is a bit softer now that he's calmed down. "I'm good at my job and I *don't* make dumb rookie moves."

When he looks up at me, I see something I've never seen before. Darkness. Owen's eyes are peering into another world—something beyond me—that's filled with pain. It's his history, the past he never speaks of.

"Look, I should have given you more warning. I'll concede to that." I touch his arm. "But you don't have to worry about me, okay? I was trained by the best."

"I can't *not* worry, Anderson. It's why I left." He stalks over to the kitchen and flicks on the coffee machine with such aggression it's like the appliance has personally offended him.

"What do you mean?"

His back is to me. The black leather jacket makes him look even bigger, tougher. Blue jeans cup his ass and thighs, shaping his muscular legs to perfection. The back of his wavy blond hair is mussed. He's run his fingers through it one too many times. God, he's beautiful. From every angle. But spending this much time with him has shown me there's a tenderness beneath the joker exterior. A damaged part he does his best to hide.

The silence is broken by the hum of the coffee machine. "Owen?"

"I left because I couldn't handle the thought that I might…lose a friend on the job." He still hasn't faced me. "And I was right, wasn't I? How long after I left did we lose Ryan in that raid? It happened within weeks."

I remember the story like it was yesterday. Ryan was a young officer on the rise—smart, action-oriented, brave. He, Max and Owen were nicknamed the Three Stooges during our academy days. But Ryan was killed during a raid because he went against orders, thinking he heard a child crying inside a drug lab. His story was a warning to recruits— don't be impulsive, *never* disobey an order. In fact, Max had taken Ryan's death so hard he'd also left his job for a period of time, following Owen to New York City. Difference was, Max returned home to give it another shot.

"Why didn't you come back for the funeral?" I ask.

"I couldn't." He turns around, his jaw tight. Eyes faraway. "I couldn't stand to be around death anymore. It follows me everywhere."

I want to run to him, because my heart is shattering into a million pieces. I want to fix him, put him back together. I want to do whatever I can to make him whole.

"Don't." He holds up a hand. "Don't look at me like that."

"Like what?"

"Like you think I'm a project."

"What happened to you?" I'm closer now, as though someone has my feet connected to a remote control. As though he's a magnet and I'm being drawn to him against my better judgement. "When you were young, what happened?"

"You really want to know?" His eyes are so blue it almost hurts to look at them. But they're red-rimmed now, wild and angry and sad and terrified. "You want every sordid detail, huh? Well, I should have fucking died the night my parents did. I should have been gutted and robbed like they were."

"What?" I shake my head.

"My father was working in Papua New Guinea for a big bank. We were supposed to be there for two years while he was CEO. One night we were going to a charity gala. My mother was dressed to the nines and covered in diamonds, and my father looked at her like she was the most beautiful creature in the universe." He swallows, his hands curling into fists. "My brother and I were going with them. It was the first time we were able to go, because there'd been threats against us. Kidnapping threats. It was common, we were told. Desperate people trying to make money any way they could."

My stomach swishes and I clamp my hand over my mouth. "Kidnapping?"

"And worse. The night of the gala I was sick, and my mother wanted to cancel. But she was already dressed up, and my brother was so excited. I convinced them to go, told them to have a good time because I wanted to stay home and play video games on my own without my little brother bugging me." His jaw twitches. "Since my ticket wasn't going to be used they took Lillian."

"Who's Lillian?" I search my brain for the name but come up empty.

"She was my girlfriend. Her dad was my father's chief of staff, and so when he took the job in PNG, her family came with us. She was…" He swallowed.

"She was my first everything. I was so in love with her, I'd told my father I was going to marry her the second I turned eighteen. In fact, I was the one who suggested they take her with them that night—because she had this new dress and she looked so fucking beautiful in it. I wanted the world to see how beautiful she was."

Oh no. I feel my eyes well, the path of his story laid out like a horrible, twisted road in front of me. I can see when he talks about her, that he *was* so in love. That he's still so in pain.

"Their usual driver was sick, so they had a different guy. Apparently he went off the approved route, and they were stopped by a group of men. They robbed my parents, but something went wrong. Maybe my father fought back? They ended up killing everyone in the car. My mother, my father, my brother, my girlfriend…everyone I cared about."

I can only stare for a minute while my brain catches up. It's like I'm swimming through mud, trying to understand how Owen is even standing right now. How he's even functioning. My mum ran off with another man when I was twelve and it shook me to my core. But it also shaped me—made me determined to be the best person I could be. Determined to show the world I was fine without her, and that my dad and brothers were all I needed. It made me driven, ambitious, hardworking.

But to lose one's entire family… I can't even comprehend what my life would be like. What *I* would be like.

"I don't want your sympathy," he says. I feel like I'm seeing Owen for the first time now—I'm seeing all his scars and bumps and bruises. All his pain and suffering. His outer shell is so shiny and so tough, I'd wager there are few people who ever get to see him like this. "I…I know I should have trusted you to handle yourself back there. But I'm not good at letting go when I think someone I care about might get hurt."

"You care about me?" My gut is filled with swirling, conflicting emotions. I've never felt like this before, not with anyone.

"Of course I do, we're friends." He cringes as my face drops. "Fuck. This is why I didn't want to go there with you. Why I shouldn't have touched you. I'm damaged goods."

Even in all of this, he's still worried about me. Sure, I'm pissed that he charged in and tried to act like I was a damsel in distress. But I get it. I get him more than I ever have before.

The worst part of it is, I *want* him more than ever before.

CHAPTER EIGHTEEN

Owen

I LOOK AROUND the kitchen and realise I'm standing in the kind of place I would never own. Marble countertops, gold hardware, custom cabinetry. Expensive coffee machine. There's a painting hanging in the kitchen and a small chandelier above our heads.

A fucking chandelier in the kitchen.

I loathe the idea of being rich because it's the easiest thing to blame for that night. If we'd never had money—if my mother hadn't been wearing those diamonds—I might still have my parents. My little brother, who'd annoyed the shit out of me when we were kids, I'd give anything to get him back. And Lillian…

Hannah looks at me with her big brown eyes and those long silky lashes. Compassion pours off her, because that's what she does—she cares. I don't want her to care. I don't want her to hug me and tell me everything will be okay. Because it's not okay.

It's never going to be okay.

But the second her hand comes to my chest, it's like the demons in my head go quiet for the first time in years. She holds eye contact, unblinking. So sincere I almost have to turn away.

"I want to make you feel better," she says.

"My problems can't be solved by fucking," I say. Damn, if only the people who'd called me a player and a lady-killer could hear me now.

But that's the thing, *this* is me. The person that I haven't let anybody see…except her.

"But they can't be made worse, right?" Her hands glide up my chest and she presses closer. Her hips are flush with mine, and when she rises onto her toes, her whole body rubs up against mine. I'm hard in an instant, my mind swinging like a pendulum between what I want and what I know is right. "Maybe blowing off some steam will do you good."

"What happened to one night?" I turn us around and lift her up onto the kitchen countertop. Sliding my hands up her thighs, I part her legs. She's wearing tight black jeans and a pretty silk blouse that's the inky colour of the sky at night. She's got this glossy stuff on her lips that makes it look like she's been sucking on a red icy pole and *that* makes me think of how she sucked my cock after having that cold water in her mouth.

"I wanted one night to be enough." Her eyes are hooded now, as I rub my hands up and down her legs, getting so close to the sweet spot between them. "I'd hoped that if I gave in, then I'd feel satisfied and…"

"And?"

"It's only made me want you more."

"Hannah…" I rest my forehead against hers.

"Don't feed me that bullshit about me falling in love with you. I'm in control of that and I won't let it happen." She nails me with a confident stare.

"So it's nothing to do with me being a sap and pouring my heart out?" I know she's only saying this stuff for my benefit…but it works.

"Nope. You're hot, that's all." A wicked smile curves on her lips. "I can gag you if it'll make you feel better."

"You're the one who's always yappin'. Maybe *I* should gag you." I lower my mouth down to hers and she tilts her face up, inviting me closer.

"Maybe you have to make me feel so good I can't speak."

Challenge accepted. I kiss her hard, drawing her to the edge of the kitchen counter so I can stand between her legs. I lean into her, my cock almost bursting behind the fly of my jeans. Underneath the soft material of her blouse, she's bare except for a tiny scrap of lace masquerading as one of those soft bra-things. I like it—no hooks. My palm cups her breast and I rub in slow circles, kissing down the side of her neck. There's a soft *thump* as her head lolls back against the kitchen cabinet and a delighted *hmm* as I find her hardened nipple with my thumb.

"You make the best sounds." I peel the blouse over her head and she lifts her arms without me asking. The soft bra is next, and her rosy nipples beg for my mouth. "So sexy."

"It's hard not to make sounds when you're doing that." Her fingers drive through my hair, holding my head at her breast. "Although I had a guy once tell me I was too loud."

I look up, my face screwed into an expression of disbelief. "What a dickhead."

"Right?" She laughs, her cheeks pink now as if she's embarrassed to have told me that. But I love how open she is. How vocal. "It's not like I *try* to be loud."

"What about when it's just you?" I move my head to her other breast and she arches into me.

"When it's just me?" A small, self-conscious laugh escapes her lips. "It's usually more the sound of the vibrator I have to worry about."

Holy hell. The thought of pretty little Hannah Anderson with her legs spread wide while she works herself over with a vibrator is possibly the hottest thing I've ever imagined.

"Tell me you brought one with you. I *need* to see that for myself."

There's a beat of silence, and when I look up she's even pinker than before. "Well, I didn't *mean* to bring it with me, but I got a travel one at a hen party one time and…I kind of left it in my suitcase."

I wrap my arms around her waist and pull her down from the counter. "Go. Now."

She's shaking her head and laughing, one hand covering her face like she's half mortified but half loving it. I'm *one-hundred-percent* loving it, obviously.

I follow her into the bedroom and she digs around in her suitcase. The item she retrieves looks almost like a lipstick—slim and silver. But when she twists the base, it buzzes.

"Get on the bed."

She sucks in a breath and does what I command. "What now?"

"I want you naked."

She places the mini-vibrator down and works on her jeans—popping the button and drawing the zipper down so she can shimmy out of the fabric. She takes her underwear with it. I palm my aching cock through my jeans. This is going to be one hell of a show.

With an almost shy smile, she crawls back onto the bed, grabs the vibrator and sits up against the headboard. "You want to watch me play with myself, Owen?"

"God, yes."

"Do you want to watch me come?" She's using this soft, breathy voice that's doing all kinds of crazy things to me. I'm so hard I could hammer nails, but I resist the urge to get out of my clothes. Anticipation is going to make this so much better.

"Yes."

Slowly, she parts her legs so that her knees bow to the side and rest against the bed. It gives me a perfect view of her sweet, pink pussy. Taking her time, she runs her hands up and down her inner thighs, as if warming up.

"Nervous?" I ask.

She shakes her head. "I never thought I'd be the

kind of person who wanted to put on a show…but I really do."

"You're a vision, Anderson."

"Hannah." It's not the first time she's corrected me, but her message is loud and clear. Now, in this room, we're not role-playing as husband and wife. We're not role-playing as high-flying businesspeople in town for one night only. Heck, we're not even role-playing as friends who like to wind each other up. Because we moved past that the moment I walked into that bar and took her up on her offer, and she's not going to let me forget it.

"Hannah." It sticks in my throat, almost drowned out by the thumping of my heart. "I want to watch you."

She looks up at me with smouldering eyes, and the second she twists the little silver bullet and a vibrating sound fills the room, the air around us is electrified. But she doesn't rush into it—oh no, she's a master of anticipation. First she runs her hands up and down her thighs, dragging the nails of her free hand hard enough to make faint pink marks on her porcelain skin. They disappear within an instant, but the sensation is enough to make her shiver.

I'm stock still. A statue rooted to the ground of the plush bedroom. Sucking on her lower lip, Hannah drags the vibrator lightly over her sex. She sinks back against the mountain of cloud-like pillows in varying shades of expensive white cotton and silk. Her dark hair makes a striking contrast, the slightly frizzy curls creating a halo effect around her pretty face. She's all big eyes and pink lips, all delicate fingers and softness. The silver vibrator hums as she continues to build up to what I've asked her to do—to put on a show for me.

"Ready?" she asks with a wicked glint in her eye.

If I were any *more* ready, I'd be stripping out of my clothes quicker than I could say my own name. But I am not going to waste this experience with her, so I shut my mouth and nod.

Hannah rubs the vibrator against herself, lowering it down to her entrance where she pushes it inside just a little. The sight of that shiny silver disappearing into her pussy is enough to fry my brain. She works it in a little, then back out. Repeating this motion until she's dripping. Then she uses the vibrator to drag that moisture up to her clit.

With one hand, she holds herself open, and the other works the buzzing device in slow, even circles. God, yes. Her cheeks are flushed pink, and it goes everywhere. To her ears, and down her neck. Her eyes flutter shut and her mouth falls open, and that's when I'm hit with the full force of her power. The sounds coming out of her—keening moans and panted little yeses—are everything.

I strip off my shirt and shoes and socks and jeans, dumping everything unceremoniously into a pile. Hannah hasn't even noticed; her eyes are still clamped shut and now she's sunk her teeth into her bottom lip as she works the vibrator faster. She rolls her hips, as if simulating what she wants to come next. It's glorious. Vulnerable and yet strong, and so honest.

That's the one thing I have always admired about Hannah…she is who she is. Unlike me, who's so far deep into character that I don't even know who I am anymore. Being with her is like having a light shone on the darkest, most damaged part of me.

For a moment I consider walking away and denying myself because it's the easiest option. As if she senses my swirling thoughts, her eyes slowly open and she looks at me through her lashes. "Come here."

I sink to my knees on the end of the bed, but she beckons me closer still. I crawl up beside her and run my palm over her legs—up her shin, over the curve of her knee and up her thigh.

"I want you to touch me while I do this." Her voice is soft, whispered. But her gaze holds me prisoner and I know I'd never be able to deny her. "It's better with something inside me."

I can't help but moan, and I trail my hand over the curve at her hip and dip down over the slick lips of her sex. I brush past the vibrator and down further, noticing how she angles herself to me. Encouraging me.

"Yes, there." Her eyes are shut again and I rub my fingertip against her entrance, coating myself in her. When I push my finger inside, she lets out a satisfied gasp that makes heat surge through me. "Fuck me with it."

I slide my finger in and out, slowly at first. Testing her. But her head turns and she whispers in my ear, urging me on. Her sex is hot and tight, and I'm so wound up I want nothing more than to sink my cock in her. But I want to see her come first. So I stroke her harder, faster. Following the rhythm she's set and soon she's shaking. Her thighs tremble and her muscles clench around my finger.

"Oh God, Owen." She turns, pressing her forehead to my chest as she starts to come. "Yes, yes."

She works the buzzing device over her clit until she's cresting, and I sink another finger inside her at the last second. She shatters, crying out my name so loud I *know* the neighbours must hear us. And that doesn't bother me one bit. Because the second she comes back down to earth, those big brown eyes locking on to mine, I know I haven't been this happy in years. Not for most of my life.

But I don't want to feel like that. I don't want to have those "what if this could be it?" moments. I'm terrified by the way she makes me feel. Absolutely, utterly fucking terrified.

"I turn into an animal around you." She presses her lips to my chest and I stroke her hair, taming the fluffy flyaways that frame her face. "I lose all sense of myself."

"Or maybe you lose all sense of who you think you're supposed to be." I tilt her face up to mine and kiss her long and slow. "Maybe this is *exactly* who you are."

A curious expression flitters over her face. "And this is exactly who you are, isn't it?"

"A guy who likes sex?" I try to hide myself with a cocky smile, but it's too late. I've shown too much.

"That crap won't work anymore." She presses her

hands to my chest and pushes me back against the big bed.

With lazy, languid movements she straddles me, her knees digging into the covers on either side of my hips. My worries are dulled now, smoothed over by the feel of her warm body as she grabs my hands and tugs them up to her breasts. I love this confidence in her. It's the ultimate turn-on.

And I love her breasts, obviously.

"I see you." She arches into my touch, letting out a satisfied hum as I flick my thumbs over her nipples.

"And?" I can't help but ask, even though I know it's only going to lead down the wrong path.

"I like it. I like knowing who you really are, under all the smiles and the jokes. You're a good person, Owen."

No, I'm not. I'm a broken guy with crippling survivor's guilt who abandoned his grandmother when she needed him most. The only thing I've ever been good at was my job as a police officer, and I couldn't even handle that.

I am *far* from "good."

I want to correct her, but her hands slither down her body and reach for my cock. When she touches me, I can't focus my brain on anything else. Her hands slide up and down, squeezing me. Working me over. I let my head sink back into the pillows.

"Feels good?" she asks, her voice husky and low. Her hands continue to play with my cock.

"That's a rhetorical question, right?" I'm mesmerised by her fluffy cloud of hair and the intense expression on her face—her pink-flushed cheeks and sooty lashes and her kiss-roughened mouth. "Yes, it feels insanely good."

We pause to grab a condom and she's back on top before I can miss her—rolling the rubber down my length. Dragging the tip of me back and forth through her slick folds, she teases me for a second before she finds the right spot. Then I'm entering her. Both of us groan when she hits that point—where I'm all the way in, and she's totally filled by me.

Hannah swears under her breath, moving tentatively at first. "Oh God. That feels…"

"Fucking incredible."

The gentle rocking of her hips is like sweet, sweet torture. It's too slow and too much and too everything. "Owen." My name is a sigh on her lips. "I think I'm ruined."

"Me too, Hannah."

She leans forward, lining my chest with her body and settling her lips against the curve of my neck. "Say it again."

"Hannah."

I reach down and fill my hands with her ass, coaxing her to fuck me faster. I thrust up into her, my hips bucking against hers and I lose myself in the moment. In her. In the stupid denial that we can walk away from all this, unscathed and unchanged. But it feels too good to be true. Too much like I've come home for good.

"Fuck me," she whispers in my ear. "I want to feel you for days."

So I give her what she wants. I sit up, pulling her with me so she's settled in my lap and I'm still deep, deep, deep inside her. I hold her tight ass and thrust up into her. Her breasts graze my chest and she moans—a long, low sound that will penetrate concrete and plaster. A sound I never want to stop hearing.

A sound that will haunt me.

But I'm lost now, buried inside her. Wrapped up in her. Filling my heart and lungs with her.

"That feels so good," she pants.

I'm chasing the edge of oblivion, and I reach for the silver bullet that's still sitting on the covers. With one arm around her waist for leverage, I use my free hand to guide the bullet between us, so it's hitting her most sensitive spot. She gasps, shuddering at the sudden stimulation. When she explodes, it's perfect—loud and honest and so fucking hot I can't help but follow her over the edge. I thrust up into her as deep as I can go, and come hard. My cock pulses and I abandon the vibrator, choosing instead to wrap both my arms around her and hold her as tight as I possibly can.

CHAPTER NINETEEN

Owen

HANNAH IS ASLEEP. I'm standing alone in the ensuite, staring at my face in the mirror. Staring at my shell-shocked expression.

The condom broke.

I didn't notice it when I pulled out of her, too enraptured with her hazy, smouldering gaze. Too busy falling head over heels for her. But when I came in here to clean up, I saw it. The split latex. The fact that my whole world could be turned on its head with one tiny little rip.

I never wanted to be a dad. I never wanted to have a family.

I can't be that guy.

I'm *not* that guy.

Fuck.

My heart is pounding like a drum, and the sound of blood rushing in my ears makes me want to scream. I grip the edge of the basin so hard my knuckles are snow white. What do I do?

What if she gets pregnant?

I'm being sucked down a vortex, my thoughts building on one another like an avalanche. I splash my face, but it does nothing. The universe is determined to mess with me, by taking something good and turning it into my worst nightmare.

And what about Hannah? She just made detective. This would not be a good time for her to get pregnant, I'm sure of it. But I don't know what she thinks about the whole having kids thing. She's always struck me as a family girl—the way she talks about her dad and her brothers.

Oh God. I can't do that.

I check on her for a brief moment, not daring to touch her in case she wakes. I dress silently as a ninja, holding my breath each time I take a step. My head is a war zone—and I need space to think. What I also need is to get my head back in the game.

Work always calms me. And the quicker we figure out what's going on at 21 Love Street, the sooner I can get back to my life in New York.

But what if Hannah is pregnant?

I can't think about that now. Being home has reminded me that I tend to get close to people when I shouldn't. And even though I live alone in Manhattan, I've made friends at work. Like my boss, Logan, and my colleagues, Aiden and Quinn and Rhys. I care about them all.

Maybe it's time to go someplace new. Start over again and do a better job at not getting attached. The idea of being able to pack up at any time and move on is so freeing—I need to know that I can escape. That I can pull the ripcord.

I'm panicking like a trapped rat.

But the thought of leaving Hannah after what we've shared settles like a stone weight in my stomach. It's going to suck, but I *did* warn her. If there's a baby involved… Christ. I don't know what I'll do.

I go down to level three to see if Matt is home. Maybe talking to him will help me get out of my own head and back onto wrapping this job up as quickly as possible. The elevator pings and I step out in time to see Matt entering his apartment.

"Hey!" I call out and it looks like he's trying to scurry away from me. Coward. "Wait."

I rush him, jamming my foot between the door so he can't close it. This bastard didn't say a word while Hannah stood there, that ugly-faced brute grabbing her like she was a piece of meat. And he didn't say a damn thing when I came barging in, having to pretend to be some dickhead husband happy to degrade his wife in order to get out of trouble.

"What do you want?" Matt growls. That's when I get a good look at his face—he's got a black eye and a split lip.

"What happened to you?" I plant my hand against his front door and invite myself in. The place smells like a dorm party— beer, pizza and BO covered up with cheap cologne. "You should get some ice on that."

"No shit," Matt grumbles. His good eye is bloodshot, like he's been on something.

"Someone's done my work for me." I fold my arms and lean against his wall. Matt seems to take the hint that I'm not leaving, and lets the front door swing shut behind him. "It's not much fun giving someone a black eye when they've already got one."

Matt grabs an icepack from the freezer and wraps it in a tea towel. "This about what happened before?"

"You're a regular fucking Sherlock, aren't you?"

He eyes me warily, and I lean into my persona. Owen Essex is a spoilt rich boy who grew up without anybody crossing him.

Matt sighs. "I don't want any trouble. Your wife interrupted my business. Trust me, I did her a favor pretending I had no idea who she was."

"How do you figure that? Looked like one of your mates was feeling her up."

"They're *not* my mates." Matt winces as he presses the icepack to his eye. "Be pissed if you want, but the fact that they don't know either of your names is a good thing."

I watch Matt's movements—he's defeated. His shoulders hunch forward as he leans against the breakfast bar. He's stocky in build, like he might have been muscular at one point but now he's out of shape. I spy multiple empty Coke bottles dry and open around the couch. Two pizza boxes on the slick glass coffee table. It's a jarring sight given that the apartment has very expensive things—a Bose sound system, giant TV...and one of Celina Yang's sculptures.

"You playing with a rough crowd?" I ask, my eyes continuing to scan the room for any useful information.

"Why do you want to know?" Matt asks warily.

"I might be looking for some new friends."

"These guys don't make friends." For a second I see real fear in his eyes, and my suspicions that he's got anything to do with the jewellery theft ring are dwindling by the second. He doesn't look like he'd have the stomach for it. So I switch tactics.

"I see you've got one of Celina's pieces." I walk over to it. It's huge —almost comes up to my waist and stretches out at least three feet— and made of a white material that's so smooth I can almost see my own face in it.

"Not for long. She's going to pick it up." He comes out of the kitchen area and walks over. "Never mind the fact that I helped get her started. I funded her first show, paid for a space back when no galleries would take her. I paid for the catering and a photographer. I helped launch her."

His bitterness is toxic.

"Why did you break up?"

"Artistic differences. I wanted to settle down and have a family, and she didn't."

I think back to the conversation I overheard at the gallery, when Celina accused him of doing things that were "dangerous and wrong." "And she had a problem with you stealing shit."

Matt's eyebrows shoot up. "What's *that* supposed to mean?"

"I'm not stupid, Matt. I know you're into something with those guys and Celina didn't like it."

"Did she say something to you?"

I lift one shoulder into a shrug. "Not to me."

Matt takes the bait and shakes his head. "Fucking women. Always talking, talking, talking. Look, it's not like that. I made some mistakes, got myself in trouble and now I'm getting myself out. But I'm not a criminal, no matter what she says."

"Stealing makes you a criminal, doesn't it?"

"I didn't steal those goddamn earrings." He pulls his icepack down and his eye is swollen and puffy. "I won them."

"You won them?"

"The guys in the alley have a high-stakes poker game once a month. I cleaned one of them out, after they brought me in thinking I'd be easy pickings. He lost all his dough, so he bet the earrings and I won them, too." Matt frowns. "I gave them to Celina because I was trying to win her back, but she figured out I didn't buy them."

Ah, so *that* was the unethical activity. Matt had himself a gambling problem.

"And then the guy and his goons started turning up at the pub and hanging around at the restaurant where I was working until they got me fired."

It wasn't the first time I'd seen this play before—the poker game might've been a set-up. Get some sucker in, let him win and then extort him afterward. But that would only work if the diamonds were fake, and my gut told me that wasn't the case. Maybe one of the Romano crew stepped out of line. Got greedy, lost to Matt, and now the higher-ups were demanding their cut.

"Why don't you give the earrings back?" I ask.

"Serge doesn't want them back. He wants help."

"What kind of help?"

Matt shook his head. "I can't say."

Should I let him know that I have suspicions about who's working him over? That I know these people won't stop until they get what they want…and then some?

"You're in deep shit, Matt." I say it so seriously he turns to me, his face going white. "I know those guys, okay? They're not going to leave you alone."

"Wh-what do you mean?"

"They're part of a crime gang. Ever heard of the Romano family?" I watch as Matt sways. "You had no idea, did you? They're into a lot of things. Drugs, jewels, cars. Diversification, that's how they keep funds coming in. When one operation goes down, they've got the others to keep the cash flowing."

"How do you know all this?"

"I know people." I lean forward, doing my best to intimidate the poor guy. I feel bad for him, since he obviously has no idea what he's gotten himself into, but I can't let it show.

"What do you want?"

"The diamonds." I place a heavy hand on Matt's shoulder. "Go to Celina, get the earrings back and give them to me. Or you're going to have more problems. But, if you help me, then all this will go away."

"You only want the earrings?" he asks, his voice shaky.

"Just the earrings. If you help me, I'll help you."

"Here." Matt rushes over to a unit on the side of the room and yanks a drawer open. He plucks out a blue velvet box and thrusts it at me. "Take them. I wish I'd never seen these damn things."

I take the box and flip the lid open. Inside are two perfectly cut square diamonds suspended from a ring of smaller shimmering blue stones. Now I know exactly how we're going to lure the Romanos out of hiding.

CHAPTER TWENTY

Hannah

I DON'T KNOW how long I slept, exactly. But what I do know is that it was the deepest, most peaceful sleep of my entire life. I barely remember Owen leaving the bed. He sent me into a bliss coma and I've awoken more rested and more satisfied than ever before.

It's a problem. Because I'm not someone who has sex purely for pleasure's sake. I don't judge anyone who does, and I've wished in the past that I *could* be more like that. But the fact is, I'm not. I *need* a connection. And for all the teasing and taunting and the playful antagonism I've shared with Owen over the years, I *do* like him. A lot. More than I should.

Because falling for Owen is a fool's game.

He's a ghost. A guy who flits in and out of people's lives because he can't bear to get close. I understand why, now. But it doesn't change how he behaves. Only justifies it.

I head to the shower—filling the room with steam and the scent of lemon soap. I glide it over my body, over all the places he touched and with each new spot, I remember how it felt with him.

I've been dragging my heels with this case, focusing on sex more than my job. It's so unlike me, because my career is everything. But in this particular instance, career success means losing Owen. The better I do my job, the faster he'll leave.

I want to explore this thing between us—this insatiable, burning chemistry that makes my body glow. That makes my heart glow. I want to know if it will burn itself out, or if there's something special and lasting underneath the attraction.

The taps twist silently beneath my fingertips, shutting the water off without the squeak I'm used to back home. I step out of the shower and drape myself in one of the many fluffy white towels that fill the linen cupboard, using the long ends to get the excess water out of my hair.

In the mirror, my face is pink and happy. There's a crinkle to the corner of my eyes that isn't usually there when I'm working an important case. That's his influence—he lightens me, grounds me.

The sound of a door slamming on the other side of the apartment fills me with trepidation. I hear the keys hitting the glass bowl and then footsteps.

"Owen?" I don't bother to dress right away, instead wrapping myself up and heading into the living room, damp hair trailing a few scant water droplets over my shoulders and chest. "Where did you go?"

He turns when I come up behind him, his blue eyes a little wild. It takes a good ten seconds for him to drink me in, but the warmth we shared earlier is gone. There's a hardness to his handsome features now, a remoteness. This is Owen's MO: at the first signs of connection, retreat.

"I paid our friend Matt a visit." He digs his hand into his pocket and pulls out a small velvet box. Inside are the earrings I'd seen on Celina the night at the gallery. "He didn't know about the connection to the Romanos, though. He won these in a high-stakes poker game."

"Not entirely surprising." I peer at the earrings, dazzled momentarily. "Where there's organised crime, there's gambling."

"Right." Owen closes the velvet box. "Something has been bothering me since the alley. But I couldn't put my finger on it until I spoke with Matt. He mentioned the name Serge."

Oh shit. "You think it's…"

"Sergio Benedetti? Yeah. We haven't heard anything about him since he was a kid, so that's why I didn't recognise him. But he looks a hell of a lot like his dad, now that I think of it."

The Benedettis were deeply embroiled in a crime gang responsible for some of the worst drug trafficking Melbourne had ever seen in the '90s. Mostly amphetamines, but they also had a hand in protection rackets, illegal gambling and prostitution. Eventually Sergio's father was murdered by a rival when he was only five years old. The Benedetti crime family folded and Sergio was sent overseas to live with relatives in Italy.

I shake my head. "Maybe he's back trying to climb the ranks with the Romanos. That's how his father started out—joining an existing family and then getting powerful enough to branch out on his own."

"That's exactly what I was thinking," Owen said. "We'll get that info to Max and see if we can confirm it's him."

"And then we try to draw him out."

"Do you think Sergio has been dipping into the merchandise?" I worry my bottom lip between my teeth. "Maybe he's skimming off the robberies to fund a gambling habit."

"Quite possibly."

"We have to get ourselves an invite to the next poker game." I'm excited by this new lead, and intuition tingles in my blood. We're on to something.

"*I* have to get an invite to the game," Owen says, stuffing the box back into his jacket.

"Excuse me?" I narrow my eyes at him. "Since when is this *your* assignment? I won't be left out."

Owen rakes a hand through his hair and exhales through his teeth. Something's wrong—I can feel it in my bones. When he left our bed, he was loose and relaxed. Now he walks like a tiger who's been caged, with agitation rippling through his muscles and a slight hunch to his shoulders.

"It'll be dangerous, Hannah."

The way he says my name is like a knife straight into my heart. It's tender and terrified, and not at all how I want it to sound. "This whole job is dangerous, which is why we have procedures. I *did* listen during my academy training."

"I know, I know." He walks to the big windows that overlook South Melbourne. It's a clear, cloudless evening. The sky is purple-tinged and the last streaks of sunset paint the horizon in coral and gold.

"What's wrong?" I go to him. I want to draw him close to me, but I'm confused—wanting what I shouldn't and in far too deep to avoid getting hurt. "If this is about before, I promise next time I'll communicate better. I saw the opportunity, but I should have told you what I was doing."

"It's not that. You made the right move."

"Then what? Is this because we've had sex?" I shake my head. "I know you've got this impenetrable wall about you, and I understand why. But us having sex has nothing to do with our job, and it certainly doesn't affect my ability to be a good detective."

"The condom broke."

For a moment there's nothing—no blood in my veins, no air in my lungs. No contractions of my heart. I'm a shell, unable to comprehend what's going on. "Wh-what?"

"The. Condom. Broke."

I step back, bracing one palm against the glass to steady myself. How had I not noticed? How had I not instinctively felt that crucial change? It's never happened before—not once. Not when I dated that dropkick I should've ditched after the first date, and not when I tried to convince myself to love the guy who was so right on paper, but failed to give me sparks.

I've always wanted to be a mother…but not like this. "When were you going to tell me?"

"I'm telling you right now."

My head is spinning like a top. I press my hand to my stomach, realising I'm still dressed in a towel. "Why didn't you come straight back to bed and tell me?"

"I…I don't know. I freaked out." Owen looks at me with panic in his eyes.

"I'll go to the pharmacy." I sound *way* calmer than I feel, but my dad always said I was like a duck in a crisis: calm on the outside, and moving like mad beneath the surface. Was medication one-hundred-percent guaranteed to work? What were the chances I would end up pregnant? I had no earthly idea.

"If for whatever reason it…doesn't work, I'll take care of you and the baby."

The sincerity in his voice melts my heart. A baby now would be the worst possible timing, but if I *do* end up pregnant then I'll make it work. No matter what. I have to admit that knowing Owen would be involved makes me feel a smidge better. "Thank you."

"Seriously, whatever you need. I…I haven't touched my parents' money. It's sitting in an account because I wanted nothing to do with it, so if you need a new place, baby stuff. I'll get you anything."

I blink. "You're talking about money?"

"Well, yeah. I know babies are expensive. It's probably the *only* thing I know about them." He rakes his hand through his hair again. "And you'd need your own place, too. Somewhere safe, which means well…shit, I don't know what the stats are like anymore. Maybe we can get hold of the crime report— "

"Owen." I hold up a hand, halting him. "I don't want your money."

"What?" It's like I've shaken him out of a trance. He's gone into solution mode, thinking about living arrangements and baby supplies, but all of that is second-tier stuff. "I can't let you manage that alone."

"But what about *you*? Not your bank account or your family's money. I mean you…if you were a dad." I grip the towel hard against me, feeling suddenly like I'm standing on a cliff face, with a sheer drop below. "If I end up pregnant, what are you going to do?"

"I'll be back in Manhattan. I'm leaving the second this is all over." The words come so automatically, it's like salt on an already raw wound. He didn't even hesitate for a second. All of this—being home, being with *me*—hasn't given him pause about his life.

I wasn't expecting anything different, but it still hurts. "Right."

"Fuck, I didn't…" God, this is so awkward. "I can't stay here, Hannah. You know that."

I bite the inside of my cheek, trying to keep all the words and feelings inside. He's right, I *did* know that. We argued about it the night of the gallery, where he tried to draw boundaries because he predicted I'd want more. And he was right.

He'd been right all along.

"Not even if you'd fathered a child? You're telling me you'd want nothing to do with us?"

"I'm not cut out for that life. I don't…do the family thing." How is it possible that he's so handsome, even now? Even with all that anguish on his face? "This is exactly why I tried to keep things professional."

"It takes two to tango, Owen." Sure, I encouraged things along, but he still said yes. He still walked into that bar and sat down next to me, knowing where it would lead. He still came to bed with me today. We're *both* party to this.

"I'm not blaming you. I'm setting expectations." When he looks at me, it's like being lanced through the heart. "I like you…a lot. Too much, in fact."

"That is the biggest load of bullshit I've ever heard."

"It's not. The whole reason I tried to steer clear was because I knew how risky it was. You're my kryptonite. You're like sunshine and fucking fairy floss and fireworks and I will suck that all out of you."

His voice is ragged. I know he believes himself—that he'll bring me down or be forced to relive the loss and pain he experienced as a boy, in some way. But it's a cop-out. A protection method. And I deserve more.

I deserve a man who's not afraid to commit. And even though I know there's something between us—something I want to explore more than anything—I won't put myself in a situation where I get discarded because he's too scared to try.

"You don't get to say that stuff unless you plan on acting on it." I look up at him, doing my best to hide my feelings away. I've shown him too much already. "I'm going to the pharmacy now, and you're going to figure out how to get us *both* into that poker game. Then we're going to pretend like none of this ever happened."

Owen turns back to the window, stony and silent. I don't know whether he's annoyed at me for calling him on his bullshit, or whether it's a self-reflection thing. Either way, I have to do my best not to care.

CHAPTER TWENTY-ONE

Owen
One week later...

I CAN'T EVEN count the number of screw-ups in my life. They range from stupid things, like putting my foot in my mouth when dealing with a client, to bigger things, like assuming the most important thing about a potential accidental pregnancy is the money.

It's the easiest aspect to tackle because money is black and white. It's unemotional and removed. Which is exactly why Hannah is pissed. It's not the conversation we should have been having, but every time I imagine her pregnant my brain shuts down.

I don't have it in me to be a dad or a husband. Because I'd wrap my child and my wife in bubble wrap, stifling them with my fear. I have to stop myself doing it now, as Hannah and I step out of the taxi next to an alleyway that's black as midnight. She looks like a million bucks wearing a little black dress that hugs every mouth-watering line of her body, a sparkling clutch bag, my mother's topaz ring and the earrings that Matt gave to Celina.

I didn't want her to wear them. It will be a flashing red cape to Serge. But the higher-ups are getting antsy, and they want more information. So we're taking the provocative approach.

In the past week, we've confirmed a few things. Number one: Serge is, in fact, Sergio Benedetti. He's been back in Australia for two years, mostly laying low and building his network. He runs the monthly poker game, along with the goon who'd had his hands on Hannah the day of the alley incident. But word is that he's a loose cannon and isn't playing by the Romanos' rules. So we might be able to get something out of him.

Number two: according to building records, five apartments at 21 Love Street have residents who moved in less than six months ago. We suspect the reason this building was chosen by the Romanos was due to its proximity to several "old money" suburbs. In addition, residential buildings are not only subject to higher privacy restrictions but they also attract a hell of a lot of attention when it comes to police activity.

Which is why my old team had struggled to get information prior to our undercover op.

Hannah walks into the alley without waiting to see if I'm following. The past week has been like this between us—tense, quiet. Her forging ahead while I overanalyse everything.

"Hannah." I catch up to her, encircling her wrist in my hand. "Stop for a minute."

"What?" She keeps her beautiful face neutral and looks up at me between sooty lashes. Her makeup is dark and smudgy, sexy as hell. Her lips are glossy and have tiny flecks of glitter on them. God, I want to kiss her right now. Every night when I go to bed alone, I wake reaching for her.

"We're a team. We play this together, okay?"

She nods. "I know."

"That means no flying solo."

Her eyes search my face. "Are you worried I'm going to lose all your money, dear husband?"

There are footsteps behind us. I feel like we need to get on the same page, but we're out in the open now. And at home—in our "marital" apartment— she treats me like a stranger.

"I trust you." I pull her toward me and she doesn't resist.

The footsteps get closer and I lower my head to hers, fully expecting her to turn away. But instead she opens, her lips parting and her chin tilting up, and she readily accepts my kiss. Her lips taste like vanilla and she smells like fruity heaven. Her arms wind around my neck and she rises up on her toes, brushing her incredible body against mine.

I wish we were back home, so this kiss could go somewhere. My hands find her back and the sweet, gentle curve at the nape of her neck.

The footsteps continue right past us. The second they're out of earshot, she pulls away and smooths her hands over the bottom of her dress. Her eyes look a little wild.

"Come on." She reaches for my hand and tugs me forward. "We're late."

In truth, I have no idea of the etiquette of an underground, illegal high-stakes poker game. But I can't imagine they're sticklers for punctuality.

The instructions I've been given were vague—a red door down this alley. How far down? I have no idea. But everything is in place. Matt suggested us to Serge and his crew, planting the idea that we're dumb and rich and looking for a thrill.

"Is that it?" Hannah slows as we come close to a door that looks like it could be red if it wasn't entirely hidden in shadows. "It looks deserted."

"On purpose, maybe?" The door is set slightly back, with a single step raising it from the ground. We're about twenty metres from the main road to our right, and to our left the alley continues on in semi-darkness. "Let's see what happens."

We knock once on the door—a loud, single rap that feels like a gunshot in this quiet place—as we've been instructed. I count to five and then knock again, twice this time. The door immediately swings open and we're greeted by a giant hulk of a man. He's built like a house, with tatts and a dark, thick goatee.

"Who invited you?" he asks.

"Matt, but he got Serge's approval." I meet his eye, unwavering. Cocky. "We want to make some money."

The doorman grunts, a slight smile lifting his lips. "I hope you're prepared to pay up."

"Won't need to." I give him a wink and drag Hannah through the door. "I never lose."

I catch his amused expression as he shuts the door behind us. No doubt Matt sold us well—I get the impression he's been expecting us. Now we're in what looks like the bowels of a commercial building—concrete walls and concrete floors and more concrete above. A tag in black spray-paint is the only thing that breaks up the endless grey as we walk toward a door at the other end of the hall; the only one that's not marked with a sign. Hannah's heels click and the sound bounces around us.

"You good?" I ask her as we make it to the unmarked door, and she nods. Her eyes flick to mine and stay there for a moment, but she says nothing.

Should I know, somehow, if she's carrying my child? Should there be some instinctive certainty in my gut? I have so many questions, and I've been bottling them up for the past week. But worse than the questions is the niggling feeling that I *want* to know what's going on…and not so I can manage my exit.

I like Hannah. A lot. And the more times I say it in my head, the stronger the feeling gets. Since Lillian, I haven't been with another woman who made me question the way I lived my life. Who made me reconsider what I wanted for my future.

Except her.

Hannah is a balm for my soul and at the same time, she's a prickle under my skin. I can't shake her. I don't want to shake her. But I don't know how to navigate it because the only thing I've ever been good at is running away and starting over.

"Stop looking at me like that," she says under her breath as she follows the same knocking pattern we used outside. "You're making me self-conscious."

If only she knew how far beyond sex and attraction this was.

You could tell her that...

But I can't. Not right now, when we're walking into an environment we can't control. Tonight, though, I'm going to lay things on the table. I don't have any promises to give, but I want to at least be honest. I want to do the one thing I've never wanted to do before—talk about the future.

"You're my wife, why wouldn't I look at you like you're the most beautiful woman in the world?"

"Touché," she says softly. "Sometimes it's hard to tell what's real and what's in my head."

Before I can respond, the door is pulled open. The contrast from the harsh, grey corridor to the inside of Sergio Benedetti's gambling playpen takes me aback. It isn't quite as sleazy as I'd thought—there's music and the walls are a rich red, covered in old-fashioned wallpaper with a faint print like one might imagine of a speakeasy. There's a heavy chandelier in the middle of the room and tables set up with everything from blackjack to poker to mahjong.

We're greeted by the guy who grabbed Hannah's arm the day we caught Matt and Serge together, and he wastes no time in sliding his gaze all over her body. My fists bunch by my sides and I have to fight the urge to crack this guy in the jaw. But Hannah reaches down and slips her hand into mine, the gesture bringing me back to earth in less than a second.

I regret bringing her here, having her be in harm's way.

"Welcome," the beefcake says. "Serge isn't here yet, but he's looking forward to meeting you in more polite circumstances."

Polite? I want to scoff.

"The feeling is mutual," Hannah replies smoothly, squeezing my hand. "But for now I'd love to see how the cards will treat me."

"What's your poison?" His eyes aren't quite on her face.

"Blackjack. And champagne?" She offers him a coy smile and he immediately signals for a guy in all black.

We're shown to a table with three other people already seated—a woman in a red dress and a sparkling necklace, and two dark-haired men in suits. They appear to know one another, but the woman is playing alone. Hannah slides into the empty seat and I stand behind her, one hand protectively on the back of her chair.

We'd agreed up-front that Hannah would play most of the games. After a few practise runs, it was clear she could hold her own *much* better than I could. I'll survey the room. Our guess was that if she tried to walk around, she might get approached, but I will be able to move around less noticeably.

Given there were probably fifty-something people in the room and I could count the women on one hand, it appears our assumptions were correct.

But the thought of leaving her here, alone, fills me with an ice-cold dread. This room is a viper pit. The men running the show are standover guys, hired guns who couldn't give a shit about the lives of the people inside. All they care about is the money. About making sure the house wins.

"Welcome, Mrs. Essex," the dealer says as Hannah exchanges her money for a stack of chips. He knows our names. Interesting. "It's a pleasure to have you at my table."

Hannah nods. "Thank you."

"Please place your bets into the betting square in front of you. This table has a thousand-dollar minimum."

I immediately sense the tension in Hannah's posture. This minimum bet is much higher than we'd anticipated, and our budget from HQ won't stretch that far. So I lean down and place a hand comfortingly on her shoulder, as though whispering sweet nothings in her ear.

"You got this. I'll bankroll us if need be."

Something flickers across her eyes as she turns her head toward me. She looks at me differently now—like I'm not the person she thought I was. I regret telling her about my parents' wealth, but we might need to rely on it now. Five grand won't take us far, and I refuse to walk out before we meet with Serge.

"All minimum bets are reached." The dealer waves his hand over the table and settles it onto the top of the deck. "All players will be dealt two cards, face up, and the house will receive one card. If you receive two cards of the same denomination, you may choose to split the cards by placing a second bet, equal to your first."

The dealer places the cards out, one by one, with the fluid motion of someone who's done this action thousands of times before. Hannah receives a pair of eights. It's not great—starting with sixteen points means a sixty percent chance of losing the round.

"I'll split," she says and the dealer slides the two eights apart. Hannah counts another small stack of chips and places them into her betting square. It's risky, going hard on the first round, but it's also the move a confident gambler would make—and that's exactly how we have to come across.

I have no doubt Serge will be watching us.

The woman to the left hits twice, and busts. One of the men stays at eighteen. The other hits and brings his total up to nineteen. I hold my breath as the dealer turns back to Hannah. She hits on her first eight—takes it to twelve, sixteen and then bust. The second hit results in a score of fourteen. Hannah taps the table again and another six comes out. That's twenty.

I can almost hear her sigh of relief. "I'll stay."

The dealer has a five to start with. Then a picture card for a total of fifteen. He needs a six to beat Hannah, or anything less not to bust. His hand glides

over to the deck, his deft fingers pulling another card
from the neat pile.

It's a six.

"Blackjack."

Shit. A flute of champagne has appeared beside
Hannah, but both of us were concentrating so hard
on the game that we hadn't even noticed its arrival.

"It's just a warm-up, my love." I pretend to whisper the words, but say them just loud enough that the
men beside her will hear. "I'm going to take a look
around. Will you be okay?"

She nods and pretends to sip her drink, my mother's ring winking in the light. "Don't be long."

I bend down and plant a kiss against her cheek.
"Let me know when you're ready for a bite to eat."

It's our code, if she needs me to pull her out. I
touch her shoulder for a brief moment, and then wander through the tables as though I'm trying to figure out what to do next. Most of the men here are in
custom suits, with expensive shoes and even more
expensive watches. For a moment, I'm transported
back in time to the parties my mother would throw
for all the other overpaid expats and corporate fat
cats. I remembered seeing them at the funeral, having them shake my hand. Wondering if anyone really cared or if it was all for show.

They named a boardroom after my father in the
bank's Sydney headquarters. Journalists hounded my
grandparents for their comments about the deaths and
whether they would sue the bank. They never did.

I often wonder what my parents would think of me

now—with no ties and my affinity for fresh starts. I've done well in every job I've had. I was a great cop and a high-performing security consultant. But my careers, like my relationships, are short-lived.

I rein the memories in, pushing down the pain and channelling it into something greater. My gaze catches Hannah across the room, looking like the only flower in a field of weeds. She's the only person since Lillian who's made me wonder whether it's worth the risk to wish for more. In her arms, I could pretend I had what I'd taken for granted as a child—family, security, love.

Love? I know it exists. But what I feel for Hannah is unlike anything else I've experienced. I can't compare it to teenage love, when that feeling was so pure and untainted. What I feel for Hannah is more… complex. Complicated.

Unwanted, but nonetheless there.

"Excuse me, Mr. Essex?"

I turn to find one of the beefcakes looming over me. "Yeah?"

"Please follow me."

CHAPTER TWENTY-TWO

Hannah

I TRY NOT to think about the fact that I blew two grand in a single round of blackjack. I try not to think about how much that money could help people in our community—how many meals or school uniforms or books it could buy.

You're helping the community by bringing down organised crime.

But it doesn't ease the sting. And without Owen's calming presence behind me, I'm adrift. The dealer asks us to bet on the next round and I slide my chips forward, fighting a disgusting sickness in my stomach. This time I receive a ten and a two. When I hit, I immediately bust.

Three grand gone. I'm panicking. We've only been here fifteen minutes and I've lost over half our money. I push up from my chair and thank the dealer, almost tripping over my own feet in order to get away.

I scan the room but can't find Owen. This place

is bad, bad, bad. But so far, our poking around 21
Love Street hasn't yielded anything and we can't get
a search permission for the entire building without
something to go on. This is our best shot.

"Hannah."

I turn when I hear my name, coming almost nose
to nose with Sergio Benedetti. Tonight he's the slick
power-player in a fitted black suit, black shirt and a
blood-red tie. Devil's colours.

"What a pleasure to see you again." He reaches
for my hand and brings it to his lips. I resist the urge
to pull away.

"Thank you for the generous invite." I tilt my
head, feeling the earrings brush against my skin.

"You're a vision. I admire a woman who has good
taste in jewellery."

Unlike most men here, his eyes don't drift to my
cleavage. Oh no, Serge only has eyes for the sparkly
things in my ears.

"Where did you get those spectacular earrings?"

I smile, bringing my hand up to fiddle with the
diamonds, remembering how Owen coached me to
play it. "Oh, these old things? I've had them forever."

Serge's expression hardens for an instant. "They
suit you."

"Thank you."

"I've got a bar set up out the back for my VIPs.
I'd love for you to join me."

My senses immediately prickle at the invitation—
something isn't right. I'm not a VIP. Well, other than
the fact that I've given the house three thousand dol-

lars. But compared to the people who come here regularly, that would be nothing.

"That's very kind of you to offer—"

"I'm insisting." Serge smiles and it's like a dog baring its teeth.

"Why don't I find my husband and then—"

"He's already received the invite."

My heart stalls for a moment. They have Owen out the back already. But how? I'd only played one more round after he went for a walk. I swallow against the fear mounting in my throat. If I walk away now, Serge will know something is up.

"I would love a drink." I hold my hand out, allowing him to lead me away from the safety of the full room.

We weave through the tables, slowed by wannabes basking in the sunshine of Serge's attention. Here, he is king. The master of his domain. The criminal underworld is full of men with god complexes. It's why there's so much bloodshed. Greed, pride, fury. Retribution. They don't care about anything else.

"I was very pleased when Matthew told me about you and your husband." Serge's lips are close to my ear—and it's nothing like when Owen whispers to me. Now I'm fighting every feminine instinct that tells me to run, reasoning with myself that this job will never *not* be dangerous.

And what happens when you have a baby at home?

Hell, I don't even know if I'm pregnant. I'd promised myself I'd never let having a child frighten me

away from this career—my dad didn't. My brothers
didn't. Max didn't. But I can't deny there's a tiny little seed of doubt unfurling in my gut. Would I walk
into this potential ambush if I had a family waiting
at home?

I honestly don't know.

We reach a door at the back of the room. With
each step, my head is screaming louder and louder
for me to get away while I can. When I falter, Serge's
grip tightens. He says nothing and neither do I. Before I know it, we're leaving the gambling room and
heading into a dimly lit corridor. The heavy door
swings shut behind us, cutting off the music and general din with guillotine precision. We're in a soundproof area and soon I know why.

A keening wail comes from the other end of the
corridor, behind a closed door.

"This doesn't sound like a VIP experience," I say.
God, what if that's Owen?

"Oh, but it is." Serge's grip tightens further and
the pretense is dropped. "I knew the second you
walked in here I'd need to deal with this."

He seems angry now, and it makes his Italian accent more pronounced. It's almost unnerving how he
can switch back and forth between sounding Australian and Italian, like it adds another level of mys-
tery about him.

"I have no idea what you're talking about." Rule
number one of being undercover: never blow the
cover yourself.

"If you think I'm stupid enough to fall for Matt's

suggestion that you would be an easy target, then you're very *very* wrong." The rolled *r*s sound like a motor trying to start. "I take my business seriously, Mrs. Essex, and I do *not* appreciate people trying to cut into my profits."

Okay, so he doesn't know we're cops but he thinks we're…competition?

"Excuse me?" I try to pull out of his grip but I'm rewarded with a sharp yank that I feel all the way up to my shoulder.

"Enough talking." He drags me to the room where his men are waiting. Someone is slumped over in a chair—dark hair, heavier set. Shit, it's Matt.

"What have you done?" I try to rush forward but Serge calls one of his men over and he pins my hands behind my back.

Matt lifts his head and I can see blood caked around a cut on his forehead and on the side of his mouth. His eye is almost completely swollen over. There's a man standing behind him, who grips him by the hair and pulls his head back. For a moment I'm stuck; there's a detail here I'm missing. Something that catches at the edge of my brain. A memory.

The man who's holding on to Matt looks so familiar…

Then it hits me. He's the concierge employee who helped us the day we moved in, the one who showed us up to our apartment. He joked with Owen about being married. We've seen him several times since, manning the front desk of the building.

He must be intercepting the jewels. He would

know who lived in every apartment of the building. If anyone saw something suspicious they would likely tell the front desk…and he could keep it quiet. Having someone on the building staff made perfect sense. They'd hear gossip, complaints, reports… everything.

But he wouldn't have heard about an undercover operation going on in the building. Which means Owen and I might get out of this.

I look at Serge with narrowed eyes. "Are you trying to prove a point? Fine. Consider it proven."

Serge's smile widened. "People tend to forget points unless they are made very clearly."

The concierge guy holds Matt's head back and Serge swings an open palm in his direction. The cracking sound echoes in the small office and Matt spits blood onto the floor. My heart is racing—Owen isn't here, which means Serge lied…or they're holding him somewhere else.

Please don't hurt him. Please don't hurt him. Please don't hurt him.

"Where's my husband?" I ask through gritted teeth. "If you've done anything to him…"

"What? You're going to blind me with your diamonds?" Serge sniffs. "If you want to operate in this world, you need to toughen up. Privileged little princesses don't last very long, you know. Their stupid husbands don't, either."

If something happens to Owen, I don't know what I will do. I'm still angry at him for offering me money instead of having a *real* discussion about what a pregnancy could mean. I'm frustrated that he's so unable to connect unless we're in bed.

But it's funny how fear clears the fog surrounding my feelings. I don't want Owen to go. I want him to stay...with me...forever. Baby or not.

That's only if we get out of this alive.

CHAPTER TWENTY-THREE

Owen

THE SECOND I realise what's happened, I feel sick. When I left Hannah at the blackjack table, I was cornered by a beefy suited guy who tried to convince me that Serge wanted to take me to some VIP lounge out back.

Not a good sign so early in the night. If Serge was really looking to get his money out of a couple of dumb schmucks, he'd let them play the tables for a bit. He'd show off. Make them want him.

But getting us out the back as quickly as possible means he wants to avoid us interacting with people. Aka witnesses. So I decline the invite, saying I promised Hannah a drink. Only now I see her heading through a door on the other side of the room on Serge's arm.

Fuck.

I pretend my phone is ringing and bring it up to my ear, turning my back on Serge's henchman. The second he looks away I hit the speed dial for the number Max set up for us.

"Hey, sorry we can't make it tonight. Hannah isn't feeling too well." It's the code we've instigated for the operation. I've just told the team that Hannah is in danger.

"Oh no, has she been sick long?" The female officer on the other end of the line is checking for details.

"No, it hit her very suddenly. Just a moment ago. But I haven't caught it yet."

"You should keep your distance then." She's telling me not to go after her, which goes against every fibre of my being. "Hopefully she's feeling better soon."

The cavalry is on the way. Max was informed that we were coming here tonight, so the team knows where to find us.

The thought of leaving Hannah feels wrong on every level. I know I shouldn't go after her—and before this assignment I would have been a good soldier. Followed orders. But if anything were to happen...

The memories swirl again—identifying my family's bodies. God, my little brother. Seeing them lying on those cold, silver trays almost killed me. It definitely killed something inside me. Something vital and precious. Something that would have let me live like a normal person.

If I lose Hannah...

I can't even bear the thought of it. Tonight is a preview of what our life would be like if we were together. Hannah won't stop being a cop, and I haven't got it in me to sit at home and worry.

I can't risk anything happening to her, even if it means putting myself on the line. I turn to the henchman and gesture to the door across the room. "Looks like my wife went ahead of me."

I can't live with the threat of the past repeating itself over and over. It will destroy me and, in turn, I'll destroy her. So I'm going to get her out now and then I'm done. I'll head back to New York, quit my job and figure out where to go next.

Clean start, no attachments.

"This way." The henchman leads me to the back of the room, through a doorway and down a corridor. There are voices—crying. I strain to listen. It's not Hannah.

"Doesn't sound like the kind of bar I usually go to," I say.

The henchman grunts. "This is a special bar. VIP service."

There's a sound of something hitting flesh, followed by a groan. "Very important prisoners, huh?"

He grins. He's got a gold tooth, a shaved head and the kind of cold eyes that look like there's nothing behind them. "You're funny."

He opens the door to an office. There's a map on the wall with pins and Post-it notes, half of which are dangling by one corner, their glue strips long dried up. In the middle of the room, Matt sits in a chair. There's blood on the floor and on his chin. He's taken a few punches and he's going to have another nasty shiner, but thankfully he's breathing and conscious.

Hannah stands on the other side of the room,

hands behind her back. Her face is a mask of fury, not fear. A rush of emotion overwhelms me, pride and terror and something warm and perfect and uncomfortable.

Love. It's been so long I almost didn't recognise it, but there's a pounding in my blood that tells me I would take a bullet for this woman. I would stand in between her and hellfire. And judging by the look on Serge's face…I might have to.

"What's this all about?" I take the approach of playing dumb.

"This idiot thinks we're trying to compete on his turf." Hannah rolls her eyes, cutting in before Serge has the chance to speak. She's trying to tell me not to blow our cover…he doesn't know we're cops. But he will, the second the SOG—special operations group—turns up.

"You clearly don't know my wife very well," I say. "She's not exactly built for…working."

"But you are, aren't you?" Serge comes forward and I stand strong. The henchman is behind me, blocking the exit, and something cold and hard presses into my back. "You approach *my* people and ask questions about my fucking business." He glances at Matt. Shit. I should have known he'd get scared and talk. "And your wife happens to stumble across a meeting, pretending to be drunk."

If Hannah is shocked that he knew it was an act, she doesn't show it.

"I was going to play it nice, let you off with a warning. Then you turn up tonight, showing off *my* jewels." He slams a palm against the wall and the sound vibrates in the cold concrete building. It feels miles from the plush gambling room. "I will not be disrespected in my own house."

"What do you want, huh? We came to play cards, not to get into an argument." I make myself sound as bored as possible.

"Matt told us everything. You said you could help him." Serge comes forward, his eyes black like coal. He has a frantic energy about him, an aura of instability that has me on edge. "How do you intend to do that if you simply want to play cards?"

Fucking Matt. The guy had no idea what he was getting himself into—his gambling addiction made him weak, vulnerable to people like Sergio Benedetti.

"Look at him, you believe a word coming out of his mouth? A guy like that will say anything to get what he wants." I gesture to the hunched-over man, as if he means nothing.

"But you just want to play cards, right?" He reaches into his jacket and pulls out a gun. It's small calibre, easily concealable. Probably has the serial number filed off so it won't be traceable if they need to dump it. Now I have two guns on me—one in front, and one behind. I don't say a word and mentally beg Hannah to do the same.

All I have to do is stall long enough that the SOG guys get here.

"Don't! Please." Hannah's voice is wire-tight. "It was all my idea, not his."

Serge raises a brow. "Isn't that sweet."

"Shut up, Hannah." My voice is rough.

"Seriously." She stands, both hands in the air in front of her in a gesture of surrender. "Owen wanted nothing to do with it, but I thought I could win big. I thought I could come here and show you up."

Fuck. What the hell is she doing?

Serge slowly rotates so his gun is on Hannah. "Really?"

"Yes." The way her lip trembles makes my insides twist. "Please, let him go."

Serge closes in on Hannah, his gun aimed directly at her forehead. The easy smugness is now gone, replaced by rage and something swirling and uncontrollable. He backs her up against the desk, pressing the gun right into her skin. If he pulls the trigger, there won't be anything left of her.

"She's a cop." The words come out of my mouth before I can stop them, and they suck the life from the room.

"What?" Serge looks at his henchmen and then me.

"If you kill her, you'll have the full force of the Victoria Police hunting your ass down." I suck in a breath. "But I'm not a cop. So I'm your better option."

"He's lying!" Hannah is looking at me with huge eyes.

"I think you're right." Serge stares at me. "He *is* lying."

"We're not really married." I grit the words out. "We're colleagues. I'm a security consultant who was brought on to track a jewellery theft ring at 21 Love Street. Hannah is not my wife."

"Then why put yourself on the line for her, huh? You think I'm stupid." He shakes his head. "I know what two people in love will do for one another. They'll say *anything* to protect the other person. I would know if either one of you was a cop."

I can't breathe. Panic has seized my chest and I know I have to do something, or else there's a very real chance one of us will get shot before backup arrives. I will not allow it to be Hannah.

The gun is back on me, thank God. Hannah is shaking her head at me, like I've lost the plot. I have. I left protocol in the dust the second I exited the main room.

"There's only one way for you to get out of this. Go now, before our backup gets here."

Doubt flickers across his features. He doesn't know whether to believe me. "You're bluffing."

"Nope."

"Well, then there *is* only one way out of here." He turns back to Hannah. "And the only good cop is a dead cop."

A sound outside makes everyone crank their head to the door. There's screaming and shattering glass, and chaos is coming from the gambling room. The door to the corridor must be open. Backup is here, but until I see the unit of men and women in their tactical gear, I'm not safe and neither is Hannah. I use the moment of distraction to lunge forward, grabbing Serge's gun and wrenching his arms up. It goes off, shattering the light overhead, and plunging us into semi-darkness.

There's a sound of gasping, a scuffle and another shot goes off. I hear shouting, but something doesn't feel right. There's a pain in my side. But I keep going. I'm on top of Serge, holding him down. We're struggling. I throw a fist, but I'm starting to move slower.

A second later the SOG members filter into the room.

CHAPTER TWENTY-FOUR

Hannah

MY EYES FEEL completely raw. After exhausting my-self trying not to cry in front of my colleagues, I eventually took a shower so I could do it in peace. Last night should have been a bad dream. But now, I'm curled up in a hospital chair waiting for Owen's eyes to open. I want to take him home so he can wake up somewhere that smells like life—like bread and coffee and fresh sheets.

He got shot trying to protect me. The doctors told us the bullet missed his organs, but he lost a fair bit of blood. If the special ops team hadn't arrived when they did, the outcome could have been very differ-ent. I could have watched him bleed out on the floor. I could have watched him die.

The thought brings on a fresh wave of tears. My knees are drawn up to my chest, and I wrap my arms around them. I don't know whether it should make the situation better or worse, but this morning I got my period. Yep, not pregnant. I took one of those early-signs tests just in case, but the results were clear as a bell. Over the past week I'd grown curious about the idea of having a child, enough to know with certainty it's something I want in my future.

The problem is, I also know with certainty it's something I want with Owen.

Last night, when I thought Serge was going to shoot Owen, I was beside myself with fear. It's made me understand him a little more. Nearly losing him has messed me up inside. I'm jittery and tense and I snap at anyone who comes within a metre of the room.

He lost his whole family and the girl he loved. It must be this same feeling times a thousand. Times a million. I don't know if I would be strong enough to go on with life, like he has. And now I can see why he keeps running away from people. I understand it.

A tear slides down my cheek and I swipe at it angrily with the back of my hand. I feel totally and utterly useless, and it's so foreign that I want to scream. Normally I'm the person who knows what the next step is. I'm the person with the plan and the to-do list and the solutions.

And now I have…nothing.

"Are we still man and wife?" Owen's voice is scratchy.

"Nope, just another statistic." I try to force a smile, but it's watery and weak.

"Then what are you doing here?" He cringes as he tries to sit up, so I rush to get the bed's remote. When he pats the space next to him, I sit.

"Being a good partner."

He's pale and has rings under his eyes. There's a cut on his cheek and another on his temple. He looks like an anti-hero, the broody bad boy in some Hollywood blockbuster. Hotter than hell, even after it all.

He tilts his head. "What are you staring at?"

"Just wondering how on earth you can get shot and still look better than me." I want to keep things light, but I'm feeling as if there are concrete blocks on my feet.

"Shut up, Anderson. Everybody knows you're the pretty one."

Anderson. He's playing the joker again, retreating into his shell. "I um…the SOG guys went to 21 Love Street last night before word could get to the rest of the Romano crew."

"And?"

"They found a whole lot of jewels. Drugs, too. The guy who was holding me last night worked the concierge desk, and he's intercepting the jewels. Max got him to cave and we figured out which apartment they were operating out of." I trace a rip in my jeans, watching the frayed edges of the denim move under my fingertip. "Now they've got security footage from the building to back it up. They're bringing in the staff for questioning over the next few days."

"So you did good."

"*We* did, you mean."

Owen closes his eyes for a moment as he tries to move. He's in pain and I'd be willing to do anything to make it go away. "You're the brains, Anderson. Own it."

"Max says they're confident Serge will talk. It will really help with the wider Romano case. Between that and what we got from the concierge guy, there should be enough to put a task force together now—the jewel theft, drugs, illegal gambling. It's solid evidence."

"That's great."

"Which means we're done with the assignment. The doctor said they want to keep you here for a bit, make sure you're healing up okay."

His expression says it all. Owen knows I'm stalling. "What are you dancing around?"

It's like the air has been sucked out of my lungs— I have so much to say and no idea where to begin. My thoughts are a traffic pile-up, one bumping into the next until it's nothing but a jumbled mess. "I thought we should talk about us."

He looks at me with those endless blue eyes and this time there's no sparkle. No smirk. Maybe I've picked the wrong time, but if I know Owen, he'll get himself the hell out of here the second the doctors allow it. Then…I might not ever see him again.

"I was really scared last night." Saying this is like ripping myself open. I've always been strong at work. There are unspoken rules for women, even these days. You can't admit to being frightened. You can't cry. You *have* to be strong. Always. But right now, I'm not at work. I'm not here for my job. I'm here for him, and for myself. "I thought you might die."

"I thought that, too."

"You risked your life." I curl my hands into fists.

"So did you. You tried to convince a gangster to shoot you instead of me."

"Didn't work, did it? I'm obviously not very convincing." I almost jump out of my skin when Owen's hand covers mine. "I went into that room alone, because I thought you were in there, which was a mistake. I could have ruined everything."

"And I followed you in there against orders, so I think we can call it even."

The silence between us is broken by the hustle and bustle outside the hospital room and the intermittent beeping of the machines tracking Owen's vital signs and administering his pain relief.

"I'm sorry I made the whole baby thing about the money," he says. "It was the only thing I could make sense of, to be honest. I know you wanted us to talk about the realities of having a kid, not just the finances."

"I overreacted." I shake my head. It feels like such a dumb argument now, with last night hanging over us as a reminder of what's really at stake. "I was feeling vulnerable, so I snapped because it wasn't what I'd hoped to hear."

"What did you hope to hear?"

I swallow. There's a lump in my throat that feels as big as a boulder. "That maybe you'd want to stay and see what happened. Maybe we could be more than a fling."

His jaw tightens, but I don't know if it's pain or

frustration or something else. Owen is Fort Knox with his emotions. But I need to know how he feels.

"It's going to sound like a fucking cliché to say it's not you, it's me. But it's true." He sighs. "You're perfect, Hannah. You're kind and smart and a total badass. You're the best cop I know."

"But?" It almost kills me to say the word, no matter how much I know it's coming.

"Your job puts you in danger every day and…I don't think I could take it." He shakes his head. "It's my weak spot, not yours. I'm already screwed up about relationships and loss, and knowing you've got the kind of job where you're in the literal firing line would make me crazy. Last night, I would have taken a bullet for you."

"You *did* take a bullet for me." I'm crying now and the tears won't stop. They start slow—fat drops that well and fall, until they come faster. Owen reaches up, even though I can see it pains him, to brush them away from my cheek.

"I would have taken ten bullets. Twenty." His blue eyes hold me captive and I want to promise him everything…but I can't.

"I'm not going to quit my job," I say.

"You shouldn't. Victoria Police is better with you in its ranks." His hand squeezes mine. "You're amazing and I'm broken."

"You're not broken, Owen."

"The second I thought something was going to happen to you…" The worry that streaks over his face is raw and so stark it makes my breath catch in my throat. "I have purposefully stayed away from you ever since I started at the academy, because I knew I'd fall for you."

"How could you have known that?"

"I just did. You had this spark about you, the way you told all the boys that one day they'd be reporting to you."

I laugh, in spite of the tears. I'd gone into the academy believing I needed to assert myself—I was young and plucky and more than a little obnoxious. But Owen had never made me feel like I needed to prove myself. He made me feel…respected. Equal.

"Why do you have to be so damn charming while you're rejecting me?" I swallow, trying to stem my emotions.

"I'm sorry. I want more than anything to be the kind of guy who makes you happy…but it's not me. You don't want someone who wakes up with night terrors, who feels like running away is the most natural thing in the world. You don't want someone who's going to bring you down."

"Don't tell me what I want, Owen." I pull my hand out of his grip and stand, my body filled with mixed-up, conflicting emotion. "One minute I'm perfect and the next you're pushing me away and trying to act like you know what's best for me."

"I'm saving us both a lot of pain."

"It doesn't feel like that. It feels like you're not willing to give us a chance even though we both want to be together." I look up to the stark white ceiling of the hospital room as if I might find answers there. "And I do…want to be with you."

"Is this about the…that you might be pregnant?"

Shit. It almost slipped my mind that he doesn't know—I've been too focused on what happened last night. "I'm not pregnant. And yes, I'm sure."

He looks at me as if waiting for me to elaborate.

"I don't know how I feel about it, either," I add. "I'm both relieved and also disappointed, if that's even possible."

"You want to have a family."

"I do." I shake my head. "I think this whole thing solidified it. I want to be a mother. And it's crazy but when I think about having a family, I see us. I know that's like the quickest way I could make you run, but these last few weeks…we fit together. I don't know what it is yet, but my gut tells me it's worth fighting for. We *have* something, Owen. This connection isn't something I've ever felt with anyone else."

He turns his head away, so I can't see what he's thinking. "I know exactly what this is and that's why I'm running scared. I don't want to hurt you. I don't want to hurt myself."

"So that's it? I'm in the 'too hard' basket?"

When he turns back to me his eyes are red. There's no tears on his face, but I've never seen him so close. I've never seen the weight around his neck as clearly as I do now.

"I'm not going to say something dumb and false to push you away," he says, swallowing. "But I'm telling you as honestly as I can, I can't do this with you. I'm sorry."

I'm shattering into a billion jagged pieces. The floor tilts beneath my feet as fresh tears prick the backs of my eyes. I knew this is how it would end, but it still hurts as if he's taken a shotgun to my heart.

"I understand." I stick my hand into my pocket, where I've stashed his mother's ring. The stone glints in the light, as if mocking me for even having a glimmer of hope that we might make it. "I'm really sorry this didn't work out."

"Me, too."

I place the ring on the table beside his hospital bed and turn to head out of the room. There's a nurse waiting and I have no idea how much she heard, but I duck my head and keep on walking. Inside, I'm falling apart.

No matter how illogical it is, I know exactly how I feel. I love Owen and I wanted this to work so badly it makes me crazy. But I won't pursue someone who can't take a chance on me.

I can't do that to myself.

CHAPTER TWENTY-FIVE

Owen

BY THE TIME the hospital lets me out, I'm feeling like an animal who's finally been released into the wild. A still-hurting, probably-going-to-get-feasted-on-by-a-lion animal, but I am free, nonetheless.

I'm on antibiotics and painkillers and moving at a snail's pace up the driveway to my grandmother's house. She's lived in the same house since before I was born. It's a squat place with thick canvas blinds that protect against Melbourne's dry, hot summers. The garden is small but neat, with roses and begonias and agapanthus. When I was a kid, she made me help with the weeds, teaching me all the flower names and how to care for them. It was a lost cause, since I've never owned a plant.

I knock on the security screen, rattling it against the front door. There's the sound of the television inside—a game show, judging by the cheering. A second later, the door swings open.

"I don't want whatever you're selling," she says,

her voice as husky and deep as I remember. I hadn't realised it until now, but God, I've missed it. A cheeky smile tugs at her lips. "What's the secret password?"

"Lamington." It was my favourite sweet as a kid—a fluffy square of sponge dipped in chocolate and rolled in coconut. "It hasn't changed, right?"

"No." Her smile falters a bit when she sees I'm moving slowly, and when she reaches up to hug me it's with far less vigor than I remember. I'd called her this morning to let her know I was coming by, and to warn her that I wouldn't be in great shape. "Does it hurt?"

"Yeah. But they've dosed me up on meds."

She steps back and holds the door, her small frame wrapped in a chunky sweater and wool skirt to ward off the chill. The house is toasty and smells like home. I know she's been baking all morning; the evidence lingers in the air with the scent of coconut and sugar.

She leads me through to the kitchen, which hasn't changed a bit. "It was nice to bake something knowing you were coming over. I don't do it much anymore. It's not the same when it's just for me."

I don't know whether she means because I left or because my grandfather died. Probably both. I had no illusions of not feeling like a piece of shit today, but we certainly came to that point quicker than I'd anticipated.

"You want a coffee?" She heads straight to the kettle, almost as if it were a rhetorical question.

Within minutes, I've got a steaming mug in front of me and a perfectly square lamington.

When I take a bite, I send pieces of shredded coconut skittering all over my plate. "So…"

"So." My grandmother isn't going to give me an inch.

"I'm sorry I haven't called."

Her eyes are a little cloudy these days, but she has the kind of stare that could reduce a grown man to a snivelling mess. "You should be."

"How have you been?" I feel like a dumbass, trading questions like one might with an acquaintance. "I've missed you."

Her expression softens. "I've missed you, too."

"Are you doing okay?"

"It's been hard, but I keep going. It's what your grandfather would have wanted." She bobs her head and her eyes suddenly well. "I think about him every day."

In contrast, I've actively tried to suppress my memories of the strong man who stood with his arm around my shoulders as we buried my parents and brother. He and my grandmother were the stuff of relationships goals—they'd battled hard times, struggled with money when my mother was a kid, and were so utterly and deeply in love until the day he passed away.

"Would you change any of it, knowing how it would turn out?" I sip my coffee, relishing the bitter warmth.

"Do I wish your parents hadn't left the house that

night? Of course. But wanting to change the past is a fool's game. It won't lead anywhere good." Her cup shakes slightly in her hands. She's eighty-five now. The same age as my grandfather when he died. "You don't think every single person in the world has something bad happen to them? We've suffered, but we're not alone."

I am. I'm alone because it's how I've made myself—refusing to commit, refusing to set down roots. Seeing every damn part of my life as a temporary stage before the next move. I thought it's what I wanted because it was safer. Easier.

But watching Hannah walk out of the hospital room was the hardest thing I've ever done.

"Here." I pull my mother's ring out of my pocket and set it on the table. "I'm returning this to its rightful home."

"I don't want it." She stares me down, looking like she wants to dump a cup of coffee on my head. "In fact, I was thinking about getting rid of all your mother's jewellery."

"Why would you do that?"

"I have no use for it. It's gathering dust and your mother always believed that diamonds were made for wearing."

"If it's about the money, I can—"

"Owen Graham Fletcher." Her voice is like ice and I'm still as a statue, suddenly reverted to being a kid again. "After your parents died, I ended up with enough for several lifetimes. I had to tell you not to forfeit your own inheritance by giving it to me. It's not about the money."

I'd forgotten that. I'd tried to get my grandparents to take it all, but they'd put it in a trust until I was old enough to access it.

"Then why sell the jewels?"

She sighs. "Because I'm getting older and I know you won't want to be bothered dealing with it all when I'm gone, so I figured I would take care of it now."

I reel as if she's slapped me in the face. "You're talking like you're already gone."

"And you *act* like I'm already gone."

Her words slice through me, cutting bone and flesh. And I don't have a single defence against it, because she's totally right. I haven't been there for her. At all. I've ignored her voice mails, messaging back only when I know she'll be asleep so I don't have to experience the pain of facing my own flaws.

"I understand why." She reaches across the table and places her hand over mine. She's cold, like always, and her knuckles are more arthritic than I remember. But her grip is strong, sure. "Owen, what you went through…it's a hell that no child should ever have to experience. But at some point you need to understand that the past is the past. It's okay to hurt. It's okay to be scared. But you act as though you also died that day and you didn't. You're alive, so start living."

She's almost vibrating with emotion—frustration at what she sees as time I've wasted, and anger that

I've treated her so poorly. Shame trickles through me, like icy drips along my spine. If only the people who think they know me could see me now. At the security company in New York I'm the one who makes everyone laugh, I ease tension when things get tough and I play pranks on my colleagues. My old academy friends came in droves to the hospital over the last few days, clapping hands on my shoulders for a job well done. Praising me.

But my grandmother sees through it all. She *knows* me…and so does Hannah. The fact that I even told her about my past should be a sign that I trust her more than anyone.

But what if one day I'm here—like my grandmother, grieving every day.

Aren't you already here?

"I know you boys are often raised not to show any emotion, and if I ever contributed to that I regret it," she says. "But maybe you should talk to someone. A professional."

I recoil at the idea. People over the years have suggested counselling and therapy and God knows what other hippy-dippy things. Tarot cards, or some shit. The idea of sitting in someone's office being asked to talk about my feelings makes my skin crawl.

"I don't want to talk to anyone."

"I know you don't," she says. "But it's something to think about. When is your flight home?"

I swallow. "Haven't booked it yet."

The surgeon had suggested that I stay in Melbourne a while longer, so they could check on the wound and ensure it healed correctly. But it wasn't exactly phrased as an order. I was lucky that everything went smoothly in the ER—the bullet didn't ricochet and hit anything important. The surgery to retrieve it was straightforward. It could have been a lot worse.

In reality, I could go home now.

But something happened as I lay in the hospital room, the space around me filling up with cards and teddy bears and bunches of flowers. I spoke to a lot of people about how lucky I was to be alive. The surgeon, and nurses, my old colleagues and, of course, Gary Smythe. Max came to visit, too, and he showed me pictures of Rose and the baby.

And all the while I thought about Hannah.

Hannah, the woman I could have been killed trying to protect. The woman who was there when I woke up, who sat on my bed and poured her heart out. Hannah, my undercover wife who'd lain on that fancy bed and given me more pleasure than I'd known in years. The woman who continued to break through my shell, even when I dissuaded her at every turn.

"I would have thought you'd be rushing to leave." My grandmother tilts her head.

"I did get shot, you know," I quip drily.

She shakes her head, her sharp blue eyes—my mother's eyes and my eyes—piercing through me. "I know not to take the joking answer as the truth."

"I thought about not going back to New York at all. I could pick some place new and start over again." At the time it had seemed logical, but now the words felt wrong. "But then what? I keep doing that every four or five years until I run out of places to go?"

"You tell me."

Everything feels wrong now, all my old ideals and goals. All my old avoidance tactics. But the only thing that doesn't feel wrong—staying here and trying with Hannah, rebuilding my relationship with my grandmother—is fraught with risk.

"Why do you find it so easy to work in an environment where people shoot at you, yet the thought of having a meaningful conversation has you running away like a terrified animal?" Her question isn't sugar-coated at all, because that's not how my grandmother plays.

"Because I'm not scared of death." The words pop out of my mouth before I can even consider them, and I know it's my deepest truth. "I'm scared of surviving."

"Hmm." She leans back in her chair and crosses her arms over her chest.

If a little old lady could mic drop, then that's what my grandmother just did.

I stand, slowly and painfully, curling into my injured side. This conversation has stirred up everything and I need to get away to think. If I'd really wanted to leave Australia, I would have booked my ticket on the hospital Wi-Fi. Because that's how I am.

This revelation is making me question everything, and my grandmother's words are swirling like a tornado in my head. The possibilities I've never allowed myself to consider are gathering steam. I've been changed by this experience—by living with Hannah, by getting shot. By this very conversation.

You're alive, so start living.

"It would kill your mother to see you wasting your life." My grandmother comes around the table and pulls me into a hug. "Don't do that to her."

"What if it's too late?"

"It's not." Her head barely comes up to my chest and I look down at the curly grey hairs covering her head, and the tops of her shoulders covered in a thick, fluffy wool. She's small and frail and I've almost made the mistake of wasting the years she has left. "And Owen?"

My throat is so clogged I can barely speak. "Yeah."

"I forgive you. I hope you can forgive yourself."

CHAPTER TWENTY-SIX

Hannah
One month later...

I FIND MYSELF walking along Clarendon Street in South Melbourne, heading in the direction of Love Street. It's my day off and I'm utterly restless. My head's been in a fog at work, and I'm stumbling over my words in meetings and missing basic things. It's grief over losing Owen, and I need to distract myself. Instead, I've wound up here. I look up at 21 Love Street—at its chic, modern design and fancy glass-and-chrome entry.

Maybe I've come here to say goodbye. Who knows.

"Hannah?"

I turn at the sound of my name and see Drew striding toward me. She looks the same as she did the night of the barbeque—long platinum hair that swishes by her lower back, all-black outfit and a wicked glint in her silvery eyes.

"Oh, hi." I struggle for what to say—how much do the people in this building know about who I really am? Do they know my marriage was a fake?

"I haven't seen you around much." She smiles and comes up beside me, her arms folded tight against her chest over the front of a studded leather jacket. "I wondered if you and that hunky husband of yours had moved out. But then I heard about the redecorating."

"Redecorating?"

Drew looks at me a little strange. "Yeah, I bumped into Owen this morning and he was telling me about all the changes he's making."

I shake my head. How could she have bumped into Owen this morning when he was supposed to be back in New York? When he *was* back in New York a week ago…not that I was bugging Max for updates or anything.

Glutton for punishment.

"Is everything okay?" Drew touches my arm and peers at me. "You look a little pale."

"I'm just…" I don't even know what to say. Am I imagining things? Is this one of those moments where I'm about to wake up any second and realise I'm alone in my bed, with my roommate banging around in the kitchen?

"Don't you faint on me, girl." Drew wraps an arm around my shoulder and steers me toward the entrance. "Let's get you a glass of water and somewhere to sit down."

I allow myself to be propelled forward, my heart pounding and my head swimming. I've tried so damn hard not to think about Owen in the last month since

I left him in his hospital bed. So damn hard I've given myself a headache over it. Daily.

But the fact is, I've been miserable without him. Just like when we finished our training at the academy and I knew I wouldn't see him as often. Just like when I found out that he moved away to New York and that meant I had to let go of my fantasy that one day we'd bump into each other and find some spark between us.

"Here, sit." Drew pushes me down onto one of the plush velvet chairs in the foyer. "I'll get you some water."

She heads over to the front desk and talks to the concierge. I think about making a break for it. I could be up and out the door before Drew has a chance to catch me. And it's not like I'll have to see her again.

But then what? If Owen really was here, then I had to know what was going on. Why had he come home? And, more important, of all the places he could live…why here?

My stupid heart was hopeful. Too hopeful.

Because I still wanted him. Deep down and with all my heart, I want to go back to that time where I got to pretend he was mine and I was his. To that night where he walked into the bar and made all my wildest fantasies come true.

Drew is back in a flash with a bottle of water from the vending machine in the building's management office, and she presses it into my hands. "Here. Drink."

The liquid is cool against my heated throat. "I don't have my keys."

"Are you okay to walk? I'll take you upstairs. You're not...?" Her eyes drop to my stomach and I shake my head.

I'm not pregnant, but I've thought about it a lot. About the family I want to create, about the kind of mother and wife I want to be. But none of it makes sense without Owen.

Each step toward the elevator makes my pulse race. Drew chats happily as we ascend to the top floor, catching me up on the gossip of the building. Hook-ups and flirtations and how she suspects that this building puts a spell on people. 21 Love Street...the place to find a happily-ever-after. She seems lighter than when I first met her, happier.

When the elevator door chimes and I walk out into the hallway, I'm hit with memories. The taste of Owen's kisses, the feel of his hands at my waist. The way he looks first thing in morning—with hair rumpled and an easy, sexy smile.

And the way he looks when I'm seeing something more. The vulnerability he shows no one else.

The door to our old apartment is open and music plays. There's a bang and a rattle inside, and when I get closer I see the place is nearly empty. It's all white walls and plastic on the ground.

I step inside and clamp a hand over my mouth. Owen is shirtless. Faded jeans sit low on his hips, highlighting his trim waist and cut abs. And *God*, those vee muscles that point down into his waistband.

Something white—probably his T-shirt—is hanging out of the back pocket of his jeans.

Drew mutters something and laughs, nudging me with her elbow before turning and leaving me. Owen hasn't noticed me yet because he's focused on a spot on the wall where he's gently sanding. Then, almost as if he senses that crazy, electric feeling running through me, he looks up.

"How long were you going to wait to tell me you were back?" The question flies out of me. I didn't know it was possible to feel horny and hurt…but here we are.

"Long enough for me to get this place repainted, but before I started buying too much furniture." He cocks his head, looking at me curiously. "You had to go and ruin the surprise, didn't you?"

I laugh, in spite of my crazy, mixed emotions. "What surprise?"

"I wanted to do things the right way this time." He rakes a hand through his hair. It's longer now, and it curls around his ears. There's flecks of dried paint in it, and over his hands. "Set down roots. Make a home."

But for how long?

As if he sees the questions dancing on my lips he says, "I'm not running anymore. I'm going to own what happened to me and move forward, instead of continuing to look back."

"So you bought this place?" I look around. It's a shell now, without any of the furniture that was here before. "What about your job?"

"I am now happily unemployed." He looks it, too. Happy. Content.

"So this is...for now? Forever?"

Forever isn't even in Owen's vocabulary. That was always the issue—he wanted freedom to run and I'm the kind of woman who commits. I pick something and stick to it. He avoids attachments. Not exactly a match made in heaven.

"Is anything forever?" He gives me one of those Owen shrugs, but this time it feels honest. Not like an avoidance tactic. "If I could have my way and know how the future would turn out, then yeah. But I don't even know how tomorrow will turn out."

Ain't that the truth.

"All I know is that this place made me the happiest I've been since I was a kid." He jams his hands into his pockets. "Being with *you* made me the happiest I've been since I was a kid."

I don't know what to say. I'm stunned. "But our conversation in the hospital..."

"I was still processing everything. I thought I had my whole life figured out. I was going to keep running, keep avoiding. Easy peasy. Then you came along and my head got all messed up. My heart got messed up. I started wanting things I thought I didn't deserve. And when we thought you were pregnant..."

When his voice cracks it's like someone reaching into my chest and squeezing my heart.

"I was terrified, honestly. But I kept thinking about it—what it would be like to have a family. How I knew you'd be an amazing mum." His smile is charming and sexy and just a little bit shattered. "And I wondered if maybe I could be a good parent, too. If I could be a good dad and a good husband."

"Of course you could be." He has no idea how much goodness is in him. "Just because something bad happened to you doesn't mean it was your fault."

"I know. I, uh…my nan convinced me to speak to someone."

"That's really great, Owen. How was it?"

"Weird. Uncomfortable." He laughed. "I hated it, honestly. But I'll keep at it because I know it'll help in the long run."

My eyes are swimming and my heart is hopeful, because the man I see before me is a man who's turned a corner. He's got so much to work through. But now he's trying. He's moving forward.

He comes closer and I try not to stare at how incredible his body is. I'm trying to be supportive, but *damn*, it's not easy. "Eyes up here, Anderson."

"Then put a bloody T-shirt on." I fold my arms over my chest, turning away because I know my face is now the same shade as a tomato. My ears are burning, too.

He grins. "What are *you* doing here, anyway?"

"I happened to be in the neighbourhood." It comes out way more defensively than I want it to. "I bumped into Drew and she brought me up here."

"You didn't tell her we're not married anymore?"

"It didn't come up in conversation. Anyway, she said she spoke to you earlier today and it sounds like *you* didn't say anything, either."

"Didn't come up in conversation," he echoes.

"Funny that."

We stare at each other for a minute, like two dogs eyeing one another up. There's a crackling tension between us—it's vibrant and exciting and I feel better than I have in weeks. Better than I have ever.

When I'm with Owen I feel powerful and excited and…I feel like I can conquer anything.

God, I want this to work. I want with all my heart to go on this crazy, magical ride with Owen and see where it takes us. Because my gut tells me this feeling I have—this fluttery, terrified, glittering feeling is special. It's love. There's a path before us that leads somewhere beautiful, if only we have the courage to walk it.

I can see myself growing old with Owen. I can see it as bright and vivid as if it were a photograph in front of me. I know him, know his quirks and his pain and his heart.

But I can't sacrifice who I am—my career or my desires for the future—because he's afraid. If we're going to do this, then it'll be with dreams intact and hand in hand as equals. Fear and all.

CHAPTER TWENTY-SEVEN

Owen

I KNOW WHAT I want but trying to put it in words is like dangling myself over the edge of a cliff. The potential consequences roar inside me. The difference now is that something else is louder—hope. Standing in this empty apartment, with Hannah's big brown eyes watching me, is surreal. I never thought I'd get to this point.

But going back to New York solidified it all. I quit my job to a hearty slap on the back from my boss, Logan, and the warmest of wishes from his wife, Addison. I gave up my rented apartment and didn't feel even an ounce of doubt. When I told my accountant I was finally going to use my inheritance to start a new life, I could practically hear my mother's voice urging me on. Encouraging me.

One day you'll understand, she'd said to me a lifetime ago. *Real loved ones stand in your firing line, and you in theirs. They see the very best and worst of you, and they love you anyway.*

Hannah *has* seen the worst of me. The ugliest parts of me. And yet here she is, standing with her hands knotted in front of her and sincerity shining out of her face.

"I don't think I'm going to be very good at this," I say. "But I'm going to try."

My hands are still in my pockets and my mother's ring is in there. It's become comforting to me, in these last few weeks, because every time I look at it I think of the two women who've made me understand what it means to be a good man. I've kept it in my pocket since the day I visited my grandmother, needing to know my family was close, even if only in spirit.

"I've taken the easy route since my parents died, thinking it was the smart thing to do. No one calls me on my shit because I'm so good at hiding all my scars most people don't even know they're there. Most people don't look very closely."

"But I did." Her words are soft.

"You did. You looked closer and kept asking, and I *knew* you'd be like that. Ever since we were in the academy, I knew you were smarter and more perceptive than most people. You *saw* me and I didn't like that." I shake my head. "But I realised after being here, in this apartment with you, that I'd been flying under the radar so long that I didn't even know who I was anymore. I wasn't a cop, because I quit that. I wasn't a grandson, because I deserted my grandmother. I certainly wasn't a son or a brother. I wasn't…anything."

"We're all *something*, Owen." Hannah steps forward, as if she wants to touch me. But her hands stay fluttering by her sides. "Even if we don't know what it is yet."

"I had to figure out what I wanted to be. Start from scratch. Pretend like I had all the options in front of me when my parents died." I pull the ring out from my pocket and her eyes glitter like the diamonds surrounding the big, beautiful smoky-coloured stone.

Unusual and pretty, like Hannah.

"And I figured that maybe I could be your partner. Maybe I could be a guy who deserves someone like you." My throat is all tight and the feeling is foreign and strange. "Maybe we could start over at 21 Love Street for real."

"I'm not going to quit my job, Owen. I know it's probably going to stress you out and make you worry, but that's who *I* am." A tear plops onto her cheek and she brushes it away before I even have the chance. That's my Hannah, independent to a fault. And damn if I don't love that about her. "But that doesn't mean I don't want this. I do, I want it so bad."

"I'm not asking you to quit your job. I won't lie and say it won't worry me sick when you're working a case, but you're doing what you're supposed to be doing in life." I swallow. "And I want to come back. To Melbourne, to you, to the force, to my grandmother. I want to give my life a second go. And I want to do it all with you by my side."

"You have no idea how happy that makes me." She comes closer still and throws her arms around my neck, pressing her lips to my skin and her body to mine. "We fit, Owen. We make each other better. When I'm with you, I feel like I can take on the world."

"I hope the world is shaking in its boots, then." I grab her hand and hold the ring, my eyes locked on to hers. "My mother would have loved you, you know."

Hannah blinks rapidly, trying to stem her tears... and failing. "If she raised someone as amazing as you, then I'm sure I would have loved her, too."

"Will you be my partner in this crazy adventure? I have no idea what I'm doing and I'm one-hundred-percent certain I'll screw something up. But I promise you I'll always listen, and I'll always put you first. Before anything."

"Owen, none of us are perfect. I'll screw up, too and that's fine. But the main thing is that we love each other as best we can...and I already know this feels right. It feels good and beautiful and perfectly imperfect. I knew how I felt about you a long time ago, and learning about your past didn't change that. It only made the feeling stronger."

"So we're doing this, for real?" Excitement fizzes in my veins at the thought of waking up here, day after day with Hannah in my arms. I've never wanted anything as much as this.

"For real," she says with a nod. "I won't even complain about having to be your wife this time."

I laugh and it's like a weight has been lifted off my shoulders. She watches as I slip the ring onto her finger.

"I can't wait to marry you, Hannah," I say.

She's taken the world and painted it with better colours. Given me hope and happiness and purpose. "I can't wait, either. I guess this means you'll have to stop calling me Anderson."

"You want to be a Fletcher?" I didn't think my heart could be any fuller.

"Of course I do, Owen." Her eyes glimmer. "There are plenty of Andersons running around in the rest of my family. I figured we could even your side up by one...or maybe two?"

A baby. It's the very thing that terrified me a month ago and now it's something I want. Sure, it's still daunting, and still something that's guaranteed to knock me on my ass. But I'm not afraid of that anymore. Not now that Hannah and I are a team. A family.

"Hell yeah, I want it all with you. I'm all in." She kisses me long and hard and I don't know how I ever got to deserve her. "I guess we've got some explaining to do to the neighbours. They're going to be mighty confused if we suddenly get married... again."

Hannah hugs me close and presses up on her tip-toes, a wicked smile curving her lips. "I don't care about what they think, since I have a *way* more pressing concern."

"What's that?"

She starts to lead me toward the bedroom, her eyes full of fire and love. "I'm hoping you've still got a bed in this place."

Damn. I'm the luckiest man alive.

* * * * *

FORBIDDEN SINS

J. MARGOT CRITCH

MILLS & BOON

For my mom, Marilyn. My biggest fan.

Thank you for loving and supporting me.

Even though I'm well into my thirties, you always make sure I'm eating, and wearing my heavy coat when it's cold out.

I couldn't do any of this without you.

I love you.

CHAPTER ONE

IF THERE WAS ever a time for Gabe Foster to be content, it was right now. He had everything a young man could want—wealth, prestige, a successful career and promising future, any woman he wanted and good friends. He'd just returned home to Las Vegas from a month-long work trip to Hong Kong, where he'd helped facilitate a merger of one of his biggest clients. The trip had earned him and his firm, Burnham & Associates, a significant amount of money, and because of it, he was a shoo-in to become a senior partner, the position he'd been groomed to take since he'd been a young adult.

"Your shot, sir." A voice at his side broke his reverie.

"Sure, thanks." He covered for his lack of attention, reaching for his glass.

"No, you're still the shooter." The stickman gestured once more to the pair of dice on the craps table in front of him.

"Oh damn, sorry!" Gabe snatched up the dice and surveyed the table. Just like him to zone out in the middle of a heater with nine hundred dollars at stake.

Everything was going well for Gabe. He should have been on top of the world. But there was something missing. But with a table full of gamblers, he didn't exactly have time to consider what it was. Introspection was for quiet mornings over coffee, not at a craps table during a winning streak.

He rattled the dice in his hand and tossed them down the table, expertly bouncing them off the end. Five and three.

The dealer flipped the button to the eight on the felt-top table, his hands moving nimbly as a flurry of bets descended on the surface. A pair of frat brothers were clapping their hands, praying for protection from "Big Red," the seven roll that would end this streak. To Gabe's right a retired dentist and his wife were having the time of their lives in a real Vegas moment.

Gabe was flying solo tonight. He'd met with his friends, the Brotherhood, at Di Terrestres. But they'd all gone home early in the evening—heading home, or to the office.

Gabe hadn't wanted to stick around Di Terrestres—the erotic club they owned, where people could come together, socialize without having to worry about their extracurricular activities and more basic, biological proclivities being reported by the press or gossip blogs. Of all of the businesses owned by the Brotherhood, Di Terrestres was the crown jewel. The ultra-exclusive club, which boasted clothing-optional areas and playrooms catering to more erotic tastes, had made them all millionaires many times over, and made them a hot commodity among the rich, famous and influential.

It wasn't his problem that all his friends had headed home to wives and fiancées, or had chosen to work on his first night back in the city. He was a young, single, rich and reasonably good-looking man in one of the hottest party destinations in the world. He could find fun on his own. He looked up at the crowd that had surrounded the table, all winning, urging him to keep playing. Strangers who he held—their chips on the table—in his palm along with the hottest pair of dice he'd ever encountered.

He looked past the group, across the casino floor, as two women left the nearby nightclub. Speaking of the hottest he'd ever encountered. Both were gorgeous, but one held his attention. She was tall, her long dark hair falling past her shoulders to the center of her back. Her fair skin told him she hadn't spent much time underneath the scorching Las Vegas sun. Definitely a tourist. The women stopped at the nearby casino bar. The brunette turned her head, and somehow, their eyes connected over the frenetic energy of the floor. He smiled, and so did she, before she turned back to her friend and sipped from the glass the bartender had brought her. The noise, the chaos, the bright lights dimmed, and all he could focus on was the elegant, beautiful woman in the short strapless dress, as she said something to her friend and again looked in his direction. She smiled. Gabe knew a signal when he saw one.

Taking a step back from the table, Gabe handed

the dice to the dealer. "I think that's it for me tonight," he told everyone. "It's been fun." He started to turn away and, removing his phone from his pocket, checked the time—the night was still young and so was he. The man who'd been standing next to him— the one who, thanks to Gabe, had won a substantial stack of chips—called to him as he walked away. "Hey, buddy, what about your chips?"

He looked down at his own newly won stack and pointed to the man. "You're up. Let it ride."

Ellie Carrington wiggled her toes in her stiletto booties. Her feet were tired, her toes most likely covered in blisters, but the two straight hours of dancing with her best friend, Rachel, had been worth it. "That was so much fun," Ellie told her. "I can't believe I almost spent the night at the office."

"Aren't you glad I convinced you to ditch work and party?"

Ellie thought about the unopened emails filling her inbox and tried to contain her grimace. Since the day she'd started work at her father's law firm two weeks ago, she'd gotten right down to work, aiding some of the more senior associates with their clients. "Despite the things I'll have to catch up on tomorrow, yes I am. But just this one time, though." This was just one small step back for her, a slip back into the world of *old Ellie*.

"Why were you working anyway? I thought you had dinner plans with your father," Rachel said.

Ellie's laugh was short and humorless. "He canceled."

"Again?"

"Yup. That's the third time."

Ellie had arrived in Las Vegas two weeks ago. After completing law school, she'd started working at her father's law firm as a junior associate.

Her reasons for coming to Las Vegas had been threefold. She mentally ticked them off again in her head, as she'd done dozens of times before: 1) to practice law and work for her father, one of the most prominent and well-regarded lawyers in the state; 2) rehab her image—the celebutante party girl she'd been had finally grown up and gotten her life together. She was an adult, she had a career and hopefully the gossip blogs would forget about her forever; and 3) most important, to rebuild her relationship with her father, Charles. Ellie had figured that number three would be the easy part. "I don't know what he wants. I moved here to work for him, hoping we would have the relationship we never had, but it turns out I'm still the daughter he never wanted."

Rachel put her hand over Ellie's. "Don't think like that. It's his loss. But that means that your weekend has been freed up, doesn't it? What do you say tomorrow night we stay in? You can do whatever work you need to catch up on, and then we'll power up Netflix, throw on our pj's and indulge in some pizza and prosecco? Been a while since we've done the Three Ps."

Ellie laughed. Ellie had met Rachel years ago, back

in their wilder, party-hopping days. Rachel had been a popular teen music sensation in a self-destructive downward spiral, and in her, Ellie had found the perfect outlet for her own teen angst and partying antics. Together, they'd had some wild times, and then both cleaned up their acts. Ellie chose law school, and Rachel had taken to acting. They'd stuck together into adulthood, and despite it all remained the best of friends.

"Sounds like fun," she said, and sipped from her wineglass. She looked around the casino. She was new to Vegas, but she loved it. Ellie fed off the energy, and she smiled. The chaos fueled her, and for the first time in a long time, she felt at home—she was built for Vegas.

It was a different world to her. In Vegas, she could live her life without paparazzi following her every movement. Nobody tried to get photos of her or Rachel being drunken messes outside of nightclubs, or even when either of them made a trip to the grocery store, just because she had been the rebellious teenage daughter of an aging D-list actress who couldn't leave the spotlight. In Vegas, Ellie blended into the crowd, and in a weird way, the wild debauchery of the crowd made her feel safe. Shouts from a nearby craps table caught her attention. Someone was on a winning streak. Unlike in LA, regular people could be the center of attention in Las Vegas. Everyone was only a roll, a hand, a pull of a slot machine away from celebrity or notoriety. She looked at the excitement at the table and she saw the man behind the ruckus.

His excited smile turned serious when his eyes met hers. She was too far away to see what color they were, but from her seat, she could tell they were more vibrant than any flashing light in the casino. His white shirt was open at the collar, revealing tanned skin. He was gorgeous. She looked away and turned back to Rachel, who was watching her.

"You might as well go talk to him," Rachel said.

"Nope. This is a girls' night. No boys allowed."

"Who made that rule?"

Ellie looked back to the man and saw that he was still watching her. She smiled again, knowing she had him. She watched him pass the dice to the dealer, and walk away from the table to the disappointed groans of the other patrons.

Ellie stood. "I'll be right back," she told Rachel, and headed in the guy's direction. Rachel said something she didn't hear over the din of the busy casino, and she turned her head. "What was that? Oof—" the air rushed out of her lungs as she smashed into a hard, male chest. She was unsteady on her high heels, but he reached for her, dropping his phone and catching her before she fell, while his cell phone cracked against the floor instead.

"Oh hey," he said, his strong fingers gripping her upper arms, supporting her. "Are you okay?"

"Yeah, I'm fine." Ellie looked down and saw the cracks that lined his screen. "I'm doing a lot better than your phone, at least."

He looked down. "Oh, dammit."

"Sorry about that," she told him as he released her and picked up the device.

"It's okay. I really should have been watching where I was going. It was time to get another one anyway." He shrugged. "I was on my way over to talk to you, so mission accomplished, I guess." He extended his hand to her in introduction, and when he looked at her, she could see the interest in his eyes. "Gabe," he said, a grin producing deep dimples below his chiseled cheekbones.

She shook his hand. His fingers were large around her own. "Hi, Gabe. I'm Ellie."

"Ellie," he repeated, as if indulging in her name. "That's pretty. Are you here alone?" he asked, looking around.

"She's here with me," Rachel said from somewhere behind Ellie. She couldn't believe she'd completely forgotten about her friend, who'd been sitting at the bar.

When Gabe's eyes widened, and he smiled, Ellie could read the question in his expression. "Not like that," she clarified. "We're *here* together. But not here *together*."

He reached past Ellie and extended his hand to Rachel. "I'm Gabe."

"I heard." She shook his hand. "Rachel."

"Why so interested if I'm here alone?" Ellie raised a playful eyebrow.

"I was wondering if there was a boyfriend around here who would try to kick my ass for offering to buy you both a drink."

"What makes you think we won't try to kick your ass?" Ellie asked him. She already liked the guy, and would definitely have a drink with him, but that didn't mean she didn't want to give him a hard time. He had to earn her time.

"I think you might try," he concurred. He cleared his throat. "At the expense of my physical well-being, would you ladies like to have a drink with me?"

Ellie looked at Rachel, who was doing something on her phone, ignoring them, and she knew her friend wasn't interested in being part of the conversation. She turned back to Gabe. "Excuse us," she told him, and took Rachel's arm, pulling her a few feet away from Gabe.

"What's up?" Rachel asked, looking past her in Gabe's direction.

"Would you mind going home without me?" Ellie asked, looking over her shoulder at Gabe, who was watching them.

"Are you sure?"

"Yeah, I'm sure. I'll be fine."

"You think that's a good idea?"

Ellie shook her head. "Probably not. But when have I ever been a fan of good ideas?"

Rachel shrugged. "All right, I'm not your mother—although, your mother *would* be all over this—so I'm going to go. But you have to promise me you'll be careful. You don't know this guy."

"I've got pepper spray in my purse, and I'm not afraid to use it."

Rachel nodded, and walked past Ellie to Gabe. "Hey,

Mr. Smooth-Talker. Let me see your driver's license."
Following behind, Ellie laughed at her friend's brash-
ness.

"What?" he asked, clearly taken aback.

Rachel held out her hand. "Let me see it."

Gabe didn't argue, and Ellie watched as he produced his ID.

Rachel was lightning quick in snapping a picture
of it with her phone. She grinned at Gabe. "Now if
anything happens to my friend, I'll know right where
to send the police. Ellie, text me later so I know
you're safe. Let me know anytime if you need me
to pick you up."

"Cross my heart, I will." She watched Rachel leave,
and when she was out of earshot, Ellie turned to Gabe.
"Sorry about her."

"It's fine," he said with another amazing smile.
"She's just looking out for you. Being a good friend."

"She is. She's amazing. We've known each other
since we were teenagers."

"That's nice. It's good for someone to have your
back."

"She's like the only person," Ellie muttered. She
hadn't meant to say that, but the words were out of
her mouth before she could stop them.

He frowned at her, and she knew she'd inadver-
tently revealed too much. "How about we get that
drink?" He reached for her hand, but she pulled back
from him.

"Why are you so sure I'm eager to go anywhere
with a stranger?"

"Because you let your friend go home without you."

"That's true," she conceded.

"All right, why don't I tell you a little about myself? Then I won't be such a stranger."

"Okay," she said, leaning casually against a cement pillar. "Tell me. You from here?"

"Yeah, I grew up here. Proudly battle-born-and-raised," he told her, referencing the Nevada state nickname. "Except for the time I spent in England for university."

"How nice."

"What do you do?"

"I'm a lawyer. Business law," she answered, still not used to saying the words. They didn't feel natural.

His eyes widened, then narrowed in scrutiny. "Me, too," he answered. "Strange we've never crossed paths before. I would have definitely remembered meeting you."

"I've only been here for a couple of weeks. I just finished school back east."

"New to the city," he said with a nod. "I'd pegged you for a tourist. So, you're brand-new and fresh-faced?"

"I guess so."

"I guess it makes sense that we haven't met. I just returned from Hong Kong, myself. I've been working over there the past couple of months."

"Oh nice. So corporate law isn't all filings and research."

"It's all of those things. But sometimes they let you go to exotic locales to file and research. How do you like practicing so far?"

"It's a lot of work. Which I don't need to tell you." She started to think about her father, and how he would more than disapprove of her night spent on the Vegas Strip instead of in her office. She pushed it aside. "You know, can we not talk about work? I really need to take a night off."

He looked relieved at her suggestion. "That sounds good to me. Can I buy you that drink now?" He held out his hand to her and looked around the busy casino. "I know a great place here. It's quieter. We'll be able to talk some more."

She looked Gabe over. The smart, sensible thing would be to thank him for the offer, catch up with Rachel and go home.

But for one night, Ellie didn't want to be smart. She wanted to have fun. Between her years in law school and her new job, she'd been working so hard lately, in her sensible suits, that it was time to finally release old Ellie for one more wild night. *One more night of fun, that's it.* She'd earned it. And as she watched Gabe, with his cocky grin and mischievous eyes, she knew that he was the way to do so. Curving the corners of her lips upward, she put her hand in his and said, "Sure."

As her fingers interlocked with Gabe's and her palm flattened against his, an electric shock shot through her body, and she looked up at his profile. He must have felt her gaze on him, because he looked down at her and winked. It was dumb, reckless even, to go off with a stranger, something that she'd never done before. But something about Gabe made her brain shut off and follow her intuition—it told her that she was right where she wanted to be.

The crowd seemed to part before them as they made their way across the casino floor. Ellie was barely aware of the people around them as Gabe led her through the throngs, expertly navigating the crowd. She wasn't sure if she was imagining many of them looking in their direction. She stiffened, wondering if any of them knew her from the days when she topped the gossip blogs, or maybe they knew Gabe, or maybe they were just admiring him, paying attention to the sexiest man in the room. He had certainly gotten her attention, Ellie reasoned.

She was surprised when he didn't lead her to the trendy nightclub, but instead bypassed the lineup and led her to a staircase that took them to a quieter area above the casino floor. The bar had an air of sophistication and exclusivity. Class. It was quieter, less chaotic than the casino below. The place felt like Gabe.

After he shook the hand of the doorman, palming him some amount of money, an attendant led them to a secluded corner at the far end, a semicircle booth ensconced in a nook built into the wall to ensure them privacy. Ellie settled into the rich, leather booth, as Gabe did the same. When the server came to take their order, Gabe plucked the menu from the table.

"What's your poison?" he asked, passing her the drink menu.

"I'm not picky," she told him.

After a brief deliberation, Gabe ordered a bottle of champagne for them.

"A bottle?"

"Well, they don't exactly sell the good stuff by the glass," he told her with a sly wink.

"Champagne, though?"

He shrugged casually. "I don't know about you, but I feel like celebrating."

She sat a little closer to him, bringing her knee in contact with his thigh, pivoting her upper body to face him on the couch. "What are you celebrating?"

"I have a feeling I'm going to become the newest partner at my firm," he told her.

Ellie's eyes widened in awe. Gabe was clearly a young man, and making partner at a law firm was quite an accomplishment. "That's awesome. Where do you work?"

He shook his head. "I thought we weren't going to talk about work?"

"You're right," she said.

"But I guess there's something else I'm celebrating," he told her, his voice dropping to a dangerously low and sexy murmur, as he tilted his head toward her.

She inhaled another lungful of his light, but spicy cologne. Ellie had never been a connoisseur of male cologne, but she needed to know what Gabe used, so she could cover her pillow and everything else she owned in the scent. "And what's that?" she asked, her voice an almost breathless whisper.

He grinned and leaned closer, bringing his lips to her ear. "Meeting you," he said with a whisper. His breath warmed her skin, dancing over the sensitized nerve endings of her throat.

The sheer cheesiness of the line made her eyes roll. "Oh please." Ellie laughed and lightly pushed his shoulder. But touching him proved to be a mistake, because instead of removing her hand, she smoothed her palm over his chest, under his jacket, over the fine material of his shirt. His chest was firm, warm, solid muscle. The man worked out. But when he put his hand on top of hers, stopping the movement, trapping her hand in the spot over his heart, she could feel a gentle thrum travel through her, until it settled in a pool of desire between her thighs. So in tune with Gabe was she that she was sure she could hear the beating of his heart—maybe it was her own—and their eyes connected as the rest of the room disappeared.

Ellie's mouth went dry and a heat radiated from her chest upward. Gone was the moment of levity they'd shared, the air heavy with sensuality. She was so caught up in the man—the stranger—sitting beside her that she failed to notice the server approach. She backed up and, startled, reluctantly pulled away from Gabe, as the waitress presented the bottle and poured them each a glass before placing it in the ice bucket and quietly walking away.

Alone again, Gabe passed her one of the glasses

and took the opportunity to sit closer to her, shifting to more fully face her in the center of the booth, placing his arm across the back. Even though he wasn't touching her, she could feel his proximity, his gravity forcing her closer, drawing her near. She couldn't fight it if she wanted to—she didn't want to—so Ellie pivoted her body in his direction, crossing her legs, bringing her calves into contact with his shin. They didn't speak, but Ellie could feel the waves of sexual tension that radiated between them.

Gabe held his glass aloft. "To us."

"To new starts," she added, clinking her glass with his.

They sipped their champagne, watching each other over the rims of their glasses, and she sighed when Gabe made the first move, dropping his hand on her thigh.

"You know, I'm pretty sure you're the most beautiful woman I've ever seen," he told her.

High-class club or dive bar, men, it seemed, were the same all over. She rolled her eyes. "That's original," she told him. Ellie wondered how many women fell for a line, especially when it was uttered by a man who looked like Gabe. He would have to do better than that.

"Okay, what if I asked you if your legs were tired?"

"Or if it hurt when I fell from heaven?"

"Well, that's it, I guess." He moved his arm away and shrugged. She missed his warmth almost immediately, and all she wanted was for him to put his arm back, to touch her again. "Those are all of my good lines." He laughed, a deep, rich sound that filled the space around them, and he raised his glass to his mouth and drained it. He leaned toward the table and poured himself another. "More?"

"Yeah. Thanks," she said, holding her own now-empty glass out. He filled it and she sipped again. The carbonated bubbles tickled her nose.

Gabe's hand found her thigh again, and some-how, through the lust-and-champagne-heavy fog, a moment of clarity shone through. Ellie backed away slightly. "Wait a minute," she said, and he removed his hand, leaning away from her, thankfully giving her the space she needed, where she wasn't under the influence of him and whatever cologne he was wearing. But when she caught her breath, all she longed for was another indulgent breath of him.

But she didn't do this. Ellie Carrington didn't fall so hard for men. She didn't chase them. She didn't jump into bed with just any good-looking guy. She needed to keep her cool. She wanted Gabe, and she could tell he wanted her. But he was going to have to work for it. She couldn't let him know that he'd already won her over.

"What's wrong?" he asked.

"Don't think that just because you got us this table and forked over way too much money for this bottle of champagne, I'm going to sleep with you," she warned him. Even though Ellie would probably end the evening riding him like a cowgirl, he didn't have to know it would be that easy.

A quick grin split his face. *Those dimples again.* "What makes you think I'm going to ask to sleep with you?"

She could still feel the ghost of his touch on her thigh. "The way you're looking at me, the expensive champagne. Stuff like that normally comes with a price, if you know what I mean."

"Oh, I know what you mean, but maybe I'm thirsty."

"I'll bet you are." She quirked an eyebrow and he laughed.

"Maybe I wanted to share a drink with a beautiful woman." He took a drink from his glass, as if to prove his point. "But so we're clear, Ellie, there's no obligation on either of our parts here. We can just sit here, two strangers sharing a bottle of champagne. And if the evening leads to more—and I hope it does—that's great. If not…" he shrugged and drank again. "Who knows, later tonight you might be begging me to fuck you—" she nearly crumbled at his use of the word, but he shook his head "—and I'll just put you in a cab to go home."

Ellie laughed, knowing he was full of it. She could see the way that he looked at her, the way he'd caressed her thigh, and knew that if she was willing, there was no way he'd be putting her in a car. At that moment, Ellie knew that she would end up in bed with this man that evening. There was no other option. She felt powerless to the hold he had over her, his captivating emerald eyes, the upward curve of his lush lips. Ellie didn't make a habit of sleeping around, or having one-night stands—nor would she judge anyone who did—not since she'd left her partying days behind her, but as she watched Gabe over the rim of her glass, she knew she would make an exception for him. Ellie was intrigued by Gabe, and she liked him already. So, she decided not to fight whatever was happening between them, and drank her champagne instead.

After an hour, the lights at the bar had dimmed a little, setting a more intimate mood. Gabe poured the last few drops of champagne into his glass, returned the bottle to the ice bucket upside down, and settled back in the booth, feeling as mellow and relaxed as he possibly could with the intense hum of desire buzzing through him. Ellie had kept her position, turned facing him, her long legs curled so her feet were underneath her, knees resting on his thigh, dangerously close to his dick.

He wasn't sure when he'd last enjoyed the company of a woman like Ellie. She was gorgeous and sexy, but she was also smart, quick, funny, and they shared some sort of connection that had eluded him for a while now. She was easy to talk to, and when the server came back, he didn't want to leave so they ordered another bottle.

"So, what are you doing on the Strip tonight?" she asked. "I might be new in town, but I know that this is mainly a tourist place."

Gabe thought about his response. With his friends all busy with their own lives, he had headed out on a solo mission. Not wanting to be alone in his empty house, the Strip seemed like a good way to kill a night. He'd been right. He'd been craving excitement. Something different. Something new. Something wild before he signed his life away to Charles Burnham, his boss and mentor, and as he looked over at Ellie, he knew he'd found it with her. "I came here tonight because I knew I wouldn't see anyone I know here. I was looking for something different."

He could feel Ellie watching him and he knew he'd revealed too much. "It feels like there's a story there," she said.

She'd hit the nail on the head, but he felt like a spoiled fool for complaining about all of his blessings and the success he'd had in his career. "There is. But not one I'm interested in telling."

She leaned closer to him, as if she were studying him. The air between them had become even more charged. Heated. It was a point of no return for him, as they both moved in slow motion. With his fingertips, he caressed her smooth jaw and drew her closer. He wanted to kiss her more than he wanted his next breath.

The second her lips touched his, he was a goner. A gentle caress at first, testing her boundaries, he took her bottom lip between the two of his and nipped. Her sigh urged him on, and he stroked his tongue against the seam of her lips, before she opened to him, allowing him access to her hot, wet mouth. Soon, the kiss wasn't enough. He grasped Ellie around the waist and lifted her, settling her onto his lap, so that her thighs straddled his. She moaned into his mouth and the sound shot straight to his dick. He was hard, and she ground against him, and she felt so good, it stole his breath when she tilted her head and deepened the kiss.

His hands went to her ass, and he held her in place and controlled her movements as he ran her hot core against his length. Christ, Gabe wanted her, and he pulled away. He surveyed their surroundings—the walls of the nook kept them obscured from the view of the other bar patrons. He could take her right there, but a part of him held back. That sort of behavior would be welcome at Di Terrestres—he cursed himself for not bringing her there—but not in a booth at a public club. Whether or not they were in Las Vegas—Sin City—public decency laws still applied. "Fuck, I want you, Ellie," he breathed against her skin, his fingers digging into her waist. He cursed his more practical, law-abiding side.

"I thought I was supposed to be the one begging."

"You aren't yet. But you will be. Let's go somewhere where I can do everything I want with you."

Ellie nodded. "Good idea."

Gabe took some bills from his wallet and threw them on the table to cover the cost of the champagne and tip. Ellie and Gabe stood and casually walked outside.

Gabe pressed his hand against Ellie's lower back, leading her to the taxis waiting outside of the casino entrance, but on the horizon, something caught his attention. The High Roller, the giant observation

Ferris wheel that had been added to the Las Vegas skyline a few years before. He had an idea. Just as bad an idea as he'd had within the confines of their cozy booth in the club—but one that would be even more fun.

"Where are we going?" Ellie asked, as they bypassed the waiting cars and crossed the street.

"I've got an idea."

CHAPTER TWO

GABE TOOK ELLIE'S hand and, with a brisk pace, all but
dragged Ellie toward the huge Ferris wheel that rose
high into the sky. On her dangerously high heels, she
could barely keep up with his long-legged stride.
When they arrived at the ride, she looked up. Groups
of probably ten to fifteen people boarded and gathered in each of the large observation pods, taking in
the view of the lights of Las Vegas Boulevard with
drinks in their hands and smiles on their faces.

Ellie wondered why—when she was about to hike
her skirt up a few minutes ago and have sex with him
in a private booth—he would suddenly want to show
her the view high above the Strip. There was a small
lineup of groups waiting to get on but Gabe held
back, waiting until the line dwindled. Ellie almost
squealed when Gabe grabbed her ass. She looked up
and saw the wicked grin that had perched upon his
lips. And she knew exactly why Gabe had brought
her there—what his intentions were.

When all the other groups had been escorted to
their pods, they walked up to the attendant. Just like

with the host at the club they'd visited, Gabe palmed a bill to the attendant. The man knew how to operate, to get what he wanted. "We'd appreciate it if we could ride alone," he told the other man.

The attendant winked at Gabe. "I'll see what I can do."

They were escorted into an observation pod, and instead of bringing in another group, the attendant closed the door after them—ensuring that they were alone in the round pod, which had a maximum occupancy of forty people. The pod was large, luxurious and even featured a bar on one side. Go Big or Go Home was Vegas's motto, it seemed.

The wheel continued on its way upward, and the lights inside the pod were dimmed, to allow its occupants to fully appreciate the nighttime Strip view. For a brief moment, she found herself drawn to the view. The lights of Sin City twinkled as she took in the Eiffel Tower, the beam atop the Luxor pyramid, the neon lights of the Flamingo... The crowds of people reveling in it. The energy of Las Vegas Boulevard was incredible, infectious, and it fed her.

But she forgot about all of that when Gabe came up behind her, cupping her hips with his large hands, watching the view over her shoulder.

"It's incredible, right?"

"Yeah," he whispered.

"I can't believe I live here."

"I've lived in this city almost my entire life. I've never seen it quite like this."

She turned in his arms, forgetting the outside view

and focusing on the one inside the pod. "How long do we have in here?"

"A half hour or so," he told her, his lips grazing her neck. "Still not enough time," he whispered against her skin.

She shivered under his touch, and smoothed her hands over his chest. "Well, we'd better get down to business, then," she said, pushing him backward until he landed heavily on the cushioned bench that stretched along the opposite side of the pod. Reminiscent of how they'd kissed in the booth, she mounted his lap, bracing her thighs on either side of his. Tugging on the front of his shirt, it was her turn to kiss him. And she did so, using more roughness than she needed to. She couldn't get enough of Gabe. His full lips, his insistent tongue.

He gripped her thighs and ventured upward underneath her skirt, and when his hands found her ass, he cupped her, his fingers digging hard into her flesh. But still, he pulled his mouth away. "Goddammit," he muttered, throwing his head against the back of the bench.

"What is it?"

"I don't have a condom." His chest heaved with what she imagined was frustration.

"Is that all?" She asked. "It's okay." She dismounted from his lap to fetch her purse. Reaching inside, she pulled out the condom she'd put in her makeup bag and resumed her position, straddling his thighs. "I've got you covered. Literally."

The relief on his face was obvious as she moved

in to kiss him again. He plucked the condom packet from her fingers as his lips trailed across her jaw and down her throat.

He went to her again, taking her face in his hands, kissing her sweet lips, tasting her champagne-flavored tongue. "This isn't very romantic," he said, between kisses.

"Are you kidding?" she breathed. "Look at the view. It's incredibly romantic."

"What view?" he asked. "All I can see is you. You deserve better than a quick fuck in a tourist attraction."

"Don't worry about me. Right here with you. This is exactly where I want to be."

His hands skimmed over her skin. "Next time, I'm going to take my time with you. So I can explore every inch of your body."

Ellie looked forward to that. Those were nice words. But she wouldn't count on another round with Gabe. This was a one-night stand and she knew it. So she focused on the present, and having Gabe for the next thirty minutes or so. She covered his mouth again with her own for another scorching kiss, before it was time to get down to business.

"Oh Christ," Gabe whispered against her. Her fingers made quick work of his belt and the button on his pants. She unzipped him, and reached into his boxer briefs to his cock. He was so hard. So thick. She wanted to fall to the floor between his knees and taste him, but there wasn't time for that. She wanted him inside of her more than anything.

Ellie plucked the condom back from his fingers, opened it and rolled the latex over his length. At her touch, he closed his eyes, wincing. He was so hard, and she was ready for him. She thought she might burst if she didn't feel him inside of her. Gabe pushed up the short skirt of her dress, and thankfully she'd skipped panties when she'd dressed for the evening, because there was now no barrier between her and Gabe. She held him by his base, and guided herself down over him.

Ellie exhaled as he filled her, and she shuddered against him. She rose again, withdrawing almost all of his length from her, before lowering and taking all of him again. With his fingers digging into her waist, he guided her as she bounced in his lap.

The lights of the Strip danced in her periphery, but all she could see was Gabe, and she was only somewhat aware of the glass on either side of her. "Can people see us?" she asked, through heavy breaths.

"We're pretty obscured right where we are," he told her. Pulling down the top of her dress, taking her bra with it, he exposed her breasts. He bent over, taking advantage, and took one beaded nipple into his mouth, as he pinched the other between two fingers. Ellie yelled out and arched her back, pushing her chest against him. Gabe took the lead and, pushing up with his hips and holding her aloft, he pumped into her, again and again.

Ellie felt her heart rate ratchet higher, and heard the hitch in his breath. She was close, and she could tell from the way that he clutched her, how his fingers dug into her waist, that he was, too. He turned her attention to the view, which slowly descended toward the earth. They didn't have much time. But they didn't need much more. Wrapping her arms around Gabe's shoulder, Ellie felt the beautiful crescendo of her climax, and she screamed out her release. Gabe released her waist and about growled against her shoulder, as his body tensed, and then loosened. He lifted his head and looked at her. They locked eyes, their connection fierce and unbreakable.

Startled by her closeness with this stranger, Ellie's breath caught in her chest. It was too intimate a moment for her. This was supposed to be a onetime thing with a sexy stranger, but she already wanted him again. "We're close to the ground," she whispered, willing her body to move away from him.

"Yeah," he agreed and released her. She pulled up her dress, covering herself before she stood and came into view of the other riders and people on the ground, while Gabe stood and discarded the condom in the garbage near the empty bar area.

"Well, Gabe," she said, fixing her hair in her dark reflection in the mirror, trying to not look like she'd been fucked senseless on a Ferris wheel. "That was something else."

He came up behind her and turned her head in his direction, gaining access to her lips. Gabe kissed her until she ran the risk of running out of oxygen. "Yeah, sorry about how quick that was," he said, his voice husky with desire. "I don't know what got into me."

"Well, I know exactly what got into me," she said, turning in his arms to face him.

"Next time, it won't be like this, though," he promised her.

Her heart fluttered at the prospect of another time with Gabe. "Next time?"

"Yeah, I already told you that. You can guarantee there's going to be another time. Definitely tonight, probably in the next thirty minutes." He looked around the observation pod, as it neared the ground and the end of their ride. "But it won't be in here."

She sighed and leaned into him. "I've got some stories, but this might be the wildest thing I've ever done."

"Me, too," he admitted.

She looked at him, and one corner of her mouth ticked upward. "A guy like you? A city like this? I find that hard to believe."

"It's true. Compared to everyone I know, I'm the straitlaced, boring one."

Frowning, Ellie brushed her lips lightly to his. "You sound sad about that."

Gabe shrugged. "I sometimes wonder how much time I wasted in my twenties with my nose in the books, working and studying." Ellie understood that; while she'd sown many wild oats before she'd been legally allowed to drink, or be admitted into clubs, she'd spent many of the past few years doing the same.

"Not that there was anything wrong with being diligent and working hard, and I've certainly learned how to have fun since then," Gabe continued. "But when I think of myself as a younger man, I can only imagine myself in a dark corner of a law library."

Ellie watched him carefully. "I can already tell that working hard has made you successful, but life has to be about balance, right?"

"Sometimes I just wonder what sorts of things I missed out on when I should have been young and stupid."

Ellie took his lapels in her hands and pulled him closer. "You're in luck," she started. "Because young and stupid is one of my specialties. Wonder no more, Gabe. Why don't we take the rest of this night, and we'll make some stories?"

"I like the sound of that. Why don't we get a room?" he suggested. She almost said yes. Spending the rest of the night naked in a hotel room with Gabe would be one hell of a way to spend a night—and they would no doubt be there in a few hours—but she wanted to show him a wild, stupid, reckless night. She couldn't help it. Old Ellie was on the loose, and she couldn't be leashed yet. "As tempting as that idea is, no way. We're going to have a little clothes-on excitement before we do that." She winked. "Then you can ravish me all you want."

"Deal. So where to now?"

"More drinks?" she asked. "It's still kind of early. We can hit a nightclub. How do you feel about dancing the night away? And we can see just how much trouble we can get into," she suggested, hoping he wouldn't say no.

His chuckle was low, husky. "That sounds good to me. The night is young, and so are we."

"Come on." Taking the lead, Ellie grasped his hand in hers and pulled him toward the door of the pod. When the attendant unlocked it they exited, and Ellie knew that based on their rumpled appearance and flushed cheeks, it was probably obvious to everyone in the vicinity what they'd been up to five hundred and fifty feet above the Las Vegas Strip. "Sorry, ladies," Ellie whispered to a group of women looking to board next, as she tilted her head in Gabe's direction. "But look at him. Can you blame me?"

Gabe chuckled as some of the women in line laughed and cast him interested looks, but Ellie pulled him away before he could say anything. They were on a mission. A stupid and reckless one.

CHAPTER THREE

THE SECOND GABE opened his eyes, he regretted it. The sun coming in through the open blinds was far too bright, and the room sat tilted on an axis. He squinted as he took in his surroundings. He wasn't in his own bedroom. He was in a hotel.

He pushed himself to a sitting position and tried to fight off the nausea caused by moving, while he attempted to make sense of where he was. Piece by piece, through the fog of his hangover, it came back to him. Meeting Ellie, drinking champagne, sex in the High Roller, more drinks, gambling, the penthouse suite, more champagne. More Ellie. More sex. Then even more champagne. He looked down at his left hand, and saw the band around his fourth finger.

Getting married.

"Fuck."

It all came back to him. Somewhere between the roulette wheel and making their way to the Bellagio penthouse suite, where he currently found himself, they'd decided it would be a *really crazy idea* to hop in a car and go to a twenty-four-hour wedding

chapel at the north end of Las Vegas Boulevard, to
be married by a later-in-life Elvis impersonator in a
polyester, rhinestone-studded suit left over from the
seventies. In a sex-and-champagne-fueled night, he'd
gotten drunk and gone and done one of the dumb-
est things he'd ever done—married a stranger. That
drunk, it couldn't have been *legal*, right?

"Ellie?" he called. The suite was silent. In the
need to cut loose a bit, he'd gone to an extreme.
After years of hard work to reach his goal, he was
so close, and he'd just fucked it up beyond all reason. Ellie had brought out something wild in him,
and even though the hangover that ravaged him
made him wish he was dead, she'd helped him feel
alive. When he was with her, he'd felt like a different man. He couldn't blame Ellie, though. He'd unleashed his own uncontrollable beast in the quest to
have an out-of-control night away from the office.
After they'd had sex in the High Roller—one of the
craziest things he'd ever done outside of the walls
of Di Terrestres—it had been his idea to up the *wild*
ante. To do what was most unexpected of him—to
go to the chapel and make the lively, strange, fun,
amazing woman his wife.

His head pounding, he looked around. "Ellie," he
called again, and was met with more silence. With
a groan, he pushed himself up from the bed and
looked throughout the suite. Ellie was nowhere to
be found. He did find his phone, however, and then
remembered shattering it the night before when Ellie

had crashed into him—and into his life. "Dammit. Right."

He didn't know the time, or even what day it was until he went to the smart TV that was mounted on the wall, and was shocked by what it told him. *Saturday. Five p.m.* He'd somehow slept through most of Saturday. And Ellie, his wife, was nowhere to be found in the suite. He pushed back his hair and pulled on his boxer shorts, which he'd found at the foot of the bed. Then he saw it on the desk—a second platinum band, smaller and thinner than the one on his own finger, diamonds encircling it, on top of a piece of hotel stationery that bore the words *Gabe, I'm sorry—Ellie.* She'd walked out while he was sleeping.

It was stupid—he barely knew the woman—but her abandonment still stung him like a great loss. He lifted the note, and underneath it was an official marriage certificate. Goddammit, their marriage had somehow been legit.

Walking through the suite, he saw the remnants of what looked like a wild night—his clothes strewn about, empty champagne bottles on the floor, liquid soaking the lush carpet—he remembered pouring it over Ellie's body, and lapping it from her smooth skin—and a room service cart told him at least they'd managed to eat at some point.

The penthouse suite was empty, but not as empty as he felt. He wasn't sure if it was the hangover, or disappointment from her absence. But he pushed past the sadness, the stupidity, the disappointment, when he thought of the legal ramifications of a marriage. Off the top of his head, he couldn't recall Nevada's marriage laws, but he knew that it would be a lot more than just signing some annulment papers. But not only that, Ellie, being a lawyer herself, through some legal maneuvering, could be entitled to his assets, and the Brotherhood's assets. He could fight it, but so could she. Ellie wouldn't come after him, his money, his house, the Brotherhood, would she? Gabe had no idea. He didn't even know her.

"Oh God." This is exactly why he never walked on the wild side. He'd potentially screwed up everything. He had to protect himself and his friends. He and Ellie had been beyond drunk, and he could argue intoxication as grounds for annulment. But he had to find her first. He checked the name on the marriage certificate. Ellie Carrington. He would have to look her up, find her. But first he had to get home, and figure out how to make everything right.

Ellie sat on her bed, her door closed, the blinds drawn and the lights off. She plucked a multigrain cracker from its sleeve and nibbled on a corner, trying to keep her stomach from revolting. She hadn't had a hangover this bad in her life, and not only was she hungover, but once again, her drunken exploits had affected her sober life. She'd done quite a few questionable things under the influence, but when she'd awakened that morning, Gabe's arms wrapped around her and a diamond-encircled wedding band on her finger, she'd panicked, slipped out of bed and, as quietly as she could, gathered her things and bolted.

She had somehow lost a night, and most of Saturday, with Gabe. Her head throbbed just thinking about it. It was a wild, incredible night. If only she could remember any of it.

It had been a long time since she'd had a night like that. Not since the hard-partying days of *old Ellie*. The party monster with whom she'd been acquainted in her past had once again reared her ugly head and made *overindulgence* the word of the day. She'd been drunk on alcohol, and drunk on Gabe. She had only the barest recollection of whatever had passed for their wedding ceremony, vaguely remembering Gabe slipping the diamond wedding band on her finger, and the Elvis impersonator declaring them husband and wife, and wishing them a "rocking life together."

This is so fucked-up. How was she going to get out of it? They could get an annulment, but she would have to find Gabe—why had she taken off without waking him and not stayed to talk about what they'd done? "Like an actual adult," she muttered to herself, reaching into the sleeve for another salted cracker.

Ellie had had an amazing night with Gabe, and when she'd woken up that morning, she felt the need to get out of there. To put her slip back into *old Ellie*'s world behind her.

She'd needed to leave, and hoped he would forget about her, or that their wedding hadn't been real, or legal. But that morning, as she'd zipped her dress, and took one last look at his sleeping form—that incredible, strong body—her only regret was that she wouldn't get one more night with him.

A knock on the door made her wince, the noise vibrating around inside her head, against her brain. Knowing it was Rachel, she said "come in."

Rachel opened the door a crack. The light coming into her darkened room made her squint her eyes shut. "Just get in here and close the door."

"Are you okay?"

"Do I look okay?"

"You do not. What time did you get in last night? Or should I say *this morning*? I was thinking about calling the police with Gabe's information, but you sent me this." Rachel produced her cell phone. Ellie looked at the screen and a picture of Gabe, Elvis and herself, smiling and standing in front of an altar left over from 1979, holding a small bouquet of wilted pink carnations.

"What happened to you last night? You got married? You're lucky I had to work this morning, because I would have definitely come out and hauled your ass home."

"Yeah. I kind of wish you had."

Rachel picked up Ellie's left hand. "Where's your ring?"

"I left it in a penthouse suite at the Bellagio."

"This is unbelievable. I don't even know what to say. You're married."

"Don't remind me."

"I take it you aren't a thrilled blushing bride."

"Why would I be? It was stupid. A drunken mistake. We need an annulment."

"What did you guys decide to do?"

Ellie winced again, and the pain in her head now had nothing to do with her piercing hangover. It was regret. "Nothing. I snuck out before he woke up."

Rachel's mouth hung open. She picked up a small pillow and threw it at Ellie. "You…did a walk of shame after your own wedding night?"

"It wasn't a *walk of shame*." She tried to defend herself, but knew it wasn't going to work. "It was a bad decision. I didn't know how to face the guy. I needed to get my mind right, organize my thoughts, before I see him again."

Rachel looked at Ellie, and laid down on the bed next to her. She took a cracker from the package and popped it into her mouth. "This is you organizing your thoughts?"

"As soon as the room stops spinning, I'll start organizing."

"What's happened to you? You're Ellie Carrington. You're fucking fearless. You stared down the paparazzi, tabloid reporters, anyone who crossed you. You don't run away."

"Maybe I don't feel much like that Ellie anymore. What do you think my father would say if he finds out that my first couple of weeks in the city, I end up getting married to a one-night stand?"

Rachel frowned. "That's what this little pity party is about, isn't it?"

"What do you mean?"

"Your father. You're worried about his opinion."

"Of course, I am."

"Sure, you married a stranger. You fucked up. You made a mistake. But that's your own problem to deal with. Why does it always come down to him?"

Ellie had to think about it. Why was his opinion so important? She settled on her typical answer. "He was instrumental in me turning my life around."

"Since when do you care what anyone—any man—thinks of you?"

"It's more than that. This is supposed to be my opportunity to have a relationship with him."

"All right. What's your next step?"

Ellie sighed. "Put on my *big girl panties* and deal with this, right?"

"That's right. And first?"

"Find Gabe. Talk to him. I don't even know how to find him."

"Girl, I can help you out there," Rachel said, scrolling through the photos on her phone. "I might know more about your husband than you do. I took that picture of his driver's license, remember?"

"You're smart," Ellie told her, taking her phone. She looked at Gabe's photo. It was ridiculous, but she found herself missing him. She regretted walking out on him this morning. She dedicated his home address to her memory and handed the phone back.

"That is one handsome husband you have there," Rachel said with a laugh, but then she turned serious. "So, you're going to go see him?"

"Yeah, I kind of have to, right?"

"You do."

"What do I say?"

Rachel shrugged. "I guess you can start with 'Hey, hubby.'"

"You're a jerk."

"I know, but you love me anyway."

With a plan in place, her hangover had dissipated, and she felt ready to tackle her problems head-on.

"I do. That's my problem," she said, smiling at her friend. "Okay. I'm going to go. But first I need a shower." She turned on her bedside lamp and took in her reflection in her mirror. "I can't go see my husband looking like this."

Gabe, freshly showered, somewhat hydrated but still feeling horrible, sat at his kitchen table in front of his opened laptop and tossed both platinum bands down next to it. He didn't know what to do with them. But he felt somehow closer to his missing wife when it was near.

Where was she? Why did she leave without saying goodbye? He'd been with his fair share of women, acquaintances, strangers he'd never see again, familiar lovers he'd seen multiple times, but he'd never married any of them in a sex-and-booze-filled stupor. He'd known the minute he saw Ellie, with her huge, dark eyes, and lush, full mouth, that there was something about her. He tried to shake her. But he knew he wouldn't be successful. Not until he saw her again. He had to find her.

Normally, the type of anonymous, one-night arrangement he'd shared with Ellie was fine with him. It was the kind of thing he sought out at Di Terrestres. Last night was different, and now he couldn't get sweet, sexy, wild Ellie—*his wife*—out of his mind. He had no idea how he would get on with his day and focus on anything but her, and figuring out a way to find her.

Gabe needed advice—needed to talk to his friends, to let them know that he'd royally screwed up and put them all at risk. With his phone still shattered, he turned to his laptop and started up a video chat with the other members of the Brotherhood. One by one, his four friends' faces filled his screen as they answered.

"Gabe!" Alana was the first to speak. "Where have you been? You've been completely MIA." It had been only twenty-four hours, but she was right. He hadn't been out of contact with any of them, especially Alana, for that long, in years.

"I smashed my phone last night. I haven't been out for a new one yet."

"You look like hell. What happened to you?" she asked.

"I may have lost most of the night—and today— in a Bellagio penthouse, after too many bottles of champagne to count." Stunned silence met him in every chat window on his screen. Within the group, Gabe was the straight man to every joke, the serious one, the quiet one. The studious one. The one who avoided scandal at every turn, while his friends had all found themselves embroiled in it at one time or another. "And that's not all."

"What happened?" Brett asked.

Gabe grabbed the marriage license and held it up to the screen. "There's also this."

"What the fuck is that?" Alex asked.

"I got married."

More stunned silence. But Alana was the first to crack, and she laughed. Soon, it was echoed by a chorus of deeper, more masculine laughs. For a moment, as he took in their glee, Gabe hated his friends.

"So, who's the lucky lady?" Alana asked, when she caught her breath.

"Her name is Ellie," he started, and made a show of looking at the certificate, "and it seems as if her last name is Carrington."

"Where is she?" Rafael asked. "*Who* is she? I didn't know you were seeing anyone."

"I'm not," Gabe responded, his voice flat. "And *who* and *where* are both questions I would love to have the answers to, as well. She was gone when I woke up this morning. She left her ring, and an extremely short Dear John letter."

As the rest of the group seemed to digest what Gabe had told them, Rafael spoke again. "Gabe, we all think this is pretty funny, but do I have to ask if there was any sort of prenup? I'm guessing there was not."

He shook his head. And he was certain he could hear the sharp intakes of breath from each of the corners of the city. They now understood the seriousness of the situation."

"Can you get it annulled?" Alana asked.

"I'm going to try. With the level of intoxication, it would be grounds for annulment. I've looked it up, and it'll only be a minor headache. My biggest problem is that I can't find Ellie to serve her with it."

"Use my PI," Rafael told him. Gabe could see he was already on his phone to get the information. "Harrison's the best. This Ellie, is she local?"

Instead of responding, Gabe just stared into his laptop's camera for a moment, urging his brain to remember any details she'd told him about her life. Then it hit him. "Yeah, she just moved here. She's a lawyer, too. But I have no idea where."

"Jesus Christ, Gabe," Alana said with an exasperated sigh.

"I know. I fucked up. But it shouldn't be too hard to track her down. Rafael, send me your PI's contact info. I'll call him."

"You guys swinging by the club tonight?" Alana asked them, thankfully taking the attention off him. They discussed their evening plans while Gabe thought about Ellie. He needed to find her, and not just for the annulment. But because he wanted to see her. He genuinely missed her, and the longer he went without seeing her, the quicker he reverted to *staid and serious Gabe.* He liked how she made him feel, and he wondered how he could get that feeling back. *You know, without the whole drunken Vegas wedding thing...*

"Coming by tonight, Gabe?"

He shook his head. "No. I've got to figure this out. See if I can find Ellie, and put it all behind me, before Burnham gets wind of it." He hadn't even thought about the repercussion his indiscretion would have on his career, or his staunchly conservative boss's opinion of him. He had to end the marriage. Now.

"Well, keep us posted," Alana told him.

"And guys, I'm really sorry about this. I'll make it right, though. I won't let my slipup put us at risk."

"It's not the first time one of us has slipped up," Brett assured him. "It'll all work out."

"But I've got to say, I never thought it'd be you," Alana said with a smirk.

"Yeah," he muttered, signing off.

He closed his video chat and opened Facebook. In the search bar, he typed her name. Several Ellie Carringtons showed up, but he had no trouble finding the woman he'd married. He clicked on her profile. It was secured, so he could only see her profile picture. It was an older photo—maybe like him, she hadn't updated her profile in a long time. He couldn't see anything so, not knowing what to do, he sent her a friend request, hoping she'd see it and get in contact. He navigated away from Facebook.

He turned to Google and ran another search on her. He saw the blog posts, the headlines, read through her wayward past as a troubled club kid. He scanned the headlines from more than five years ago, the teen daughter of an aging horror starlet, stumbling out of nightclubs, yelling at photographers, drinking. It felt wrong, looking into her past like that. It felt like a betrayal, and he wished he could protect her, and scrub it from the internet entirely. But still he perused the sites, hoping he'd find something that would help him find her today.

One hit brought him to the website for Stanford Law School. She was part of a group photo of the most recent graduating class. He found her, in the second row, with no problem. She was like a beacon. She looked more like the woman he'd married the night before, and nothing like the troubled teen she'd been. Her eyes were bright, her smile proud. As she should be with her honors degree. Gabe was impressed and kept looking, but no matter how much he looked, he couldn't find a way to contact her.

With a frustrated sigh, he shut his laptop. Gabe felt impotent, unable to fix the situation he'd found himself in. He called Rafael's PI and left a message for him to call him back. But for the moment, there was nothing else he could do. He wandered down the marble hallway. Being a lawyer had certainly lined his pockets, but it was the money that he'd earned as part of the Brotherhood that had given him the finest of luxuries. At the end of the wide hallway sat his piano. He hadn't played in months. Between his work trip to Hong Kong and the ungodly hours he spent at the office, he had had little free time, most of which he spent at the gym or at Di Terrestres. He sat at the bench and lifted the cover revealing the shiny black-and-white keys. He placed his fingers on the keys, but before he could apply any pressure, his doorbell chimed.

Gabe wasn't expecting company, nor did he feel like seeing anybody, but he stood, and as he made his way down the hallway, the doorbell chimed again.

"Hold on, I'm coming," he said, even though he knew the person on the other side would not hear him through the heavy door. His head still pounded, and the third chime of the bell tested his patience.

He whipped open the door, not sure who he was expecting to see, but he was about to give them a piece of his mind. But his angry tirade stopped in his throat, and he was shocked to see Ellie standing on the other side.

"Ellie," he whispered.

"Hi, Gabe."

CHAPTER FOUR

ELLIE WASN'T SURE what sort of reception she should expect. But she stiffened when Gabe asked her, "What are you doing here?"

"We need to talk about...well, everything. Can I come in?"

That seemed to shake him free, and he stepped aside and held open the door for her. "Yeah, sorry. Of course. Come in."

Ellie walked into Gabe's home. His place was modern, yet classic. Spacious, light, with large windows, clean lines. Not only was it uncluttered, but it looked as if nobody lived there at all. She ventured farther inside. She walked down the spotless marble floor, her high heels clicking as she went, and passed a large media room—his man cave, she assumed—where lush leather furniture was pointed toward one of the largest television screens she'd ever seen. She pictured Gabe and his friends watching sports in front of it, and wondered which sport was his favorite, or if he even liked sports at all.

"Can I get you anything?" he asked.

"Water's good," she told him. She still felt fatally dehydrated from the night before, and just looking at Gabe had made all of the moisture evaporate from her throat.

"Sure thing. Kitchen's on the left," he told her. "Make yourself at home."

The kitchen was like the rest of the place—large, clean, devoid of the clutter and knickknacks that littered her own living space. It said a lot about Gabe, that he lived a neat, ordered existence. And she did not. Her life, ever since she'd been a child, was chaos—a wild ride—with brief detours into ordered and serious. They might have gotten married, but they weren't husband and wife. She took a seat at his table, wishing that it wasn't too dark to see into what was probably a beautiful backyard, judging by the house.

Gabe poured each of them a glass of water from the fridge dispenser and passed hers over while taking a seat next to her. "We need an annulment," he said, his voice firm.

"That goes without saying," she agreed. "I'm not familiar with divorce law in Nevada. What do we have to do?"

She could see the change in Gabe's demeanor as he launched into a speech about law. He looked at ease, and no longer volatile. "The first step is to file a complaint for annulment, which includes basic information about both of us, and the grounds for an annulment—intoxication should cover that. It won't be the best reason the court has seen, but that's what happened." His smile was lopsided and wry. "I can file it and get the papers ready by tomorrow.

"After you're served, you file an answer, the court will schedule a hearing within ninety days and a judge will schedule a hearing to determine whether an annulment is appropriate. It's not ideal, but at the hearing, we'll have to testify before a judge."

"Ninety days? Testify at a hearing?" Ellie's panic began to rise again. "That's a bit extreme, isn't it? There isn't an easier way?"

"We could have not gotten married," he said, with a grim smile. "But it's too late for that."

She didn't appreciate his attempt at humor. "God, this is the longest one-night stand in history."

He left the table and came back with a notepad and pen. "I can draw up the papers and have someone serve you with them on Monday. Where will I find you?"

Ellie knew that like every other workday, she would be spending most of the day and night at the office. "I'll be at work," she told him.

"Okay, where's that?" he asked, poised to write.

She started to tell him, but she could picture the rumors that would be started if someone saw her getting served with legal papers at the law office. Word would ultimately reach her father, and there's no way she could explain that she'd drunkenly married a stranger at a cheesy twenty-four-hour wedding chapel. "Can we meet somewhere else?"

"Yeah, sure." He seemed to think for a moment,

before writing down an address. "Why don't you stop by here sometime tomorrow evening?"

"Where is this?"

"It's a club."

"I work late," she told him.

"It's open late," he assured her.

Ellie raised her glass to her lips, and Gabe did the same. They watched each other over their glasses, letting the silence enfold them, just as they'd done before. And just this once, Ellie allowed herself to revel in the memories she'd made with him the night before. How Gabe had touched her, how they'd connected, and she could tell from the way his pupils dilated, darkening his eyes to a deep emerald, that he was also thinking about the same.

Gabe put down his glass and exhaled. "You know," he started. "No matter how it all turned out, I really did have one of the most fun nights of my life with you."

"It really was a lot of fun."

"I don't think I'll ever think of the High Roller in the same way again."

Ellie laughed. "I still can't believe we did that. We could have gotten arrested."

"That would have been pretty embarrassing, huh?"

"At least we probably would have skipped the cheesy Elvis wedding."

They laughed together. Such a simple moment between two people, but Ellie could feel the still present sexual tension between them, just as surely as she could feel the desire that caused her to clench her thighs together.

"Oh." Gabe stood, suddenly disrupting the moment. "I should give this back to you."

"What is it?"

He reached into a bowl that sat on his dark marble countertop. "Here," he said, extending his hand. She stood in front of him, and it took her a moment to see what he'd pinched between his thumb and forefinger. It was the elegant, delicate band she'd had on her finger when she'd woken up that morning. The overhead lights splintered off the diamonds that encircled it. It was stunning. But he was trying to give it to her.

"That isn't mine," she insisted.

"It is."

"It must have cost a fortune."

He shrugged. "Probably a small fortune," he said with a wink. "But you should have it. I mean it."

She wasn't going to keep the ring. Even though, judging by his house and lifestyle, Gabe had money, it wouldn't be right. But it didn't stop her from reaching out. She took the ring, but as she did, her fingers grazed his. Their eyes connected over the band. She couldn't have known who made the first move, but in just two seconds, the ring had bounced on the tiled floor, and their arms were around each other. And the ring forgotten, she went to him.

She wanted Gabe again. This time, she couldn't blame intoxication. It was all him, the way he moved, the way he laughed, the way he looked in his grungy

T-shirt and fitted jeans. Her lips crashed to his, their mouths parted, and his tongue found hers—*oh God, the way he kissed.*

Ellie pushed her hands underneath his T-shirt and scratched her fingernails along his rippled abs, then tracked them upward to his nipples. Her tickles sent a shudder through him and he chuckled into her mouth. He pulled his mouth away only long enough to reach his arm behind his head and pull his T-shirt off, treating her to the view of his upper body. He was all tanned skin, firm muscle, and soft golden hair that peppered his chest and stomach.

Their separation was short-lived, however, as he pulled her close again, kissing her so hard that she knew his lips might bruise hers. His fingers found the hem of her shirt and pulled it over her head, and before she knew it, her shorts had followed suit, and sat in a pile at her feet. Their kisses were frantic. Their hands frenzied as they traveled and became reacquainted with each other's bodies.

Ellie undid his jeans and pushed them over his hips. He lifted her onto the table. She reached for her purse that was hanging on her chair and pulled out the condom she'd hopefully put there before leaving her bedroom.

Gabe chuckled, taking it from her. "You're so helpful," he murmured against her lips.

"Always be prepared," she told him. "That's my motto."

"Good motto." All humor vacated his expression, and he took his place between her knees. She watched, riveted, as he lowered his pants and boxers. She watched as his cock sprung free, released from the tensile material, and he covered himself with the latex.

With his free hand, he grasped for the band of her panties, and she lifted her hips obediently so he could peel them away from her. He tossed the satin to the floor. Taking her ankle, he rested her foot on the tabletop, and then the other, so that her legs were spread and she was revealed to him. He grabbed her hips, aligning her with him, and pushed inside of her.

Ellie sighed with the sweet relief of him filling her, stretching her to his size. He stilled for a moment, and she was grateful for it—she needed to learn how to breathe again.

"Ah, Ellie," Gabe muttered, his voice thick and heavy with pleasure. "You feel fucking incredible. I didn't think I'd get another chance with you."

"Neither did I," Ellie concurred. "But if you don't move soon, I might explode."

"You got it," he promised, pulling back, extracting most of his length from her, and then filling her again, drawing a loud cry from between her lips.

Increasing his tempo and the force behind his powerful thrusts, he took her hard, furiously, and his hips slammed into her. He leaned over her, kissing her—his lips brushing against the sensitized skin of her jaw, throat, shoulders, setting her nerve endings ablaze. Gabe buried his face in the delicate crevice between her shoulder and neck, and Ellie inhaled deeply, pulling his scent—a heady mix of soap and sweat—deeply into her lungs. In an attempt to preserve it, keep him with her forever, she held her breath, until pleasure forced it from her lungs.

The slap of his flesh against hers and their bodies against the wall mingled with the sound of their heavy breaths and curses to make an erotic orchestra of sound that filled his kitchen and surrounded them.

The table was sturdy, but Ellie wasn't sure it would survive their impact as their still-filled water glasses fell to the tiled floor, sending water and splinters of glass everywhere. The mess barely registered to Ellie, however, as all she could focus on was Gabe's delicious assault.

Ellie tried her best to keep her feet on the table, but with the wild movements of his driving hips it was difficult, so instead, she locked her legs around his waist and pulled him in, pulled him deeper. She closed her eyes and felt him all around her, pressed against her. She was completely wrapped up, surrounded by him—the feel of his touch, his moans in her ear, his taste all combined to completely take her over.

Ellie felt the beginnings of her orgasm tremble low in her belly and in a desperate attempt to chase her own pleasure, she lifted her hips in time with his, and Gabe's own movements became faster, more erratic, as he cursed helplessly in her ear. The pleasurable, exhausting warmth took over and Ellie felt herself breach the point of no return, and she cried out. With just a couple more pumps, Gabe followed her over the edge with a coarse shout, his neck stretched, veins protruding, before he stilled and collapsed over her.

As Ellie caught her breath, Gabe pushed himself from her body. Ellie sat up and took in the broken glass on the floor and their clothing thrown about the kitchen.

Gabe tossed the condom and pulled on his pants and boxers. "Sorry about that," he told her, his shoulders rapidly rising and falling in an attempt to catch his breath.

"I wasn't complaining." Ellie stood on the floor.

"Watch the glass," he told her, grabbing a broom and dustpan from a tall cupboard.

She gingerly stepped around the table, collecting her clothing and dressing as Gabe cleaned up. "Why are you sorry?"

Gabe disposed of the last bit of glass. "I just lost control there." He shook his head and wiped his hands. "It seems to happen quite a bit around you."

Ellie paused before pulling on her shirt. She looked at Gabe, wavy hair tousled, shirtless, wearing his worn, low-slung jeans. She was just feeling the glow of her orgasm dissipate, but she wanted him again. "You bring it out in me, too."

Ellie exhaled, forcing all of the erotic thoughts from her psyche. She couldn't let a man, no matter how amazing Gabe was, sidetrack her image rehabilitation, her relationship with her father, or any of her goals. She'd known Gabe for less than twenty-four hours. And already she'd married him, and had been reduced to a needy, quivering mess around him. She took one final look at his shirtless form and grabbed her purse. "Uh," she stammered. "Listen, I'm glad we're on the same page with the annulment. But I need to leave. Thanks for the water," she said feebly. "And everything else."

He frowned. "You sure?" He took several steps and came to stand in front of her.

"Am I sure about what?"

"About leaving. Why don't you stay?"

She couldn't. She had to leave, get away from his influence, before she threw everything away for the man before her.

"Come on," he said, reaching for her hand. "You are my wife. We're still married, at least until we get before the courts."

Despite herself, Ellie smiled, and the spark of desire within her rekindled as he stroked the pulse point on her wrist with his thumb. And with one small action, several short words, Gabe had almost won.

Almost.

Ellie gripped her purse strap in her fist and took a step back. She wanted nothing more than to stay, but she couldn't. Gabe's power over her was dangerous, but she had to focus her attention on her goals, her future. And the sooner she put this incident behind her, the closer she'd be to everything she wanted.

"I have to go."

"I'll see you on Monday, then."

"Monday?" she asked.

His smile was crooked. "At the club," he told her. "I'll give you the annulment papers."

Ellie was dumbfounded by how she'd managed to forget her reasons for meeting him again. But she would have to keep her senses about her. There was no way she could let herself fall for his charms again. Everything was riding on it.

She hoped she was strong enough to resist him.

CHAPTER FIVE

IT MAY HAVE only been 8:15, but Ellie was already running late for work on Monday morning. Not a great start to her week. She ran a brush through her tangled hair and leaned close to her mirror, examining the tired dark circles under her eyes. Her complexion was dull—the result of a lack of sleep and dehydration, and she hurriedly applied some concealer and blush. With just enough time to pour some iced coffee into her travel mug, she was on the road before traffic hit gridlock time.

The quiet confines of her car, however, again let her mind drift to Gabe. She had to see him that night, and while she was glad to put their massive mistake—their marriage—behind her, she knew that if she saw him again, she probably wouldn't be able to stop herself from fucking him. Her track record showed that. She blew out a heavy breath and tried to stop thinking about him. She turned the corner toward Burnham & Associates. It was time to get her game face on, and get to work.

As she'd learned during her first weeks at Burnham & Associates, most of the junior attorneys worked long, tough hours. That was fine with her. She'd made it through law school; she knew how to function with little sleep, and coffee was her new best friend. This was the career she'd chosen. She would do it, and she would do it with a smile on her face.

Twenty minutes later, she pushed into her office and saw an email from her father, requesting her presence at a meeting in his office at 8:45 to meet her new mentor at the firm. It was the first time her father had summoned her for anything professionally. Ellie had to dismiss the voice in her head that told her that it was only because her father was one of the founders.

"You graduated at the top of your class," Ellie said aloud in her empty office, as a reminder to herself that there was a reason she'd been hired, beyond nepotism. "You're here because you're good at what you do, and you have a promising career ahead of you." Sure, she had secured a spot at a top firm because her father was a founding partner. But she'd still interviewed like anyone else. She'd studied hard and gotten the grades just like anyone else. "You deserve to be here," she told herself.

She took a deep breath after her pep talk, as she won today's daily fight against imposter syndrome. Some mornings, it worked; others, it didn't. And those mornings just made her work harder. But that didn't mean she didn't see the looks from the other associates, or hear their cutting words, that she owed her success to nepotism, or that she was a *daddy's girl*. They had no idea how far from the truth that was. Keeping her head down, and not getting involved with office gossip and jealousy, she would do her work. She had a lot to prove—to her father, to her coworkers and mostly to herself.

Gabe drank his coffee and rubbed his tired eyes. The past weekend had taken a lot from him—physically, emotionally, mentally. Sleep had eluded him. Every time he'd closed his eyes, he saw Ellie. He could still smell her in his kitchen, feel her, like she was still there.

He'd started the filing for their annulment, and hopefully when it was all settled, he could put it and her behind him. Not because he didn't want to see her, but she affected his focus. He was on the cusp of getting everything he wanted, everything he'd worked for, and he couldn't screw it up now.

It was his first day back after the Hong Kong trip, and looking over his agenda, Gabe saw the one-hundred-and-one things to do that day, and every day for the rest of the week, the month. That was fine. He'd been working sixty-hour weeks since he'd started at Burnham & Associates as a junior associate, just out of law school. And making partner wouldn't reduce his workload any. Research, filings, client meetings came with the territory, and he was ready to get back to it.

He tried to start in on his to-do list, in an attempt to make at least a small dent in it. But he couldn't seem to keep his mind on track. He drummed his restless fingers on his desk. And that didn't make the stack of files miraculously become any shorter. He looked at his computer monitor. The blank document he had open mocked him. It was barely past eight thirty, and already he was restless, bored and he wanted to get the hell out of his office. Maybe he should have taken a personal day, *but potential partners didn't take personal days.* He could have hit the gym, or the road on his motorcycle. Both things normally helped clear his mind. But it was nowhere close to quitting time, especially on his first day back. All he could think about was Ellie—*his wife*—who had quickly fled his house after he fucked her on his kitchen table.

"Focus, goddammit," he chastised himself in his empty office. He really had to get to work, or he wouldn't have a job to worry about.

He knew the meeting he was about to have with Charles Burnham would probably change his career. But he couldn't shake the flashes of Ellie that cruised unabated through his mind. His gut clenched in response and he blew out a harsh, frustrated breath. Why had she walked out on him? In a moment of weakness, he'd asked her to stay with him, and he knew it was for the best that she didn't—but tell that to his empty bed as he'd spent Saturday and Sunday night tossing sleeplessly.

It would be stupid to think that there had been something special between them. Hell, they'd had a one-night stand—well, a two-night stand—and he'd been so taken by her, he'd gotten drunk enough to suggest heading to the chapel.

An annulment was the only option; getting married after too much champagne was perhaps the stupidest thing he'd ever done, and he had to put it behind him quickly and quietly before Charles or any of his clients found out. The works were in motion, but it would have to wait—he checked his watch—it was time for his Monday briefing with Charles.

Tension formed a tight band across his forehead, and Gabe rubbed his temples, reached into his drawer and shook a couple of aspirins into his hand. He popped them into his mouth, swallowing them with a mouthful of hot, black coffee.

Gabe took the elevator up to Charles Burnham's office. As his father's partner, Charles had been a fixture in Gabe's life since he'd been a child. He'd become Gabe's professional mentor, and with Charles, he shared perhaps a closer relationship than he had with his own father.

Charles's assistant let him into the office. The older man was sitting behind his desk. He stood, and gestured him toward a sitting area on the other side of his large office. As Charles greeted him, Gabe again found himself distracted by thoughts of Ellie. He took a deep breath and blinked hard, again finding himself trying to banish her image from his mind. He had to focus on work. The work, and nothing else. This was it.

Since leaving law school in London and moving back to Las Vegas, he'd had a very clear career path—sure, it was one predetermined by his father and Charles Burnham—that had led him to where he was, and he knew that he would be the next partner at Burnham & Associates. Becoming partner was the smart thing to do—the responsible thing. He sighed. Part of him was sick of doing the right thing. He thought again of his time with Ellie. And how it was the most fucking fun he'd had in a long, long time.

"Gabe, how are you?" his mentor asked, walking to the wet bar in his opulent office, and even though it was well before lunch, he poured each of them a finger of scotch from a crystal decanter. He paused, midpour, looking at Gabe's face, studied him and frowned. "You look tired."

"I'm fine," Gabe insisted. Charles was a smart, observant man. It was as if he could see the debauchery of his weekend written on his face. But instead he moved on.

"I just wanted to see how you're settling in since returning from Hong Kong. You did fabulous work there. It must have been a nice change of scenery for you."

"It's not like I had a chance to see much of it," Gabe admitted. "I spent most of it in the suite working. Now I have to play catch-up on everything I missed here."

Charles smiled. "That would have been my response, too. How's the workload?"

"It's fine. Nothing I'm not used to."

"It's admirable what you accomplished while you

were away. Fantastic job on the merger," Charles told
him, moving on and concentrating on the scotch.
"You've made a lot of people very happy, and very
rich."

"Thank you, sir."

"It's spectacular how far you've come at such a
young age. You know after the partners vote, you'll
be the youngest partner in the history of the firm."

"Thank you, sir." At Burnham & Associates, the
path between being an associate and a partner was
long and intensive. And partners were long-serving,
not leaving many opportunities to join their ranks.
Charles's smile was large, and dimpled his cheeks.
Weirdly, it somehow reminded him of Ellie. God,
he had to get his head in the game. This was what
he'd worked toward his entire life. Why couldn't he
think about anything but the woman? He cleared his
parched throat and sipped on the scotch. "And I'm
grateful for the opportunity, so early in my career."
In his own ears, he could hear that his words weren't
sincere. They sounded hollow—foreign—coming
out of his mouth. As he thought of Ellie, lying below
him on his table, work was the furthest thing from
his mind.

"Gabe, in your short time here, you've brought in
some extremely valuable clients. That's made you
an asset to us, and I know that you are the future
of this firm."

Gabe did have many clients, and many of them
were rich and powerful, trusting Gabe with their
legal matters. But from the small way Charles's face

changed minutely—his narrowed eyes, the almost imperceptible downturn of his lips, the way his voice became clipped—Gabe knew that Charles was talking about the Brotherhood. Gabe represented each of their business and personal interests, and it was known that they were his friends, but what wasn't as known by Charles and his family, all staunchly conservative, was that Gabe was also part owner in the group's businesses. He'd kept that strictly under wraps, hidden from the general public, especially from his boss and family, and his other clients. He was pretty sure that none of them would appreciate the fact that the firm's newest partner was one of the owners of the city's most popular erotic venues.

"Of course," Charles continued, his indulgent smile returning. "The partners all have to vote, but unless you do anything to change my mind, I think you'll fit right in at the top."

"Yes, sir," Gabe said. He sipped his scotch, knowing that the past weekend would, no doubt, change Charles's mind.

"But I have to warn you, one of the other partners has put forward Ian Smith for the position."

Gabe frowned and leaned forward. "Is that right?" Ian was an asshole, a suck-up, a bootlicker, with a face that just begged to be punched. Gabe was damned if Ian Smith was going to deter any of his plans.

"I don't think you have to worry about him, though," Charles assured him. "It's basically your position."

Gabe had woken up that morning *knowing* that he would be the newest partner, the goal he'd worked for his entire career. He was a better lawyer, and was more well liked, than Ian, but he would prefer if the promotion was a sure thing. He didn't know what sorts of sneaky tricks and manipulation Ian had up his sleeve.

Charles moved on as if he hadn't just dropped a bomb on Gabe. "But the reason I wanted to meet with you this morning was to tell you about my daughter, who has just joined the firm."

That made Gabe start. He'd known Charles his entire life. How had the fact he had a daughter been hidden from him? "I didn't realize you had a daughter."

Charles looked sheepish. "She's illegitimate. The result of an irresponsible affair with an actress years ago. I wasn't involved with her upbringing, but I should have been." He shook his head. "The child was a mess. Always getting into trouble. I didn't approve of her lifestyle, while her mother applauded it—whatever kept her name in the headlines. And when my daughter ended up in some trouble, I helped her out and offered her a way to turn her life around. But I was careful to keep her under wraps."

Men like Charles Burnham were experts at portraying a clean, conservative image, while covering up the scandals and indiscretions of their buddies. Gabe figured he was much the same. He, himself, had several secrets he wouldn't want to get out.

Big secrets.

"Is that right?" he asked.

"I bailed her out, literally. But we made a deal—she had to clean up her act, and I would put her through law school and offer her a job."

"Great motivation to turn her life around," Gabe said.

"I think you'd be a good fit for her. For the mentorship program."

The Burnham & Associates mentorship program paired junior associates with those more senior, to show the new attorneys the way the firm worked. It had been a while since Gabe had been paired with anyone, and he wasn't especially sold on the idea. "It sounds like you want me to babysit your daughter and make sure she doesn't get into any trouble."

Charles's head tilted. "Huh. I never thought of that. But I suppose you might be right. At least meet her before you discount her. I was as surprised as anyone that she'd done a complete one-eighty turn-around. Despite her trouble, she's just like you. She's young, sharp and she just might impress you."

Gabe was skeptical. In his years at the firm, he'd met every type of clerk and newly minted lawyer—the lazy ones, the super-ambitious ones, the ass-kissers, the spoiled ones—and he wondered which category Charles's daughter would fall into. "Fine. I'll meet her. But I'm not promising anything."

"That's as good as any response I was expecting from you."

"I haven't made my career being nice, Charles."

"No, you made it by being a smart-ass," he said

with an indulgent, avuncular smile. He continued, "I believe Ellie will find herself on a similar career track as yours."

Gabe's head whipped upward at the mention of Ellie's name. *No, it can't be.*

"…If she performs as well as I believe she will, we expect her to make partner also. Maybe in the future you'll both be running Burnham & Associates—maybe it'll even be renamed Foster & Carrington, by then," he finished with a chuckle.

Carrington? His worst fears confirmed, Gabe blinked and finished his scotch in one swallow. An image of Ellie flashed again in his mind. Carrington. The lawyer, who was new in town. Just out of law school. The memory of her flushed his cheeks, the image of her full breasts, luscious curves making his breath catch. He shook his head. It couldn't have been Ellie. Not his Ellie. That would be too much of a coincidence. And Gabe didn't believe in coincidence.

Charles continued speaking, and Gabe tried to follow, but again part of his mind kept drifting back to Ellie.

He looked up and saw that Charles had his expectant eyes on him. *Shit.* "I'm sorry?" he asked, trying to recover, prove he was paying attention. His world had just imploded. He'd put a wedding band on the finger of his mentor's daughter.

"I was just telling you some more about Ellie."

"It's nice that you're reconnecting," Gabe said, not sure what he could add. Needing to straighten his legs, he stood. He could feel the scotch warm his blood, bypass his twisty stomach and go straight to his head. He felt just a little wobbly as he made his way across Charles's office and looked out the window to the desert and the mountains in the distance. He turned his head, and saw the woman on the other side of the glass wall of Charles's office. The fair brunette, who stood next to Rosa's desk, smiling broadly, was the woman who'd completely rocked him. The woman he barely remembered marrying. The woman he'd fucked on his kitchen table. It was his Ellie.

"And there she is!" Charles announced, turning and seeing her, as well.

Gabe's breath halted in his throat. He didn't need to look far to find his new bride. He'd drunkenly married his boss's daughter. He turned back to the window, unable to face the situation in front of him. He took deep, careful breaths in an attempt to steady himself. It didn't work. In only five seconds, his life had gone from just merely complicated to catastrophic. There was no way he'd find his way out of this. He was 100 percent royally fucked—personally, but even more professionally. There was no way Charles would make him partner, or even keep him at the firm, knowing what he'd done with the man's estranged daughter.

Gabe felt the walls close in on him as Ellie stood before him, locked in an embrace with Charles Burnham. When she turned away from her father, she finally looked up and saw him. He caught the brief falter of her smile, and her eyes widened momentarily, but then returned to normal, covering her apparent surprise, before her lips turned upward in a gracious smile.

She was beautiful, sexy and, even though he had intimate knowledge that she was anything but, she looked absolutely demure in her conservative black suit. He could still see the lush curves she attempted to conceal in the heavy material. She couldn't fool him. She took several steps toward him and extended her hand. He shook it. He had to restrain himself from pulling her to him and kissing her to make up for the time they'd lost when she'd left him on Saturday, but instead, he released her hand. "Mr. Foster. Nice to meet you," she said, not letting on that they'd met before.

"Call me Gabe," he corrected. "I hear we'll be working closely together." He was unable to remove any hint of innuendo, directed only at her, from his voice.

Charles explained to her what he'd just told Gabe—that he'd be working with her as her mentor. Her eyes widened again at the news—it was unexpected to her, as well—and even though Gabe knew it would be a bad idea to be her mentor, he was just so goddamn grateful to be in her presence again.

They exchanged pleasantries, but Gabe couldn't take his eyes off Ellie. He could tell that she was trying to make her escape. Gabe caught how expertly Ellie disengaged from the conversation as she took a step back. "It's been great meeting you, and I can't wait to start working under you." Gabe almost laughed out loud at her words, as unintended as he knew they were. He could sense her discomfort; it matched his own. "I should go. I've really got to get back to work, anyway. I've got lots to do today."

Charles beamed at her. "That's my girl. Nose to the grindstone. Maybe you are like your old man, after all."

Without responding, she nodded, turned quickly on her heel and all but ran from the room. Gabe watched the door she'd vacated, unable to take his eyes from it.

He put his glass on the table in front of him. "Thanks for the breakfast scotch, Charles. It's quite a substitute for coffee," he said. "And thanks for everything, but I should be going. I've got a lot of work to catch up on, as well."

Charles nodded. If he suspected there was anything going on between Gabe and Ellie, he didn't let on. "I'll let you know when the partners are planning to vote."

"Please do," Gabe said, shaking his boss's hand, before turning and all but sprinting from the room after Ellie.

For what was probably the tenth time, Ellie pushed the elevator button. "Come on, come on," she muttered, willing it to come. How was it taking so long? Her heart was still pounding in her chest, and her breath wheezed out of her lungs. She had almost choked on her tongue when she walked into her father's office and saw Gabe standing there.

She was currently living in her nightmare. Why did she think that having a one-night stand would be a fun little distraction before she could get on with turning her life around? It was one of the stupidest things she'd ever done. But as she considered Gabe, and the time she'd spent with him, nothing about how Gabe had made her feel was stupid.

She thought she'd covered her reaction to Gabe well enough. Her father didn't seem to have any idea that she'd met Gabe previously. *That's good.* Having a relationship with her father was new to both of them. But despite the rough start they'd had, his absence and the trouble she'd caused as a teenager, she knew they could be close, if they both tried. Ellie couldn't screw it up, though. Even though she was a grown adult—with a job, her own bills—she couldn't help but crave his approval.

But tell that to the lust that curled up from her core at just being in the same room as Gabe. The passion she'd felt two days before had been reignited. She'd run away from his house on Saturday, not wanting to deal with the reality of wanting him, but little did she know that fate had other plans, and played a cruel hand by putting him in front of her as her father's associate—her new mentor.

Ellie hit the elevator call button again. "Goddammit, come on." She needed to get off that floor, and get back to the safe confines of her small office. Away from Gabe, until the time came for them to actually work together.

Someone joined her in waiting. "This one is always slow," he said, his voice low and so familiar that it was imprinted on her brain. She turned her head and saw that it was Gabe.

He said nothing for a while, but as they watched the light indicating the approaching elevator, he cleared his throat.

"I'm surprised to see you here."

Her short, curt laugh was humorless. "Likewise."

"I'm chalking it up to coincidence. Am I correct in doing so?" He still didn't look at her. "Or did you plan this?" He paused and looked at her, his eyebrows pinched together skeptically. "Or did someone put you up to it?"

She turned her head to look at him, incredulous that he would accuse her of—what, exactly? "What are you talking about? Who could have put me up to it?"

"Never mind. Forget I said anything."

"What is taking this elevator so long?" she asked, just wanting to hide back in her small office on the bottom floor.

"It's an older building. And this elevator is slower than the rest."

The bell chimed, finally announcing the elevator's arrival. The doors parted and they both stepped inside. She let them close before she turned to face him. "I assure you, Gabe, this is a totally unfortunate coincidence. How could I have ever planned this? Why would I? What would be the benefit?"

He pushed the emergency button, halting the elevator's course downward. "I don't know why you might have. Remember, I don't know you at all. But if you're playing some kind of game here, or working with someone else, you can forget about it. I've worked too goddamn hard to get where I am. I need to know that I can count on your discretion. No one can know what happened between us—that we got married."

"You don't have to worry, Gabe. I won't say anything. This looks just as badly on me."

"Aw fuck," he murmured. "I just need to make sure I lock it down, and get the votes before word gets out that we'll be in court. But listen to me. It won't get out. I'm used to keeping things under wraps. This is no different."

Ellie wasn't sure why, but because of the way he looked at her, spoke to her, she believed him. She nodded.

"Sounds good to me."

Ellie reached out and pushed the emergency button again, restarting the elevator. It jolted to life, but stuttered to a halt, as the lights dimmed.

Flattening her palms against the wall, she looked to Gabe. "What just happened?"

"Shit," Gabe muttered. "This happens sometimes. It's stuck."

"Stuck?" Ellie tried to calm the hysteria that edged her voice. "I can't be stuck in an elevator."

"It's okay," he said, putting a hand on her arm, attempting to placate her. "It's fine," he told her in a calming tone. She pushed the emergency call button, but Gabe shook his head. "The button doesn't work. It hasn't for years."

Ellie tried to get her breath, but the panic won out, and she leaned against the wall to stop the small box from spinning around her. "We're going to die in here."

He laughed, his deep chuckle both soothing and irritating. "We aren't going to die in here. Claustrophobic?"

She shook her head. "Just afraid of plummeting to my death in a small, metal box. Or, best-case scenario, getting chopped in half during a rescue."

"I think we're a way off from either of those outcomes." He laughed again.

"Did you plan this?" she asked, mimicking his earlier words.

"I guarantee I did not," he insisted before laughing again.

"This isn't funny," she repeated, slapping him on the chest.

"It's a little funny."

She looked around. "Okay, we're stuck, and the call button doesn't work. How do we get out of here?" Looking up, she saw the ceiling tiles, and briefly considered climbing onto the top of the elevator and scaling the wall to safety.

"We call the front desk. They'll get the service people in." Gabe took out his cell phone. His frown wasn't encouraging. "Dammit. No signal." He shrugged. "We'll just have to chill out here until they realize we're in here."

"Are you kidding?"

"Afraid not. But it won't take long. There are only

two other elevators. They'll soon realize this one is out of commission."

"Okay, fine. What do we do in the meantime?"

Gabe faced her, and a moment passed between them, where a flicker of heat ignited. "I'm sure we can find something to pass the time," he said, his voice smooth as silk. When she looked up at him, his eyes connected with hers. He was just as sexy as he'd been the night she'd met him when he'd taken her on the Ferris wheel, and the night after that when they'd had sex in his kitchen. Before Ellie could stop herself, she reached out and grabbed his tie, pulling him to her, kissing him. He seemed surprised at first, but then his arms wrapped around her waist. The kiss was hot, all-encompassing, and when she pushed her hips against him, she could feel his rock-hard length against her stomach. He groaned and pressed her against the wall of the elevator, and his hands landed on her thighs, just above her knees. He slid them underneath the material of her dark skirt and cupped her ass in his large, strong hands, and squeezed. But it was the movement of the elevator finally kicking in that separated them, reminding them of where exactly they were.

They pushed apart, and Ellie fought to catch her breath.

"Jesus," she heard him whisper, as he brushed back his wavy, golden hair from his forehead.

She straightened her skirt and clenched her shaking hands into fists in an effort to regain control, just as the doors parted on his floor. He stepped out, but she stopped him from walking away. "Just so we're clear, I'm just as much at risk here as you are. And I'm not playing any game. This is my life, and I'm not going to fuck up my career, or any relationship I could have with my father, for anything. So, let's just forget anything ever happened between us, okay?"

He looked her up and down. His body was tense. "Fine by me." But then his expression changed. "I'll still see you tonight?"

She held the door open with her hand and nodded. "Yeah, I'll meet you at the address you gave me. I don't think I'll get out of here until later. Can I meet you at nine?"

"I'll be there."

She smiled. "Thanks." She stepped past him, out of the elevator, and into the hallway.

"Where are you going?"

She walked away from him. "I'm taking the stairs the rest of the way down."

CHAPTER SIX

GABE TAPPED HIS fingers repeatedly on the manila envelope. He looked over the balcony from his spot at the Brotherhood's table at Di Terrestres, watching for Ellie. He couldn't sit still, and a restless energy made him fidget in his seat. He wasn't nervous, but he wasn't completely sure why he couldn't sit still. Maybe it was leftover sexual tension from their kiss earlier. Maybe it was because knowing that she was his boss's daughter, and he her new mentor, meant that he couldn't touch her again.

He checked his watch again—it was a little past nine. She was late, and as his friends started arriving, and taking seats next to him at the table, he wished that he'd asked her to meet him anywhere else.

Alex got there first, holding the hand of his fiancée, Maria. Gabe stood to greet Maria with a light kiss on her cheek. "So, where's your old lady?" Alex asked Gabe, as he held out a chair for Maria.

Gabe rolled his eyes, and flipped Alex his middle finger.

"Dude, do me a favor and shut the fuck up."

In the next several minutes, the table filled. In the past couple of years, the Brotherhood had to add several chairs to their private table that sat above the club, as three members of their group—Brett, Rafael and Alex—had settled down with the women they love. It had been unexpected, but his friends were happy, and the women a welcome addition.

"I can't believe you, of all people, had a quickie Vegas wedding," Rebecca said, settling into her seat, as Brett sat beside her.

"Yeah, I don't think anyone would have put money on you being the next to get married," Jessica Morgan, the mayor of Las Vegas and Rafael's fiancée, said with a hearty laugh. "Especially in a chapel on the Strip at 4:00 a.m."

"Yeah, it's so unlike you," Maria was next to comment.

Gabe frowned. That was his reputation in the group. He was the reserved one, and although they would never say the word, the *uptight* one. He looked over at the happy couples seated around him at the table. Brett had fallen head over heels for his former rival, and had tried to take over her company. Now they were happily married. Rafael and Jessica had both run competing campaigns to be mayor of Las Vegas. They'd survived a high-pressure election and sex tape scandal, and somehow had defied the odds stacked against them, and were living together. Alex had fallen for Rafael's younger sister Maria, and it had almost destroyed their friendship, and the group. Despite all of the trials, scandals and hard times, all of his male friends had fallen deeply, madly, irrevocably in love, and Gabe wondered if there was something he was missing.

He and Alana, his closest friend in the group, were the only single members of the Brotherhood.

"Just you and me left, eh?" she said.

"Yeah." He eyed the annulment papers in front of him, not sure what else to say. He wasn't *technically* single. He'd gotten married but he'd missed all the steps that normally preceded it—the first date, getting to know each other, living together. He ran his thumb over the envelope that contained the annulment papers, and the rest of the group fell away into his periphery as he thought of seeing Ellie again. When he looked up, he saw that even though the rest of the group had begun talking among themselves, Alana was watching him.

"What's that?" she asked, pointing to the envelope on the table.

"Annulment papers," he explained, blowing out a heavy breath. "Ellie's meeting me here and we're going to begin proceedings to sign our ill-conceived marriage into oblivion."

"You had to bring her here?" Brett asked. "You couldn't do that in your office or anywhere else?"

Gabe shook his head. "Too risky. It's a small office. We couldn't risk serving her with papers there, and someone seeing it. Charles can't see her there, or catch us doing the paperwork. He would have a lot of questions. And I've seen the man asking questions. He's relentless." He explained that he and Ellie had agreed that it would be best if Charles never found out about their indiscretion.

"Whoa, whoa, whoa," Alana interrupted. "Why are you so concerned about Charles seeing you together?"

Gabe blinked, realizing that he'd revealed far more than he'd meant to. "Turns out Ellie is Burnham's daughter."

Stunned silence met him, and Gabe blew out a breath. He'd been hoping to avoid the topic altogether. But again, he'd been sloppy. Seemed screwing up was his specialty lately.

"You drunkenly married your boss's daughter?" Rafael asked.

"Apparently so."

"Explains why you'd bring those here, and not around Burnham." Alana nodded in agreement. "Yeah, there's no chance he'd be seen anywhere near here," she said, rolling her eyes.

Gabe huffed out a laugh, thinking about his very conservative boss, who had no idea that his youngest partner had a stake in an erotic club. Charles Burnham had even formed a group who'd lobbied the city to shut down Di Terrestres, citing propriety laws. Gabe knew that if the news of his marriage got out, he could kiss partnership, and probably even his job, goodbye. "Plus, I technically need a third party to serve her with the papers," he said, taking Alana's wineglass from her hand, tilting it in her direction, and drinking from it himself.

"What, you want me to do it?"

"Yeah, why not?"

She took her glass back. "There are lots of third parties here tonight."

"Ah, Lana, but you're my favorite one."

Alana rolled her eyes. "Fine," she said, snatching the envelope from him. "I'll do it. Don't say I never do anything for you."

"You're getting an annulment, eh? Not going to stick it out? What about the sanctity of marriage?" Brett chided him with a laugh, eliciting the same from the rest of the group.

Gabe chose not to answer. Unlike his friends, he'd always kept himself clear of scandal, and being the center of attention was not something he enjoyed. When he looked down at the floor again, his breath stopped. He saw Ellie in the crowd; his eyes were drawn to her. "She's here," he whispered to Alana, hoping to not raise the attention of his other friends.

No such luck.

"Whoa, is that her?" Maria asked, following his gaze to the woman standing near the bar. "She's gorgeous."

"Yeah," he said, without paying much attention to the reactions of his friends. He couldn't take his eyes off her. He'd hoped that the night could just be business, starting their annulment proceedings. But looking at her, he didn't think so. He'd been rigid and tense since that kiss in the elevator. As he watched her from above, his body betrayed every command given by his brain. He had to keep his distance from her. Not do anything stupid. He had to think about becoming partner. Not his dick, and everything he wanted to do with her. Gabe wasn't sure how he'd be able to do that, being assigned as her mentor.

"Invite her up," Alex suggested.

Gabe shook his head. "I don't think so."

"Come on, we'll be nice," Jessica insisted with a grin.

"Yeah, I'm sure you will be. Now if you'll excuse me…" He trailed off, drained his glass and stood. "Come on, Lana. Let's get this over with." He looked at the rest of his friends. "I'll see you guys later."

"Oh boy," Ellie muttered to herself, as she looked around the main floor of Di Terrestres, the club where Gabe had asked her to meet him. She'd heard of the place, and a quick Google search told her it was exclusive, expensive and—she took a look around the room, where people were drinking, laughing and touching each other intimately –*definitely sexy*. Why Gabe had insisted she meet him there was beyond her. What would he have had to gain? What was he up to? What sort of game could he be playing with her?

Both she and Gabe knew the importance of signing the annulment papers and putting their drunken marriage behind them. Maybe he wanted to sign the papers—she looked around again at the amorous patrons—but not before they had another night together. She could certainly warm up to the idea. If that kiss in the elevator was any indication of the passion that still simmered between them… "Oh boy," she whispered again, her throat drying and her stomach fluttering. She definitely needed a drink.

Dodging interested looks from both men and women, she made her way to the bar. A little liquid fortification was needed before she faced Gabe Foster again. Just five years ago, she would have felt completely at home in a place like this. But that was the old Ellie. Since bumping into Gabe on Friday night, nothing she'd done was indicative of her change, and the great strides she'd made. She'd grown up, put her wild ways behind her. But one night with Gabe was all it took to turn it around. It seemed that no matter how hard she tried to grow up, she'd reverted to her old ways.

Nudging her way around a small group of men who all looked at her with interest, she ignored them and took a seat at the bar. The bartenders were busy, but the cute one caught her eye. "Be with you in a second, doll," he told her with a wink, his hands busy making cocktails.

When she felt someone come up behind her, her spine stiffened instinctively, knowing who she would find when she turned around. "Can I get you a drink?" he asked.

She turned her head to look at Gabe. "They're a little busy at the moment. I'm still waiting my turn."

"Don't worry about it," he assured her, raising his hand and getting the same bartender's attention. "What are you drinking?"

She hadn't even thought about what to order. "What do you recommend?"

"Based on our history, can I suggest champagne?"

"You think that's smart?" The last thing she needed was to end up drunk on champagne while they should be keeping their wits about them.

"Nope. But I'll try to control myself if you do," he said with a chuckle. "Phillip," he called to the bartender. "A bottle of Dom."

"Yes, sir. Coming right up," he said, pouring three cocktails from a shaker and placing them in front of waiting patrons, and then immediately moving to get their champagne. He retrieved the bottle and two stemmed glasses and handed them all to Gabe.

Ellie could barely pull her gaze away from Gabe when she heard a throat clearing next to her. She turned and saw a stunning blonde woman.

"Ellie Carrington?" she asked.

"Yeah."

"Here you go," she said, passing her an envelope. "Happy annulment," she said cheerfully, before casting a more serious look at Gabe and walking away.

"Friend of yours?" she asked Gabe. He nodded.

"Are these what I think they are?"

He nodded again. "A third party serving the complaint is procedure."

She nodded, too. "Makes sense." All of the sparks that had previously snapped between them just minutes ago had sizzled. She understood what this was—not a chance for a second night together, but business. On his turf. "Makes sense." Part of her was disappointed. She'd been looking forward to seeing him again, outside a work setting. Another part of her

was embarrassed; she should have known that Gabe
would be eager to get the annulment underway. He
wasn't thinking about sex. Plastering a stiff smile on
her face, and ignoring every hormone that screamed
at her to rip her clothes off and jump him, she knew
what was the most important thing—signing the annulment papers and putting this whole embarrassing
episode behind her. "Let's do this."

"Let's get a table. We can talk," he suggested,
barely looking at her.

Gabe, with his long fingers on one hand wrapped
around the neck of the champagne bottle, settled
those of his other hand on her lower back, guiding
her toward a bank of tables on the other side of the
room. His touch, both light and commanding, was
filled with so much promise that she almost came
from the unspent sexual tension since the elevator
incident earlier that afternoon.

"Quite a table," she said, as they slid into the
plush leather semicircle booth. She looked around
at the other booths, filled with people who kissed and
touched. A spell of erotica filled the air and blan-
keted everyone in the room. This place was brazen,
carnal, and Ellie was intrigued as to what she was
doing there. There were literally hundreds of places
where they could have met. With a third party serving her the papers, as per protocol, he didn't have
to be present at all. But still he brought her to what
she'd learned was an erotic club. What was his goal?
She couldn't figure him out. Like hot and cold, Gabe
now looked at her with the same fiery desire he had

earlier, and she wondered if he was also warring with his body to resist her.

Reminiscent of the last time they'd shared a booth, he slid in next to her. Their thighs touched, and she breathed through desire that clenched her chest.

"You must have connections here."

He chuckled, and she watched his hands as he opened the bottle of champagne. His capable hands withdrew the cork with a small, careful pop. "Yeah, you could say that, I guess."

Her eyes narrowed. "What's that supposed to mean?"

Gabe shook his head. "Why don't we get down to business?" he asked, pointing to the envelope in her hands, without answering her question. She opened the envelope and looked over the papers as he spoke. "I've filed a standard annulment here. We were both intoxicated, so we could both argue diminished capacity. We both leave the marriage with what we had coming into it," he explained. "The sooner you answer the complaint, hopefully the sooner we can have our day in court."

"Sounds good to me."

He reached into his breast pocket. "And I believe this is yours," he said, putting the platinum and diamond band on the table. The one he'd tried to give to her on Saturday.

"Gabe, I told you. I can't keep your ring," she said.

"It's yours," he told her. "I don't have any use for it. I mean until my next drunken wedding, I guess. But then I can always get another ring." He cracked a small smile. "Seriously, keep it. It'll be a great reminder of a weekend we'll never forget."

"If only either of us could remember." She laughed. She examined the delicate band and the small, flawless diamonds that encircled it. "Thanks. It's really pretty."

"I don't remember picking them out."

"You insisted we hit the Tiffany & Co. at Caesars Palace."

"So said my credit card statement. I used my account activity to piece together what happened that evening. We bought the rings right before we got a cab to the chapel, where I only paid for the best wedding ceremony two drunk people could want at $24.95."

"A lot of that does sound familiar," she affirmed. "Let me at least pay you for some of the night—the rings, the champagne, the suite."

"Don't worry about it." He laughed. "I still can't believe we got married. Why would they ever let people that drunk sign any sort of legal papers?" He sobered, and she felt him shift away from her. "It's so strange how fate threw us together this way. You're Burnham's daughter. And he wants me to mentor you."

Dismissing any confusion she'd felt about what Gabe expected from their night, Ellie pushed down any desire she was feeling. Gabe had just laid out their professional relationship, not leaving any room for sex. Even though Ellie had tried to forget their professional ties, Gabe had put it on the table. Knowing where they stood, Ellie was relieved, but also disappointed. Part of her had wanted another night with Gabe, but it was for the best. She sipped her champagne and smiled. "It's such a crazy coincidence. I didn't know the world worked that way. But you should have seen your face today in my dad's office."

"You were no less shocked, honey," Gabe told her.

"Really? I thought I had a pretty decent poker face."

He tilted his head, and made a show of appraising her. "You were pretty good," he conceded. "But I saw the flash of recognition in your eyes," he said, his voice dropping in volume. She had to lean in to hear him over the music and the din of the club. "I saw the small, surprised O you made with those lips," he continued, brushing her bottom lip with his thumb. He sat back quickly, changing his demeanor. "But I don't think we need to worry. Charles didn't suspect a thing."

"Thank God." She laughed again. "The less he knows about this the better."

"I'll have you know that your father loves me. I'd be an excellent son-in-law."

Ellie scoffed, having fun bantering with him. "Sure, he loves you. You didn't spend the majority of your teen years publicly embarrassing him."

Gabe sat back and watched her, and she knew that she had revealed too much. "Sounds like there's a story there."

She blew out a heavy breath at the memories that flooded her. "Is there ever."

"Tell me."

"No," she said, shaking her head. "It's too embarrassing."

"Come on, Ellie, we've already shared so much. At least let me have one embarrassing story before we get annulled."

She looked at Gabe, and took a drink from her glass. The champagne reminded her of drinking with Gabe on Friday. "Okay," she said. "When I tell you this, you have to promise you won't judge me based on who I was as a teenager."

"I promise." He crossed his heart with a solemn, but joking, look on his face.

"Picture the most self-absorbed, obnoxious underage party girl who has ever gotten into the hottest LA clubs, and at least twice as many celebrity gossip blogs."

His eyes widened. "Done."

"Multiply all of that by at least one hundred, and you would have me. Or who I was." She took a deep breath. "My mom is an actress."

"Oh really?"

"Yeah, she was a serious D-lister. She was in a few horror movies, and her star was set to rise—until she met Charles and had me after what I've learned was a very brief affair. So instead of being a success—which she's sure she would have been—her star burned out. And she's never let me forget that it was my fault."

Gabe dropped his hand on her thigh. She could feel the heat from his touch reignite the flames of want that licked at her from the inside. "You know that's not true," he told her.

"I know that—now. I was raised in Hollywood, with all of those child stars. But much to my mom's disappointment, I was never talented or charismatic enough to be an actor or singer—where my talents lay was in having a good time. I was underage, but people still kept letting me into clubs. Partying basically became my job." He started to rub her thigh, making small circles with his fingertips. His touch did something to her. She tried to breathe through the sensation so she could keep talking, instead of moaning.

"When we met on Friday, I was just stoked that you didn't recognize me. But I was right up there with the likes of the Hiltons. People knew me, and it wasn't good."

"I never really followed any celebrity news," he told her. "Although I would have definitely remembered you. So you liked to party. That isn't so bad. What kid doesn't?"

"*Partying* doesn't really cut it. There was the wild partying, the paparazzi obsession, the upskirt photos, more partying, the drunk driving arrest—which was the stupidest thing I've ever done—rehab, repentance, boredom. More partying, the shoplifting charge, another arrest, mugshot, more partying and rehab again." She regarded the champagne flute in her hand. "I guess it didn't really stick. Meanwhile,

dear old Mom stuck by me—in nightclubs and court-
room appearances, posing for photographers, thrilled
that her pictures were finally front page–center
again. There's no such thing as bad publicity, right?"

His hand stilled, but he didn't remove it from her
thigh. She wondered if she had driven him away.
Turned him off by telling him how messed up she
actually was. "That's quite a résumé. What happened
then?"

"My dad bailed me out." She shrugged. "He used
to send checks every month, and presents for my
birthday and Christmas, but that's all I ever heard
from him. I hadn't seen him in years. But he convinced me to smarten up, and he gave me the chance
to turn my life around. He offered to pay for my
college and law school, if I got in, as long as I kept
my grades up. I knew it was my only chance to get
away from Hollywood's—and my mother's—influence. And I did well, so he offered me a position at
the firm. It gave me the opportunity to be close to
one of my parents, at least. Maybe I can prove to him
that I'm not the same teenage screwup I always was."

"I think he knows that, otherwise he wouldn't
have hired you."

Ellie wasn't so sure, but she knew that she didn't
want to talk about her father anymore. "So, what
about you?"

"What about me?"

"Any stories of embarrassing teenage indiscretions you want to share?"

He laughed. "No."

"Come on, your stories can't be any worse than mine."

"That's just the thing—I don't have any. I was telling you the truth when I told you that on Friday."

"Really?"

"Yeah, I'm pretty boring. I've always just studied, worked, followed the rules, kept to myself. My parents were strict. Like your father, very conservative, formal, cold. That's how I grew up. I didn't have a lot of leeway for wild times."

Ellie watched Gabe for a moment. "I find that hard to believe. You might look reserved, but there's some real passion bubbling beneath your surface." She leaned in, pressing her breasts against him. His eyes drifted downward, and she shifted in her seat a little to alleviate the pressure of need, but it just made her nipples bead as they brushed against the inside of her bra as she moved. "I know," she whispered. "because I've seen it. You can let loose when you want to."

"I do know how to cut loose. But with the exception of last weekend, I do so in a controlled environment."

"You like control."

He nodded.

"And we aren't just talking about sex, are we?"

"No," he said, with a brief shake of his head.

A silence fell over them and Ellie looked around the club. She could see the things going on around them. Among the other patrons, inhibitions were low, and the soft, golden lighting, the music, the champagne all had an effect on Ellie. She didn't care that sex with Gabe was inappropriate because of their working relationship. "Interesting place you asked me to meet."

"You've never been here before?"

"No. What is this place? It's not a normal club."

"No, it isn't."

She crossed her legs, and the tight fabric of her dress rode up and revealed some of her thigh. She caught the downward shift of his eyes, checking out her legs. When he looked up, he saw that she was watching him, but he wasn't embarrassed at being caught. He smiled. It seemed to encourage him.

"You know," he started. "If I was a smart man, I would stand up, call you a car, say good-night, and go home and jerk off in my shower." He paused. "This isn't a good idea for a lot of reasons. Because of work, because of who your father is, because of what he means to my career." He pushed his fingertips through her hair, brushing it behind her shoulder. He smoothed two of his fingertips down the line of her jaw and down her throat.

Ellie closed her eyes and swallowed hard, luxuriating in his touch, as he drew his fingers across her shoulders. "Why don't you go then?"

Gabe paused, and Ellie hoped against hope that he wouldn't follow through. But instead, he reached for his champagne flute and drained it. "Because I'm not a smart man," he said, before moving in and laying his lips over hers. She parted hers immediately and snaked her tongue out to trace his. She could feel his shudder, hear his moan, as his mouth covered hers.

In the booth, she kissed him like her life depended on it, as his fingers smoothed over and gripped her thighs.

Ellie was certain that Gabe could feel the shiver that traveled through her body at his touch. With the fire that just his fingertips lit within her, the desire he inspired, she closed her eyes and remembered the other talents the man possessed.

The annulment papers forgotten, he leaned closer, and put his lips to her ear. She heard him inhale, felt his intake of breath. She could smell his cologne. It was deep, rich, masculine, and immediately she was transported back to memories of the weekend before, flashes of skin, hard, lean muscles, lips, tongues, hands ran through her mind. "What do *you* do here?" she asked. His fingers crawled up her thigh. She had to bite back the sigh that formed in her throat. Gabe's touch was more potent than anything she'd ever felt.

Using his fingernail, he lightly grazed her inner thigh, and she unconsciously uncrossed and parted her legs to grant him easy access. "Depends on how adventurous I'm feeling," he told her. "There are a few options," he said with his breath brushing her cheek. "How adventurous do you want to be?"

Gabe had tried to give her the impression that he was boring, but she knew that was a lie. There was nothing cold or reserved about the man next to her, the one whose fingers elicited such an intense reaction from her.

Ellie drew her lip between her teeth. She saw Gabe's gaze drop to her mouth. It had been a long time since she'd done anything close to what could be characterized as *adventurous. Until the night she'd spent with Gabe, that is.* The man brought out the wild in her, that's for sure. As she looked into Gabe's emerald green eyes—they held such promise, and such mischief—all she wanted was to indulge her long-buried, not-so-forgotten uninhibited side again.

"Ellie?" he asked brushing her lower lip with the pad of his thumb. She closed her teeth, and gave the flesh a playful nibble. He laughed. "What do you say?"

"Show me adventurous," she whispered.

CHAPTER SEVEN

GABE COULD HEAR his heart pounding in his chest. He'd meant what he'd said to her. None of this was smart—inviting her to Di Terrestres, ordering champagne, touching her leg, kissing her again—he was in too far, way over his head. He was fucked, he decided as he led her across the floor of the club.

"This is the main floor," he said, through a fist-sized lump in his throat, gesturing to the large room they were in. He tried to keep his voice steady as he gave her a tour like one he would give a regular guest. But Ellie wasn't a regular guest.

"This is generally where the evening begins. Our guests come here, have a few drinks, loosen up. There's also entertainment—stage shows, erotic demos, all sorts of things." The crowd had certainly grown more amorous as the evening had worn on. They touched, caressed, stroked. Some were even in the beginning stages of being undressed.

"It looks like things are getting a little wild in here."

"It happens."

"I'll bet it does."

They crossed the floor, until they stopped at the host's stand in front of a large staircase. A set of stairs went up to the private rooms, and Gabe wouldn't have minded taking Ellie up there, but she'd asked for adventurous.

Andre, the host on duty, greeted them. "Mr. Foster. How can I help you tonight?"

"I believe we're going to head downstairs, Andre," Gabe told him. "Is that right, Ellie?"

"What's down there?" she asked almost cautiously.

"We have some rooms and suites upstairs," he told her. "Where we can be alone. But downstairs are some exhibition and demo rooms if you're feeling a little bolder."

"Define *bold*."

Gabe smiled at her interest. "We cater to polyamorous groups, BDSM enthusiasts, fetishists, exhibitionists and voyeurs. Anything an adult could want in a safe, consensual environment can be found within this building. Up or down? It's your call."

Ellie didn't say anything. The red lights that led downstairs cast a rosy glow on her fair skin. Gabe knew how disorienting Di Terrestres could be on a person's first visit, but he wanted her answer. She looked around them. He wanted her attention. And he got it when he turned on her and pushed her against the wall. He pushed his fingers underneath her skirt and cupped her sweet heat, satisfied when he felt how wet her panties were as he stroked her. Ellie spread her legs, opening herself up to him, while still standing. "Make a decision," he commanded, moving her panties to the side. He easily slid a finger inside of her, before withdrawing and plunging inside again. She moaned. "Gabe, everyone—"

"They don't matter. Tell me what you want."

"I want you to keep touching me."

"And I will." He took her hand, and led her downstairs.

Gabe watched Ellie as his eyes adjusted to the large, darkened room. The lights were always kept low downstairs, with strategically placed wall sconces that mimicked candlelight.

"What the...?" Ellie whispered.

"This is our playroom," Gabe offered. "People can meet up and get down however they like."

"Like what?"

His voice turned serious, as it did whenever he discussed the club's features and offerings. "As long as everyone is safe and consenting, the possibilities are endless," he finished with a wink.

Ellie let go of his hand, walked away from him and drifted toward a scene where a woman, who Gabe recognized as one of the city's most powerful CEOs, was on all fours on a cushioned platform in the center of a circle of men. He came up behind Ellie as she watched for a while. He put his hands on her shoulders, sliding them down her smooth arms, and she leaned against him.

Soon she moved away, and he knew that as it was

her first time in the playroom, she was trying to see everything. They walked to another scene across the room, where eight people cavorted in a small orgy. One woman held out her hand to Ellie; he could see the interest in her smile as she approached. The woman kissed her, and Gabe watched with growing interest as Ellie kissed her back. Gabe wanted Ellie to himself, but if he had to share her with this woman, then hell, that was a sacrifice he would gladly make. But Ellie backed away from the woman. "Thanks for the invitation," Gabe heard her say. "But I should go."

"Come back anytime, and bring the guy," the woman replied, blowing kisses at them both. They looked around, and watched a few scenes. Gabe was already rock hard, and felt as tightly wound as a spring. He enjoyed showing Ellie what Di Terrestres had to offer, but if he didn't have her soon, he might burst.

"What's behind that door?" she asked, pointing to a heavy wooden door.

"The dungeon," he responded.

She raised an eyebrow in question, but said nothing.

"It's not really my scene, but it's where the BDSM enthusiasts hang out. Do you want to see?"

She nodded.

Gabe took her hand, and pulled open the door. It was a typical night. A man was shackled to an X-shaped St. Andrew's cross, as a woman struck him with a wooden cane. Against another wall, a woman was bent over, and a man paddled, then soothed her reddened ass. It wasn't his thing, but the dungeon was one of their most popular features, and who was he to put down another person's kink?

"Wow," Ellie said in a whisper.

"This is what Di Terrestres is all about," he told her, as they ended up in the main room. "People can come here, and enjoy whatever gets them off." He walked her to a leather chaise.

"And what gets you off, Gabe?"

Ellie knew when she asked the question that there was no way she was leaving Di Terrestres without having Gabe again. "I think you like control."

He took her hand, and laid it on his dick. She squeezed him and she felt the vibration of his body run through him. "Turn around," he told her, his voice low. She didn't move for several beats, not used to being told what to do. But she decided that she should let Gabe boss her around for a while. She dropped her purse to the floor, and did as he'd instructed her. "Bend over and grab the back of the couch."

Maybe she wasn't comfortable with him taking complete control. "Gabe, wait," she said.

That got his attention, and he righted and took a step back. "You okay?"

"Yeah, I guess I'm not used to being such a passive participant."

"You won't be passive. But if you don't want to do this, we can just leave, and go our separate ways, and only connect at work."

"I don't want to go anywhere."

"Are you sure? Do you want to be here?"

"I do."

"And you're okay?"

"Yes," she vowed.

He put his lips to her ear. His breath tickled her. "Then bend over, grab the fucking couch and don't let go."

She would have done literally anything Gabe said at that moment. So she did what he told her. She bent at the waist, and gripped the leather couch. The movement pushed her ass against Gabe's cock. He stood behind her for several moments. Completely still, silent but for his jagged breath as he inhaled. He dropped to his knees behind her, pushed his hands under her dress, and hooked his fingers underneath her panties and lowered them to the floor. With his fingers on her inner thighs, he spread her legs and leaned close. "Fuck, you're soaked," he murmured against her skin. She could feel his breath on her bare lips as he breathed over her. She gasped when she felt his tongue drag across her seam. With his mouth still on her, he moaned appreciatively, and the hum pulsed through her.

As Gabe feasted on her, Ellie righted herself, standing straight, turning to watch him, forgetting his instructions, and everything else but the way he made her feel. But he soon corrected her when his palm smacked heavily against her ass. The crack reverberated throughout the room, over the noise of the other occupants.

"Grab it," he told her. His demand sent another

shiver down her spine, and she obliged him. He wrapped his large hands against the tops of her thighs, pulling her to him, and holding her in place, as he went back to work. Ellie could barely breathe as his tongue, lips and teeth worked in tandem, driving her crazy. Soon Ellie was panting, shamelessly pushing against his face as his greedy mouth ate from her, his moans of satisfaction somehow matching her own of desperation.

Ellie turned her head, and saw their reflection in the large mirror on the nearby wall. She was bent at an angle, her dress around her waist, with Gabe on his knees, behind her, his face almost completely obscured by her thighs and ass. In all of her days, including her wild past, it was the single most erotic sight she'd ever seen. Her heart thudded against her rib cage, and she gripped the couch tighter, her fingers clenching the leather, hoping it wouldn't rip under her grasp. Her breaths became shallow, and her toes curled as he plucked at the strings of pleasure that ran throughout her body. She felt her muscles become taut, and as he pulled her closer, his lips closing over the bud of her clit, she became uncoiled as her orgasm tore through her.

When the room stopped spinning, she felt him take a standing position behind her. "How was that?" he whispered, his voice husky and darkened by desire. He grasped her jaw, turned her face toward him and kissed her roughly. She could smell and taste herself on his lips. He took his hands from her. "Stay right there." She heard the clang of his belt buckle.

His hands worked behind her, and when she caught his reflection in the mirror, she watched him pump his fist over his cock several times before he rolled a condom over himself.

Turning her head over her shoulder, she saw that he was still fully dressed, down to his button-down shirt and suit jacket, his pants resting on his muscular thighs. As she looked at them in the mirror, he was lining himself up with her from behind, and was inside of her with one solid thrust.

"Gabe!"

While he stood, grabbing her hips, he pushed in and out of her. His thrusts were quick, powerful. He was rough, and she knew he would probably leave bruises on her. But she didn't care about that. It was hard, dirty, everything she wanted. She was on the brink of her second orgasm, and from Gabe's frenzied movements, she knew he was close. She moved her hand between them, found where they were connected and touched both of them simultaneously. Her eyes snapped to his in the mirror, and for a moment, there was something else to their connection. Something potent that went beyond biological urges.

Keeping her eyes locked with his, she rolled the pad of her finger around her clit. The sensation was enough, and she came again, and felt herself clamp around Gabe's length. He yelled out, stilled and leaned over her, covering her body with his. He groaned roughly into the crook of her neck as he spasmed inside of her, filling the condom.

She felt the quake in his strong legs as he removed the condom and tossed it in a nearby trash can. Ellie looked up, and she saw that they'd gained an audience. Now that the show was over, the crowd dispersed.

Gabe helped Ellie straighten her dress, and he picked up her purse for her before then escorting her to the staircase. "What'd you think?"

"That was amazing," she told him. "Thanks for showing me around."

"No matter how any of this works out, anytime you want to come back, just let me know. I'll put you on the list." Back on the main floor, Gabe reached into his breast pocket, pulled out his cell phone and was transfixed by the screen. She knew that she'd lost him when he frowned.

"Everything okay?" she asked him.

"Yeah, it's fine," he told her, not looking up, his thumbs moving over the screen. "Excuse me for a minute, would you?"

Gabe saw the missed call notifications the minute he'd retrieved his phone. He wished that he hadn't replaced the damn thing after he'd smashed it on Friday night. Charles had called him while he'd been in the playroom with Ellie. Seven times. Left voice mails and several texts for Gabe to call him. He took several steps away from her and dialed his voice mail.

"Gabe, I need you to call me," Charles said in the first message.

He skipped to the next. "Gabe, where the hell are you?"

The messages got more urgent. "I need you to get your ass over here now."

"Everything okay?" Ellie asked him.

"Your father," he told her, dialing his mentor.

"Where the hell have you been?" his boss demanded, when he answered.

He took a look at Ellie. "What is it?" If Charles had any idea where he'd been…

"We need you at the office right now." Gabe listened as Charles told him how one of the firm's top clients had initiated a multimillion-dollar takeover of another company.

"What? You need me there now? Aren't there clerks that can handle that sort of thing?" Frustration had him biting the words at his boss.

Charles was silent for a moment, as if stunned into silence. "He's your client, and he wants you here now. And as a *potential* future partner, you'd better get here ASAP." And there it was, Charles dangling his promotion over his head like a carrot on a string. He sighed and looked at Ellie, not wanting to leave her, but work had to come first. "Fine. I'll be there in fifteen minutes."

He slid his phone back in his pocket and saw the look that Ellie gave him. "Ellie, I'm sorry."

"You have to leave?"

"Yeah. A big client wants me in the office now. Some kind of crisis, apparently."

Ellie straightened. "Yeah, of course. Well, thanks for that," she said, gesturing down the stairs. "I'll talk to my lawyer about the papers and get them back to you." It felt like Gabe was losing Ellie already. But he didn't want to let her go. Whatever was between them—he wanted to hold on to it.

She started to move past him, but he held out his hand, stopping her.

"Ellie, wait."

"Yeah?"

He had no idea what he wanted to say to her. He just wanted her to stay with him. He didn't want to say goodbye to this aspect of their relationship. "You know, we'll still have a while before the marriage is officially annulled," he told her.

"Yeah."

He huffed out a breath, and took a step to stand right in front of her. "You can't deny that we have a certain physical connection. But as long as we're waiting for the annulment to be official, we might as well, I don't know," he stammered. "Hell, I'm usually better at this." Words and presenting his case was his livelihood, and Ellie turned him into a stuttering fool. "Why don't we keep seeing each other?"

"You want to still play husband and wife?" she asked him. "Like, sexually?"

"Yeah. Let's give this—whatever this is between us—until then."

"Gabe, that's insane."

She was right. It was insane. "I know it is. But I don't want to let you go tonight without exploring what there is between us. What's the worst that could happen?" Both of them could be ruined; that was a pretty heavy *worst*.

She didn't say anything for a while. She looked at the staircase as if to leave, and then she turned back to him. He couldn't read the emotion that was on her face, and he hoped that he hadn't just laid everything on the line, and made himself look like a jerk, by saying the stupidest thing he'd ever thought.

"What about work?"

"We'll keep it separate. Keep it secret. Especially if I'm going to be your mentor."

"That's still on?"

He should say no. As soon as he'd said the words, he felt guilt punch him in the stomach. But he didn't want to trust her career to anyone else. He was the best man for the job. "Yeah. It's still on."

"But—"

"I like you, Ellie. You're smart, fiery, strong. I'll bet you're a really good lawyer to boot. If I can learn to keep my hands off you at the office, I do think we'll be a pretty good match. Whatever is between us physically won't affect either of our careers. What do you say?" he asked her, trying to not let desperation creep into his voice.

"Okay," she said. "To both."

"I'm glad." He wanted nothing more than to go home with his *wife*. But his boss—his unknowing father-in-law—was waiting for him. For the first time in his life, he didn't want to jump up and go to work. He turned serious, reached out and cupped her jaw. Her skin was smooth and warm. "I'm sorry I have to go. This is not how I wanted to spend this evening, at the office, working on a takeover."

"I changed my mind," she told him. "I do believe that maybe you are the boring one."

He laughed. "It's true. Maybe you should have known that about me before you married me," he told her, winking. He cupped her face with his hands. "I want to see you later, but I really don't know what time I'll be done tonight."

God, he wanted nothing more than to ignore Charles, his client and the millions of dollars at stake, and take Ellie to his house and spend the night exploring her body. For a man who normally held on to control with a firm hold, he felt it start to slip from his grasp.

"That's okay." Her casual shrug made him wonder how she was so unaffected. "Thanks again for the tour. I had fun."

"Me, too," he assured her. He reached out and cupped her cheek in his palm, before drawing her near and placing a chaste kiss on her lips. He turned away from her while he still could. He had to get to the office.

CHAPTER EIGHT

GABE WAS ON the conference call from hell with Charles and his client, and had been for three hours and counting. The other men were talking, but all Gabe could think about was Ellie. He'd gotten home from the office well after midnight the night before, after saying goodbye to Ellie at Di Terrestres. His quiet, empty house wasn't the comfort it always was. He'd wished that Ellie was there. He'd almost called her, but he figured that it was too late. Was Ellie a night owl? An early bird? Again, he cursed himself for not knowing anything about her. But he went to bed without calling or texting her, even if he'd had to leave his phone downstairs in the kitchen to stop himself from contacting her from his bed.

Finally, the call ended, all matters of the takeover having been discussed. Gabe knew that Charles had noticed he'd not been an active participant in the conversation, and had made several points of it during the call. It bothered Gabe that he was unable to focus on his client. It bothered him that he couldn't get Ellie, who was probably in her own office several floors down, off his mind. He'd emailed her earlier with some tasks, and he wondered how she was doing with them. Maybe he'd take a trip down there to see if she needed a hand. But he stopped himself. They'd agreed to keep their work separate, and Gabe knew that the minute he was in her office, he would lock the door and take her.

He needed to cool down. He needed to get out of his office. He walked to the lunchroom to get a coffee. Sure, he had a machine in his office, and he could have sent Kellen, his assistant, out for a cup, but he preferred to get his own. But when Ian Smith entered the lunchroom, he wished that he'd left the building and gone to the café around the corner.

"Gabe," he said. "How's everything?"

"Pretty good," Gabe responded without much enthusiasm. He'd known Ian since they'd both started at the firm. The man was an ass-kisser, not one genuine bone in his body, and would do anything to get ahead. He was always jealous and resentful of Gabe's connections within the firm—his father and Charles. "And yourself?" he asked, not because he was interested, but because the social contract between coworkers dictated it.

"I'm good, man, good. I hear you've got Burnham's daughter working under you now."

Gabe stiffened at the way Ian spoke.

"I'll tell you what, I wouldn't mind having her under me."

Gabe's hands formed into fists at his sides. "Stay away from her."

"Or what?" Ian asking, glancing down at Gabe's clenched hands. "It's not a good idea to deck a partner."

"You aren't a partner," Gabe reminded him.

"I know they're looking at one of us to come on board at the top." Ian leaned in and lowered his voice. "I know you and the old man are pretty tight. But I have my connections, too. The partnership is mine. Stay out of my way."

The look in his eyes made Gabe understand that Ian was trying to threaten him, but he didn't succeed. Ian was hungry—for power, money. But so was Gabe, and even though he didn't need to work—the profits from his stake in the Brotherhood's businesses was more than enough to live luxuriously—as he looked at Ian, his competitive nature took over. It was never just about the job for Gabe, it was about *winning, being the best.*

Gabe chuckled. "Here's the thing, Ian. Everyone knows you're a snake. There's no way the other partners will take you seriously enough to vote you as a partner."

"Is that right? I think you're going to be sorry for that, Foster. I know you're a golden boy over here, but you're done. Don't cross me."

Gabe stayed cool, figuring that not visibly reacting would bother Ian more. He was right. Ian glared, before pushing past Gabe and leaving the room.

Gabe had to grab the handle of the nearby fridge to stop himself from stalking after him. But Ian was right, he couldn't pummel the man—not on company property at least. He could handle himself. But he was angrier on Ellie's behalf. Ian wasn't going to get anywhere near Ellie.

He wasn't sure if the tension roiling through his body was anger or lust. Every time he tried to focus his mind, it just made his body recall the way Ellie had felt underneath him, surrounding him. How she'd kissed him back in the elevator, how it felt to drive into her from behind in the playroom at Di Terrestres. It was barely noon, and he had to get out of the building. He'd always been a workhorse, making him an asset to his employers and clients. Since meeting—and marrying—Ellie, however, his work ethic and productivity had plummeted.

He looked out the window. It was another hot day in Las Vegas, and while his air-conditioned office was a relief, he needed to get outside. He made his way back to his office, changed out of his suit and back into the jeans and T-shirt he'd worn that morning, and made his way to the parking lot.

He jumped on his motorcycle and put on his helmet before starting it up. The motor vibrated, coming to life between his thighs, and he pulled out of the parking lot and onto the road. He drove for a while; the wind was cool on his arms, but the sun was hot as he drove away from the city and into the desert. Taking a ride on his bike was normally the thing that cleared his mind and helped him focus.

But this time, it didn't work. Like always, Ellie dominated his thoughts, and when he managed to push her aside, he thought about the firm and his future. He was so close to attaining his dreams, he couldn't blow it now. And if word got out that he'd drunkenly married Charles Burnham's daughter, he'd be finished. There's no way Charles would forgive him. And there was no way Ellie would see the reconciliation with her father that she'd craved. It had been selfish, asking her to continue their relationship until the annulment was finalized. And he'd put her in jeopardy.

His phone vibrated in his pocket and Gabe pulled over to the dusty shoulder to answer it. It was a text from Alana.

I'm at Thalia, doing some work. Up for late lunch?

At the mention of food, Gabe's stomach growled, and he realized that he'd skipped breakfast, and had only had coffee so far that morning.

Hell yeah. I can be there in twenty. Of all the members of the Brotherhood, Alana was his best friend, and if there was anyone he could trust to give him brutal honesty and clarity on his current predicament, it was her.

He turned the bike around and headed back to the city, weaving in and out of traffic, expertly gliding his motorcycle over the asphalt. At Thalia, he parked next to Alana's red vintage Stingray, loosened his helmet and hung it over the handlebars. On his way to the door, he let some well-dressed businessmen go inside ahead of him. They looked him up and down in his jeans and T-shirt. Gabe was definitely underdressed to dine in their restaurant—which had a dress code—but he assumed, with a chuckle, that as one of the restaurant's owners, management would make an exception for him.

He held the door open for the men, and smiled while they barely regarded him. He followed them to the hostess stand, and Libby, the gorgeous woman standing behind it, broke into a huge smile, much to the surprise of the men. "Gabe," she greeted him. "Alana is just inside at her usual table. Behave yourself because she isn't having an easy morning."

"Thanks for the warning, Libby," he said gratefully, as he made his way inside. Alana had already been seated. She had her tablet and a stack of papers in front of her, and her phone to her ear.

"That's completely unacceptable," she told the unfortunate person on the other end. She looked up at Gabe and winked. "Get back to me in two hours with a better response," she said, and promptly hung up the phone.

Gabe took a seat and helped himself to her half-filled wineglass. "What was that about?"

"Oh, you know, the usual. We need some work to be done on the hotel. The contractor is trying to dick me around because I don't have one." She shrugged and bit back a yawn.

He watched her. She'd been working herself like crazy the past few months, especially since the Brotherhood had opened their latest hotel, in which they'd taken the erotic themes of Di Terrestres and created a full-service hotel around the concept. Alana had taken on most of the management of their hospitality businesses, and he knew that the work must be piling up on her. "Everything okay?"

"Just peachy," she said with a smile that Gabe knew wasn't as genuine as she tried to portray. He also knew that pushing Alana on the issue would make her push herself harder, work more, to prove him wrong.

He reached across the table and put his hand over hers. "We know you're working hard lately. You can reach out, you know. The guys and I can help lighten your load."

"Yeah, especially now that Brett is off enjoying married life, Alex is also planning a wedding and Rafael is working on the campaign for his senate run, on top of their own workloads. Yeah, they have all the time in the world to help out. Don't worry, I'm fine," she told him. Her voice was firm, and told him that she was close to getting angry. "Give me that," she said, reaching out and plucking the wineglass from his fingers, and drinking from it.

The waiter came by, and Gabe asked for a beer. Alana put away the stacks of paper and the tablet, and the server returned with Gabe's lager. He tasted it. It was cold and crisp, the bubbles reminding him of the champagne he'd lapped up from Ellie's body the night they'd married. *Jesus, get a grip.* He sighed, rubbing his eyes with his thumb and forefinger.

"I think the better question is, is everything okay with you?" Alana said.

He didn't look at her, instead taking another mouthful of his beer. He sighed again.

"Bad day so far at work?"

"It's fine," he told her.

Alana clearly wasn't convinced. "What's going on? Did you get those annulment papers filed?"

"Yeah. But there's more." He took a deep breath and told Alana everything. What had transpired between him and Ellie the night before, and how he'd told her he wanted to keep sleeping with her, at least until their day in court.

Alana was quiet for a minute, and Gabe hated the way she watched him—so critical. "What? Why would you do that?"

"The sex is really good?" he answered, searching for a reason.

"You've had good sex, dude. And I'm sure you can find it again with someone who isn't your boss's daughter."

"It's not only that," he told her. "Ellie is…" He tried to find the words. "Ellie is special."

"Well, that's nice for you. But you married your boss's daughter when you were drunk. And we both know I hate to be the person to say it, but is she worth destroying your career and everything you've worked for? Because that's what's going to happen when Burnham finds out."

That was why he'd gone to Alana. She was the voice of reason. He knew that Alana wasn't just giving him a hard time. She was helping him talk through his problem. She was good at that. "I know, and I know if I make partner, I'll be set for the rest of my career. But when I'm with Ellie, Jesus, I don't know, it's like I lose all control. I don't care about anything but being with her again." Alana smiled, and it annoyed him. He failed to see the humor in something that could seriously fuck up not only his career, but his life.

"What?"

She shrugged and sipped her wine. "Nothing. It's just that I've never seen you in anything but complete control. You're in quite a bind over this woman."

He wanted to tell her that she was wrong, but he couldn't. Already he was seeing that he didn't pull the strings when it came to Ellie. It scared him. "So, what do I do?"

Alana narrowed her eyes at him, as if considering her response. "Honestly? I think you might be going through a typical late quarter-life crisis. Seeing all your friends settled down and married off has got your own biological clock ticking. You should be careful. But just remember, Gabe, you've worked too damn hard to screw up your career. Don't throw everything away because of a pretty face."

He nodded. "Maybe you're right." Had his desire to have what his friends had driven him to marry Ellie, and then ask her to stay in his bed until the annulment? And that was why he'd gone to Alana. He could count on her to give him a straight, practical answer that wasn't governed by matters of the heart. "Thanks. I knew that's what you would say."

"And that's why you came to me instead of one of the guys?"

He smiled. The rest of their friends seemed to have fallen in love with amazing women. Good for them. Any one of the guys would have probably advised him to stay married to the woman, to have babies and live happily ever after. He was grateful that Alana understood that not everything was about that dreaded four-letter word—*love*. "You know me too well."

"And don't you forget it."

"Thanks, Lana. But there's something else, though," he started, not looking at her. There was one very big piece of information he'd left out.

Her eyes narrowed. "What?"

"Her father assigned me as her mentor."

Alana blinked. "Christ, are you serious?"

"Yeah."

"That's messed up. Forget for a second that she's Burnham's daughter. Forget even that you married her. You're responsible for this woman's career, and you took her down to the playroom last night?"

Gabe had no excuse. "Yeah."

"That's not okay—"

"Everything between us has been consensual," Gabe told her. He'd made sure of that.

"The problem is with the imbalance of power. She's young, just out of school. You're supposed to guide her. Help her. You can't do that if you're unzipping your pants."

"I know," Gabe admitted and put his head in his hands. "You're right."

"You have to quit being her mentor, or quit sleeping with her. Which is it going to be?"

Which indeed?

"I'll find her a new mentor."

Alana's lips pursed in a way that annoyed him. "Interesting."

In any other life, he could see being with Alana, and while they'd fooled around a little in the past, they'd thankfully decided that they were much better as friends.

"So, in the meantime, what do I do?"

She shrugged. "I find it hard to believe that you don't have more self-control than that. But, in the same breath, I can't believe that you're here looking for advice about women. This is new territory. I think you should avoid her until a judge signs off on the annulment, instead of playing the happy honeymooners. There's no sense in prolonging the inevitable." She paused. "Unless you see a future with her."

Gabe looked into his beer, saying nothing.

"Do you see a future with her?"

"I don't know," he admitted. "I know I like being with her. We have fun. I think that's why I wanted to see her again—getting to know each other, see if there's something worth salvaging between us."

Alana hummed, and took a sip of her wine. He couldn't tell what was happening behind her eyes.

"What?"

"Nothing. You hungry?"

"Starving." Gabe picked up his menu, ignoring her knowing gaze. He'd told her his problem, and she'd given him some good advice—not that he was sure he'd be following it. He was done with the conversation. "How's the tuna today?"

"It's amazing, as usual," she told him, still watching him carefully. "I'll drop the subject if you want to drop it."

"I want to drop it."

"Another round?" she asked, gesturing to her empty glass.

Another round? His life was a complete mess. He needed at least another *six* rounds. He could always take a car back to the office. "Yes, please."

CHAPTER NINE

ELLIE SIPPED HER coffee and looked around the large conference room at the assembled associates and staff of the law firm. She scanned the faces—most somewhat familiar—trying to tell herself that she wasn't looking for Gabe. With the exception of a few emails back and forth, she hadn't seen him all day. But really, she hadn't seen anyone. She'd sequestered herself in her tiny office on the first floor, barely breaking to eat a sandwich at her desk, one by one ticking each item off the list of things Gabe had asked her to do.

She wasn't about to complain about the work. She didn't want to be accused of skating by just because she was the firm founder's daughter. She was willing to do more, stay later than anyone just to prove that she deserved to be there. She drank from her mug again. Just coffee. Not wine or spirits like everyone else. There was no way she was going to let her father catch her with a drink in her hand at a work party.

She looked around at all the people gathered, their rigid postures jovial, but there was no way they were having fun. It didn't take a keen observer to see the discomfort, the stilted smiles, the awkward interactions. Everyone on their best behavior. It wasn't the type of party she was used to. "I used to be so good at this," she muttered to herself in her corner, away from what *might* be called the action.

Ellie heard Gabe before she saw him. She looked to the doorway, where she watched him enter the room, laughing with another one of the senior associates. He slapped his colleague on the back, and looked up to search the room—his eyes finding hers immediately—and in several long strides, he crossed the room to her.

"Ellie, I'm glad you made it up this evening."

"Yeah, I just finished up."

"Sorry if I piled on too much."

"Don't worry about it. It's nothing I can't handle."

"You did excellent work," he told her.

Ellie lowered her voice. "I even took care of that other matter we discussed last night." Her answer to their annulment.

He blinked quickly. "Good." His voice lowered. "Now it's in the judge's hands until we get a court date, and it'll all be behind us." She nodded, and he shifted closer to her. "Now that that's taken care of, there's something else I wanted to discuss with you."

She noted the way his voice lowered, his eyes hooded.

"And what's that?"

Covertly, he looked over his shoulder. "I want you to come home with me tonight."

"And then what?"

He leaned in. "I'm going to rip that dress right off you later, my darling wife," he whispered in her ear before pulling back.

"Is that right?" she asked, when she found her voice, shocked by Gabe's quiet, but bold declaration. She looked over Gabe's shoulder and saw another man approach them.

Gabe turned, and she saw the briefest flicker of a frown before he covered it with a polite smile. "Ian."

"Gabe," Ian said. "Who is this lovely young lady? Is this Charles's daughter?"

"Yes. Ellie, this is Ian. Ian, Ellie," Gabe introduced them.

She offered her hand to him, and he gripped it almost too hard, as if exerting his dominance, and Ellie watched him give her a once-over. She instinctively backed up a little. But he didn't release her hand, and she knew at that moment that she didn't like Ian. And even though she was standing next to Gabe, she didn't feel safe with this other man anywhere near her. She cast a look at Gabe, who was also watching the interaction, his eyes narrowed and trained on Ian.

"Ian, how are you doing?" Gabe physically put himself between her and the other man, and offered his own hand, knowing that, per the social contract, Ian would have to release her and shake it. Jarred from the interaction, Ellie stood back farther from the conversation and drank her coffee, completely rattled from the seemingly innocent interaction. Ian ignored her, but Gabe kept his eyes on her until he saw that her cup was empty, and then he reached out to her. "Why don't we get you another coffee, and I can introduce you to some people you haven't met."

With Gabe's broad, warm palm spanning the width of her lower back, she finally felt safe. His touch wasn't cold, threatening, like Ian's. "I saw the way he looked at you," he whispered, his voice tinged by anger. "Are you okay?"

Ellie nodded. "Thanks for getting me out of there, though. That guy really creeped me out."

"Yeah. Your instincts were correct. I've heard some of the stories, and he isn't a good guy. A real asshole." He grimaced, but then turned on a charming smile to greet his colleagues as they walked by.

"Can we get out of here?" she asked.

"Yeah. I can't wait to make good on my promise to you."

"Gabe!" she heard someone shout. It was her father; he was quickly approaching and didn't look happy. Gabe quickly removed his hand from Ellie's lower back. She was already humming with anticipation of another night with Gabe. Desire pooled between her thighs. They were almost out—so close to the door to freedom, and more than likely, more orgasms than she could count.

"Sir," Gabe greeted him. "Great turnout this time."

"Yes, everyone's been working so hard lately. Which is why I'm sorry to have to do this to you tonight. I just got off the phone. There's a problem with the Hong Kong takeover you've been working on."

"What is it?"

Charles went into a long, drawn-out explanation about a spooked board of directors, and dissension among their ranks. He needed Gabe to assist them and provide counsel to help them come up with a better deal, and renegotiate the terms of their acquisition. Ellie knew those sorts of things could go on for days, weeks, and from the many details she knew about the deal already, Ellie knew that Gabe had already worked his ass off on it.

"They know you, and trust you. You need to take care of it. Ellie, you know some of what is going on. Give Gabe a hand. Help him with anything he needs."

"I can do that," she promised. So much for the sex-filled night she'd planned on. Her hopes were now deflated as she knew that she would be spending the night not in Gabe's bed, with her ripped-up dress on the floor, but in the office. She would still be with Gabe, but he had turned back immediately into the diligent, serious partner-to-be. Gabe was already on his cell phone. She smiled at her father, but he was already turning around and moving on to the next cluster of people.

"There's an empty conference room down the hall," Gabe told her. "It might be better for us to spread out over there. Go get what you need from your office." He blew out a heavy breath, and she knew that he was just as frustrated as she was. "It's going to be a long night."

Ellie nodded, and left the conference room to head to her office. If she and Gabe weren't able to sneak away for a night at his place, maybe the night wouldn't be a complete bust. Maybe Gabe was on to something when he said they could *spread out* in the conference room.

And as she promised her father, she would give Gabe a hand with anything he needed...

A few hours later, Ellie found herself sequestered with Gabe in one of the firm's conference rooms to deal with the problems happening in Hong Kong. Ellie watched in awe as Gabe spoke in Cantonese with his client—the CEO of the tech company that was embroiled in the takeover drama. They'd spent their time making international calls, and researching and brainstorming with people around the globe. Normally, a company like that would have in-house counsel but Gabe had explained that he'd known the CEO and founder, now one of the world's richest men, since he started out. That was why the task of smoothing out the takeover fell to two young Americans half a world away.

Ellie released the pins and elastic that had been holding her bun in place. She shook her head, and her dark hair fell to her shoulders. Gabe watched her, then disconnected the call, put down his phone and rubbed his eyes with his fingertips. "What a clusterfuck," he said.

"No luck changing the board's minds?"

"Not yet. They don't believe the takeover is in the best interest of the firm, nothing that we've presented is changing their minds and Tsai is ready to go ahead with it anyway, the opinions of others and consequences be damned."

Ellie rolled her chair closer to him. "You did your best. We both did. You provided counsel, guidance. And we'll go ahead and file whatever papers your client needs us to." She put her hand on his thigh. "I didn't know you spoke Cantonese."

He turned his head and looked at her. His golden, wavy hair was tousled and fell over his forehead. He'd long abandoned his tie and jacket, and his sleeves were rolled up over his corded, tanned forearms. He was a gorgeous man. "Are you impressed?" he asked, flashing his white teeth.

"A little, yeah." She crawled her fingers up his firm thigh, and she felt him stiffen underneath her touch. He blew out a breath.

She squeezed her fingers into the hard muscle. He tensed again, but he made no movement to remove her hand. So, emboldened, she moved her hand upward, toward his fly, and found his dick, already hard and warm in her palm behind the fine material of his pants. She smoothed her palm over him. His lips were pressed together, and he moaned under her touch.

Ellie looked up. Through the frosted glass walls of the conference room, she could see their colleagues milling about in the hallway on the other side of the glass. She assumed that the mixer had finally cleared out, but there were still a few stragglers.

He looked at her out of the corner of his eye.

"Ellie," his voice was a low, dangerous grumble. "What are you doing?"

She shrugged her shoulders, still palming, stroking his rigid length through his pants. "You look tense. My father told me to give you a hand."

There was a giggle in the hallway, and they could see someone's form lean against the clouded glass. Ellie gasped, but she didn't move her hand.

Gabe chuckled, and put his hand on top of hers. Instead of moving her hand away from him, he squeezed it and flexed his hips forward in his chair, the minute movement putting him more fully into her hand. He was hard, thick and hot. She squeezed him before finding and pulling down his zipper. She felt his abdomen twitch, and he covered a moan with another cough, which was enough to catch the attention of the people in the hallway. The glass was definitely not soundproof.

The person in the hallway turned toward the glass, but instead of leaving, he reached for the doorknob and opened it. Ellie let out a startled gasp, as one of the guys from family law—Ted, she thought his name was—poked his head in. Ellie and Gabe both straightened, Ellie pulled her hand away from Gabe's crotch. "Hey, guys. Sorry, we didn't know you were in here."

"It's all good," Gabe told him through clenched teeth.

"See you guys tomorrow," Maybe Ted told them with a jovial smile and a finger gun.

Ellie nodded. "Yeah, tomorrow," she agreed.

"I'll let you get back to work, I guess."

"That'd be great," Gabe told him.

"You okay, Gabe? You look a little tense."

"I'm fine. We're just trying to finish up here." Gabe's body was so rigid that Ellie was certain he might snap in half.

"You know, you'll work yourself to an early grave."

When Ted closed the door, Gabe straightened and removed her hand from him. "Jesus, Ellie," she heard him mutter under his breath. "You know I'm about to make partner. This is too important for me to screw up. I can't be embroiled in a scandal any more than I already am."

He was right, but that didn't mean she had to like it, or that she was even done. Ellie released him, stood and walked deliberately to the door, making sure to put a swivel in her hips, knowing he was watching. "You don't think that my job is important to me? I've got a lot on the line right now, as well." She watched him over her shoulder from across the room and saw that he was still in the chair, his legs spread. He'd made no attempt to stuff himself back inside his pants. Watching her with lust-darkened eyes.

She smiled and flipped the lock on the door, ensuring they wouldn't be interrupted again. She turned to face him. The large table separated them, and they watched each other.

Slowly, Ellie reached back behind her and found the zipper of her dress and lowered it. The material loosened, and she pushed it past her shoulders and down her hips, until it fell to the floor. Gabe stood straight.

"What are you doing?" he asked, almost breathless. "We have a lot of work to do."

"You're the one who still has your dick out," she pointed out. "Want me to take care of that for you?"

His response was a low grunt, as he settled into the chair.

In her matching bra and panties set, stockings and high heels, she took several deliberate steps toward the table. "I'm not sure there's much more we can do tonight. Plus, the way I feel, I'm not sure if I could concentrate on it right now. You won't believe how wet I am, right now, just thinking about you."

She came to the edge of the table, and instead of walking around it, she used more grace than she knew she had, and climbed on top of it. Half crawling, half sliding, she made her way across the table until she came to meet Gabe at his end, and she knelt upright, above him, her thighs spread at his eye level. Their mingled breaths were the only sounds in the room as they watched each other. More conversation filled the hallway and captured both of their attention, and they both looked to the glass.

Ellie held her breath. All someone would have to do is try to open the door, see it was locked and they would raise suspicion. What if her father came by to check? When the hallway was empty again, Ellie turned back to Gabe.

"This is insane," he told her. She thought he would

zip up and tell her to get dressed. They *were* at work. He was right. It *was* insane that she was kneeling on top of a conference room table in her underwear, and Gabe was sitting in the chair with his cock out.

"Should we get back to work?" she asked. "Or should we finish whatever we've started here?"

Ellie held her breath, waiting for his response. He stood from the chair, and made no effort to zip up his pants. He put his hands just above her still-spread knees and slid them up her thighs, over the nude-colored lace at the top of her stockings. His touch made her gasp, and a warmth traveled throughout her. She needed Gabe, and needed him now. If he turned her away, she might explode from need.

His chest rose and fell with his breath, and he looked long and slow up her body, until he reached her eyes. "Let's finish it."

Thank God. She breathed out a sigh of relief.

Gabe helped her step down from the table, and once her feet were on the floor, she put her hand on his chest and pushed him back into his chair, following him down, straddling his thighs. Gripping his lapels in her fists, she leaned in and grazed his ear with her lips. "Here's how this is going to work, Gabe," she whispered. "I know you're big on control, but now it's my turn." She kissed his lips hard—she held the power now—and before he could say anything in response, Ellie slithered off his lap, and onto the floor, to kneel between his knees.

"Ell… You don't have to do this," he murmured, but her fingers gripped him and slid up and down his length. He pushed his hips forward into her fist. "Oh Christ," he sighed.

"Don't worry. I want to," she assured him, before her lips closed over the head of his dick. She brought her head down, taking as much of him as she could, before rising, stopping at the crest before taking him all the way again.

"Fuck," he said, putting his hand on her head, wrapping her hair in his fist. "That's incredible." She used one hand on his shaft, but when she cupped his balls with her other hand, he began thrusting into her mouth. She could feel his desperation, knew he was close, but before she could bring him to completion, he put his hands on her cheeks and gently pushed her away.

She got the hint and rose up to straddle his lap again. She licked the side of his throat, and then trailed up to his ear. "Why did you stop me?" she whispered, before taking the lobe between her teeth. He groaned. Ellie knew that she was killing him.

He pulled her close, and the contact brought his hard dick against her still-clothed pussy. She rocked her hips against him, her clit throbbing with the light contact. "Because I couldn't wait another second to have you." Shifting slightly, he reached for the table, where he'd put his wallet. He pulled out a condom. In seconds, he'd ripped the foil, and had the latex rolled over his pulsing shaft. With a rough tug, he pulled Ellie's panties to the side, and she lowered herself over him. At the contact, they both stilled, but then Ellie went into action, raising and lowering herself over him.

Gabe pulled down her bra and closed his lips over one of her nipples, nipping her, making her cry out. He spread his palms over her back, holding her close as she rode his cock, taking every ounce of pleasure she could, and giving it back to him. Riding him, the wonderfully rough friction of her lace panties against her clit, and the way he filled her quickly brought her over the edge. She gripped his shoulders, and in a move to stop herself from screaming out, she dug her teeth into the warm skin of his throat.

In her ear, he grunted his release and he stiffened beneath her.

"God, Ellie," he whispered against her bare shoulder, breathing against her sensitive nerve endings. "That was amazing."

"Yeah," she said, realizing that she had to disengage from him. He let her, and she stood on wobbly legs, walking to the other side of the room to collect her dress. She could feel his eyes on her as she straightened the material of her dress over her body.

"That probably shouldn't have happened here," Gabe told her. "I know we promised to keep this separated from our jobs. But, Ellie, you make me lose all control. I just can't help myself around you. But I don't regret it."

"You're right," Ellie agreed. "Even though we had an agreement, it was fun, wasn't it?"

"Doesn't mean it won't happen again," he told her with a smile. She took it as almost a warning.

"I know," she agreed, and took several steps until she was standing in front of him. Her hands flattened against his chest, while his found her hips, pulling her closer. "I know that we agreed this would be temporary, just until the annulment." She shook her head. "There's no way to stop this, is there?"

Gabe paused and kissed her. Already his lips and taste were familiar. She wasn't sure how the man had already imprinted himself on her senses. "I don't know how," he muttered, before turning serious. "But I feel like we need to talk about something first."

"What is it?"

"If we're having this relationship, or whatever this is," he added too quickly for her liking. "I don't think I can, or should, be your mentor."

That made Ellie pause. She and Gabe worked great together. "Why not?"

Even though she knew the reasons why, Gabe listed them—propriety, office politics, it was risky to both of their careers. He had a power imbalance over her. She knew all of that, but Ellie didn't care. She couldn't fight the way she felt around Gabe.

"I agree that what we're doing is inappropriate," she said, carefully choosing her words. "I know it puts us both at risk. But there's no one else I would rather have by my side in my career. I can learn a lot from you, professionally. So if you think we have to end one aspect of our relationship, either physically or professionally," she took a deep breath, "it needs to be the physical." As she said the words, she felt a pain in her chest. She wanted Gabe in every way. But if he was making her choose, she could still make the right decision for her future.

"Is that what you want?" he asked her.

"No. It isn't at all. I want both. And Gabe, I'm not some young ingenue, I know exactly what I want. You."

He didn't say anything for a moment. But then he nodded again, his serious frown turning upward. "Let's go to my house."

Ellie couldn't wait to go to his home. To see the kind of person he was outside of the walls of the law office. She wanted to know the real Gabe. But as she smiled, watching Gabe collect their things, his words rang through her head.

I know this is temporary...

Yes. It was temporary. They were just having fun until their annulment was finalized. Gabe finished up, putting his laptop in his shoulder bag.

He smiled at her. "Ready to go?"

Ellie nodded. For once she wished she'd met Gabe under different circumstances. That she didn't work at his firm, that he wasn't so close to her father. That they hadn't had a drunken Vegas wedding. Whether or not they were temporary, it didn't mean that she wouldn't enjoy every second that she could get with Gabe. "Yeah," she told him, wishing she could take his hand as they walked out of the building. "Let's go."

CHAPTER TEN

ELLIE STOOD NEXT to Gabe as he unlocked his door using a pass code, and when he opened the door, she walked inside ahead of him. She'd been in his home before, the day after their wedding.

"I'll be right back," he told her, disappearing around a corner.

She turned her head, and then she saw it. *Speaking of knowing nothing about him.* She walked to the grand piano, shiny and black, and sat at the bench in front of it. Did Gabe play the piano? She pictured his long, capable fingers, his grace, his beauty—she knew that he must have been a skilled player, and she longed to hear him play.

She lifted the lid and pushed one of the keys. The sound filled the hallway, and echoed off the marble. She hit the next key. Then she played a little song that she remembered from childhood.

When she looked up, she saw Gabe watching her from the hallway. She was surprised to see him, having not heard him approach, but not as surprised as he looked to see her sitting at the piano.

"Do you play?" he asked.

Ellie shook her head. "That's about the extent of it," she told him, standing. "But based on this, I'm willing to bet that you do."

"Some," he explained, not moving from the hallway.

"You any good?"

Gabe shrugged. "I'm okay."

"Will you play me something?"

"Later," he told her. "But now I'm hungry. Want some food?"

Ellie realized that she hadn't eaten since lunchtime. "Yeah. I'm starving."

"Let's go to the kitchen," he suggested, taking her hand and leading her through the house. "How do you feel about a very, very late breakfast?" he asked, opening the fridge.

"Sounds great."

They weren't going to be together forever—sex was just a fun diversion for them. There was no way they would be able to maintain the pace they'd set, keep the fires burning as hotly. But being in his kitchen as he opened the fridge and pulled out a selection of fresh vegetables and a carton of eggs? Well, it felt nice.

"Well, I'm about to make you the best omelet you've ever had."

"Oh really? That sounds like some big talk."

"Not just talk. You should know by now that I'm amazing at everything I do."

Ellie laughed. "You're not wrong. Want any help?"

"No, you take it easy. You've worked hard to-night," he said with a wink. "Want a drink? There's some wine in the cellar over there." He gestured over his shoulder to a door off the kitchen.

"Sure, what kind of wine goes best with eggs?"

Chuckling, Gabe cracked one into a bowl. "Surprise me."

Ellie went into the wine cellar, and picked a bottle of red that looked appealing. She poured them both a glass and handed one to Gabe. The small act of domesticity made her smile.

Just temporary... Just temporary... Just temporary.

Ellie knew that she and Gabe had no chance of a future together. She watched his back as he whisked the eggs, and mentally ticked through the list of reasons why they couldn't stay together—their career tracks, her father. The fact that they were so freakin' sexually compatible couldn't stand up to those things. But still, she liked Gabe, and wanted to get to know him. "Tell me about your friends," she said.

"What do you want to know?"

"You've told me about your business interests, Di Terrestres, but who are they? What are they like? What drew you all together?"

"That's a lot of questions," he told her, his hands busy chopping vegetables. "My friends and I are tight. I met them when I returned from London after finishing law school. We did everything together. Went into business together, each of us using our strengths to ensure the success of the group.

We share everything. We were like a wolf pack, the Brotherhood."

"The Brotherhood. Sounds like one of those secret societies, with the robes and rituals."

He laughed. "Not quite. We don't have nearly enough robes and rituals," he told her. "Brett and Alex are real estate developers, Rafael is the politician, Alana runs Di Terrestres, Thalia, our new hotel and the rest of the entertainment properties."

"And you?"

"I'm the lawyer."

"You put out all the fires."

"We all work together to put out the fires. We did everything together." He artfully flipped the omelet, with a flick of the pan.

"Did?"

"One by one—first Brett, then Rafael, then Alex—they fell in love with amazing women. They're better for it, of course. These women challenge them, love them. I've never seen any of them happier or more complete. It wasn't what I thought I wanted, but…" He trailed off, as if searching for the words. "Sometimes I wonder if that's what I've been missing."

Ellie heard the words he was saying and wondered if that was the reason he'd drunkenly suggested they head to the wedding chapel.

He turned back to face the stove where the omelet cooked. "I can't believe I said all that," he told her, with a shake of his head. "My friends are great, kind of jerks sometimes. You'll meet them officially tomorrow. They're coming into the office for our monthly briefing."

Gabe plated their omelets and put hers in front of her, and they ate in near silence. She hadn't eaten since lunch, and just realized that she was starving. Ellie watched Gabe as he ate. It was the quiet moments they shared—not just when they were having sex—that she enjoyed. Just talking about his friends, sharing a meal with him, getting to know him. It was those moments when a small amount of hope told her that she and Gabe might have a future between them. But more than once, he'd laid out the temporary, inappropriate nature of their relationship. Especially once he became partner, they would never be able to see each other.

Ellie frowned. And if her father found out, there would be no chance of them reconciling. There was no happy ending for her and Gabe. Watching him eat, she pushed her plate back, no longer hungry.

Gabe must have noticed her shift in mood. He put his fork down and looked up at her. "You okay?"

"Yeah," she lied. "I'm just full."

Gabe ate the last forkful on his plate. She could tell from the way he looked at her that he wasn't convinced. But he didn't say anything. Instead, he took her hand and stood. "Come on," he told her. "Let's go to bed."

CHAPTER ELEVEN

ONLY A DAY after he and Ellie had had sex in the very chair where he was sitting, Gabe looked around the conference room at Brett, Alex, Rafael and Alana. The Brotherhood had gathered, as they did every month, to discuss their business interests and to brainstorm ideas for new revenue streams. The group went through their joint portfolios, analyzing their profits and deciding where to allocate funds and re-invest in the business.

There was a knock on the door. Gabe hit the switch that turned the glass wall clear, and he could see Ellie standing on the other side.

He smiled, as he found himself doing when she was near, and waved her to come in. "Gabe, I just wanted to let you know that Charles just got off the phone with Hong Kong and he wanted to let you know that Tsai and the board came to an agreement. They're going through with the acquisition. It's all because of your work last night."

Gabe could have kissed her. He put another big client in the win column, and it would definitely ensure he was brought aboard as a partner. He could almost picture himself sitting behind his new desk in the office next to Charles's that his father had vacated the year before. "That's amazing! And it was *our* work. I couldn't have done it without you."

He heard a throat clear behind them. He'd completely forgotten his friends were there. He turned and saw four amused smiles. "You going to introduce us?" Rafael asked.

He sighed. "Yeah, Ellie, take a seat. These are my friends—" he went around the table "—guys, this is Ellie."

"The new Mrs. Foster," the bigger one, Alex, said, extending his hand across the table.

"Stop," Gabe warned him.

"You told them?" she asked Gabe. "I thought we agreed to keep it secret."

He shrugged. "Of course, I told them. We share everything. These people are my closest friends. You didn't tell your closest friends?"

She thought back to the conversation she'd had with Rachel. "Yeah, I told Rachel, my best friend," she explained. "You met her the night we met, if you can remember."

He heard a snicker and he wasn't sure who it came from—hell, it could have been any of them, as a look around the table told him that they were all enjoying the show.

"Ah, yes," he said, recalling the woman who'd snapped a picture of his ID. "I told you that these guys are my business partners, too. My business is their business. But a few nights ago, they had explicitly promised that they'd be nice," Gabe said. "Although I don't really believe that."

"That was Jessica who said that," Brett retorted. "But we'll behave," he added, winking at Ellie.

"How are you liking Vegas?" Alana asked her.

"It's nice. Unfortunately, I haven't been able to see much of it—with work taking up so much time—"

"And getting married," Alex commented. "Huge time commitment. I'm planning a wedding, and it's a lot of work. Although I think we're skipping the Elvis impersonator."

"Dude. Be cool." Gabe's voice was rich with warning.

"It's fine. I can take it," she assured him.

"I'm just having fun. Sorry, Ellie."

There was another knock on the door, and Gabe looked up to see Charles Burnham. He expected to be summoned, but instead the man looked at Ellie. He didn't look happy. "Ellie, may I speak to you?"

"Yeah, sure," she turned to the group. "It was nice meeting you all." Gabe watched her leave the room and walk down the hallway with Charles, a bad feeling clenching his gut.

Ellie followed her father down the hallway to his office. He didn't say a word, not until they were inside with the door closed.

He turned on her, his face twisted with disgust. "What were you doing in that conference room?" For a brief moment, she thought he had somehow found out what she and Gabe had done in there the night before. She had no idea how she would talk her way out of that one.

"Why were you sitting in on that meeting?"

"I wasn't. I told Gabe the news about the Hong Kong acquisition. He introduced me to his friends."

"I don't want you associating with those people," her father commanded.

Excuse me? "And why not?"

"They're a group of degenerates," he said dismissively. "You have no idea what sorts of business they do."

"They're nice. Gabe was just introducing me."

"They're his clients. But I don't care for the association with them. Gabe's a hell of a lawyer, and he brings in a lot of money. Money from *them*. But I don't have to like it. I've worked to shut them down for years, without success. They have a lot of powerful connections. But they're smut peddlers."

Ellie shook her head at the unfairness of her father's tirade. "Their money is good enough for you, but you think they're degenerates and want to shut them down?"

"Don't be smart, Ellie. I don't want you to be seen with them—especially not here. Are we clear?"

"You can't tell me who I will or will not associate with." She paused. *"Are we clear?"*

Charles looked like his head might explode. Anger turned his complexion a bright red, and she was willing to bet that no one had spoken to Charles Burnham like that. "I want to have a relationship with you, but I'm a grown woman, and you don't get to dictate my life to me." Holding her head high, she brushed past him and headed out of the office.

Ellie could barely breathe as she walked away. The scene with Charles reminded her that even though she was his daughter, that Gabe was one of his favorite associates, it didn't matter. If he found out about what had happened between her and Gabe, they would both be ruined.

She didn't get far before Gabe stopped her farther down the hallway. He must have seen the emotion on her face, because he frowned. "Ellie, what's wrong? What happened with your father?"

"Nothing," she told him, unsure of how to tell him what her father had said.

"I'm fine," she said, trying to move past him.

"Where are you going?"

"I have work to do."

Gabe moved in close to her, blocking her way. "Ellie, tell me. What happened? If he said something to you—"

"It's nothing," she insisted. "I have to go. I still have to look up those property deeds for you, and that's on top of a dozen other things. I'll bet you have the same."

Gabe nodded. "Yeah, you're right. It's time to work."

The dust in the oldest section of the Burnham law library made Ellie sneeze. She had been sent down there by Gabe to look up some old property deeds for land on Las Vegas Boulevard, but she hadn't realized that no one had been down there in probably fifteen years, or she might have taken some allergy medication. For the first time in the whole afternoon, she heard the heavy oak door open and close, and footsteps got closer to where she was seated. Some other poor sap had been sent down to do some research, she assumed.

"Thought you could use some coffee." She was surprised to hear Gabe come up behind her, startling her. He placed a coffee cup on the table.

"Thanks."

"I also wanted to make sure everything is okay. You were acting a little strange earlier."

"Yeah, it's just the conversation I had with my father."

"It was about my friends, right?"

"Yeah."

"I know he doesn't like them, and he's led campaigns against the businesses."

"Why do you work for him, especially since he has a vendetta against your businesses?"

"As a group we decided it was still best for me to work here, especially on my partner track." Gabe sipped his coffee. "But enough about me. How is the workload? I haven't been too hard on you with this task, have I?"

"No, not at all. This is what I want. I don't want to be seen as someone who's here because of her father. I want to be treated like everyone else."

He took a seat across the table from her. "Want

some help?" he asked. The golden halo of light surrounded him and he looked devastatingly sexy. She felt her desire rise. God, Ellie couldn't control her hormones around the man at all.

"I've got the work under control. But there's something else I could use your help with."

"Yeah? And what's that."

"I think I'm in need of a little stress reduction."

He smiled, but knew exactly where she was going with it. He laughed and pushed the books aside, and stood, moving around the table to sit her on it in front of him and hike her skirt up. She spread her legs. "How about you put that smart-ass mouth of yours to some good use."

"What? Right here?" he asked.

"Scared?"

"Of you?"

"Of losing control. Doing something wild."

"Never."

He kissed her, standing between her spread knees. She could tell he was game, but something made her pull back.

"Are there any cameras or anything down here?"

"No, nobody comes down here, as you can probably tell."

She hadn't seen another soul come down in all of the time she'd spent there. "Are you sure?"

"If I didn't know better, Ellie, I'd say you were all talk." He put his hand under her skirt and stroked her through her panties. She leaned against him and moaned. "How's this?" he asked.

"I don't want you to stop, but I need you right now. Hurry."

"You got it." His grin was cocky and satisfied, and he moved in and kissed her with a fierceness that she'd come to associate with Gabe and the passion with which he did everything.

His tongue traced her lips, before diving inside her mouth and brushing against her tongue, in a dance more like a duel. Her panties now gone, Gabe dropped his hand to her center and circled her clit with his fingertips. He inserted two fingers and continued his work. And Ellie shuddered against him, her body completely sensitized. Helpless to anything but climbing higher, she braced her hands behind her on the table, leaned back farther, as his fingers brought her closer and closer to heaven. She was close, her breathing became short, and she squeezed her eyes shut, but still saw the blinding white light as she came, her screams echoing against empty stacks of the library. She fell back on the table, and she was barely able to catch her breath, watching him through hooded eyes, as he unzipped his pants and withdrew his dick. She couldn't take her now alert eyes off him as he handled himself, giving himself a few lazy pumps, as he leaned over her.

"Ready for more?" he whispered, leaning over her, before placing a kiss on her lips with a grin. He reached into his back pocket for his wallet, and took out a condom. He quickly covered himself.

She shrieked when he gripped the backs of her thighs and yanked them, lining her up with the edge of the table, and entering her with a loud groan. He pulled back and then thrust back into her again. Several more thrusts, and she could feel the desire inside her coil tighter once again, as he stoked another fiery bout of passion within her. She reached for him, but she was too far away from where he stood, so she sat up and wrapped her arms around his shoulders, unable to concentrate on anything but kissing him.

The position, and the public nature of the encounter, reminded her of their first night together, the night they'd met. In the Ferris wheel, overlooking Las Vegas Boulevard. It had been only a short time since then, but how things had changed. They'd been strangers that night. They'd gotten drunk, and then married. Gabe was now more to her than a sexy stranger. She'd learned many of his intimate secrets, and she wanted to know more. She wanted to know everything about Gabe.

Their eyes connected, and something passed between them. A flash of closeness. She knew Gabe felt it, too, but he buried his face in the crook between her neck and shoulder, as he pumped into her several more times before she felt his body stiffen in her arms, and he came with a harsh grunt against her skin. She felt a clutch in her chest as Gabe held her close. If she wasn't careful, she could see herself falling in love with Gabe.

It's already too late. The thought scared her, especially when it was followed by his words from just a short time ago. *It's only temporary.* With their hearing date quickly approaching, she felt a small hollow grow in her chest. Each time with Gabe was more outrageous and more exciting than the last, and she wasn't sure how she could go to just being colleagues once the ink dried on their annulment.

When their breaths quieted, she was certain she could hear the pounding of their hearts echoing off the dusty stacks of the law library, and she was brought back to where they were—the very public basement floor of their law office. The heavy slam of the door made them both jump.

"Oh my God." Ellie scrambled down from the table, straightening her skirt. "Did someone see us?"

"No, it must have been something else," he said. But his worried frown told her that he didn't think that. "We would have heard them come in."

"Would we? I'm going to be honest, I was only paying attention to you."

"Don't worry about it," he told her, rubbing her back. "It's fine. No one saw us."

Ellie wished that she could believe that.

CHAPTER TWELVE

GABE WAS EXHAUSTED when he took a seat at the one empty chair left for him at the table at Thalia. He was meeting the rest of the Brotherhood for dinner. He'd spent most of the night up with Ellie, and then after she drifted off, sprawled across his chest, sleep had eluded him.

He'd discovered that day that the board would be voting tomorrow for either he or Ian to be the new partner at Burnham & Associates. He'd be lying if he said he wasn't nervous. Only a stupidly cocky man would consider it a sure thing. He'd been a ball of tension all day.

"Where's Ellie?" Alana asked, when Gabe took his seat. He could hear the annoyance in her tone. What was her problem with Ellie?

"Working."

"Typical," Alex said with a laugh. "You go out for dinner and get the juniors to do your work."

"So, the annulment papers must be close to being signed?"

"We have our hearing in a week."

"That's a long time," she muttered into her glass, before taking a drink.

"What's your problem, Lana? I'm getting really sick of your attitude about all of this. What's your problem with Ellie?"

"I don't have a problem with Ellie. But do you want to talk about what I'm sick of? You—all of you—risking everything we've built here. You married a stranger without thinking about the businesses, or any of us, or how much we could have lost."

"Ellie isn't after our money."

"How do you know that? You don't even know her. You drank a couple of bottles of champagne and then took her to the chapel."

"Alana, hold on—"

"No. I'm not done." She slapped her hand down on the table. "For the past few years, I've watched you all do it. Brett almost ruined Collins/Fisher initiating a takeover to get Rebecca to notice him."

"Hey!" Brett protested.

"Raf scuttled the election because of Jessica, and Alex almost destroyed the group to be with Maria. Don't get me wrong, I love those women like sisters," she said. "But pardon me, Gabe, for worrying that you're thinking with your dick here."

Gabe fumed. "I'm not thinking with my dick, Lana. I made a mistake, and I've dealt with it."

The rest of the group stayed silent, knowing it was better to let them work out whatever was going on between them. "You're still sleeping with her!

You call that *dealing with it*? You should have just cut and run."

"What is this about? Are you jealous? Are you afraid that I'll end up staying married to Ellie, and we'll live happily ever after, and then you'll be left out in the cold alone?"

She gasped, and the stunned silence at the table told Gabe that he'd gone too far. "I'm sorry, Lana—"

"Don't," she said, slamming her glass down on the table. "You know what? I'm going to go. I've got work to do at the club tonight. Somebody has to."

They all watched her leave. It was more than thirty seconds—that felt like minutes—before anyone spoke.

"What the hell was that?" Gabe asked. He and Alana had never fought like that.

"Something she's been holding on to for a while, I guess," Brett said.

"She's wrong," Rafael told him.

"No, she's right," Alex announced. "But not for the reason she thinks."

"What?" Gabe asked.

"Do you love Ellie?" he asked outright.

Gabe didn't answer. Didn't know how to answer.

"Your silence speaks volumes, man."

"We all took huge risks when it came to the women we loved. Could have lost everything. But we didn't."

"Love is about taking risks, being stupid," Brett said.

"That's ridiculous," Gabe said.

"Exactly."

"I think Alana's just upset that for so long you two have served as the coalition of reason in this group when the rest of us fucked up. Don't worry about it. She'll get over it eventually."

Gabe nodded, but he watched the door Alana had vacated. He hoped so. But he wasn't so sure.

With one hand on the wheel, and the other drumming impatiently on the console—a habit she knew she'd picked up from Gabe—Ellie pulled up the driveway to her father's house.

The more time she spent with Charles Burnham, the more she wondered if building a relationship was even worth it. They hadn't had a conversation since the day he'd caught her chatting with Gabe's friends. He'd been rude, controlling, and she'd walked out on him. He hadn't spoken to her at work the day before. She wondered why he would call her to meet him for dinner. What could they possibly have to talk about? But she wanted to try, if only to say she made the attempt.

She parked her car and walked to the front door of her father's house. She knocked on the door, and he opened it quickly, as if he'd been waiting for her on the other side. "Ellie," he said with a smile, drawing her in for a hug. "Thanks for coming."

"Hi, Dad. Thanks for having me over."

He led her through his home, bringing her to the formal dining room. "Please have a seat. Dinner will be ready in a few minutes. Want a drink?"

"Water is fine."

He poured her a glass from the crystal pitcher on the table and handed it to her. "Ellie, I would like to apologize for the way I spoke to you in my office the other day. It was uncalled for."

She nodded, surprised that he'd even apologized. She had a feeling that it didn't happen very often. "Thank you. It was inappropriate. Why did you not want me to meet Gabe's friends?"

"The entire city might have been won over by that group. But I'm not so easily swayed. They make their money in lascivious ways—even by Las Vegas standards."

"You're talking about Di Terrestres?"

"And that hotel they own, and God knows what else they're into."

"They're clients of your law firm," Ellie reminded him.

"I know. But if they didn't bring in so much money, they wouldn't be."

"They were very nice to me, more welcoming than almost anyone else has been since I've arrived in Vegas."

Her father's cook chose that moment to come into the room with their dinner. They sat back and she placed their plates in front of them. When they were alone, he took a bite of his steak and turned back to her. "I just don't want you falling in with a bad crowd again, like before."

"Like before? Goddammit, I was a teenager. I'm

an adult now. I'm not the same person I was back
then."

"A leopard can't always change their spots that
easily."

She gaped at her father. "Unbelievable. Sure, I
was a mess. I made a lot of stupid mistakes and you
helped me out. I cleaned up my act, I went to college, I pay my bills, I got a job."

"At my law firm," he needlessly reminded her.
"And I don't need any more of the embarrassment
that you caused me when you were younger. I'll ask
you to not get involved with *those people*, not while
you're representing me or my firm."

Something in her father's words rubbed her the
wrong way. Her skin crawled, and she wanted nothing more than to leave and go to Gabe, fall into his
bed, his arms, and spend the rest of her life wrapped
up in him. "Is this why you invited me here today?"

"No, I thought we could have a nice meal together
without you acting like a child."

"And you think this is a nice meal?" she asked.
She couldn't stand to look the man. She didn't know
why she bothered. Sure, he had paid for her education, had given her a job. But that didn't mean the
old asshole owned her. She stood. "You know, thanks
for the invite, but I'm leaving."

"Ellie, stop being so dramatic. Sit down and eat
your food."

"Pardon me if I don't feel so hungry anymore,"
she said, throwing her napkin on the table and walking out of the room, leaving her food untouched.

* * *

Back in her car, Ellie blinked back tears of frustration and disappointment. If Charles thought that she was such an embarrassment, then why did he invite her back into his life? Why had he given her the impression that he was at all interested in starting over with her? Was it all just so he could control her?

She started to drive with no destination in mind. But she knew that there was only one person she wanted to see. *Gabe.*

Pushing a button on her dashboard, she called him. He answered after only one ring. "Ellie, hey," he said. As his smooth voice filled the interior of her car, she could picture his lazy smile as he said her name. She closed her eyes, savoring the sound of her name on his lips. Only a couple of weeks had passed since she'd met him, but already she was starting to feel as if she couldn't live without him. She didn't know if it was love, but at this time in her life, she needed him. His presence reassured her.

"Hey," she responded, so filled with relief at hearing him say her name, she tried to keep her voice from cracking.

He must have heard the emotion that she'd tried to cover. "Are you okay?" he asked.

"Yeah," she said, shaking her head, knowing he couldn't see her. "I just want to see you. Are you busy?"

"Never too busy for you. Where do you want me?"

"Can you meet me at Di Terrestres?"

"Ellie, you don't sound good. Where are you? Let me come to you."

"Meet me at the club," she insisted.

"Okay. I can be there in," he paused and she pictured him consulting his expensive watch, "fifteen minutes. I've put you on the list, so you can just go on inside."

"See you there."

Ellie disconnected the call and drove straight to the downtown building that housed Di Terrestres. While a valet parked her car, she walked to the door. Gabe had been right; the doorman let her on inside. She saw Alana, speaking with some of the servers. When the other woman looked up, she waved and made her way over to her.

"Ellie, hello," she said. "What brings you by?"

"I'm meeting Gabe here."

"It's only seven. Pretty early for him to come by."

Ellie shrugged. "Yes, I needed to see him."

Alana smiled, but it didn't quite reach her eyes. Ellie could hold her own, but next to Alana's critical gaze, she felt like a small child. "Can I get you a drink?"

"Yeah, sure." After her ill-fated dinner with her father, and now whatever was causing her chilly reception with Gabe's closest friend, Ellie needed a little fortification. They took a seat at a nearby table and a server came by to take their order.

Alana was quiet for a moment, before she pursed her lips and then spoke. "So, you and Gabe...?"

"Yes?"

"You're still married." It was a statement, not a question.

"Yeah, we are. Unfortunately, an annulment in Nevada isn't as cut-and-dried as one would think. We're still technically married for at least the next two weeks. We have a hearing with a judge, and he'll decide if an annulment is appropriate in our case."

"Is that what you want? An annulment?" When Ellie didn't respond, Alana went on with a good-natured smile. "Sorry, I don't mean to pry."

"I think you did mean to pry. Because why else would you ask such a personal question?"

Alana smiled. "You're right. I am prying. It's just that this is all so weird. Gabe. Married. I just don't understand, and for once he won't talk to me about it."

"What are you asking? If I want to stay married to him?"

"Gabe is my closest friend. I want to know what's in it for you? I need to know that you aren't just screwing with him to get at his money, or to get back at your daddy for some reason. I need to know he won't be caught in the cross fire if you have any nefarious plans."

"Are you worried about him, or his career track?"

"Of course, I'm worried about him."

Ellie sat back and looked at Alana, simultaneously surprised and impressed that Alana asked the question. "I'm not using him. I don't know Gabe well, but I really like him." She wouldn't reveal to Alana that she was in love with Gabe. "We're having fun together. But I assure you, it's only temporary."

Alana nodded, and inspected her cuticles. Ellie could see the woman was an impressive, intimidating figure. "That's good. Because if you hurt him, I'll hurt you."

"You don't have to worry about me," Ellie said. "I won't hurt him."

"Good."

Ellie talked a big game about wanting her father's approval and forging a relationship with him. But Alana had made her realize something. Was being with Gabe her way of sticking it to dear old Daddy? Her heart broke in two when she realized that maybe Alana was right about her. Maybe she *was* going to hurt Gabe.

It wasn't hard to find Ellie once he entered Di Terrestres. She was sitting at a table with Alana and it looked like the women were engaged in a serious conversation. He frowned, and wondered what Alana could be saying to Ellie. They hadn't left on the best of terms at their last meeting, and he hadn't spoken to her since. He'd seen men crumble under Alana's examination, and he knew that Ellie was tough, but he hoped she was faring well.

He jogged over to them. "Ladies," he said, more alerting them to his presence than greeting them. He could tell that the air between them was tense. "Everything okay?"

"Everything is fine," Alana told him, her voice still cool to him.

He turned to Ellie for confirmation. She nodded. "It's fine." She stood and wrapped her arms around his neck and kissed him, her lips parting for him immediately.

Her mouth was warm, wet, willing—full of promise. As his tongue lapped around hers, his arms encircled her waist, and he pulled her closer to him.

Oblivious to Alana, he kissed her without restraint; his hands cupped her ass and she pushed against him and his already hard dick.

"Let's go downstairs," she whispered to him.

He nodded and searched her face. Whatever had been bothering her when she called him had seemed to evaporate. But there was something dark and wild in her eyes.

When she picked up her purse, he looked again to Alana who gave him a curious shrug. He wondered what was going on behind her unwavering eyes. But he could get to the bottom of it later. For now, he had Ellie, and he needed her. "We'll talk later?" he asked her.

"Yeah, sure," she said with another shrug. He took one last look at Alana, and wondered what was on her mind, but he couldn't pay that any mind, as he watched Ellie head across the floor to the downstairs.

"We can get a private room upstairs," he told her when they got to the landing of the staircase.

"Why would we do that?" she asked, pulling him downstairs.

Gabe frowned; something strange was happening with Ellie. But he'd be damned if he knew what. Then he remembered. "You met with your father today. Did something happen?"

"No. Nothing that matters or is any sort of surprise."

He stopped. "Ellie, what are we doing here? What happened?"

She turned, and he could see the wildness in her eyes. "It doesn't matter."

"You're acting so strangely."

"I'm acting like me. This is the real me." She leaned in close, and ran the point of her tongue across his lips. "Don't you want to be with the real Ellie?"

He couldn't argue with her. He wanted Ellie any which way he could have her. "What do you have in mind?"

"Nothing. I haven't been thinking. But that's what I want. Wild, uninhibited."

"It's always wild between us. No matter where we are."

"Exactly."

He watched as Ellie took in the room, searching for inspiration. In a place like Di Terrestres, she could have anything she craved, but when her eyes returned to Gabe, he saw that he was what she wanted.

The people in the room moved around them, as they looked in each other's eyes. Gabe raised his hand and rested it on her shoulder, and then trailed his fingers back down her arm. Her skin was smooth and so soft, he could have spent the night caressing her. Gabe's hands rested on her waist, and surprising her, he lifted her. Her legs wrapped around his waist, her ankles locking behind him.

Ellie giggled against his mouth before his lips took hers in a kiss.

"Where do you want me to fuck you?" he said, his voice hungry. For her. But it didn't matter to her what they did, where they went, as long as Ellie was with him.

She pulled back from him, and twined her fingers through his hair. He saw the change in her demeanor. She'd softened. The change gave him whiplash. "I think I've changed my mind." She frowned and looked around the room. "Why don't you take me home instead? I want you in your bed."

"I'd love to." Gabe released her, unsure of what was happening to Ellie inside. But they could talk when they got home. "Are you sure you're okay? You can tell me, you know."

"I'm okay," she insisted. "Let's go."

They walked upstairs together. When they reached the top, he saw Ian Smith standing across the room, watching them with a cocky smirk on his face that Gabe wanted to smack off.

"Just give me a minute," he told her. "There's someone I want to talk to."

"Yeah, sure. Is everything okay?"

"Everything is fine," he assured her. Not sure if he believed it himself. "I'll be right back."

"Okay. Just don't be long."

He frowned as he walked toward Ian. Gabe knew he didn't have a membership at Di Terrestres. In fact, Gabe was certain the man's clients would also be downright scandalized to see him there.

"Gabe, how are you?"

His grin was slick. "Fantastic, and yourself?"

"Very good." Done with the social contract that told him to be civil with his foe, Gabe got to the point. "Strange seeing you here."

"Yeah, I came with a friend. Quite the place isn't it?"

"It is."

"Is that Ellie Carrington over there?" He pointed to where Ellie stood. "Burnham's daughter."

"Gabe, are you ready to go?" Ellie asked, coming over. It was apparent to Gabe that she hadn't seen Ian over Gabe's height, because her face blanched and her eyes widened when she saw the man.

But Ian saw her. "You're here together?"

"Yeah, I've just been showing Ellie around Vegas."

"And you bring her to a sex club? I wonder what Charles would have to say about that? Or what it would do to your chances of making partner."

Gabe chuckled. "You son of a bitch. You wouldn't dare."

"Wouldn't I?"

Gabe chuckled. "You go right ahead, if you think you aren't talented enough to beat me in a fair fight? I knew it. You were always jealous of me."

"Is that so? Well now you can be jealous when Charles makes me partner."

"You'd better get the fuck out of here, Ian."

"Or what?"

"Or you won't make it to see partner." Blocking Ellie from his view, Gabe stood tall and faced him. He wasn't afraid of Ian, or what he would do to him. Gabe was a better lawyer, he brought in more money, people liked him. He wasn't afraid for himself, but the man could cripple Ellie's career before it even got started.

"Sounds like a threat, Foster."

"It's more than a threat. It's a promise."

The plainclothes security officers that Gabe recognized must have sensed the brewing trouble and converged on their small group without interrupting or becoming obvious to the rest of the patrons.

"Everything okay, Mr. Foster?" one asked.

"Yeah, it's fine. I was just telling Mr. Smith where the exit is."

"I'm leaving. But wouldn't Charles be interested to know his darling daughter is here with his associate."

"Get the fuck out of here." Gabe shoved Ian's shoulder. Security swarmed them, and covertly pulled Ian away.

"Ellie, I'll be in touch," he said.

"You'll stay the fuck away from her."

Ellie grabbed Gabe's hand. "Oh my God. He's going to tell everyone that we were together."

"It doesn't matter," Gabe assured her. "I'll deal with it."

He turned back to Ellie, giving her his full attention. But she looked distracted, worried. "You okay?"

"Can you just take me home?"

"Yours?" he asked.

"No. Yours."

Home. More and more, he liked the idea of it being their home. Their annulment hadn't yet been finalized, and even though he knew the day was quickly approaching, part of him didn't want it to come. Their arrangement would end and they would just go back to being colleagues. He'd be her mentor, and that would be it. They'd given themselves this grace period to have sex—it was supposed to be purely physical, but now that it was nearing the end, Gabe wasn't looking forward to it. He didn't know if he could go back to life before Ellie.

Gabe unlocked the door to his house, and moved aside so Ellie could enter ahead of him. They walked in, and Ellie dropped her purse on the mostly decorative table by the door—just as was becoming her habit. The simple act smacked of domesticity, as the more he looked around he could see signs of her. Her things had begun to clutter his space. He'd never had a woman stay at his home. It warmed him, but also scared him a little.

He'd never imagined himself getting married, but whether it was traditional or not, Ellie was his wife. At least for now.

"Are you worried about Ian?" she asked, uttering his name for the first time since leaving the club.

"No," Gabe lied. Whether he wanted to admit it or not, Ian now held a power over Gabe. Gave him leverage. "I don't want to talk about him now."

Ellie turned on her heel to face him. "What do you want to do?"

Gabe all but growled, and went to her, shucking his suit jacket and his shoes, phone, glasses on the way, caring not how or where they landed, or about the crunch that followed his phone hitting the tile floor, the glass and plastic splintering into pieces.

"I think you're going to need another phone," she told him with a laugh.

"I don't care about that right now." Gabe cupped her face and drew her to him in yet another blistering kiss. But this one was without the ferocity that had come with each of the previous kisses. There was no hurry, no urgency this time. He took his time kissing her, until he stooped and picked her up, and brought her up the stairs to his bedroom.

Still carrying her, Gabe knelt on the mattress, and laid her in the center of the king-size bed.

He went back to kissing her. This time, his lips traveled over her jaw, down her neck and over her shoulder. He pushed the strap of her dress aside, and kissed her.

"Gabe, I want you now. Quicker."

"I don't think so," he told her, his lips grinning against her skin. "I've got you here, and tonight I'm finally going to take my time with you."

"I don't know if I can take it any longer," she told him.

Gabe put his hand on her knee and pushed up her thigh. "I haven't even started yet." His hand tangled in the material of her dress, and he groaned. "But first I have to get rid of this dress." He grasped her waist and surprised her by raising her up. He reached behind her, lowered the zipper and then peeled her dress down her body.

"God, you're beautiful." She looked in his eyes, and believed every word. "All I could think about tonight was taking this dress off you, revealing your amazing body, all this smooth skin, inch by inch."

He laid her back flat and settled between her thighs. He loosened the cuffs on his shirt, removed his watch, and she watched, riveted, as he unbuttoned his shirt and threw it on the floor. He covered her again—chest to chest, bare skin against bare skin. God, Gabe was amazing. She could feel his hard dick against her stomach as he kissed her again. He trailed down her body, stopping to play with her nipples, each kiss, tug, lick sending zings of pleasure throughout her body.

He licked his way down her midsection, taking a moment to dip into her belly button, before going farther south. His mouth landed on her, and he licked up her seam, before plunging his tongue into her. His lips and tongue played at her clit—bringing her higher and higher, until she came, pushing herself shamelessly into his face.

"Gabe, now. Please!"

He moved away from her and reached into his bedside table, pulling out a condom. He shucked his pants. He rolled the latex over himself and then settled over her. He entered her in one solid, fluid thrust. He buried his face in her hair, and she heard his rough exhale. He pulled back his hips and thrust inside of her again. He kept a steady pace. His rhythm brought her to climax once again. Her hips rose to meet his thrusts, and she came a second time, just as she felt Gabe stiffen above her, before his body loosened and he came.

Once their breaths returned to normal, he rolled away from her and pulled her over on top of him. Ellie felt so right, fitting perfectly against his body.

She hummed as he trailed his fingers up and down her back, and lightly placed kisses on his chest. "What do you want to do now?" she asked him.

"How do you feel about a soak in my tub?"

She sighed against him. "Sounds wonderful."

"Come on," he said, picking her up and slinging her over his shoulder, and walking with her into his master bath. She giggled as he quickly turned into his bathroom, depositing her on her feet on the ceramic floor.

While he turned on the hot water, Ellie busied herself looking around in the cabinet beside the mirror. "Hey, nosy," he called to her.

"I'm your wife, aren't I? Shouldn't I be allowed to look in your medicine cabinet? Unless I'm going to find something weird."

"Nothing too weird," he assured her, as she picked through his skin care products.

She laughed. "It's like you live in a Sephora over here."

"What are you talking about?" he asked, turning around.

"Double cleanser, toner, moisturizer with sunblock. Serum?" she read through the labels on the narrow shelf.

He walked over to her and framed her face with his hands. "Listen, none of this is an accident. I've got to look after my skin."

"I only use makeup remover and a night cream."

"That's because you're twenty-four and haven't spent your life in the harsh desert. Wait until you're old and grizzled like me."

Ellie turned around and faced him. She reached up and smoothed her palm over his cheek. "Hmm… Not so grizzled."

He reached behind her. "That's because of the serum," he said, pouring some bubble bath into the tub under the water. And that was why he liked— *loved?*—Ellie. It wasn't just the sex, although that was incredible. She was smart, funny, tough. But there was more to her—to them. They had fun together. They laughed. And that was something he'd never shared with a lover. No matter what Ian said to Charles, no matter what the consequences for him, being with her was worth it.

She looked at his reflection in the mirror without turning around, frowning as she studied him.

"What?"

"Were you ever young, Gabe?"

"What do you mean?"

"Were you ever young and stupid, impulsive?"

He wondered where the line of questioning had come from. If it had anything to do with her father, or her small outburst in the club earlier, and he recalled the story she'd told him about her turbulent younger years. "Like you, you mean?"

"Nothing that extreme. But you're just so serious all the time. When was the last time you let your hair down?" She reached up and ran her fingers through his golden waves, disheveling his hair.

Hardly ever. He stood from the tub and folded his arms as he faced her with a playful smile. "Need I remind you that I co-own an erotic club?"

"When was the last time you got out of your bubble? Sure, you own a sex club, drive a Harley, you own a piano you won't play, but you're still very buttoned-down. It's all a front. You're so stiff. You still haven't been able to cut loose."

"Haven't you spent your entire adult life trying to erase your wilder days from memories?"

"Yeah, but at least I'm able to say that I made those mistakes, and learned from them. You've always been so sensible and in control. Me losing control as a teenager was self-destructive. You losing control can be freeing."

"I seem to remember a wild weekend where I almost drowned in champagne, a beautiful woman and telling a pretty decent Elvis impersonator that I wanted her as my wife."

"Hmm, yeah, that was you, wasn't it?"

"But maybe I was helpless under your extremely bad influence."

"You're saying this was my fault?"

"You know I don't remember, but either way, I'm glad it happened."

"Me, too."

He turned and saw that the tub had filled. "Let's get in," he suggested, as he helped her into the bathtub before settling in behind her.

Leaning back, with Ellie at his chest, he ignored the way his cock stiffened in response to the warm naked body pressed against him, and he leaned his head back and breathed a sigh of relief. He'd never had an appreciation for the tub before. Having only used it after a few stressful days at the office, or a vigorously intense workout, sharing it with Ellie was an experience unto itself.

They lay quietly for a moment, but Gabe couldn't fully shut off his brain. "Do you want to tell me about your dinner with your father?"

She stiffened against him. "Not really."

"It couldn't have been that bad."

"He told me to stay away from you and your friends."

That surprised Gabe. Charles had been one of his biggest champions during his career. "Why?"

"Your friends, because he thinks they could be my gateway back into debauchery. Like I'm the same person I was back then."

"You know what? I'll bet you were an amazing person back then, too. He was just too much of an old, conservative asshole to see it. Why does he want you to stay away from me?"

"Because he doesn't want me to destroy your future like I'd almost done my own. I'm a bad influence."

Gabe tightened his arms around Ellie. He regretted the line he'd teasingly said earlier that she was a bad influence. He couldn't begin to imagine how much hearing those words could have hurt her. And he understood why she'd acted out earlier. Her mother and father had really done a job on her. "Jesus, Ellie," he whispered against the top of her head, before placing a kiss there. "I'm sorry. I had no idea how cruel he could be."

"It's okay. It isn't anything I'm not used to from him. You know, I'd leave and forget he ever existed if I didn't need the job."

"You graduated from a good school. You can get a job anywhere."

"Please. I already know how small Vegas is. If I leave the firm, people are going to know why. Not to mention that it's pretty easy to use Google, and I know my name brings up some pretty interesting headlines."

"You can stay here. I can take care of you," he told her.

"What? You want to cancel the annulment, have me here as your happy housewife, making sure I meet you every day at the door with a martini and a pot roast in the oven?"

Gabe didn't think that would be so bad, but he didn't push it.

"I've worked too hard to get where I am. I want to keep the job. Even though my father paid for my education, I'll never say I wished he didn't. I've got a promising career. I can't turn my back on that. You know that. It's the same reason you won't leave it either."

Gabe had no response to that, so all he could do was wrap his arms around her. And he held her close, neither of them talking, until the water cooled.

In the silence, with his eyes closed, Gabe felt himself begin to drift off into sleep. He shifted, needing to get them out of the chilled water before he fell asleep. "Ready to get out?" he asked her.

"Yeah, I was waiting for you to wake up," she told him with a laugh.

"I wasn't asleep," he told her. He was sure he'd only drifted off for a minute—tops.

"Oh really? You normally snore when you're awake?" She stood and he watched the rivulets of water roll down her body. Maybe she was right, and he had napped. He was reinvigorated, his energy rising, along with his dick as he watched her step gingerly from the tub.

He followed her out and grabbed a fluffy towel. He stood behind her and drew the towel over her body, soaking up the water, following it with his lips. Her warm, damp skin was smooth under his mouth, and he kissed, licked, tasted his way across her shoulder blades. She turned in his arms and encircled his neck with her own. She kissed his mouth, and as he kissed her back, he could feel himself, naked chest to naked chest, melt into her. Kissing had always felt like a precursor to the more fun elements of sex, but kissing Ellie was different. He'd never felt anything so good or pure. He could have stood there kissing her all night.

Her body shifted, reminding him of his hard cock that stood straight up between them. Keeping his mouth fastened on hers, his tongue entwined with hers, Gabe lifted Ellie, and she wrapped her legs tightly around his middle. He made the short trip to his bed and lowered her into the center of his king-size mattress.

He followed her down and settled on top of her, between her knees. But soon, Ellie took over, and pushed him over to lie on the bed. On top, with her thighs straddling his hips, she stroked him, gripped him.

Gabe groaned his approval and let himself relax and enjoy her touch. But when she rose above him and slid her sweet, hot pussy against his dick, he thought he might explode.

"Fuck, Ell," he muttered through clenched teeth.

"You like that?" she asked. He saw the wicked smile that played on her lips. She was enjoying torturing him.

"I'd like it a lot better if you would just lie back and let me do my job."

"Your job is to just lie there," she told him. "Tonight, you're mine." She continued grinding on his dick. Her moans and quick breath told him that she was enjoying herself.

"I'm always yours," he whispered.

She stopped moving at his declaration. He opened his eyes and saw her watching him. He didn't know if he'd scared her. He regretted saying anything. He cursed his own stupidity and lack of control where she was involved.

She didn't say anything, but she raised up above him, took him in her hand, and lined him up with her opening. She started to lower herself. He was already inside of her, albeit just an inch, when he put his hands on her hips, stilling her movement.

"Ellie, wait."

"What?"

"A condom," he told her, nodding to the top drawer in the bedside table.

"No," she whispered back.

"What?"

"I don't want one. I want to feel you."

Gabe's restraint was razor-thin. He'd never had sex without protection, and as a sexually active young man, he underwent testing every few months. "Are you sure?"

"I'm on birth control, but besides that, I was tested a short time ago. I'm clean. Unless you have something to tell me."

"Not a thing," he assured her.

As Ellie lowered herself onto him, he arched his back off the mattress at the feeling of filling her with nothing between them.

Fully seated on him, she stilled and moaned. "Jesus, Ellie. If you don't move, I might die."

Her laugh was throaty and full of passion. She lifted and lowered herself, and then repeated her motion, riding him.

Not using a condom was a risky move, but as Ellie moved over him, he watched the spot where they connected. Gabe realized that he would risk everything—his career, his friends, his future, his life—for this woman. His Ellie.

He gripped her hips and slid his thumb to her clit, and rubbed her with small, gentle circles until her breath quickened and her movements became more frenzied. And when she came, her internal muscles clamped and squeezed him. It was all he needed to follow her over the edge. He pumped his hips quicker until he was completely spent. She fell over on him, and he could feel her heart beat in time with his.

"Ellie," he whispered against the side of her head. He knew what he wanted to say. He loved her. But the words wouldn't form on his tongue. "Ellie," he started again. But he couldn't finish.

"I know," she whispered, her lips against his chest. "I know."

CHAPTER THIRTEEN

GABE SAT ON the bench behind the keys of his piano. Ellie was asleep upstairs. After making love to her, she'd dozed off immediately, leaving him wide-awake and unable to sleep. His fight with Alana was fresh in his mind, as was his realization that he loved the woman now asleep in his bed. When they'd asked him, he hadn't responded to his friends, but he believed he was falling in love with her, as inconvenient as it was. They'd agreed to see each other, sleep together until the annulment went through. But the sex between them was so good, and the conversation even better.

He was tired of the secrecy. Part of him wanted to scream it from the tower at the top of the Stratosphere. He wanted to touch her in public, talk to her, hold her hand, drape his arms around her. But he couldn't. Not until she was ready. He would wait if she needed him to.

With each passing day, he found himself growing closer to her. He wanted to know everything about her, and wanted her around him all the time. Gabe had never felt that way about a woman before. He was falling deep. Was it love? How could it be? He'd only known the woman for such a short time. He'd allowed her to get closer to him than anyone else, but love? He had no idea.

With his forefinger, he stroked the middle C4 key, and then pressed it down, the noise echoing throughout the hallway. He then hit the next key—D—and ran through a scale and back several times, his hands getting used to the movement and pattern on the keys. The instrument was still in tune, despite its misuse. He dived into a tune that he'd played over the years, his fingers moving wildly over the keys, the beat of the music matching that of his heart as he played.

He looked up, his fingers stopping and clenching into fists. His breath came in short pants from the exertion of playing, when he saw Ellie at the base of the stairs, completely naked, just as he'd left her in bed.

"Sorry if I woke you."

She shook her head. "It's okay." She walked slowly toward him, and stood next to the piano. She reached for his scotch tumbler and took a sip. "You're really good."

"Thanks. I feel like I'm a bit rusty. It's been a while since I played anything."

"Why haven't you played?" she asked, taking a seat next to him on the narrow bench. He wanted her again.

"I'm just too busy. Work takes up a lot of time.

And I started seeing this woman who just demands orgasms whenever she wants."

"I've been begging to hear you play. You're amazing." She gasped. "I've got an idea. You told me that Di Terrestres does stage shows, right?"

"Yeah."

"You should play there."

"Play what?"

She rolled her eyes. "The piano, you idiot."

He shook his head. There was no way he would get on a stage and play for the people there. "No."

"Come on. Why not? You're really good."

"I've never played for anyone before, and I'm not starting there."

"What, you'll walk around naked, have sex in front of these people, but you won't play a song for them?"

"It's different, Ellie."

"How?"

"I don't know…" he trailed off, as if trying to find the words. "Sex is just sex. But when I sit behind the piano, it's more. You know? It's intimate. It's me, laying myself bare. It's scary. What if I suck?"

Ellie laughed. "You try to play the tough guy, but I know that isn't you. You're sensitive, creative, talented. What if you do it and you're incredible? You never know until you try."

"I'm not doing it," he told her, hoping his tone would end the conversation.

With a sigh, she moved on. "It's weird. I just look around this place, I look at your lifestyle. Why do you work for my dad? Sure, I know that law earns you a good living, but obviously a lot of your assets come from the Brotherhood."

"I like practicing law. It's what I'm good at. You know my dad was the other founding partner of Burnham & Associates, back when it was known as Burnham & Foster. When he retired, they took his name off, as some sort of weird challenge, like it would be up to me to see the name Foster back on the header." He shrugged.

"You know what," she said. "I think I finally get it."

"You get what?"

"I get you. Why you're so invested in the firm, and being partner, and why you're so straitlaced. It's all about living up to your parents, isn't it?"

"You're right. I guess that's something we have in common."

Not wanting to discuss it any further, he grasped her waist and lifted her so that she sat naked in his lap, her thighs straddling his. Her hot core open to him. He was wearing his briefs, and flexed his hips upward, making her moan at the contact, hoping she'd forget about the conversation. "I don't really want to talk about that right now." He punctuated his sentence by thrusting upward again, pressing his hard dick against her clit.

She moaned again. "But aren't these the kinds of things that husbands and wives are supposed to talk about?" Her eyes closed, and she ground against him.

Her moist heat was exquisite. "Their futures? Their careers? Their dreams?"

"You're my dream," he whispered against her lips.

He lifted her again, sitting her on the keys in front of him. The notes clattered, clashing against the marble floor. He put her feet on the bench and she was fully opened to him. He could feel her heat, smell her desire, see the glisten of her in the low light. He ran his thumb up her seam, eliciting another moan from her. He brought his thumb to her lips—tasting her juices. "I love how you taste," he told her in a murmur. *I love you*, he left unsaid, shocking himself. But he realized it. He was in love with Ellie. It was irrefutable.

He leaned over her and put his lips against her, closing them over the tight, needy little bud at her crest. He lapped his tongue at her until she was rigid. He knew she was about to come, and he couldn't wait any longer to have her. He stood and pushed his shorts down. He took himself in his hand and lined his dick up with her, and was inside in one forceful thrust. He withdrew and plunged into her again, and again. Over and over. The noise from the keyboard below her played an off-key tune, but he barely heard it. She felt amazing, flesh on flesh. He felt the fire burn up his spine, and his balls tightened. He came with a harsh shout as his orgasm sapped everything from him, and he collapsed over her in a heap.

He gave a few more leisurely thrusts, luxuriating in the feel of her.

Sitting on the bench, he pulled her down so she sat on his lap. "You're my dream," he told her again, kissing her on the lips.

CHAPTER FOURTEEN

GABE WALKED INTO his office. Waking up with Ellie was quickly becoming the best part of his day. All of the secrecy was starting to get to him. They hadn't talked about what they would do at the end of their marriage, and their court date was quickly approaching. But neither of them was ready to discuss it. He loved her. He was certain she loved him. But revealing their relationship—if that was something they even wanted to do—was something they needed to be prepared for. The ramifications would be serious. Gabe felt like he was ready. With each passing day, he cared less and less what Charles Burnham would think of their coupling. But he had to wait for Ellie to be ready. There was more at stake for her than just a job. For some reason, Ellie still wanted a relationship with her cold, distant father. Because the more he heard about Charles, the less he liked the man. But he would wait until the moment she was ready, and not a minute before.

He took a seat at his desk, and was about to start in on his day when Kellen buzzed in. "Ian Smith is here to see you, Gabe."

Gabe frowned. He didn't have a meeting with Ian, and he certainly didn't want to talk to him socially. He knew it had something to do with their encounter at Di Terrestres. He'd expected it earlier, but he was ready for whatever he had to say. "Send him in."

Ian walked into his office. His smirk was slick, and Gabe wanted to punch it off his face.

"What can I do for you, Ian?"

He sat across from Gabe. "We can't have a social visit?"

"We never have before."

"You're right." He passed his cell phone between his hands.

"I just wanted to see how you felt about both of us being up for the partner position. The vote is happening today."

"Yes, I'm aware."

"And I just wanted to see if you were interested in withdrawing from consideration? Telling Burnham and the other partners that you don't want it. Then we wouldn't need to waste everybody's time with a vote."

Gabe laughed. "Why would I do that?"

"I have some information that you might want to keep covered."

Gabe straightened in his chair. Did he know about his ownership stake in Di Terrestres? Have more details about his relationship with Ellie? He tried to play it cool. "And what's that?"

"That day, in the law library. I saw you with Burnham's daughter. I was waiting for the right time to reveal the information. I think that's today if you don't do what I want."

Gabe tried to hold his panic at bay. "Is that right?"

"Yeah, it was quite a show you guys put on. That Ellie looks like a pretty decent lay."

"Keep her out of this." Gabe clenched his fists and stood. "And I won't be blackmailed, especially by someone like you. You should leave," he warned the other man.

Ian made no move. "I can assume the old man doesn't know that you've been fucking his daughter. But that's not all."

If Smith exposed Ellie, he had nothing else to lose. "What else you got?"

"I've learned that you're one of the principle partners of Di Terrestres. The club that Charles Burnham is working so hard to shut down."

Gabe tried to not let his feelings show, played it cool. "How do you know that?"

"There are some good private investigators in this city."

"You son of a bitch."

"I know your old man used to run this place, but I don't think he would appreciate your ownership of a sex club. So if I were you, I wouldn't worry so much about you becoming partner. And of course, when Charles fires you, maybe I'd be down to *mentor* your girl, myself." Ian laughed and stood, then walked to the door. Gabe sat for several moments, frozen with the rage that pulsed through him.

He stalked out of his office and caught up to Ian,

who was already in the hallway. So early in the
morning, it was already full of his colleagues milling about, socializing, warming up for the day. But
Gabe didn't care about what any of them thought.

"Ian," he ground out between clenched teeth.
When the man turned to face him, his smirk was
the perfect target and Gabe couldn't resist reacting.

He reached back and punched Ian with enough
force to knock the other man back. When Ian re-
gained his equilibrium, he tackled Gabe, forcing him
against the wall, before they took it to the ground.
Screams echoed in the halls as the men scuffled on
the floor, throwing punches, and Gabe quickly main-
tained the upper hand, until they were finally separated by some other workers.

Gabe brushed off the peacemakers. He straightened and wiped his mouth, and his hand came away
bloodied. "You son of a bitch," he muttered to Ian,
who was nursing his own wounds. "You stay the
fuck away from Ellie."

"Gabe, what's going on?" he heard Ellie cry behind him. He turned and saw her on the edge of the
onlookers who'd congregated. She came to him. "Are
you okay?"

"Yeah, I'm fine," he told her, hoping that he didn't
look as bad as he felt.

"Hey, Ellie," Ian called. "Want to nurse me back
to health?"

Gabe made a start for the man again, ready to
tear him apart, but he was held back by a couple of
his colleagues.

"Gabe, no!" Ellie's hands were on his chest, holding him back, and her pleading eyes kept him from pursuing Ian any further.

"Fine," he told her. He stared at Ian, who was already looking at him. He knew his career was done, but it didn't strike him with regret like he thought it would have, when he put his arm around Ellie. "He isn't worth it."

"Who wants to start?" Charles Burnham looked between Gabe and Ian.

"I'm sorry I embarrassed the firm, sir." Gabe's jaw ached, and he knew a bruise was forming on his cheek. When he threw the first punch, he knew he would have to answer to the boss. But he hadn't cared about that when it came to defending Ellie's honor from the snake beside him.

"What was the fight about?"

Gabe paused, before answering. "It was about Ellie," he said, with a look at Ian, daring the other man to stay silent. He did.

"Can I ask what my daughter has to do with anything here?"

"She's my wife, sir." He hadn't meant to say it, it just came out.

Gabe could feel the shock coming from both Charles and Ian.

"Your wife?"

Gabe nodded.

"How— You married my daughter, and didn't tell me."

"I know I should have come to you—"

"You're goddamn right you should have. But that still doesn't explain why two of my more promising associates were grappling in my hallway."

He heard Ian snicker. "Yeah. Gabe, why did you pull that first punch?"

Charles made a disgusted sound, and hit the intercom button to his assistant. "Rosa, call Ellie and get her up here immediately."

"Yes, sir."

"Ian, get out of here. I need to sort this mess out. I'll deal with you later."

Ian stood and quickly left the office, his head bowed.

Gabe turned back to his mentor, who looked at him through narrowed, angry eyes.

Ellie put her hand on the doorknob to her father's office. She knew that the call would be coming. She entered, and both her father and Gabe watched her. She sat and put her hand on Gabe's arm in a gesture of support. When her father folded his hands together in front of his face, she knew that he was pissed.

He cleared his throat. "I'm not sure what's going on here," he said, raising an eyebrow at her hand on Gabe's. "I was told there was a physical fight between two of our most promising attorneys, who are in line to become partner, and I learn that you're married."

Ellie's mouth dropped and she looked to Gabe.

"I told him, Ell. I'm sorry."

"You're married? How? When?"

"It happened a few weeks ago."

His mouth dropped. "Weeks," he said, not a question. "And neither of you thought it was important to tell me." He was addressing both of them but his gaze fell solely on Ellie.

"It's not her fault, sir. I take full responsibility."

"Anyone planning on telling me how this happened?"

"There is no real explanation. We met one night. And we got married. I didn't know she was your daughter, or that she was working at the firm. I'd just gotten back from Hong Kong. We were on the Strip—"

Her father sat back in his chair, and he nodded. His eyes were still cold and mean. "Ah, I think I finally understand. I see the *old Ellie* has finally shown her true colors again. It was only a matter of time."

Ellie's stomach dropped. Her father's judgment of her hurt. Every move forward they had made had been lost. She realized that her father hadn't changed his opinion of her, and he never would. But she still had a chance to save Gabe. He could come out of this whole debacle unscathed. She just had to cut the ties.

She released Gabe's hand, and smiled bitterly at the older man. "You know what, Dad? You're right. I haven't changed at all. Gabe and I got drunk, we got married. Possibly the most reckless, impulsive thing I'd ever done. I was doing this to get back at you, and it was the only way to do it."

Gabe looked from Charles to Ellie. "What?" She

could see the hurt and confusion written on his face, but she ignored it. She had to.

"Yeah, Gabe, this had nothing to do with you. It was all about getting under my father's skin. You know, bad seed that I am, and all."

"Ellie, what—"

"Gabe, just stop. You're embarrassing yourself." She slid the ring she always kept near out of her pocket and put it in Gabe's palm, trying not to look in his eyes. "I'm going to get out of here. Thanks for the fun, Gabe." She turned on her heel and walked out without even looking back.

He caught up to her in the hallway. "Ellie, what the fuck was that?" he demanded.

"He's right, wasn't he? Your career has already been jeopardized by me. Just like he said would happen. You can't throw everything away."

Gabe shook his head. "But you didn't mean what you said in there. I know it. There's no way you were faking things between us."

Ellie said nothing.

"You must be one hell of an actress, but I don't think so. Because I don't believe you right now."

Ellie shrugged indifferently, making him feel like punching a wall. But he got his anger and hurt under control.

He put the ring in her hand. "But I meant what I said earlier. The ring is yours. In fact, I meant everything I said to you." He turned and strode down the hall.

"Gabe, wait!"

Instead of facing her, he waved casually over his shoulder, dismissing her, without even looking back.

Gabe stood outside of his office. His most fucked-up day was just getting worse and worse. Kellen looked up at him but said nothing, most likely stunned at seeing his boss anything but put together. He quickly averted his eyes and looked back to his computer, but his fingers didn't move over the keyboard.

Gabe put his hand on the doorknob, about to enter his office and try to see how he could even go about salvaging his career. But something stopped him. Instead of opening his door, he turned around and went back down the hall to Charles's office.

Striding past Charles's assistant, he walked right into his mentor's office. The older man was clearly surprised to see him. "Yes, Gabe?"

He watched Charles's hand shake as he brought the scotch tumbler to his lips. "I need to talk to you."

He waved at him to proceed.

"I'm in love with Ellie." Charles nodded, but didn't say anything. "It might be too late for us, but you need to rethink your relationship with her. She's kind, smart, funny, compassionate, and your approximation of her, that she's still the irresponsible party girl she used to be, is bullshit."

"My relationship with my daughter is none of your concern."

"That's where you're wrong. Ellie concerns me.

Her desire to be close to you touched every aspect of our relationship."

"You don't know what she's put me through. The headlines, the gossip."

"She was a teenager. Get to know her, sir. You won't regret it." He paused. "I don't."

"This matter with Ellie aside. You started a physical relationship with another associate. You're her mentor. You know that is highly inappropriate."

Gabe nodded. "Yes, sir."

"If I can't trust you, how could I propose you as partner?"

Gabe shook his head. "You know what? I don't care anymore."

"Excuse me?"

"You've held that goddamn partnership over my head, dangling the carrot for far too long. I don't care. I don't want it anymore. And now that I think about it, I don't even want to work at this firm anymore. Consider this my resignation." Gabe turned without saying anything else, but before he reached the door, Charles called to him.

"Gabe," he said, in a sad tone that almost made Gabe pity him.

"What?"

"What was the fight about, between you and Ian?"

"He discovered some things about me that I didn't really want you to know." Gabe didn't care about revealing the truth about himself, if it took the focus off Ellie. "Ian had me investigated and found out that

I not only serve as counsel for the owners of Di Terrestres, but I'm an owner, as well."

"You what? You own that...that...den of sin?"
Charles sputtered so dramatically Gabe rolled his
eyes.

"With my friends, yes." His chuckle held little
humor. "You know, it's ridiculous how long I was
wary of you finding out. But really, the fight was
that he saw me with Ellie, and had some comments
about her."

"You gave up on your career for Ellie?"

"I'd give up a lot more than that for her." He extended his hand to his former mentor. "But, Charles,
I want to thank you for the opportunity you've given
me here. I really appreciate it. But it's over. I'll go
pack up my office now."

CHAPTER FIFTEEN

GABE SAT BEHIND his piano, his right hand pressing a sequence of keys that should have combined melodically with those played by the left hand, if only that hand hadn't been holding a tumbler of scotch. He drained his glass, put it down and filled it again with the bottle that sat on the top, not taking his right hand from the keys.

He looked up, just as he had the night Ellie had seen him playing and they'd made love on the piano. But this time the marble hallway was empty. He sighed and swallowed more scotch past the lump in his throat.

He'd spent most of the day just as he had the others since Ellie had left him—lost, listless, drinking. Who was he? He wasn't Gabe, the lawyer. He wasn't Gabe, the husband. His doorbell chimed, ricocheting off the bare hallways. He stood and walked to the door, and saw it was Alana. He frowned, remembering their fight, and how wrong he'd been. He felt stupid. He wasn't even Gabe, the friend, anymore.

"Hey," he said, turning and leading her into his

house. He knew she followed when he heard her close the door, the click of her high heels on the floor.

He walked into the kitchen. "Can I get you anything?"

"I'll have a Perrier, if you've got one."

He passed her one, and opened a beer for himself. "Are you here to gloat?"

"About what?"

"You were right about Ellie. It was all a mistake. And guess what, she even told me that it was all to mess with her dad."

Her eyes widened. "Really. Did you believe that?"

"No. But she said it. And she believes it."

"I think I may have put that thought into her head." She looked to the floor. "Sorry about that."

"Whatever."

"Are you okay?"

"Just fucking peachy, Lana." He punctuated it with a swallow of beer. "What can I do for you?"

"That's all you have to say to me?" She sighed. "Fine. I'm sorry, okay?"

"You're sorry? Didn't I just tell you that you were right?"

"It's not about being right or wrong. I know I was wrong. You shouldn't have given up so easily. And maybe you were right, too. Maybe I was just a little jealous. You and all the guys have so much going on personally right now. Maybe I feel, sometimes, like the odd man out."

"I don't want to hear this right now."

Alana looked at him closely. He knew she saw

his unshaven face, his sweatpants. "Did you not go to work today?"

He laughed. "Didn't you hear? I quit."

"You quit your job?"

He shrugged. "Yeah, I was tired of the whole god-damn thing. The career I spent years building." He chuckled without mirth. "It's over."

"Have you been playing?" she asked, looking over at the piano, seeing the almost empty bottle and his glass sitting atop it.

"A little. Ellie said I should play at the club. Think that could be my new job? I'm not exactly looking forward to being unemployed."

Alana smiled. "You know, I think that's a pretty good idea." Her phone beeped in her purse. "Damn, I've got an appointment. But are you going to be okay? Why don't you call the guys over?"

"I'm fine."

"And think about doing a show, Gabe. Take a chance. Do the unexpected. It could be great."

Ellie was sitting in front of her television, a glass of red wine in one hand and a frosted cinnamon roll in the other, when her phone rang. Her eyes were still red-rimmed and burned, and she looked over at the papers she'd left on the coffee table in front of her. The annulment papers that Gabe had given her more than a month ago. The proceedings were wind-ing their way through the legal system. Their day in court was quickly approaching, and she didn't know if she could face Gabe in front of the judge.

She briefly considered ignoring her ringing phone, but she picked it up, and saw her father's name on the screen.

She sighed, wondering which emotional barrage to prepare herself for. "Hello?"

"Ellie."

"Yeah?" she said, keeping herself detached.

"I, uh, just wanted to ask you if you wanted to get together for dinner. So we could talk."

Picturing the last meal she'd shared with her father, she shook her head. "I don't think so, Dad," she told him.

"Please, dear. I've been thinking a lot about how I've treated you. I want the opportunity to apologize to you in person."

"Apologize?"

"Yes. I was wrong. All along. I know I've probably blown every opportunity we've had to build a relationship, but I would like to try."

"What about Gabe?"

"I don't know. He quit that day. I haven't heard from him."

"He quit?" Gabe's job was everything to him. And he'd quit because of her.

"Yes, he walked out shortly after we spoke last."

Ellie paused. "Do you mean what you said? About wanting to start over?"

"Yes. Every word."

"Dad," she tested the word, gingerly. "If you're being honest with me, and you want us to try again, then we have a lot of work to do. And this is our last chance. If it doesn't work, that's it."

"Yes, I know."

"Okay, I'll meet you for dinner tomorrow night." She hung up the phone, cautiously optimistic about her upcoming meeting with her father, and she felt part of the burden and misery lift from her. She had to make things right with Gabe. Whether that meant being with him or cutting ties, it had to be done. If her father could swallow his pride and contact her, she could no doubt do the same.

As Ellie stood, with a newfound vigor and resolve, the crumbs from her first cinnamon bun fell from her sweatshirt to the floor. She was on her way to her room when there was a knock—no, a pounding—on the door. *Oh God, what now?* She sighed. *When it rains, it fucking pours.* She went to the door, part of her hoping to see Gabe, but she was left confused and—truthfully—a little scared when she saw Alana on the other side. She stepped back, unsure whether or not she wanted to answer.

"Ellie," she called. "I know you're in there, ignoring me. And that's fine. It's your right. But please let me in. I'd like to talk to you."

Ellie opened the door and faced Alana. She straightened her shoulders, at least trying to make herself feel confident next to the gorgeous, poised woman in front of her. "You sure you don't want to hurt me?" she asked, recalling Alana's words during their last conversation. "Like I hurt him."

Alana shook her head. Her eyes looked sad. Alana

looked unguarded. "That's all big talk. I just want to be real here with you." She flashed a sad, tight-lipped smile. "Plus, I don't want to hurt a person so dear to my best friend."

Ellie moved out of the way, and gestured for Alana to enter her apartment. Alana came in and looked around. If she noticed, or minded, the clutter that Ellie had allowed to accumulate in the past few days, she gave no indication.

"How is he?"

"He doesn't look great." Alana looked her up and down. "And neither do you."

"About as good as I feel."

"I thought he'd made a mistake—in seeing you."

"Is that so?"

"Yeah, I thought you were after his—all of our money. Or that you were using him to get back at your dad."

"That's what I told him, when I saw how much his career had already suffered because of me."

"Is it true? You had ulterior motives for being with him."

"No. I said it out of anger, and I know I hurt him. It's one of my biggest regrets in my life." Ellie felt her eyes fill up when she remembered how Gabe had looked at her when he gave her back her ring, for a second time.

Alana must have seen it, and she looked away before taking a seat on the easy chair, kitty-corner to Ellie's on the couch. Ellie paused the show on the TV.

"You love him."

"Yes. But it doesn't matter now."

"You know, I'm new to having relationships with women. For so long, it was just me and the guys. I've since gained a few female friends, but I've never felt threatened by them."

"I threatened you?"

"Just a little," she smirked, holding her thumb and forefinger an inch apart. "But don't tell anyone. It could seriously destroy my reputation as a hard-ass ballbuster."

"Not likely," Ellie said. "What was it about me that threatened you?"

"I don't know. Gabe and I were always so close. And don't get me wrong, it's not like I'm secretly in love with him or anything, but I think I was kind of jealous that you managed to whirl into his life and become the center of his world. And I think that was why I pushed back so hard. All the guys have found love with incredible women, and I just didn't think Gabe was going to be one of them." Alana trailed off as she averted her eyes, and Ellie would have sworn that there was a tear hanging off an exquisitely long eyelash.

"Are *you* okay?" she asked, leaning closer.

And in an instant, Alana snapped out of her thoughts, reverting back to the *hard-ass ballbuster*. "Yeah, I'm fine," she said with a laugh that Ellie knew was forced, and she knew she was seeing a side of Alana that not everyone did. She wondered if Gabe had. "I'm here to talk to you. What happened?"

"I don't know, really. I walked up the hallway at

the office and saw Gabe and Ian fighting." She told Alana the series of events that had led to her storming out of her father's office. She sighed, reliving the hurt and anger she'd felt. "It was so selfish—the whole relationship. I knew that the blowback would be harder on Gabe than on me. He loves his job, wanted to be partner at my dad's firm. I took the fall, and I ended it. I cut the tie as easily as I could. For him."

"Why haven't you called him?"

"I don't know. Fear, maybe? A hefty dose of shame?"

"Why don't you swing by Di Terrestres tomorrow night? Before eight?"

"Why?"

"You're a smart woman, you can figure it out."

CHAPTER SIXTEEN

GABE FOUND HIMSELF behind the piano. The curtain was still closed, but he could hear the patrons on the other side. The usual hum of activity reminded him of the many people who were about to hear him play in public for the first time. He wished he'd had another drink to fortify himself. He was a courageous guy, but the thought of laying himself bare on his keyboard scared him more than any of his more adventurous endeavors. How did he allow Alana to talk him into this?

"You nervous?"

Gabe turned his head and saw Alana joining him on the stage. "Yeah," he admitted. "It's stupid, but I really am."

"Want some liquid courage?" She joined him on the bench, passing him a glass of whiskey.

He accepted it gratefully and took a drink. "Thanks."

"No problem. You're going to be great, you know."

"I just want it to be over."

"Should we put out a tip jar? Seeing as how you're out of a job and all that."

He laughed. "I think I'll be okay."

Gabe put his arm around Alana. "I'm glad we aren't fighting anymore."

"Me, too."

"And things have returned to the way things should be—the two of us doomed to our bachelor-and-spinster-hoods."

Alana shrugged and moved away from him. "I wouldn't be so sure of that."

"I'm going to try not to think about it." He stroked his fingers over the ivory keys. "At least until this is done."

Alana gave his shoulder a quick squeeze as the house lights went down, indicating a stage show, and the hum of the crowd outside the curtain quieted. He could somehow feel their eyes and attention through the heavy cloth.

Soon Gabe found himself alone on the stage. He placed his hands on the keyboard of his piano and, focusing only on the white-and-black keys, zoned out the entire room and started.

He didn't know how long he'd been playing; he'd planned for only a twenty-minute set but by the way the sweat rolled down his neck and his fingers ached, he knew it had probably been much longer. When he stopped, the crowd erupted into cheers. He took a bow, left the stage and made his way to his regular table.

Crossing the floor, he shook hands, gave hugs, but

when he saw Ellie, sitting alone in the same booth where they'd first discussed their annulment, he stopped in his tracks.

"Ellie, what are you doing here?"

"Our court date is tomorrow. I want to cancel it."

"What?"

"Let's stay married."

"Ellie, what is this? I don't have time—"

"Listen to me. I can't bear not being with you. Yes, we might have done all of this out of order. Getting married first, then getting to know each other. You showed me the comfort and safety of a real relationship. I showed you how to be impulsive. We balanced each other. But that doesn't change the fact that I fell in love with you somewhere along the way. And you fell in love with me. You can't tell me that you no longer feel that way about me. I love you."

"Ellie, I—"

"Tell me you love me, goddammit!" She demanded.

Gabe knew there was no use fighting her. He was madly in love with the stubborn, funny, sexy, beautiful woman in front of him. "I love you. I think I fell in love with you the day I bumped into you at that casino. I fell in love with you when I saw our wedding certificate. I fell in love with you when we kissed in the elevator in your father's building, when I made love to you on top of that piano. Since the minute I laid eyes on you, I haven't *not* been in love with you." He shook his head and breathed out a frustrated breath. "How did we get here?"

"I don't know. Do you think we can start over?"

"You want to stay married."

She nodded. "But I want all of the relationship trappings. I want dates, romance."

"You got it."

"I want you."

"You got me."

"I'm sorry I ran from you. I'm sorry I let my father's opinion run my life. I should have confronted him earlier. Told him what I wanted."

"I can't let you take the fall for that. I was just as reluctant to talk to him about it. I realized that life isn't what I wanted anymore."

"There's nothing in our way now, is there?"

"No, there isn't. We were fools for letting anything get in our way before." He grinned. "Come here."

When she did, he wrapped his arms around her body and kissed her, knowing that he would never let Ellie—*his wife*—go again.

* * * * *

COMING SOON!

LET'S TALK
Romance

For exclusive extracts, competitions
and special offers, find us online:

facebook.com/millsandboon

@MillsandBoon

@MillsandBoonUK

Get in touch on 01413 063232

For all the latest titles coming soon, visit
millsandboon.co.uk/nextmonth

MILLS & BOON
Desire

Indulge in secrets and scandal, intense drama and plenty of sizzling hot action with powerful and passionate heroes who have it all: wealth, status, good looks… everything but the right woman.